THE FLIRTING GAME

LAUREN BLAKELY

COPYRIGHT

ABOUT THE BOOK

My new neighbor is a hot, grumpy hockey player who works out shirtless on his porch every morning. But it's not *technically* spying if I just happen to be on my patio at the same time... right?

Imagine my surprise when the sexy grouch turns out to be the client who just hired me to redecorate the house he's giving his mom.

What's a ray of sunshine like me to do? Pretend I've never noticed his abs while we pick out furniture—since I'd never date a client. And Ford Devon? He's made it clear this is his final season, and he wants zero distractions.

Which means I need to exercise some serious resistance...

To his cool blue eyes that track my every move.

To that deep voice that makes me shiver.

And to the mouth that shuts me up one night in our shared backyard with a scorching kiss.

Oops.

We agree it's a one-time slip up. But when he insists on

being my date to my cheating ex's party...we slip up again into a *very fun* sleepover. With our dogs watching!

One fake date at a charity gala turns into another at a hockey game, and somewhere between fabric swatches and porch picnics, I stop pretending.

But how do I convince Ford that with me, he can have *both* love and hockey?

DID YOU KNOW?

To be the first to find out when all of my upcoming books go live click here!

PRO TIP: Add lauren@laurenblakely.com to your contacts before signing up to make sure the emails go to your inbox!

Did you know this book is also available in audio and paperback on all major retailers? Go to my website for links!

THE FLIRTING GAME

LOVE AND HOCKEY #6

By Lauren Blakely

1

SHARING IS CARING

SKYLAR

I'm nosy by nature.

If a couple decides to whisper their grievances across a diner table, I'm going to lean back in my booth and eavesdrop.

If someone's reading next to me on a plane, I'm going to peek at their screen to see if the hero's about to evade an assassin, rocket to Mars, or buy a chocolate shop as a gift for his heroine. I'll take the latter, thank you very much.

And when I spot my brother's cat in the mudroom with her unblinking green eyes locked on the corner of the yard, I need to know what has caught Cleo's attention at the same time every morning this week.

I can't leave well enough alone.

As my coffee works its magic, I peer through the open window leading to the luxurious catio—an enclosed patio for cats—trying to get a read on her target.

But I can't tell what it is from inside my home. Hopping onto the mudroom cubbies, I adjust my fuzzy pajama bottoms covered in illustrations of martini glasses and a threadbare T-shirt that says, *Everything is Fine Here* in a font of flames. I poke my head out, taking another drink from my steaming mug, coffee tendrils wafting into the warm October air.

"Sharing is caring," I tell the feline, but the regal tuxedo is perched on the highest shelf of the catio maze my brother built in his townhome—before he took off for an assignment in Europe six weeks ago and I moved in— and she's pointedly ignoring me.

After I set my coffee cup at the end of the first cat shelf —like I'd leave my coffee behind—I roll up the cuffs of my pajama pants.

I hoist one leg over the windowsill, brace myself, and haul my ass out. Why didn't I venture here sooner? This catio is state of the art, with screened walls keeping the kitty safe and an obstacle course of shelves giving her premium vantage points.

The catio is about fourteen feet long and ten feet wide, so I've got some distance to cover. Have I mentioned that each shelf along the catio only has about three feet of headroom?

I take a fortifying sip of coffee, then do my best John McClane impression, crawling through the catio like I'm sneaking through heating vents to save Christmas.

I wiggle forward like a caffeine-addicted snake, and finally—*finally*—I reach Cleo.

Oh. *Hello there, hot neighbor.*

My eyes pop. My pulse spikes. Hell, my coffee cup sweats.

Cleo is a naughty girl. She's been staring *for a week* at an absolutely strapping specimen on the back porch of the house next door. I've never seen him before though. Is he a guest? Or does he live there? And if he lives there, why didn't my brother tell me?

I jerk my gaze away from the vision of well-muscled glory and turn an accusatory stare to my companion. "You were holding out on me," I whisper, betrayal laced through every word. "Where is the leaning in, girl? I'm seriously disappointed."

Cleo lifts her haughty chin like she obviously doesn't care. Well, she doesn't. The greedy little thing has been keeping the hottie all to herself.

But not anymore.

I sit next to her, take another sip of coffee, and settle in to check out my next-door neighbor properly—or improperly, as the case may be—as he does porch yoga.

Shirtless.

This is the pick-me-up I needed. Earlier this week, I'd lost out on a project I busted my butt to land. The client went with a big corporate design firm instead of little old solo me. This bit of good fortune is the karmic jump-start I need this morning before I get into the badass business-babe zone to meet another potential client this afternoon.

I swing my gaze back to the man. Should I get my binoculars? I have a mini pair inside—well, they're opera glasses, technically. I found them on an epic thrifting treasure hunt a few months ago. You never know when you might need them. For birds, obviously. I spotted a red-winged blackbird in the yard just last week, and I'm seriously thinking about taking up birdwatching.

But I don't know how long the show will last, so I stay put. My gaze roams over the well-built man with all those muscles on display. He's only wearing compression shorts.

They're bright yellow. I don't love the fashion choice, but given the free view, I can set that aside.

He stands tall, his sturdy arms raised to the sky like he's trying to touch it.

I swear I can make out every muscle. The biceps, the triceps, the *make-my-jaw-drop-ceps*.

His hair flops over his forehead with just the right amount of devil-may-care messiness that begs you to run your fingers through it. Are those golden strands woven through his brown hair, or is it just the October sun haloing this Greek god? If I were the sun, I'd shine on him too.

Just look at him with that strong profile. Chiseled jaw. Roman nose. Carved cheekbones. Fair skin kissed with just a hint of tan. I sigh contentedly. Despite my head nearly bonking the roof, and my legs scrunched up cross-legged, I'm going nowhere till the curtain call.

He bends, folding at the waist, dropping his arms to his feet, and—oh my god.

There's a first time for everything, and I might need to make a T-shirt that says, "I was today years old when I became an ass woman." Because I could set this cup on that firm rear end.

I take a satisfying sip of coffee as he moves into some kind of plank, and...that pose. Dear god, that pose is doing unfair things to my lady parts. So unfair that I hum, low in my throat, and...coffee shoots out of my nose.

I swear Cleo rolls her eyes as I mutter, "Ack."

The man spins around, eyes darting left to right as if he's searching for the sound of the noise.

Mustn't have been a mutter. Could have been a shout.

I hunker down, hoping he can't see the woman spying on him from her catio like some weirdo in pajamas.

But he's a weirdo too. What kind of person does yoga without listening to music? Or better yet, a podcast? He's exercising *and* thinking?

I don't think he spots me though. He turns back around, settles into a plank, and holds it.

Stop the presses. Why have I *never* realized what a plank is a metaphor for? He lowers his pelvis while arching up his torso, and...it's official. I'm now a convert to the church of yoga. I happily settle in for more enjoyment featuring downward-make-me-stare-harder-dog and why-don't-you-warrior-with-me pose.

A whimper from inside my home interrupts the spectator sport.

My shoulders slump.

Another whimper drifts to my ears.

I say goodbye to the heathen cat and the peep show, then wiggle backward like a snake with regret.

Nature calls.

By the time I unfold myself from the catio and step into the mudroom, Simon—my little rescue dog—is practically bouncing with his legs crossed like a kid waiting for the bathroom.

"I've got you, buddy," I say to my favorite person, grabbing his harness and leash. I slip them on him—while still holding my coffee because this gal can juggle—and hustle to the front door.

I glance down at my outfit. Hmm. The shirt has a bit too much breathing room. Setting down the coffee, I reach for a jacket from the hook, not even looking at it, then snatch my life-sustaining coffee again.

Only when I step outside do I realize I'm still in my pajamas—and I've grabbed my bathrobe.

But Simon doesn't care what I'm wearing, and I have

plenty of time to make myself presentable before meeting the prospective client later today. So I shove my feet into my gardening boots from the front porch and trot down the steps, thinking about how I can fit yoga TV into my morning schedule every single day.

2

AIR DOG

FORD

The second the timer on my watch goes off, I break my Shavasana. Sixty seconds of relaxation after twenty-nine minutes of yoga—done. I hit the button to silence the alarm, push up, stretch my neck from side to side, and yank open the sliding glass door to head inside.

Zamboni waits patiently in her dog bed, her part-German Shepherd, part-Corgi head popping up, tilting slightly as if to ask, *How did it go?*

"I kicked calm ass," I say, patting her behind the ear as her black-and-tan tail thumps against the cushion.

I duck into the main bedroom, grab a pair of basketball shorts from where they're neatly folded on the bureau, and tug them on over my compression shorts before heading into the closet. After flicking through my options, I pick a gray T-shirt with my alma mater's logo, then carefully slide the hanger out from the bottom to keep the neck from stretching. Life's too short for stretched-out T-shirt collars.

When I've pulled it on, I return to the kitchen, open the counter-depth fridge, and grab the pre-sliced frozen bananas from the freezer. Next, the kale I picked up at the farmers' market. Then some frozen mango. All of it goes into the high-end blender sitting on the clean white countertop. I hit blend on the perfect concoction—kale smoothies are a party in the mouth, and I challenge anyone to prove me wrong.

As the machine chops, dices, and liquefies, I mentally check in on my goals for the day. My personal conditioning coach had me add yoga to my routine this season, so I've knocked that out first thing. It'll be time for the real work when I meet with her later today for a session. She's a hard-ass—exactly what I wanted when I signed with her at the start of the summer.

After ninety seconds—the ideal blending time for peak consistency—I stop the machine, grab a spatula, and scoop out a sample.

Yup. Perfect. Just like it is every day.

I hold out the spatula to Zamboni. "Come here, girl."

She trots over, sitting before I even have to ask. "You are the best girl in the world," I say, letting her lick the spatula clean. She asks for more, so clearly, she agrees.

"Don't worry. When I open the best smoothie shop in the city, I'm naming it after you," I promise, then send her back to her bed, where she'll wait until it's time for a walk.

I pour the smoothie into a stainless steel to-go cup, pop the lid on, then grab my earbuds from the case where I always set them. How people lose these things, I will never understand. Just put them in the same damn place when you're done. Easy.

I put them in, leash up Zamboni, and say, "Let's do it."

We head outside, where I lift my face to the sky. The sun is shining—it's warm for an October morning in San Francisco.

I take a sip of my kale goodness while Zamboni trots beside me, perfectly in stride. I toggle to my audiobook and hit play on a new book my sister, Hannah, recommended—*Own Your Time.* The premise? Treat your day like a resource and devote your hours to three main priorities.

For me, that's a kick-ass final hockey season, my family, and—Zamboni, obviously. This girl has been my main squeeze since my marriage imploded spectacularly two years ago.

But thinking of that shitshow does not align with my priorities whatsoever, so I slash it out of my head.

As I listen, I mentally check off my schedule for the rest of the day, considering how each task aligns with my priorities. The session with my conditioning coach? That's a no-brainer for goal alignment.

Another appointment with a potential decorator for the house I bought as a retirement gift for my parents? Yup. I want the best for them, but that's not easy. My mother makes Moira Rose look low maintenance. Mom's already fired, oh, I don't know, 478 designers, give or take. Last night on the phone, I finally told her I'm hiring the next qualified one no matter what. And I'll stick to it. Hopefully I can hire the candidate today since we need to get this moving.

Also, I need to hit the sack early tonight and get a good night's sleep because this year—my last year in the pros— will be my best. Screw everyone who said I should have retired last season. Hell, screw everyone who ever said I wouldn't make it in the NHL.

I proved them wrong then, and I'll do it again now. I'm thirty-six, and I plan to go out on the highest of high notes.

As I round the corner, Zamboni still in perfect heel, I catch a glimpse across the street.

Whoa.

That is one sexy, hot mess of a redhead.

Floral bathrobe. Red pajama pants with—wait, are those martini glasses?

Why the hell is that cute? It shouldn't be cute. And yet she's hard to look away from. Her coppery hair is piled into a messy bun. Actually, scratch that. The messiest of buns.

And she's walking an adorable Doxie. Or really, the Doxie is walking her.

I slow my pace before I even register watching them, considering...saying hello.

Except, nope. Not today. I'm not going to go chat up a random woman walking a dog in my neighborhood. That does not align with any of my priorities.

I snap my gaze forward, the picture of self-discipline. I turn on my block, and ten seconds later, a brown-and-tan Doxie rockets around the corner, trailing a long leash and beelining toward Zamboni. My girl whips around with an apprehensive bark—a ladylike one—as the little dog yaps out an enthusiastic greeting right in Zamboni's snout.

My pulse settles—the dog's not attacking—but I'm still on my guard even as a voice calls from behind me, "I'm sorry! He likes dogs!"

I glance around.

Oh. It's her. And damn. She's prettier up close, even when arriving in a cloud of chaos.

Freckles dance across pale cheeks. Green eyes flash with amusement as her dog wags its tail so fast it's practically vibrating. She lets out a low laugh and tugs on the tiny tornado's leash without looking up at me. "I meant—he's very friendly."

"Yeah, I see that," I say dryly.

"I should have asked first if they could say hi." She turns around, looking up and meeting my gaze for the first time. "Oh. You're the—"

She swallows her next words, leaving me guessing. Maybe she's a hockey fan. It's rare someone recognizes a player when we aren't wearing helmets and uniforms. But as she flicks her gaze over me, the inspection seems to satisfy her, as if it answered a question. Still, I don't fill in the abandoned sentence—I'll feel stupid if I'm wrong.

The woman moves on. "I would have asked first, but as you can see"—she gestures to her haphazard clothes—"the day is kind of getting away from me."

I nod at her ceramic cup. "At least you have coffee."

"It's lukewarm, but hey, it still works."

"Caffeine doesn't care about temperature," I agree.

Then I realize—she doesn't have a lid. What kind of maniac walks around San Francisco without a lid on their coffee cup?

But hey, some people like to take risks. Is talking to her a little longer a risk I want to take right now? I'm considering the question when, out of the corner of my eye, I see something I can't unsee.

Her tiny dog is no longer licking Zamboni's face.

He's mounting her. *Enthusiastically.* He's humping her like a deranged stuffed animal let loose in a strip club.

No. Just no. I point, stiff-armed, at the animal. "What the hell?"

The woman winces. "He's frisky today."

"No kidding," I say sharply.

She laughs awkwardly, and I can't tell whether she's

embarrassed or cheering him on. Her beet-red cheeks say, *Oh no!* But the chuckling says, *Go get 'em!*

"Just make him stop," I say stiffly. "That's gross."

"Simon, no," the woman calls. "Simon, that's enough. Simon, stop right now, you naughty little devil."

Her scolding would work better if she weren't laughing. The cute voice calling him a naughty little devil is not doing the trick. Nothing is. The little horndog doesn't stop. He grips my girl's hips with his tiny paws and just keeps pumping.

It's not even remotely funny. Balancing my kale smoothie, I reach for the dog at the same time the redhead does—

Bam.

Her elbow knocks into my cup. It shoots up a few feet, then plummets. I snatch it before it splatters onto the sidewalk.

Her coffee?

Not so lucky. Nor is sweet Zamboni.

The coffee spills. *All over my dog.*

"Seriously?" What the fuck has this sexy chaos demon done to my day?

"It's not hot! I swear. Also, that stopped him so...yay?" She scoops up her dog, then tries to clean my dog with the end of her robe.

Why? Just why? I should stop her, but she's mopping Zamboni's back like the fate of the world depends on getting her clean. "I'm sorry!"

"Yeah, me too," I say, grabbing her coffee mug from the sidewalk. The handle's nicked, but otherwise it's fine. "Now she'll need a bath. And probably therapy."

"Don't we all?" The woman flashes a grin that is way too confident for someone who just spilled coffee on a stranger's dog. "I got some off her, though, so double yay."

"Thanks." I hand her the mug and assess my dog. Surprise—my girl is still covered in her drink. I'll have to take care of her myself. That's usually the only way to get things done anyway.

"But nice reflexes," the redhead adds in an upbeat tone. "Is that a smoothie in there?"

Is she going to ask me to make her one? "Kale smooth-ie," I mutter.

"Good thing that didn't spill then. Shame about my coffee, but I suppose there was nothing to be done."

"Except use a cup with a lid?" I ask, bewildered. How can one person be both sexy and disastrous at the same time?

She shrugs, unbothered. "Why would I dirty another dish?"

"That logic doesn't even make sense."

"It's more environmental this way. If I poured it into a to-go cup, that would mean more water, and so on," she argues, adjusting the Dachshund mix in her arms.

Wait. I mean...the humping hound. Because the dog is *still* going, thrusting his little doggy hips as he dangles from her hands.

I stare at him. Then at her. Then back at him. "He's still humping?" Because...holy shit. Her mutt is out of control.

She snaps her gaze to the pup, chiding him too, "Simon, you're in air jail." She shifts her focus back to me, lifting her chin. "It's just excess energy. It's something some dogs do when they're excited...or overstimulated."

I arch a brow at the last word. "Overstimulated?"

"It doesn't mean *that*. It's just a thing some dogs do."

"They hump the air?" Where does she come up with this stuff?

She jerks back, as if she's offended. "Are you actually critiquing his style?"

"His style of dogging it while he's in *air jail*?"

She clutches the pup closer as he gives a final thrust, like a wind-up toy winding down. "He's just...high energy," she says defensively.

"He's just...inappropriate," I toss back.

She rolls her eyes. "Simon, let's go."

In a huff, she spins around, heading down my block.

Don't want to be anywhere near her unchecked energy, so I turn the other way. My jaw tightens as I walk. So much for my neat and orderly day.

3

FRIDAY NIGHT MONKEY

SKYLAR

I'm still fuming an hour later as I flip through a rack of vintage handbags. "Can you believe the gall of that guy, critiquing my dog's humping style?"

The thrift store smells like old books and good deals, while some kind of indie pop plays faintly overhead. Trevyn holds up a sequined silver clutch against his glowy ebony complexion, raising a *What do we think?* eyebrow. Mabel inspects a full set of Le Creuset baking dishes, which are, for some reason, displayed next to the bags.

"I stopped Simon before anything happened," I continue, still indignant at my uptight neighbor and insulted on Simon's behalf. "There was no need to insult his technique. Some dogs just have urges. My mom's Chihuahua humps a stuffed monkey every Friday night. She even calls it *Friday Night Monkey*—so what's the big deal?"

Trevyn chokes on a laugh. "I—okay, wait. *Friday Night Monkey*?"

Mabel sets down a cherry-red pan, tilting her head, her big brown eyes curious. "That's a lot to unpack. I'm not even sure where to start," she says, tucking her chestnut waves behind her ears.

"It's not like they're going to make some freaky little Chihuahua-Dachshund-Corgi-German Shepherd mix," I argue. "Simon's neutered."

I pluck a faux leather tote from the shelf next to a set of whisks. This store off Fillmore Street is nailing the gadgets-and-accessories theme. I desperately need a new bag for my meeting today—something stylish, professional, and eco-conscious. I also desperately need this job. Being a one-woman shop is hard, and it means hustling for every job. The corporate design firms keep getting bigger and gobbling up more work, so a job for a whole house is a big deal.

I waggle the bag for my friends. "Is this the one?"

Trevyn and Mabel stare at me.

"Then why are you so mad?" Mabel asks, ignoring the bag question.

I huff, lowering the bag. "It's the principle of the thing."

"The principle of not wanting your dog to be banged by a rando on the street corner?" Trevyn doesn't play devil's advocate. *He is* the devil's advocate. "Look, if someone's Yorkie tried to get it on with Barbara-dor, I would cut them with my sharp wit."

"And his wit has a razor's edge," Mabel remarks, patting Trevyn's strong arm.

"Thanks, doll," he says, flashing her a bright smile.

Ugh, I hate that they're right. "Fine, maybe Simon was…" I roll a hand, then concede, "Uncouth."

"You think?" Trevyn says with a snort-laugh.

"Just a little," I mutter, then sigh again. "It's just that Mister Porch Yoga was so…*put together.*"

"And that bothers you?" Mabel asks.

"Of course it bothers me. His dog walked in perfect heel, his clothes were neat—they were gym clothes, and yet it looked like he'd ironed them. *Ironed them.*"

"Give me his number," Trevyn says with an appreciative purr.

"So you object as someone who detests ironing?" Mabel presses.

That's not what's really irritating me, of course. Mabel stares at me, tapping her Converse-clad toe, and I can tell my friends see right through me.

"Fine," I say, tossing up my hands in surrender. "He's *irritatingly* hot. He's infuriatingly sexy. The furrow in his brow. The ruler-straight line of his lips. And the way his blue eyes are so...icy hot. But he's a dick, so now I can't enjoy staring at him every morning. He's ruined my routine."

"Your routine of checking out the hot neighbor you just discovered today?" Mabel asks, deadpan.

"Yes! And I only moved in six weeks ago, so I think I'm well within my hot-neighbor discovery window."

Trevyn cracks up, then drapes an arm around me. "You and Simon are a perfect match."

"Like this bag and you," Mabel says, holding out a faux leather tote with a little more structure to it. "This bag says *I don't have a frisky frankfurter, and I definitely didn't walk around the block in a robe while meeting my hot neighbor who hates me because of my dog.*"

I snatch it from her grasp. "Then I'd better get it."

Trevyn sighs dramatically in relief. "Thank god."

"Please, you *love* thrifting," I say. "I've seen you get lost in thrift shops."

"Not the way you do," Mabel points out.

"Well, it *is* my job," I reply. Well, specifically, my job is scouring consignment shops. As an eco-friendly interior designer, my mission is to help clients find sustainable furniture and decor. That makes me a huntress of sorts.

And this bag? It's clearly made to last a hundred years, so it represents my brand well. I don't skimp on quality when I hunt for deals.

"And since it's your job," Mabel says, "we decided you also need this blazer." She pulls a pastel sky-blue one from a nearby rack—the exact shade I love. "It's a vintage power blazer. Pair it with a T-shirt—"

"Plus nice slacks and this bag," I continue, my excitement building. "It says *I have range*. It says *I can achieve a lasting style that won't hurt the planet*. It says *I can track things down*."

Yep. A few new accessories, and I'll be ready to nail this meeting and win a new client. I slide my arms into the blazer, and it fits perfectly. I spin around, modeling it.

"Like a glove, baby," Trevyn coos.

I beam, stroking the soft fabric. "It was made for me."

Mabel nods. "I approve."

I let out a long exhale. "I feel better. Thanks, friends. I needed this."

"Good. You don't smell angry anymore," Mabel teases.

"Did I smell angry?"

"Oh, I'd say the scent of annoyance was pretty strong," she adds. "But now? You just look like a badass babe."

Mission accomplished.

I march to the register, saying hi to Hetty as I swipe my phone. Then I drop the blazer and bag into my reusable canvas tote, and we head out onto the busy block, past cute boutiques with sidewalk sales and a perfume shop that just opened and peddles the prettiest vintage bottles.

As we near the crosswalk, Trevyn stretches his arms and grins. "So, are we going to talk about the hot neighbor discovery on the podcast?"

I run a design podcast, co-hosting with Trevyn and Mabel, that just cracked eight hundred fifty—count 'em, eight hundred fifty—subscribers. Add in our video version, and it makes nine hundred thirty-one. Technically, *Hot Trends, Classic Spends* is all about how to get the look you want without the waste. But somehow, we always circle back to dating instead of design hacks. Dating is a never-ending well for content, especially since I've been single for over a year after Landon, AKA Mister We'll-take-the-next-step-as-soon-as-I-open-my-board-game-store, left me in the lurch.

Five years together—*five years*—and in one afternoon, he packed up and left. That's how I learned my biggest lesson: I deserve the best, and I'll never come in second again.

"No," I say firmly. "I won't give my hot neighbor the satisfaction. Just like I won't give him the satisfaction of me checking him out tomorrow morning."

Mabel laughs. "So you're going to punish him by *not* ogling him?"

"Sounds about right."

"Sounds like you're punishing your eyes." She squeezes my shoulder with affection. "Ever heard of cutting off your nose to spite your face?"

"Check him out tomorrow, Sky. Just check him out," Trevyn goads.

Right now, I need to go home and review my notes for my meeting. I'm going to nail this job. This gal is not going to let that happen again. I've got a new bag, a new blazer, and a can-do attitude. Try and stop me.

I say goodbye to my friends and head to my temporary home in Hayes Valley. When my brother Adam, a scientist, landed a coveted year-long research post studying efforts to reduce carbon emissions around Europe, he took it. Then he asked me to move into his home to look after his cat while he's traveling. Um, hell yes. Of course, I pay him rent too.

Adam's place is right at the end of a cluster of town-homes, which means Hot and Mean Yoga Guy's house is a little bigger than my current abode. But it's a great deal on a fabulous place, even though I have a bone to pick with my brother.

I let Simon into the tiny backyard for a bathroom break when I get home—refusing to look at Hot and Mean Yoga Guy's yard—and then call Adam.

It's evening in Amsterdam, where he is this month, so he answers with a question. "Did you break the water heater? The dishwasher? The dryer?"

I gasp. "Excuse me. I'm handier than you."

"Did you, Skylar?" he presses.

"No! I didn't break anything, and I could fix all of those if I did."

"Did Cleo escape then?"

"I don't only call when there are problems," I point out.

"Is there a problem?" he counters.

I sigh as I head back inside with Simon at my feet. "Yes, a big problem. Why didn't you tell me your neighbor is hot?"

He's quiet for a beat. Then, in a softer voice, he says, "Jessica? Yeah. She's something, isn't she?"

"No," I say, rolling my eyes at his mention of the artist who lives down the street and sometimes shares seeds with me for planting. "Though, yes, she is quite pretty and nice. I mean the guy right next door."

"Oh," he says with a snort. "The hockey player."

"He plays hockey?" But of course he plays hockey. That explains those strong thighs and the buns of steel. Plus, that to-go cup save, darting out his hand like a superhero. I hate him even more now.

"I'm pretty sure," Adam says. "I mean, we're not friends. But I did talk to him once when there was that windstorm and a tree from my yard landed on his property. He was cool about it, and some neighbors are dicks. He offered to help haul it off and plant another one."

"Really?" Ugh. I hate that he was cool about it. I double hate that he wanted to plant a tree. I mean, I love it, and I hate that I love it.

"Skylar, why are you asking? Are you causing trouble with the neighbor?"

Shoot. Adam would not be happy to hear about the argument this morning. "Of course not," I say, upbeat. "I was simply curious. I noticed him from the catio."

"Good. Because the world is community-based these days. We all need to get along with each other," he says.

He's right. Maybe I should leave, I dunno, a nice gift on his front porch to say sorry from Simon. Like some shishito peppers. Just in case one is super-hot and burns his tongue. Not that I'm being petty or anything.

"I get along with everyone," I say breezily. "Even Cleo, and you know what she's like."

"A cathole," he says with a laugh.

I smile, and we catch up on his work for a few minutes before we say goodbye. Then, I settle onto the couch to prep for my meeting while Simon snoozes on my lap. I review the notes that the potential client sent me. His name is Devon, but that's all I know about him. The job is for an old house that needs an updated look, and he and his mother love my eco-friendly approach.

And they need someone to start immediately.

I'm their gal.

I grab my stuff and head out for my meeting in Sausalito—but not before peeking at the house next door, making sure my neighbor isn't outside.

And dammit.

Mister Haughty Hockey is bounding down the steps confidently. He's wearing charcoal slacks, a short-sleeve button-down that shows off his biceps, and aviator shades. Why must he wear aviator shades? That just makes it harder not to stare at him. I give in as he strides to a gleaming silver car parked by the curb. Of course his ride is spit-shined. Probably smells like new car and efficiency. I bet the inside doesn't have a single food wrapper or rogue fry.

I growl under my breath, wait until the coast is clear, then I take off for the bus stop. On the way, I pick up a left-over cardboard takeout box from the sidewalk so I can toss it in the recycling bin.

Well, you have to practice what you preach.

4

DESPERATE TIMES
FORD

My mother clucks her tongue. "I should come down to handle this."

I drag a hand through my hair. "You don't need to," I reassure her.

"Are you sure?" She arches a brow on the phone screen. "You're running a hand through your hair. You do that when you're stressed. Just let me help. I love to help."

"If by *help* you mean fire everyone, then no, Mom." I pace the empty living room, my footsteps echoing across the floorboards of the Sausalito home I bought for her and my dad. It's been their dream to retire by the water, and you can't beat the views of Richardson Bay in this seaside town across the Golden Gate Bridge from San Francisco.

"I only fired people who weren't executing my vision. The last one didn't know what to do with her time. The job shouldn't have taken a week, even with the non-toxic paint I picked out. They do it so quickly on TV."

I stride over to the sliding glass doors. "You manage to sound so reasonable."

"I am, Ford. I'm incredibly reasonable. I expect excellence. You're the same way. You expect excellence from yourself on the ice."

She's a little bit right, but I'll never admit the similarity. My mother has been running the renovation like a reality TV show host—the kind who makes everyone cower. "Firing a dozen contractors and designers is not going to help you and Dad move in here by the end of the year."

She shoots me a doubtful look over FaceTime as she adjusts her pearls. Because of course she wears pearls while watering plants in her Seattle backyard. "Was it really that many?" she asks airily. "It seemed like one."

"It was hardly one." I watch the boats gliding along the sapphire-blue water of the bay. It's serene here and feels far removed from the events of this morning. I bathed Zamboni and worked out with the conditioning coach, gaining the necessary distance from the madness of that run-in. Did that sexy chaos demon get distance too? Has she given it a second thought?

I dismiss her from my mind and focus on the current problem. "Look, I'm meeting with a new designer, and it's going to be great. You'll be able to move in very soon."

"I should meet with this person," Mom says, setting the green metal watering can by a garden bed. "It'll be easier that way."

It'll be easier if she's not involved at all. The more involved she gets, the more opinions she has, the more issues she finds, the more problems she makes. She thinks she's being helpful, but she's steamrolling me, and I just want to do something nice for her and Dad.

I briefly remember wanting to do something nice for my ex-wife—and look where that got me. I'd arranged for a private chef when she wanted to learn to cook, only for her to shack up with him instead.

This is not the same, of course. This is for my parents. But I have a plan for this year, and micromanaging a home renovation is not part of it. Giving my parents the home of their dreams is. That's the point of hiring a designer—not that it's been easy. The last person I interviewed reeked of weed, and the person before that said her design aesthetic was actually brutalist, not environmentally friendly.

"I've got this, Mom," I say, firm but not pushy. If Mom senses an opening, she'll take it. And I can't go through a dozen more designers.

"I really should oversee it," she adds in the persuasive tone she uses to convince people to donate to the charity she works with. The Seattle-based organization brings recycling and composting initiatives to communities all over the country, including here in San Francisco.

"No, Mom, you should focus on making sure your final charity gala goes off without a hitch. Designers exist to handle the inside. I'll make sure she does everything to your standards and shows you what she selects," I say as a flock of seagulls flies by. I breathe in calmly, savoring the view.

"When are you meeting with this person?"

"Today."

She hums, doubtful. "Well, do you want to conference me in?"

I don't know how my mother is going to survive retirement. She's reduced her hours to part-time, but she's still entirely too busy. "Let me do this for you and Dad. I've always wanted to. You know that," I say. "And don't worry. The designer will be great."

And honestly, Skylar Haven better be. I reviewed her design portfolio online, and the style is one hundred percent my mom's—creative but classy, a little edgy, and very eco-conscious. So it'll be like a breakaway shot, a nice easy path to the goal.

"Call me the second it's done, Ford. *Since you refuse* to video call the whole time," she says.

I roll my eyes, making sure she sees. "Bye, Mom."

I love her. Really, I do. But she's making finishing this house harder than playing an entire hockey season on a torn groin.

Hanging up, I check the time before tucking the phone into my back pocket. The designer should arrive in five minutes, so I head out to the deck overlooking the water. In the short wait, I take my phone out again. One thing has been weighing on me since this morning—the nagging worry that I was too harsh about the Doxie's shameless display. I ask Google, "Why do neutered dogs hump?" and scan the answer.

Was the hot-mess redhead right? No way. I check another site. Then another. Then one more.

"Huh," I mutter. Apparently, yes, dogs can get overly excited, and that extra energy turns into—you guessed it —humping.

Maybe I owe her an apology if I ever run into her again while walking the dog.

I check the time as the doorbell rings. Nice. She's a touch early. I seriously appreciate that.

I stride over to the door, swing it open, and freeze. The hot-mess redhead stands in front of me, looking shockingly professional and cheery. Gone is the just-rolled-out-of-bed couture. In its place? A polished, businesslike blazer and slacks, and hair that's actually seen a brush.

The copper strands fall in soft waves, framing her pretty face and a bright smile.

A smile that vanishes as soon as recognition dawns in her eyes.

"Arc you kidding me?" I ask.

She gawks, blinks, and says almost hopefully, "I must have the wrong home."

This has to be a mistake. She can't be the designer. "Are you..." I swallow roughly, then manage to get out, "Skylar Haven?"

Her lips curl like she just ate something sour and nods slowly, as if reality is sinking in. "Yes. Skylar Haven with Haven Designs."

My mind whirls, assimilating the situation. She may be a sexy chaos demon, but her style is Mom's style, and I need someone to take on this job, yesterday.

But I can't let on how desperately I need this to work out. The thing I've learned playing in the pros? Never let the enemy see a weakness. "I didn't know you owned anything besides a robe."

She slides a finger down the lapel of her blazer, furrows her brow, then shrugs. "It works as a robe, too though. See? I'm all about using things in multiple ways."

Damn. She's good. I try not to laugh, but it's hard. I turn away, but I still open the door and let the sexy chaos demon past the threshold, hoping I won't regret it.

5

I'LL RAISE YOU A CHAIR

SKYLAR

Clearly, this is a test. What other explanation could there be for my potential new client being a man who hates me?

The man I supposedly despise too.

I mean, fine. What did he really do other than admonish my dog-rearing skills? But isn't that enough?

Still, I won't let on. I'm dressed to impress, and I'm going to move forward and dazzle him with my skills. Would a big design firm freak out? Nope. I won't either. No way am I going to let another gig slip through my fingers.

I stick out a hand, keeping my brightest business smile in place. "Pleasure to meet you," I say, ready to put the morning's incident behind us. "I'm so excited to see the house."

Maybe he'll just forget we became mortal enemies this morning.

He looks at my hand with a raised brow. Then, after a beat, he takes it. "Ford Devon," he says.

Ah. He just used his last name over email. Interesting.

"So it's not just Devon?" I ask. "Do you prefer Devon?"

"Ford will do," he says, then blows out a breath. His forehead is all bunched up. This man is so intense. "I... wasn't expecting you."

"And I wasn't expecting you," I say lightly. "Are you moving out of the house next door to me and into this one?"

He tilts his head, looking thoroughly confused. "What do you mean?"

"Well, we..."

Oh. Shit.

He doesn't realize I live next door to him. He doesn't know I spied on him from my brother's catio this morning and must not have seen where I marched away to this morning. And he definitely didn't see me this afternoon when I peeked on him from the front door.

Oh, god. Could this get any worse?

I have to tap dance my way through this. I swallow and power through. "I live on Franklin Street in Hayes Valley. My brother mentioned some of his neighbors before I moved in a month and a half ago."

There. When all else fails, blame thy brother.

My potential client's handsome face goes entirely blank. Ice blue eyes glazed. Lips parted.

Shock, thy name is Ford Devon. "You're my neighbor?" he chokes out. "My next-door neighbor."

Some luck, huh? But I smile. Fake it till you make it. "Yes, I am."

Too bad I don't have those shishito peppers right now. I could use an apology gift. But then again, do I really want to start a business meeting with an apology? Actually, maybe I should. I was probably too amused by Simon, and then too annoyed by Ford. I can't just gloss over the...*illicit encounter.*

"And I'm sorry again about this morning," I say, shifting into full-on professional mode. "But I already have some amazing design ideas for your house based on the info you sent over earlier."

"This house is for my parents, actually."

"Great, well I think your vision—integrating the natural charm of Sausalito while still keeping a modern, recycled aesthetic—is very doable." I gesture toward my bag with my tablet in it. "Would you like me to show you what I have in mind?"

He blinks, then collects himself. "Sure."

You've got this, Skylar Haven. You're a badass babe.

I click open my portfolio, and as he takes me from room to room, I pull up a range of design ideas that could work—reclaimed wood, bamboo furniture, secondhand furniture that's as good as new, and a house filled with just the right amount of greenery.

"My mom does love plants," he says, almost begrudgingly.

Bingo.

"And I know all the best places to shop," I add, my confidence surging. "From San Francisco to Cozy Valley and down to Palo Alto—there are so many great options for sustainable materials and decor." I scan the walls in the living room. They're sage green, easy on the eyes. Most of the others are a soft shade of eggshell, a relaxing, warm hue. "I see you've already painted. That's great."

Ford lets out a low huff of amusement. "My mom hated the painter. Loved the colors though."

Hmm. She sounds hard to please, but I love a challenge. "What did she dislike about the painter?"

"The timing. She wants everything done yesterday."

Ah, that's easy. I don't like to fuck around either. "I like her already."

He shoots me a skeptical but curious look. "Next, you'll tell me you can find a mid-century chair for her home office. She's been looking for one for a while."

Please. "Of course I can."

His gaze sharpens. "That so?"

"Absolutely."

He seems to mull that over, then says, "Listen, Skylar..."

I hear *it*. The tone.

The one that says he's about to let me down.

My heart sinks.

I wanted this job. I truly did. A coveted chance as a solo designer to tackle the whole house, not just a single room. And a house like this, with that stunning view of the water? It's a huge opportunity. I can't believe I'm about to lose it because my dog humped his dog.

Or, really, because I laughed at the scene.

Fine, I laughed uncontrollably.

God, I *am* uncouth.

Trevyn's voice rings in my head: *"Look, if someone's Yorkie tried to get it on with Barbara-dor, I would cut them with my sharp wit."*

I lift a hand before Ford can continue. I need to apologize like I mean it. Not like I'm trying to win a deal. "I'm sorry about Simon."

He blinks. Clearly, he wasn't expecting that.

"He's...very excitable," I add, with a self-deprecating smile. "But I completely understand that your little cutie girl wasn't into it. You had every right to be annoyed with Simon and with me. And I definitely shouldn't have laughed."

Ford tilts his head, saying nothing at first. Then, finally, he asks, "Cutie girl?"

I nod. "She's adorable. She's part Corgi, part German Shepherd, right?"

"She is," he says, and suddenly, his entire demeanor warms.

"What's her name?" I ask.

"Zamboni," he says, unsuccessfully fighting off a smile and the dimple that comes with it.

That's too stinking cute. Both the name and the dimple. But damn, the dimple is hot too.

"That is seriously adorable," I say, grinning. "You play hockey, right? My brother mentioned it."

It's the perfect cover, and I have to keep it up. While the apology was necessary, this man will never need to know I checked him out this morning. Especially since I won't do it again. If he becomes a client that'd be a bad idea.

"Yeah. I do," he says. Then he hesitates. "I thought maybe—" He waves a hand, dismissing whatever he was about to say.

"That I recognized you?" I guess, but then the moment from this morning flashes before my eyes. When I looked up, startled to see him, and was about to say *you're the yoga guy*, but I cut myself off. Good thing. Past me was looking out for present me and before he can answer I lean all the way in. "I did. Big hockey fan."

That's not entirely true. But I've been to a few games since some of my friends are dating hockey players.

"Cool," he says, then pauses, looking toward the sparkling bay beyond the windows. He's quiet for a few seconds, and I get the sense he's a man who's okay with silence. There's something attractive about that—it says you're comfortable in your own skin. When he turns back to me, his jaw is set. Is his mind set too? "What I was going to say earlier was I'm sorry too."

I blink. What? I was the offender. "For...what?"

"I was kind of harsh on the street," he says.

Oh. That. Well, yeah. He *was*. But I bite my tongue, since I don't want to say *yeah, you were, dude*.

"And I looked up what you were saying about dogs and being excited. And...you were right."

Holy smokes. *You were right* are three of the best words in the universe. The only ones better? *You got the job.*

I rein in my enthusiasm, even though I swear bubbles are flowing in my veins. Those words have to be coming next. I'm already imagining popping the cork with my friends and toasting to my new gig. Then, paying the rent. My brother's house isn't free after all. Even a good deal from family costs—gasp—money.

"Well, thank you for saying that. I'm glad we're all good," I say, and inside I'm thinking *please, please, please give me the gig*.

He extends a hand. "Thank you for coming by. I'll be in touch."

Oh. Okay. I've been dismissed. And in this industry, four out of five 'I'll be in touches' end with no touches at all. Nada. Zip.

The job's as good as gone. I swallow down the ball of failure rolling through me, say thank you, and leave.

* * *

On the bus back to the city, I replay the entire meeting. Hell, I rewind the whole day. But I keep coming back to my portfolio. Ford legitimately seemed impressed by the ideas.

He also indicated over email that he wanted to move quickly.

All I can think is that a simple apology won't do. I need to prove to the hard-ass why I'm the right person for the job. He's an athlete, so he's used to competition. I'll show him I know how to compete.

Once I'm home, I call Mabel and ask her for a particular recipe.

"You want to make *that*? It's so not you."

"I know, but sometimes you need to get out of your comfort zone."

"Okay," she says skeptically, then texts it to me.

I pop out to the store. When I return, I scour the websites of some of my favorite stores and put a hold on a very special item. Next, I find the plain white dog T-shirt I picked up for Simon at Second Time Around—sometimes he wears dog clothes on his social media feed. Usually, I just Photoshop writing onto them, but for this, I grab a fabric marker, spread the shirt out on the kitchen table, and start writing.

Simon stares at me from his spot on the floor, head tilted, waiting.

"I know you want your picture taken, but now's not the time, you camera hog."

He turns his snout the other way and waddles off.

It's past eight when I finish. Probably too late to stop by my neighbor's home.

Guess I'll have to catch Ford tomorrow after yoga. Such a shame that I'll have to watch him shirtless after all. But a lady boss has to do what a lady boss has to do.

* * *

In the morning, I keep popping onto the back porch, peering carefully around the edge of it. I can see some of Ford's deck from here too, though the view's not as good, nor am I as hidden here as I am in the catio. From the second Ford appears on the porch in his yellow compression shorts—why on earth does the man like yellow?—I peek out every few minutes as he moves through his sun salutations.

The moment he's done, I hustle to the kitchen, grab the goodies and my dog, and head to the front door.

Checking my reflection, I confirm I look presentable. Stylish jeans, cute sandals, and—I hate to admit this—a yellow top.

It's pale yellow though. The only acceptable shade.

"Wish me luck," I say to my reflection. Then I do the neighborly thing.

Well, if you're the type of neighbor who royally screwed up and now wants to win a contract.

After I leash up Simon, I head next door, swallow down the last remnants of nerves, and take a deep, fortifying breath as I knock.

After a few seconds, I hear barking. Not aggressive—more inquisitive.

Soon, I catch a glimpse of Ford striding through the home, and—my breath hitches.

He's wearing basketball shorts and a gray T-shirt. The compression shorts are gone. And I'd really better not think about the fact that he was whisking them off moments ago.

Tilting his head, he shoots me a *what the hell are you*

doing here look through the window next to the door but still tugs it open.

Simon barks once—enthusiastically. But when I tell him to sit, he plunks his butt down like a good boy.

"Good morning," I begin smoothly as Ford's dog checks us out from a dog bed several feet away. "Simon just wanted to bring Zamboni some dog treats made from kale."

I hand him a small brown paper bag full of home-made dog biscuits.

Ford arches a brow. "My dog doesn't like kale. Unless it's in a smoothie."

Damn. But no worries—I can pivot. "I did wonder if the dog and I had some things in common..." I say lightly. "But guess what? Here's the rest of the bunch for your smoothie."

I hand him the fresh bunch I picked up last night.

Ford takes it. "Thanks."

Oh. Is that a hint of a smile?

It disappears in a second only to reappear when his gaze shifts to my dog. Ford reads the T-shirt I made for Simon, then arches a brow before looking back at me. "*Not The Goodest Boy (But I'm Trying)*?" he asks.

"He's a work in progress," I say.

And here goes the pièce de résistance.

"I'm off to my favorite consignment store in Noe Valley," I say, playing it casual. "They just got a classic Eames chair in. I'd love to reserve it for your mom's home office."

His jaw falls open. "Wait. You—seriously?"

"Yes. Do you think she'll want it?" I ask, knowing full well it's *the* dream chair for mid-century aficionados.

"Yes," he says, still looking like I've just knocked him over. "Absolutely."

I smirk. "Does that mean I got the job?"

He pauses, recovers his composure, and then shoots me that cocky smile again. The one that shows off his dimple.

"I was coming over to tell you as much," he admits with a no-big-deal shrug.

I blink, shocked and thrilled. "You were?"

He scratches his jaw casually. "I decided yesterday to hire you."

Wait. Hold on. I park a hand on my hip. "Did you just want to make me sweat?"

His smile turns victorious as he waggles the green leaves in his hand. "Or maybe I wanted the kale. I need to make a smoothie after all. I'll be in touch with details."

Bending down, he strokes Simon's head, and my little dude eats up the affection, even as Ford says, "Let's keep you out of air jail."

Then he heads back inside and shuts the door.

6

THE GOOD STUFF

FORD

The penguin's almost there. One more corner in this maze, and I'll get him to the end. But the maze fucks with me, shifting ninety degrees on the screen.

Ha. I won't go down that easily.

I readjust to the new spatial orientation, maneuver the penguin through the last turn, and send him safely out.

I punch the air.

"Dude, how fast were you today?" Wesley Bryant, one of our star wingers, asks from across the locker room as he tugs on his shoulder pads.

"Thirty-two seconds," I say proudly as I stretch in front of my stall and toss my phone into the cubby.

Our goalie, Max Lambert, wiggles his fingers from his stall. "Gimme. I can beat you."

I scoff. "You wish."

He taps his temple. "I've been training my brain for a long time."

From the other side of me, Tyler Falcon snorts. "Might want to see if you can get a refund next time," says the defenseman, who became a fast friend after joining the team a couple years ago.

Max strides over, half-dressed in his chest protector and shorts. "I will kill it in this penguin game," he declares. "I do eye exercises all the time."

"Yeah? Then use your eyes to look it up on your phone. It's called—hold on," I say, waiting as he doubles back and grabs his phone, presumably opening a search bar or app store. As he looks back at me, I finish, "*The Penguin Maze That Ford Devon Owns Your Ass In*."

Max glares at me like he wants to murder me in my sleep.

It'd be a long, slow, painful death.

I'd probably deserve it.

I flash a closed-mouth grin as I pull on a yellow under-shirt. "Look, I'm happy to wipe the floor with all you clowns in the brain-game department," I say.

I've only been playing them my entire time in the pros. Anything for an edge.

Anything to prove I belong here.

When I was younger, so many people said I didn't. Well, the facts said it too. I went undrafted. After college, I had to claw my way up. I went to a training camp for the Miami team as a free agent and impressed them, but I got sent to the minors. Then I landed a shot at the Phoenix training camp. Same deal—I was an undrafted free agent too, only older. But I played hard, worked harder, and finally snagged a slot on the roster. Didn't log ice time in my first NHL game until I was twenty-four.

Nearly ancient by this sport's standards.

Definitely an anomaly, as sportscasters pointed out. Hockey pundits figured I'd be an afterthought. The player who'd spend a couple of months in the pros, fill in here or there, and disappear.

I defied the odds.

I stayed for twelve.

A career in hockey was a puzzle to solve.

And that's what I fucking do.

These brain games help with focus. And now, all my focus goes to the ice.

I pull on my jersey, then grab my water bottle—the same one I bring to every game, covered in stickers of mountains with the words Surprise Them across the side. "All right, kids. Hitting the ice for warmups," I say.

"Good plan, old man," Max calls. "Let me know if you need your AARP card to play tonight."

I flip him the bird and head out.

* * *

Look, I'm not saying the Penguin Maze warmed up my brain, but I am in the zone physically *and* mentally.

In the first period, when I'm not on the ice, I'm laser-focused on studying the Chicago defenders here in our rink and the way they try to snag the puck from our forwards.

When it's time for a line change, I hop over the boards and attack, drowning out everything but the game.

The crowd noise? Gone.

The chirping from the opponents? Irrelevant.

Every thought outside of this second, this play, this chance? Nonexistent.

Falcon snags the puck on a rebound and flicks it my way.

I escort it down the ice, taking a shot on goal.

It's nearly there, but their goalie lunges for it, snagging it just before it goes in.

Next time.

We'll get it next time.

I don't get stuck on what didn't happen in one play. The past is already written. But the future? That's still up for grabs.

When the shift ends, I hop over the boards, take a breath, and visualize what's coming.

And in the third period, I'm fucking ready when Bryant jumps on the puck, racing down the ice. I'm right by his side, but a Chicago defender comes out of nowhere, stripping it from him.

Fuck that.

As the guy spins, clearly hunting for a teammate to pass to, I reach out my stick, *thank you very much*, and take it for myself.

I race back toward the net, calculating, waiting, reading the Chicago goalie.

He shifts right.

I send the puck left, straight to Bryant, who whips it past a sliver of an opening.

Perfect shot.

The lamp lights. The crowd roars. For a brief second, I let the sound filter in.

That's another thing I've learned over time—how to block out the noise that doesn't matter. And how to let in only the good stuff since the good stuff fuels you.

Otherwise known as *how to have a thick skin*.

When the game ends with a W, I skate off the ice, grateful we're starting the season with another win.

More grateful that I feel good.

Well, mostly good.

I move through my post-game rituals. But even after a quick bike ride at the arena, and then a polar plunge for five minutes at fifty-two degrees—and doing them after nearly every home game for more than ten years doesn't make these ice baths any easier—my muscles are still sore, and my neck is tighter than a jack-in-the-box. Nothing that some time in the hot tub at home won't fix though.

On the drive there, my mind wanders to my cute and irresistibly sexy neighbor, who I'm meeting in a couple days about the renovation.

And I wonder, can I see her from the hot tub up on the second-floor balcony? Is there a view into her kitchen? Her bedroom? Her living room? I've never looked, and the whole way home, I can't stop wondering what I'd see if I did.

The thought is entirely too tempting as I walk in the door.

* * *

With board shorts on, and Zamboni watching my every move, I grab my water bottle from my bureau—the one I keep at home that my sister's kids got me for Christmas. They're just as practical as their mom but a bit more creative since they put stickers of Corgis, German Shepherds, and my dog all over it.

Patting my thigh, I say to my girl, "C'mon, Zamboni."

She trots by my side as I pad across the bedroom to the sliding glass doors, tug them open, and walk onto the balcony. I stretch under the stars, lifting my arms to the sky, shifting my neck back and forth, and keeping my gaze fixed firmly in front of me.

Not to the side. Not to my neighbor's home.

I won't look.

I definitely won't look.

I'll just enjoy the stars along with the bubbling hot tub. Setting my phone on top of a stack of towels on a small, low stand away from the water, I sink into the welcoming heat. Zamboni parks herself on the wooden deck.

As I gaze up at the inky sky and the stars winking on and off, I take a drink of water—gotta stay hydrated in the jacuzzi—then close my eyes, letting the water work its magic.

I let my mind go blank. This is owning my time, right? I'm using this moment to relax and recharge.

And it works. Hell, it's easy to keep my focus in front of me. It's late, nearly eleven, and I bet Skylar isn't even up. If I did glance next door, the curtains would be closed, the house shrouded in darkness.

Don't think about your neighbor. Think about relaxing in this final part of your post-game ritual.

But...what if I could see her?

Except, nope.

I shouldn't do that. I really fucking shouldn't. I don't watch my neighbors. I mind my own damn business.

But there's a difference between watching and just... noticing. Right?

I'm not spying. I'm just...curious.

What's the harm, really?

We live next door to each other. We've seen each other a few times already. She walks her dog. I walk mine. I'm simply sitting here on my balcony. Just...checking out the neighborhood. A safety check of sorts.

I open my eyes and look.

Hmm. Just the side of her house.

I shift to another seat in the hot tub. Nope. Still just the yard, like always.

But wait.

If I lean my head to the right…

I peer farther into her yard, and there it is—the catio her brother had built over the summer.

Huh. I've never had a close-up look at a cat playpen before. That's interesting. I wonder how many shelves it has, how far it goes, what the levels look like.

"What do you think, girl? Should I get a better look?" I ask Zamboni as I shift around, and…

Oh.

Well.

I've never sat on this side of the hot tub before.

And right here, I can look down and see the kitchen.

Where Skylar's walking around in—I squint—are those sleep shorts?

The light in her kitchen is soft, casting a golden glow on her pale skin. Her legs are long, smooth, toned in a way that makes my chest tighten. The cami clings to her just barely, like it's hanging on for dear life.

And that hair—copper waves have been braided loosely, messy strands slipping free. Like she's just casually twisted her hair into a braid, with barely a second thought. What was she doing when she swept it up? Was she talking to a friend on the phone? Singing along to an upbeat tune on her playlist? Bingeing a comedy series? No. She probably watches something I'd never expect. Like, I don't know, zombie shows.

And she's holding her phone, talking into it—a voice memo maybe? She walks to the counter a few feet away, and I can't see all of her anymore. I break my stare to grab a drink of water, then set the bottle down again.

And...hold the fuck on. She's back in view and...now she's bending over.

Heat rolls through me. I shift in my seat, adjusting myself beneath the water.

My grip tightens on the edge of the hot tub.

My neighbor—the woman I've just hired—is standing in her kitchen, wearing the tiniest fucking shorts I've ever seen.

A lot of good the water break did. I am parched.

I should look away. I should absolutely, one hundred percent, look away.

But I don't. Not sure I can once her shorts ride up, showing off the back of her legs in a way that makes my chest rumble. That sends my brain spinning in filthy directions. A sound lodges low in my throat.

This is so wrong. And yet, I can't seem to stop.

"I'm a bad, bad man," I mutter, tearing my gaze from the building next door and focusing on my dog instead.

Zamboni tilts her head, judging me. Hard. "Oh, don't look at me like that. I've seen you try to eat fifty-day-old bagels on the side of the road."

She huffs and turns her snout away from me. A second later, I'm distracted by the view once more as Skylar rises, holding her wild dog. She cuddles Simon on her left side and clasps his paw with her right hand like they're dancing.

A laugh bursts out before I can stop it. Holy shit. They're waltzing. Or is that a tango? Maybe a mix of both. She sways in a full circle with the horndog, shimmying her hips, giving him a kiss on his snout. The music must shift to a faster rhythm. Now she's club dancing with the Doxie mix, hitting some kind of groove like she's been partying all night long under purple lights and pink smoke.

After a final ruffle of his fur, she sets him down on the floor.

A smile tugs at my lips—this woman hosts dance parties with her dog late at night. What is it like to have that kind of...spirit? And to continue to move like that? She sashays back over to the counter, still swaying to some kind of song.

I really should stop watching my new decorator. But I don't.

She returns to her counter, grabs her phone, and then comes back into view. She taps it and speaks into it again.

A second later, my phone buzzes.

I jerk back like I've just got caught. Like she can see me watching her from all the way across the yard.

I stretch for my phone on the stand, checking the screen.

Skylar Haven is texting. Shit. Can she see me? After drying my fingers on the towel, I slide open the phone while rehearsing excuses—*Hey, is that an owl in your tree?* Or, *What exactly is the roof of that catio made of because it sure looks sturdy*?

> Skylar: Hi, Ford! Just wanted to check in and make sure it's okay that I mention your parents' home on my design podcast. I won't name you or your parents, but I'd love to talk about the general themes and looks.

Ah, okay. That's easy enough to answer, though my pulse is still jackhammering as I settle back into the water, keeping the phone above it.

Ford: Works for me.

There. She'll never suspect I was watching her if I keep my reply curt.

Skylar: Thank you! And we'll be meeting at Twice Loved, a consignment shop in Noe Valley, on Friday at eleven? Did your mom like the picture of the chair I sent you?

Skylar mentioned that shop when I followed up with her earlier today. Since she's seen the house already, she suggested meeting at the store that's holding the Eames chair. Mom's initial reaction to the photo was, *If that feels as good as it looks, I will divorce your father and marry that piece of furniture.* But my mother is notably capricious, so I play it safe and tap out another succinct reply.

Ford: Yep.

Skylar: Cool! I'll see you there then. I'll be a few minutes early, so buzz me if you arrive early too.

.   .   .

I frown. That's a little unusual.

> Ford: Are you planning to run away with
> the Eames chair before I get there?

>> Skylar: Not unless it fits on the bus. And
>> that's why I'll be early, by the way. I catch
>> the bus.

Wait. She's taking the bus? That makes no sense since she lives right next door.

> Ford: I can drive you. We're leaving from
> the same place.

But that's presumptuous. She might have another meeting. I tap out another note.

> Ford: But you might be coming from
> someplace else.

>> Skylar: I love carpools! I can be back here,
>> neighbor.

She adds a winking smiley face.

Neighbor? That's casual. Familiar. But does that wink mean she saw me watching her? My stomach twists. I lean over again, watching as she texts and wanders around her kitchen. But she's not staring out the window, so maybe she doesn't know.

> Ford: Sounds like a plan. Meet you out front of our homes at ten-forty then.

There. That sounds all businesslike. As it fucking should.

> Skylar: This is so much better than the bus. Well, presuming you don't watch clips of Michael Scott at top volume on your phone like the guy next to me on the bus did yesterday. I mean, I love The Office, but I don't want to hear random outtakes. Also, you don't clip your nails while you drive, right? That happened to me last week.

I cringe.

> Ford: The bus driver?

Skylar: Oh no! Just a passenger. I don't
even know how a driver would do that.
Do you?

Wow. She's hard to keep up with, but I'm ready for the
task.

Ford: Using autopilot.

Skylar: Do you have autopilot on your car?

Ford: Yes, but I don't clip my nails. Or
watch TV.

Skylar: In general, you don't watch TV?

I roll my eyes, but I'm laughing.

Ford: When I drive, Skylar. I don't watch
TV when I drive.

Skylar: But you do watch it?

She wants to tease me. I take the bait. It's making the hot
tub even more enjoyable, after all.

Ford: What do you think?

She paces her kitchen, then turns to the window. I tense—
but only for a second. Turns out she's staring at the sky—
not next door, just the sky—before returning to her
phone.

Skylar: I bet you watch how-to-make-a-
kale-smoothie videos. I bet you look up
'how to train your dog to shake.' I bet you
watch tutorials on how to fix a dishwasher
if it breaks.

I stare at the phone, then across the yard, then back at my
screen. Fuck. She's scarily good.

Ford: I like The Office too.

And I should say goodnight, but I don't. Curiosity has me
in a chokehold. Also, I need to know if I'm right.

Ford: And you? Do you watch decorating
shows? Comedy specials from women
comics? Zombie shows?

Skylar: Why women?

Ford: They're usually funnier than men.

Skylar: True, true.

Ford: And the answer?

I glance to the right, just to check. She's sitting on a kitchen stool now, I think, and...damn. Is that a smile on her face as she replies?

My chest feels a little warm.

No shit. You're in a hot tub.

Skylar: Tonight, I'm bingeing how to impress your client with the best kale smoothie ever.

I know that's not what she's doing. I could call bullshit, but instead, I grin and call her bluff.

Ford: Can't wait.

7

SEXY RENO GUY

SKYLAR

The next morning, I walk in early to the podcast studio in the Mission District—because no one ever slays by being late. My matchmaker friend Isla uses this studio for her wildly successful dating advice show, and I snagged some recording time here for my design podcast. Pretty sure she struck a *sure, we'll let your friend use the space as long as we can have you too* kind of deal, but hey, beggars can't be choosers.

In the break room, I'm pouring another cup of iced coffee when Trevyn walks in with Mabel. Her caramel-colored hair falls in perfect waves since she has perfect hair, blonde streaks and all. I'd be jealous if I didn't love her so much. She dictates into her phone as she enters: "I'm not going to tell him how to boil an egg because boiled eggs are gross." Then she hits send, looks up, and says with zero apology, "My brother. I'm trying to stop him from making an egg salad."

"You're doing the Lord's work," I say solemnly.

"She always is," Trevyn says, "and so is Simon." He waggles his phone at me then clears his throat and reads,

"*Waiting for Mom to finally take dance lessons. If she improves, maybe she can make some cash shaking it—gotta fund my posh lifestyle somehow.*"

He's reading straight from my dog's social feed.

"Simon's shameless. What can I say? He's practically begging for a sponsorship," I reply.

"He deserves one," Mabel says.

"Well, Simon Side-Eye *is* more popular than me," I admit, since my dog absolutely kills it on social media with his sarcastic commentary on our photos—like the one I took last night of us dancing. "Seriously, where does he come up with this stuff?"

"I can't even imagine," Mabel says, nodding toward the studio. "Ready? I need to meet a broker later today."

"Ooh, do you think you'll get a space finally?" I ask. Mabel's been trying to find the perfect location for a bakery.

She crosses her fingers. "We'll see." She sounds cautious, wary even, but I get it. She's been working her butt off to make the leap from selling cookies and other treats at farmers' markets, pop-up shops, and local cafés to, hopefully, having her own bakery. A few spaces have fallen through, but I'm seriously proud of her gumption and her skills. Trevyn too—he refurbishes furniture. It's a far cry from his former career as a professional pairs figure skater, but he's nailing this one just like he nailed jumps and lutzes once upon a time.

We head into the small studio and move into our seats like synchronized podcasters. I flip open my laptop, fire up the software, and hit a few buttons. After testing our mics, we're good to go. The only thing left is the camera. I pop my smartphone into the ring light in the room, hit record, then return to my seat.

"Hey there, we're back with another episode of *Hot Trends, Classic Spends.* This is your host—Skylar Haven. I'm joined by two of my favorite sidekicks—"

Trevyn clears his throat. "Sidekick? I like to think of myself as the main attraction."

"I'm bringing the headliner energy too," Mabel adds, not to be outdone.

"Fine, fine. We are all superstars here," I concede. "And I'm going to be a superheroine of eco-design since my new client wants me to do—wait for it—his entire house *and* make it sustainable."

They already know this, but Trevyn gives a "whoop, whoop," and Mabel adds, "That's awesome."

"Thank you. I'm, admittedly, a little excited. I live for this kind of blank slate. And I have big plans," I add, then share some of my general ideas for the home.

"And this is for Sexy Reno Guy?" Trevyn asks with a *gotcha* smirk.

Of course Trevyn knows the big new client *is* the hot neighbor I hated for a day. I'd never keep that kind of juicy nugget from friends. Still, I do my best to remain unfazed for the sake of podcasting entertainment, furrowing my brow as I innocently ask, "Did I call him that?"

Mabel smirks. "No, but based on the red in your face, I think the name might be sticking."

I press a hand to my cheeks. My skin *is* a little hot. "Please. My cheeks aren't red," I say, grabbing my coffee and taking a long sip. It'll cool me off.

"So he *is* Sexy Reno Guy?" Trevyn smirks, enjoying himself way too much.

"I would never use such a term," I say, acting all prim and proper.

"Doesn't mean we can't. Right, Trev?" Mabel, the little scamp, flashes a grin at Trevyn.

He leans back in his chair. "I'm all for calling it like it is."

"As I said, he's a client." *And he has muscles for days. And hair that I want to rope my fingers through. And a stern expression that I find ludicrously hot.*

"Poh-tay-toe, poh-tah-toe. He can be a client *and* hot. The two aren't mutually exclusive," Trevyn points out, always stirring up trouble. "Mabel, level with our followers. Have you ever had a hot...client? Like, the owners of the cafés and places you supply to?"

"I don't think of my clients that way," Mabel answers diplomatically, and who's the prim and proper one now?

"Oh, the tables have turned," I say to her.

"When you're hauling boxes of baked goods at four in the morning, you're not usually thinking of someone's hotness since your own hotness is in the swamp," she explains.

Trevyn snorts. "Liar. One, you're always hot, Mabel. And two, your hotness detector does not turn off even if you're a swamp."

"He's right. The radar is twenty-four-seven," I say.

Trevyn levels me with a sharp stare. "My point exactly. So the sooner *you* admit your new client is a hot tamale, the better off we'll be."

"And why's that?" I counter.

He sets his chin in his hand. "Because it's more fun for me."

I laugh, then relent slightly. "Fine, I'll admit Sexy Reno Guy is easy on the eyes. But that's not the point—"

"That's the *whole* point," Mabel says, and we spend the

rest of the show arguing about design and the client hotness scale.

Trevyn tries to goad me into ranking everyone I've ever worked with on a one-to-ten scale. And, like a perfect sidekick, Mabel encourages him.

But I stay strong. I refuse.

I've already called him Sexy Reno Guy, and that's *plenty* for now.

No need to indulge any more wildly inappropriate thoughts about my tightly wound, hard-ass, hot-as-hell client.

* * *

Some people dream of relaxing on the beach. But *my* happy place is a two-block section of the Dogpatch District that's home to design business after design business. From lighting shops to furniture stores to a place that specializes in bio-glass, I could spend all day here. Sometimes I do.

I say goodbye to Trevyn as he drops me off at the corner, then I dive straight in. While Ford and I are going to a consignment shop tomorrow, I want to do some preliminary work today on materials for countertops or bathroom sinks—I have a feeling we might need to redo a few of those in his parents' new home.

I rap on the door of the appointment-only Reflective Showroom, and Amika hustles over to let me in.

"Come in, come in. I read that Simon is demanding a steady supply of dog bones and biscuits," she says, her British accent carrying a soft lilt from her years in India.

"I work for my pets," I say.

"And why isn't he here today? I love my little Simon hugs."

"He needed to catch up on his beauty sleep. Apparently, there's a Doxie law that they must sleep twenty-one hours a day."

"Reasonable. Totally reasonable."

"I also had to do my podcast. And Simon's a little too chatty in the studio."

"He has a lot on his mind," she says.

"And you have a lot of new stuff here," I say, my eyes widening as I scan the showroom.

"We do. Let me show you around," she says, and just like that, I'm a kid in a candy store—running my fingers over smooth marble and snapping pics of shimmering glass, already picturing the perfect countertop.

I thank Amika and pop into the bamboo furniture showroom a few doors down, snapping pictures of some fantastic new chairs and stools with neat, clean lines. Next, I dart into the lighting shop, making notes on my tablet of new recessed ceiling lights and a plethora of LED options.

I can find all this online too, but nothing beats actually seeing the products you might recommend to a client— touching them too. Making sure the Internet doesn't— gasp—lie.

I also check out some vintage desk lamps for Sofia Ximena, a civil rights attorney who hired me to make some updates in her new office. It's only slightly intimidating outfitting a high-profile law practice where they all do good work in crisp navy suits as they fight the system, but hey, if I've been tasked to help them see their documents better, I'm up to the challenge. I snap some pics to send to Sofia.

When I'm done there, I pop outside and check the time. Mom should be here any minute for our weekly lunch, so I tuck my tablet into my tote bag and check my reflection in the window of a tile showroom, spotting Mom several feet away as I do. I spin around. She's sporting big sunglasses, a slouchy bag she's had forever (because, as she puts it, who needs more than one handbag?), and a warm grin.

When she reaches me, she pushes her shades into her thick mane of auburn hair, clutches my shoulder, and declares, like it's a battle cry, "I want you to know I'm going to boycott Games People Play when it opens later this month."

My brow furrows as I try to put two and two together. When it hits me, I wince. "Wait. Is that the name of Landon's shop?"

"Yes," she says, aggrieved, as she links arms with me and we head to Happy Cow, a few blocks away. "I'm on his newsletter list. I subscribe so you don't have to."

"Thanks, Mom. You're the best," I say, and really, she is.

"And even though I need a new stash of party games for game night, I will find another board game shop. I refuse to go to his store."

"They do sell them online," I say.

"Please. It's much more fun to find a local competitor to that cad—and mark my words, I will," she says as we reach the restaurant. Its white wood exterior and green awning, adorned with an illustration of a cow drinking what appears to be lemonade, is always inviting. A chalkboard menu out front advertises today's specials—a mushroom burger and a lentil salad. Yum.

"You don't have to keep doing penance," I point out as we head inside.

"It's not penance. It's parenting," she says, then turns to the hostess stand and tells a woman with a nose ring and a Happy Cow apron that we'd love a table for two, ideally by the open window.

"Right this way," the woman says as she whisks us to a bright white table that looks like it's an antique that's been repainted.

"Do you know where this is from, Dahlia?" I ask, reading the hostess's name tag. "Or can you ask the manager?"

She pauses, then shrugs. "Sure."

My mom arches a knowing brow when Dahlia takes off. "Really?"

"How will I know where to find the best deals if I'm not constantly on the hunt? Also, you're one to talk."

"You've always been my daughter," she says, resigned but proud—since, well, I am a lot like her. She's semi-retired from her work as an antiques dealer, but she can't resist still dabbling in it. I suppose I get my ambition from her.

She runs her fingers along the wood of the table. "And yes, this is a nice one. You have a good eye, Skylar."

"Thanks, Mom," I say, appreciating the compliment, like I've always appreciated her support—and my dad's too.

After we order, she returns to the Landon topic, giving me a *very sorry* look. I've seen it a lot since he broke things off. "I should never have encouraged you to take your time with him," she says, frowning. "I really thought he was a great guy."

"Don't feel bad. So did I," I say, wishing she'd stop

beating herself up for having been a cheerleader of both the relationship and the there's-no-rush-with-romance approach she advocated for me in my twenties. And that I, admittedly, followed.

"I know, but it's a mother's job to see the potential pitfalls," she says, then rolls her eyes. "I mean, I can't depend on your father for that. He wears rose-colored glasses."

"He does," I say, my voice warm with affection for him. "But Mom, it's fine. Landon broke up with me more than a year ago, and it's not your fault I wasted five years on him."

She winces. "Ouch."

"I didn't mean it like that," I say quickly, realizing how harsh that sounds when I replay my words.

"I know, sweetie," she says, smoothing her napkin over her lap. "I just wanted you to have what your dad and I have, so I told you to take your time with him. I thought he was the right guy."

So did I.

Not only was my longtime ex charming, but he dreamed big. The idea of opening a board game shop seemed like the height of kitschy charm to me. We both loved playing board games, so when he announced plans to open a shop, I did nothing but encourage him—to create a business plan, to go for it, to find a spot, to nab a loan.

And Landon was into it, making promises—*we'll move into a new place after the store opens, we'll get engaged once it's up and running, we'll get married the year after.*

But he could never move ahead. Everything was always *just around the corner.*

If I ever called him out on it, he'd tug me onto our

comfy couch, nuzzle my neck, and say, "Babe, I'm getting there. Just support me and play CATAN with me. When you push, it stresses me out."

I'd wanted to support him. It'd seemed like the right thing to do. So I paid most of the bills while he worked as a bartender by night and a dreamer by day.

One day, he met someone else. Packed up. Told me he was going to open the store—with *her*.

At first, I was too shocked to be mad. But then I was angry for a while. Next, hurt. Then just sad.

Now I'm simply smarter. More self-protective. A woman who's learned her lesson.

But I also don't want my mom to think her honest encouragement and support have anything to do with why I stayed so long. I simply picked the wrong guy but believed he was the right one. I won't be so foolish next time. I'll ask better questions at the outset. I'll spot the red flags. And I won't give my heart to someone who won't tend to it.

I meet the gaze of my biggest supporter—her brown eyes are earnest. Full of that mom worry as she rearranges her utensils.

"It's okay, Mom," I try to reassure her. "I have Simon and Cleo while Adam's in Europe, and my podcast and my friends. My business is growing, but it takes a lot of work and focus to establish myself and my brand of design in this economy. Now I've got this big opportunity...and it's best if I give that my all."

The server arrives with our food, and Mom seems to take a beat to consider all that as he sets down the dishes. "That makes sense," she says when he's gone. She lifts her fork. But before she takes a bite of her salad, she asks, "So...there's no one new on the horizon?"

It's asked gently, with no pressure.

And it's strange that an image of Ford flickers past my mind.

He's a client. A neighbor. Plus, my brother made it crystal clear that it's best to keep relationships *neighborly*, and besides...Ford's sort of a stern, gruff hard-ass.

Well, maybe not as much of one as I'd first thought. He might have a softer side underneath his sandpaper exterior.

But he's not a new romance on the horizon. I shake my head. "Nope."

As I eat my mushroom burger, I try *not* to think too much about *Sexy Reno Guy*.

That night, though, I do pick out an outfit to wear when I go shopping with him.

Not for him. Just...I like to look professional for my clients.

8

A LITTLE SPARK
FORD

Sometimes you just have to prove your point. After I grab my to-go cup—with a proper lid on it, right where it belongs of course—I say goodbye to Zamboni and head out, ready to prove a point.

To myself.

That this meeting is business as usual. That I'm simply doing a nice thing for my mom's designer. That I'm unaffected by my sexy-as-sin neighbor.

Who's...waiting on the sidewalk already, and it's not even ten-forty.

How the hell is a hot mess early? Earlier than me? This makes no sense. Skylar's supposed to be clumsy, kooky, and unable to remember an appointment. To arrive ten minutes late, clutching a huge stack of books, tripping on her feet, and landing kersplat as the books spill onto the sidewalk.

I'd sweep them up and offer a hand while she'd flash a quirky smile and apologize.

But nope.

I didn't even tell her which vehicle was mine—no

need—but Skylar Haven is already leaning against my car, all casual and easygoing, big red sunglasses on and...an infernal coffee cup in her hand. But I can't even bother to check out the mug because she's looking like the cool kid in high school, with black pants that hug her legs just so and a slouchy gray top that reveals a hint of her creamy shoulder.

And...freckles.

Fucking freckles that travel across the exposed skin by her collarbone.

What does she taste like there? Right there?

The thought is entirely too distracting. I fight it off, wrestle it to the ground, and stomp on it. Then I leave it behind me.

Play it cool. Play it like you didn't watch her in her kitchen less than forty-eight hours ago.

I stride down the steps, across the stone path, and over to her, making a show of checking the time on my phone. "You're early."

"Are you going to fire me for that?" It's asked as a playful challenge.

"Not today, Skylar. Not today."

She wipes a hand across her brow. "Whew. I was worried."

I thrust the to-go carafe at her, figuring it doubles as an apology gift, too, for giving her a hard time about her dog last week. This is what a decent dude who didn't check out his neighbor late at night would do—bring her a drink before a work meeting. Since I'm absolutely, definitely no longer thinking about how she looked in her kitchen the other night wearing those just-the-right-amount-of-short pajamas. Nope. Not at all.

"You were right," I concede.

"About what?"

"When you said I was watching kale smoothie videos. But only halfway right since I watched a video on how to make a...wait for it...pineapple smoothie. Figured that was more your speed."

The corner of her lips twitch in a grin—one that spreads like wildfire. "Pineapple? And why's that my speed?"

Because it tastes delicious, like I bet you do.

And what the fuck is up with my runaway thoughts?

I shrug, making the drink seem like no big deal, when really, it's my thoughts I'm trying to downplay. "I figure anyone who wears a robe to walk her dog likes pineapple."

Her brow knits. "Huh. Why does that feel like a dig?"

I ignore the comment, nodding to the smoothie so I can stay in control of the convo. "Try it. I guarantee it's good. It's got honey and coconut too."

"Did those seem like my speed too?"

"You know what? They did."

"Aww, thank you. You must think I'm sweet."

"Take the smoothie, Skylar," I say, keeping my tone stern, ignoring the teasing bait, even though she's damn good at doling it out.

As I hand over the drink, I glance at the mug in her other hand. Holy shit, it has a lid.

"I see you've discovered lids for coffee cups."

Her smirk is downright cat-who-ate-the-canary. "Actually, I learned how to make a kale smoothie for my new client." I take the mug from her, peel off the top and...she's not kidding. She really did make me a drink, like she'd hinted she would. And it looks good. Just the right consistency.

"You did," I say dryly, schooling my expression. I want to grin and say, *Great minds,* but I don't want to presume too much common ground when it comes to... motivation.

"Go ahead. Say it," she urges.

"Say what?"

"Say...*I was wrong.* Well, say *you* were wrong."

"How was I wrong?" I counter.

"The other night when we texted? You didn't think I was watching videos on how to impress your client with the best kale smoothie. But I was, Ford. Oh, I was. And the proof of the pudding is in the eating. Or the drinking. So bottoms up."

I part my lips to make a counterpoint—*actually, you weren't watching a how-to video. You were dancing with your dog, your short shorts riding up temptingly*, but that would tip my hand. So I shut the fuck up and cautiously try the drink.

But holy shit, it's good, with a hint of sweetness and a little peppery bitterness. It's everything a kale smoothie should be.

"You sure you hate kale?" I ask.

"I'm sure," she says.

"All the more impressive then. This is good."

Whipping off her shades, she smiles, and this time it's bright and big, like her personality. Those clever green eyes twinkle as she wraps her pretty lips around the metal straw in the cup. I didn't anticipate how dangerously sexy that'd be. The way she looks at me from under those long lashes as she drinks some of her tropical smoothie and hums.

Actually hums. Like one of those food shows where the host goes all orgasmic. I can't look away. Hot tension courses through me as she rolls her lips together, then says, "This *is* sweet." She bobs a shoulder. "Just like me."

"Good," I mutter. My brain spins with inappropriate thoughts, and I clench my phone tighter. *Focus, man. Focus.*

She turns to the car. "Ready to go?"

That raises a question. "How did you know this was my car?"

"It's neat," she says, then wiggles a brow as she lowers her voice. "Also, I saw you get into it the other day."

She's observant. Note to self: make sure she doesn't see you when you check her out from the hot tub.

I open the passenger door for her and try not to watch as she slides into the front seat. But I like the way she moves. I like the way she flicks her hair off her shoulder. I like, too, how she settles into my car, like she's comfortable being there.

When I jerk my gaze away from her, I'm shaking my head at myself.

Because I also like that she enjoyed the drink, plain and simple. Which—fuck me—means I didn't make it to prove a point to myself that I'm cool and in control.

I made it...for her.

"Your car could win an award," Skylar remarks with a whistle of appreciation as she looks around the interior, checking it out while we zip off.

"Yeah? For what?" I ask, since it feels like I'm being set up.

"Neatest car ever," she says. "This is Swedish, right? It's that new Swedish electric car that everyone's loving?"

"Yup," I say, "but I didn't get it to be trendy."

"Of course not. You got it because it's very you—form follows function," she says.

"I'll take that as a compliment," I say warily.

"It is," she says, then peers at the floor again, then at me with assessing eyes. "Look at the floor. Did you vacuum it this morning?"

"Obviously."

"Wait. Why is that obvious?"

"How is it not? Things don't get clean on their own," I say as I turn onto Castro Street.

"But you clean it every day?" She seems perplexed by this.

"No, Skylar. A magical fairy appears out of thin air with a broom."

"I'm even more impressed now that the car is cleaned with a broom," she says.

I fight off a laugh. "So it's the broom for you? Not the fairy?"

"Oh, the fairy's cool too," she says, then lifts a hand toward the gleaming dashboard, like she's about to stroke it, but she jerks her hand back a second before she touches it. "Wait. Am I allowed to touch it?"

"Why would you not be allowed to touch it?"

"Because it's so neat, so Swedish, so...excellent," she says, then takes a drink of her smoothie, making another one of those sensual purrs. I keep my focus firmly on the road. Not on her lips. Not on that sound. Looking at her mouth right now would be a serious hazard.

She cranes her neck around to the back seat, then returns to the front. "Yep. Just like I imagined."

"You imagined my car?" I ask. This woman keeps me on my conversational toes, that's for sure.

"Definitely. I had a feeling it would be like this," she says as I slow at a light. "Are you a neat freak, Ford Devon?"

I bristle. "Just neat. Nothing freakish about it whatsoever."

She nods. "Hey, neat freak is a compliment too."

I scoff. "How do you figure? It's got freak in it."

"Maybe I like neat freaks," she says, smirking, "who drive Swedish cars." With an impish shrug, she takes another sip of her drink, her lips curved around the metal straw.

My jaw tightens, and I grab the mug from the console, then knock back some kale smoothie like it's the source of my superpower. Well, I hope it is, but as I set it back down in the holder on the console, I nearly do a double take. Wait—*is that her dog giving me the side-eye on the mug?*

Quickly, returning my eyes to the road, I blurt out, "Is your dog on the mug?"

"Yeah," she says, with a delighted kind of grin. "It says *I Swear I'm Not Judging You.*" Then she lowers her voice. "But he's totally judging you. I mean, his Internet name is Simon Side-Eye."

I tap the gas pedal. "Your dog has an Internet name?"

"And his own line of merch. He even works with an eco-friendly company that fulfills his merch orders. He's quite the business dog."

And she is quite the surprise. As we wind past Twin Peaks, I don't mind that my very neat car is now filled with her...wild spark.

9

AN EVERYTHING GUY

SKYLAR

I probably shouldn't have given him such a hard time in the car. It's just...nearly impossible not to.

Besides, sometimes it seems like he *likes* it. Like he sort of enjoys being called out. Maybe I'm reading too much into the back and forth, the way he serves volleys right back to me, then waits like a badminton player on the other side of the net.

Best for me to focus on being the badass babe I am.

Ford swings open the door for me at Twice Loved—because, of course, he's the kind of guy who holds open doors—and I slide into pro mode as we enter one of my favorite places.

"Bastian—he's the manager—has the Eames chair set aside for us," I say. "And he also emailed me pictures of a few other pieces he thought might fit the style of the home. I can show you those first, or we can just wander. It's up to you. Are you the type of person who likes to discover things as you go, or would you rather I guide you through?"

Ford mulls over the question, his expression serious,

then says, "You mean, am I the kind of guy who sets out for a day in Tuscany to see what he stumbles across, or do I hire a tour guide?"

Hello, man with excellent taste. "Take me to Tuscany, please. I'd like a date with all the pasta in Italy."

That dimple of his shows up again. Everything seems to be a game with Ford—a subtle, flirting game. Or maybe I'm reading too much into it. I tilt my head, considering him. He's dressed impeccably again today, even in his casual attire—crisp jeans, a smart polo that shows off those biceps I want to bite, a pair of aviator shades hung on the neckline. His jaw is lined with light brown stubble —but it's neat. Purposeful stubble, like he keeps it trim. His hair's got a mind of its own, all floppy and wild, brown with some golden streaks. Besides the locks, everything about Ford screams *list guy*. He likes order, a plan, a strategy. But I also have a feeling he's got a well of patience a city-block wide and a control streak a mile deep, so I finish sizing him up and declare: "You're an everything guy."

The dimple deepens, fully owning his face. "Yes. I am."

I sweep an arm out to indicate the depths of the shop. "This place has several rooms, so we can wander and check out all sorts of things, but I'll make sure we see the items Bastian's earmarked."

Ford steps deeper into the main room—a maze of living room furniture, all well cared for, most pieces barely nicked and ready for a second life.

"Let's start with a couch," I say. "It's the centerpiece of the home."

"Not a kitchen table?"

"Don't get me wrong—I love a good kitchen table, and we *are* definitely going to find a fantastic one for Mama

Devon. And your dad of course too. But I think a couch is kind of like the soul of a home."

"Maybe," he says, seeming a little reluctant.

As we pass an emerald-green sofa that looks too stiff—definitely not right for him—I arch a brow. "You don't use couches?"

An image of his home springs fully formed in my mind, even though I've never seen the inside. But I bet it's mostly chrome and nickel, angles and lines, clean surfaces, deliberately bare. With some...plants though. Yeah, he's a plant guy. I just know it.

Before he can answer, I say, "Are you a total minimalist? Do you basically have a yoga mat and a couple of pillows in your living room and that's that?"

I swallow the last word, like I can swallow the entire line of questioning. Need to be more careful. How would I know he does yoga if I wasn't checking him out, catio style?

He shoots me a skeptical glance. "No, I do yoga on the back porch."

The way he says it—so serious, like it's a given—makes me roll my lips together to stop myself from blurting *I know, I know.* And even though I swore I wouldn't look at him anymore, I peered out the catio window this morning and happened to spot him on his porch in those distracting yellow compression shorts *again.* But in my defense, I thought I heard the squawking of a great blue heron in my yard, and I've been dying to see one of those beauties up close. Turns out, the squawking was just a sound effect on the comedy podcast I was listening to. But you don't want to take a chance when it comes to a great blue heron sighting.

"So, you *do* have a couch?" I ask.

He shrugs. "I don't use it a lot."

The picture of Ford sharpens a little more. "You probably don't like to relax."

His shoulders shift, stiffening a bit, but his blue eyes are sharp, trained on me. "You think I'm a neat freak who can't relax, don't you?"

I really need to be more professional. I *cannot* keep goading him, no matter how fun it is. "There's nothing wrong with being busy," I say carefully. "Not everyone's into downtime, and that's okay."

"I like downtime," he says, then flashes the barest of grins. "In Italy."

I laugh. "Well played."

His blue eyes sparkle, then he's serious again as he says, "But this is for Mom and Dad. Mom's a couch person. She likes to relax at the end of the workday. And she deserves to."

It's said with such affection and pride that my heart swells, along with my curiosity. "So you're helping your parents set it up before they move in? They're in Seattle, right?" I ask as I usher him past a few more baroque style sofas that are all wrong for his mid-century mom.

"As much as I can," he says, adding matter-of-factly, "I bought it for them."

I grab the arm of a gray sectional, stopping in my tracks. "You bought them the house?" I repeat. That's big. Really big. I had no idea *he'd* bought it. I'd thought he was simply...overseeing the redo.

A smile shifts his lips. "I did. As a retirement gift. It's all theirs."

The breath escapes my lungs. That's so generous. "Ford. That's incredible," I say, my voice breaking a bit.

"I always wanted to. I'm glad I could," he says, full of a lovely earnestness that warms my heart.

"Always? Like it was a childhood dream?"

The dimple flashes, almost boyish this time. "Actually, yes. We had a small home growing up. My mom works in non-profits, but she actually works for them—she's not just one of those rich ladies who goes to galas. Not that there's anything wrong with that—we love rich ladies who go to galas and donate. But she works in donor services," he says, then lifts a finger, his eyes twinkling. "You'd like her organization. They bring recycling and composting initiatives to communities all over the country, including here in San Francisco."

My heart pitter patters. "Love it."

"She travels a lot and organizes fundraisers, though she's working on her last one. And my dad ran a hardware store. We didn't have a ton of money or extra space growing up, and one day when I was maybe nine or ten, I had to sleep on the couch for a week when my mom's sister came to visit. I told them that someday they wouldn't have to worry about space. That someday I'd buy them a bigger home, one where they didn't have to worry about the mortgage either."

I cover my heart with my palm. I'm beyond touched. "That's so sweet." I pause, then give him a little sass as I say, "I guess *you're* the sweet one."

He waves a hand dismissing it. "It was just..."

But he doesn't finish, maybe because he knows it's sweet and he can't deny it.

He clears his throat. "They sacrificed a lot—time, money, and so on to make sure I could play hockey. To make sure I could go to college, too, and play there. And I didn't even make it into the NHL until I was twenty-four."

He stops in front of the love seats. "This was something I always wanted to do. Something special. Something meaningful. To make their lives easier. To make their dreams possible. They're pretty cool people."

"I love that you feel that way. I'm close with my parents too," I say. "I have lunch with my mom every week—she lives just outside the city. It's nice, isn't it? To get along with them," I ask, and he nods softly. "I have lots of friends who have strained relationships with their parents. I know I'm lucky. I try not to take it for granted."

"Same here," he says, patting the arm of the love seat. "So let's find them a good couch."

I step to it. "Of course we will," I say, glancing around at a few more pieces, then scanning a little deeper in the room for something in particular. But I want the discovery to feel organic. "My question for you is do we want to stick with the muted shades theme we have with the paint? Because I have a couple of ideas."

Ford doesn't answer right away. His gaze has shifted elsewhere. When I follow it, he's studying a deep purple couch a few feet away, stepping toward it, running his hand along the arm.

"Velvet?" His voice holds a note of disbelief. "Is this *really* velvet? Who makes a velvet couch?"

I join him, running my fingers across the fabric too. "It's pretty soft," I admit.

For a brief moment, we're both touching the couch, fingertips grazing the plush material, our eyes locking with each other's. The air goes still for a long beat—a beat that doesn't feel professional at all. That feels...almost heady.

I don't quite want it to end, even though this moment feels like it's tipping into something risky. I'm supposed to be working, not imagining what it'd be like to curl up on a couch with him.

"Yeah," he says, voice lower. "It really is."

He clears his throat like he's clearing away the rasp in it. "But maybe *too* soft. Besides, I don't think my mom is a velvet person."

I blink off the shimmery feeling. "Not everyone is," I agree, focusing on the job. "Velvet's an acquired taste."

He glances at me as we pass another row of couches in warm earth tones. "I bet *you're* a velvet person."

I shoot him a daring smile—but a fun one, not a flirty one. "So you think I'm all about pineapple and velvet? What does that say about me?"

He smirks right back. "I guess the same thing being a neat freak who doesn't use a couch says about me."

I'm about to tease him again when he leans in slightly, his shoulder nearly bumping mine even as he looks my way. "I'm right, aren't I?"

My breath catches. He holds my gaze, and my skin feels warmer than it should when I'm with a client. "I'd be a liar if I said I didn't like velvet," I say.

"Good. Don't be a liar, Skylar." His voice is lower, smokier than usual.

I can barely move for several seconds. Then he looks away, like he *has* to, as if looking any longer would be too dangerous. I force myself to refocus on the mission, ushering him along. We check out a few more couches, but Ford is noncommittal on most of them. He might be a man who likes control, but he also seems a little lost amidst too many choices.

Time for me to bring it home.

As if we just so happen to stumble upon it, I turn down another row, eyeing a rich brown couch several feet away—chocolate-colored, with clean, simple lines. One that complements the painted walls in the home. "How about this one?"

Ford sinks down onto it, pats the cushion, leans back, crosses then uncrosses his legs, and pronounces, "I like it."

"Good," I say, pleased but not surprised. I had a feeling, so I told Bastian to put a hold on it. "Do you think your mom will?"

Ford seems to give that some thought. "I think she will. It's a good one." But he winces apologetically while dragging a hand through his messy hair. "She *did* ask me to conference her in today and show her some things, but I figured we could do that after we pick out a handful of items. It'll be easier that way." Then, almost sheepishly, he adds, "I hope you don't mind."

"I'm looking forward to it," I say, meaning it completely. But that also means we'd better keep moving.

* * *

Like explorers who leave no stone unturned, we cover the rest of the shop, checking out armchairs and kitchen chairs. Ford finds a few he likes, and I show him the ones I've picked out too.

We visit the kitchen area, rapping our knuckles on bistro tables and breakfast tables, until his attention snags on...a lamp with a base that looks like a sloth foot.

He beelines for it, like it's the treasure he's been seeking. Or an oddity.

"What in the ever-loving hell?" Ford says, running his hand along the metal carved to look like the animal's toes. "I almost want to get this as a gag gift for one of my teammates." He looks at the ceiling, seeming deep in thought.

His phone buzzes in his hand, but he hits ignore before checking it. I can appreciate a man who lives in the moment.

"Bryant. This would be great for Wesley Bryant. He loved being pranked when he joined the team."

I laugh. "Probably made him feel welcome."

Ford blows out a breath. "It did...but would he really use it?" He sighs, then shakes his head, resigning himself. "I'll have to think of other pranks."

I pat his arm absently. "I'm proud of you for resisting getting something you don't actually need," I say, then glance down at my hand. Curled around his strong arm.

Holy shit. I just touched him.

And...he's looking at me as if he likes the contact too.

The casualness of the touch goes up in flames. *Poof.* Vanishes. I'm standing here in the store, touching him, and I shouldn't be. Really, I shouldn't.

Touching him was a mistake. Not a big one. Just...the kind that lingers in the air a little too long.

I pull my hand away like I've been burned, swinging my gaze around, hunting for a distraction—then spotting one in the next room. "But maybe you want the billiard tables. For your parents' house," I say, pointing ahead.

"Oh sure. Maybe," he says. "I do like pool."

He turns into the next room, and I take a beat to just... breathe.

Don't touch him again, even playfully.

I step toward the room when a voice crackles over the loudspeaker, like in a grocery store: "Paging Ford Devon, your mom is on the phone."

10

STEAK TO A TIGER

FORD

I wish I could say I was surprised. But this is so unbelievably on brand for her that I simply let out a heavy sigh.

Skylar's irises flicker with question marks. A worried frown curves those pretty lips.

Right. She has no idea what my mom is like. She might think something bad is happening. "This isn't the first time she's done this," I try to reassure her.

Her shoulders relax. "You're...not joking?"

Shaking my head, I beckon for her to join me as I stride through the labyrinth of tables, sloth lamps, and an umbrella holder with an elephant-head at the top (*who knew?*) toward the front of the store.

"When I was eighteen and driving to college, I was pulled over by highway patrol. Wasn't even speeding. Had no clue what it could be for. A broken taillight? Maybe my tags were out of date? But when I rolled down the window, the officer said, 'Are you Ford Devon?' I said yes, of course. He said, 'Call your mom. She hasn't heard from you in a couple of hours.' Then he walked off."

Skylar's eyes spark with an amusement that spreads across her whole face. "Noooo."

"Yessss."

"That's...fantastic."

"That's annoying," I correct.

"I meant it's fantastically diabolical."

She gets it. "Yes. All because my cell phone battery ran out somewhere in the Rocky Mountains. Mom said she wanted to make sure I was okay."

Skylar's green eyes flicker with more amusement than eyes should be allowed to hold. "How many times did she do this when you were a toddler? Were you endlessly paged in grocery stores? Did they know your name at the local super store? Did they call out, 'Ford in the toy aisle— go find your mom in tampons?'"

She sounds positively delighted. A far cry from my ex, who loathed my mother. I get it. Mom is like cilantro—not to everyone's liking.

"I wish I could tell you that didn't happen, but it did," I say as we weave past a haphazard row of reclaimed wood tables. Pretty sure that cream table is the one we picked for Mom, but right now I'm too irked by her to give it a second thought.

"I probably should actually give her my number at some point," Skylar offers, "so she doesn't worry."

That is entirely too kind. And also dangerous. "Do you want to throw raw steak to a tiger?"

"I hate steak, so that'd be a no. But why?" Skylar's eating up every detail of Mom like they're gumdrops on the path to the gingerbread house in the woods.

"You'll get stories upon stories, articles upon articles. More 'did you knows' than you'd know what to do with. Did you know you can tell the Google Hub to remind you when your laundry is done? Did you know you can compost wine corks? Did you know that *Sex and the City* is finally streaming?"

Skylar blinks. "It is? Huh. I guess I haven't looked for that in a long time. But thanks, Mama Devon, I know what I'll be bingeing tonight."

I roll my eyes, but I'm fighting off a laugh as we reach the front counter.

A man with a thick beard, horn-rimmed glasses, and a wry smile is waggling a beige phone receiver. "Let me guess. You're Ford Devon?"

"Was it the reluctant look in his eyes that gave him away?" Skylar asks, drumming the countertop in an amused rhythm.

"I'd have to say yes," the man says, then hands off the phone with a *good luck, you're going to need it* look.

Deep breath.

Chill out.

Remember your morning yoga meditations—*all is well, and I am calm.*

I press the receiver to my ear. "Mom, I know that *Sex and the City* is finally streaming. And I will get to it, I promise."

Skylar snorts, not at all delicately. It's like a full-bodied snort, and it's...kind of cute. Because it's so...bold.

"Darling, I tried calling you. You didn't answer. Is everything okay?"

"Everything is always okay. You don't page me in the middle of hockey games. Why are you paging me now?"

"Of course I don't page you in the middle of hockey games. I know you're busy then. But right now, you were supposed to be available for our video chat, so naturally, I was concerned. I also have a lunch in a little bit, and I didn't want to miss the opportunity. We probably have to switch back to your cell phone though. Did you know you can't really do video conferencing on landlines?"

I drop my forehead in my hand. "Yes, Mom, I am aware. I will call you back."

When I end the call, Skylar shoots me an *I've got this* look. "Want me to show her around?"

"Don't say I didn't warn you," I say, but I'm crossing my fingers. I hope Mom likes her style. She's been critical of other designers, but I want a win for Skylar.

"Oh, I heard the warning loud and clear," she says as we retrace our steps. I hit Mom's name on the phone, then hand it to Skylar as it rings, mouthing, "*good luck."*

When my mother answers on video, Skylar flashes her the same determined smile she gave me when she showed up on my front porch with those kale dog biscuits that Zamboni turned up her snout at.

"You must be Skylar," Mom says, effortlessly professional, temporarily hiding her dragon self. "So lovely to meet you."

"And you. Also, I'm so glad you called. Ford was getting far too distracted by the billiards table," Skylar says.

"Seriously?" I mutter, shooting her a *how could you throw me under the bus* look.

But Skylar doesn't even acknowledge me.

"Oh no, I like mid-century, not man cave. He'd better not be looking at moose heads."

"You have my word, Mrs. Devon. I will never decorate with death...or man cave," Skylar says.

"Call me Maggie," Mom says, with a smile just for the designer.

"Maggie," Skylar echoes. "May I show you the couch I have in mind?"

"Please do," Mom says, and Skylar guides her through the store to the chocolate brown couch.

"Here you go," Skylar says, voice bright and hopeful as she spins the phone around, giving Mom a tour of the sofa.

My muscles are tight. I'm bracing for Mom's reaction.

She's silent. For a long, *long* time. So long it makes my skin feel itchy. Time to sell it to her. I grab the phone and flip it back around as I sit on the couch. "It's comfortable, Mom."

Her face is stern, and she sighs—the deep, aggrieved sigh only a mother can deliver. "I despise it."

Skylar blinks. Steps back, out of view of the screen. Says *oh* quietly, low enough that Mom can't hear.

Things were going so well, I doubt she saw the smackdown coming.

"Mom, what is wrong with it? It's..." I cast about for a word, landing only on, "nice." Because what else is there to say about a couch?

Mom gives me a look like I should know better. "Ford, I detest brown. Did you not tell Skylar?"

"You don't like brown?"

"Have you ever seen me wear brown?"

"I don't catalogue the colors of your clothes," I say, sinking deeper into the couch. All this time spent here has been a waste. I glance at Skylar—she looks shell-shocked.

"I don't have a single item in brown. Not even boots," Mom continues.

"I don't look at your shoes."

"The only thing I like that's brown is chocolate," she adds, punctuating her point.

I roll my eyes. "Message received."

Skylar clears her throat, then beckons for the phone. I'm all too happy to hand it to her.

"Maggie, is it just the color?" she asks diplomatically, recovering quickly from her surprise.

"Yes! It's loathsome."

Skylar takes the comment in stride. "But the style? How do you feel about the style?"

"It's hard to see past the color," Mom admits, but there's a hint of *intrigue* in her voice—a *tell me more* kind of tone.

Skylar trots off with the phone, moving so fast through the couches I might need to jog to keep up.

I find her at...a gray version of the same couch.

"It's dove gray," Skylar is saying. "And as I'm sure you know, you can throw a pretty sage green or dusty rose fleece over the back of it to give a pop of color. That way, too, you can alter the look to feature cooler shades in winter and warmer umber-toned ones in fall."

Mom narrows her eyes on the screen, studying Skylar as she settles into the new couch now, patting the cushions, stretching out an arm along the back of it.

"Dove gray *is* pretty, isn't it?" Skylar asks.

More silence on the other end of the line, then at last, a nod. "It is. Dove gray is one of the unsung shades."

"Yes! I was saying the same thing the other night," Skylar says.

And *holy shit*...did she just—charm my mother?

I think she might have, since Mom is saying, "I like that one."

"Good. Let me show you some tables."

Skylar weaves through the store, effortlessly navigating Mom's rapid-fire opinions on the pieces we selected earlier to show her—some are dismissed outright, others earn a considering hum. Through it all, Skylar listens intently, pivoting when needed, adjusting her choices without hesitation. And the best part? I don't have to handle my mom.

Skylar's doing it perfectly.

When we finish at a pale-yellow breakfast table that Mom approves since it'll catch the sun just right in the morning, Skylar asks, "Should I arrange to have all these items delivered to the Sausalito home? I can stage them, take pictures, and do another video tour once they're in place. I have an arrangement with the store—try before you buy. If anything doesn't work in the space, we can return it."

Mom shifts to me. "Ford, why don't all stores do that? None of the previous designers offered that."

I don't bother pointing out that we never got to the furniture-shopping stage with them. "It's one of the mysteries of the universe."

Mom checks her watch, then says, "I should go soon."

Skylar leans closer, almost whispering, like she has a secret, "Before you do...would you like to see the Eames chair up close? The one I had them set aside for you?"

"I've only been dying to get another look since I saw the first photo," Mom says.

Skylar confidently guides the floating screen head of my mother through the store once again, leading us to a back room where Bastian, I presume, lets us in. Skylar spins the phone around, showing off a pink chair that looks like it's from the *Mad Men* era. "And the best part? It's a dusty-pink."

My mother gasps. "Who doesn't love pink?"

"Never trust someone who doesn't love pink," Skylar

says, running a hand over the dusty-pink upholstery on the lounge chair, set on an aluminum base, with a high back and a cushion for the head.

"Words to live by," Mom says, seeming agreeable but then...she eyes it with an arch in her brow. Judgement in her eyes. A ruler-straight mouth. Oh shit. She hates it.

I try to soften the blow. "I guess you're not proposing to it?"

"No," Mom says, and my shoulders sag.

Dammit.

But I'm not disappointed for me. I was hoping she'd love this chair Skylar found for her because I wanted Skylar to have that win.

But Skylar doesn't miss a beat. "I'll find you another one."

Mom tuts. "You'll do nothing of the sort. That chair and I? We're eloping tonight."

Skylar grins. "Congratulations."

I expected Skylar to survive my mother.

I didn't expect her to *win her over.*

And as we leave, I sure as hell didn't expect to be wishing the day wasn't ending.

* * *

On the way home, I glance at the dashboard clock more than I should. My mind races through unexpected ideas like *Want to stop at High Kick Coffee? I hear coffee tastes better drunk rather than worn.* Or *Want to walk our dogs? You'll keep yours at least ten feet from mine though, right?*

But those all sound suspiciously like dates.

And that's not what I should be doing with my neighbor, my designer, and a woman who, frankly, I don't have that much in common with.

At least, I didn't think I did before today. I'm beginning to question that assumption. *A lot.* So I fiddle around with the console, asking instead, "Want to listen to some music?"

"Sure," Skylar says, and I wonder what she listens to. If we even have *that* in common. We probably don't. "But I figured you only listen to news."

I roll my eyes, then stab the pump-me-up gym playlist Wesley shared with all of us—he's our resident music savant—to make my point.

But instead of the Bad Bunny tune that played the last time my teammates and I bet who could bench press more, a confident, soprano voice fills the car, saying: "Now, if someone requests a meeting, ask yourself—does it align with your three key priorities?"

Shit. I must have hit my audiobook app instead.

Skylar whips her gaze to me as I slow at a light. "You listen to...business productivity books?"

It's said with way too much satisfaction.

I hit *end* so fast. "Just something my sister suggested," I say, shrugging it off. It feels personal. Too personal. Like I'm letting her see a part of me I'd rather keep to myself.

Or maybe—another voice says—a part you're afraid to share?

I shared these parts of myself with Brittany.

The goals I had for myself—to excel at hockey—and for us as a couple—to grow closer. Brittany had asked me to hire a private chef to teach us how to cook together, so we could have quality time over homemade meals. She'd framed it as an investment in our relationship, a way to reconnect during the season when I spent so much time on the road. Instead, she used that time when I was gone to start an affair with the chef.

My jaw clenches at the unwanted memory as I slow at a light. I steal a glance at Skylar, unsure what to say, if anything. But I choose silence—it's easier than taking a risk. Don't want to get burned.

But Skylar's gazing out the window thoughtfully. "That's cool," she says, waving a hand at the console. "I could probably benefit from that. That kind of focus, you know?"

And...that was *not* what I'd expected her to say. "Yeah?"

"Definitely," she says. "It's a good way to look at things —what your priorities are."

And it's a reminder too—mine are hockey, family, and my dog. Romance isn't on the list. Dating isn't even close.

It's my final year in the pros, and I don't need a thing distracting me.

"Speaking of priorities," Skylar says, then shoots me a quick, hopeful look. "It would be cool to do a before and after video of your parents' home. To show on the podcast."

"It's video and audio? Your show?"

"Yep. But if that's too much to ask I completely understand. No pressure at all," she says. "If your mom doesn't want their home featured at the end, it's not a problem."

I take a beat to think it over, even though it's Mom's call of course, since she's making all the calls on the home. But probably a before and after for a big project like this would help Skylar. "I'll make it happen," I say, since it's a two-fer. It'll make Skylar happy and, well, Mom likes showing off things she's proud of.

"Thank you," she says, sounding both relieved and excited.

This thing with us is business. Just business. And her podcast is a good reminder.

When we return to our homes, I say goodbye, making plans to see her when the furniture arrives at the end of next week, and walk my dog alone.

My arms are shaking, my shoulders are screaming, but I don't care. I lower myself from the plank position to the floor again. And again. And one more time.

"All right, all right. You can do push-ups—*we know*. No more showing off," my conditioning coach, Leah, chides, beckoning for me to get to my feet.

"What? Extra is good," I say as I pop up from the floor.

"Not always," she says, then points to the barbell on the mat. "Rest for one minute. Then I want ten box back squats. Only ten."

"I can do more," I offer.

Leah Boasberg has made a name for herself as one of the top strength and conditioning coaches in the game. She worked for our intra-city rivals, the Golden State Foxes, before going out on her own. We have a strength and conditioning coach on the Sea Dogs, but I wanted a personalized program for the entire season, so I hired her for private sessions. Some of the guys on the Golden State Foxes followed her too—like Corbin Knight, who's here with me today at the gym we go to on Fillmore Street in the city.

"I can do double what this clown does," Corbin offers.

Leah rolls her eyes before flicking her thick brown braid off her shoulder. "Conditioning is not a competition, boys."

I shoot Corbin a skeptical look, then flash the same doubtful one to Leah. "You sure about that?"

She points to the weight again. "Do ten, or I'll make you do nothing."

Corbin steps back. "Whoa, reverse drill-sergeant psychology."

She looks his way with a proud grin, then points her tablet at him. "That's right. And I'll use it on you too, Knight."

With a gulp, he heeds the warning, holding up his hands in surrender.

I squat down, grab the bar, and lift it up, then squat until my ass touches the box. My legs bark at me. But if it were easy, it wouldn't get the job done.

I'm going to do everything in my power to have a phenomenal season. To ensure I can walk away from hockey, rather than have hockey slip away from me.

Like my marriage.

I blink away the unwanted thought. Brittany made her choice, and I learned from it—it's best to rely on myself and my dog.

When I finish ten reps, beads of sweat are sliding down my back, but I'm feeling stronger, and that's the goal. Once I set the bar back in place, I catch my breath before I grab my water bottle. I down some, stretching out my legs as Corbin takes his turn, obeying perfectly.

"Good," she says to my buddy as he puts the barbell away with a huff. "I'll let you keep up the training." Then to me, she adds, "But more is not always more."

"Agree to disagree," I say.

"Ford," she warns.

Corbin throws a towel at me. "Were you a suck-up in school too? *Teacher, can I have more addition problems? Can I write an extra essay?*"

I shoot him a look that translates to *I'll kill you in your sleep,* mostly because I don't want to acknowledge he's right. Of course I did extra work. How else would I have gotten a scholarship?

"I swear I'll need to get my daycare license soon," Leah says, rolling her eyes. Scanning her tablet screen, she gives us the next set of drills.

I happily do them, no matter how loud my muscles scream.

When we're done and Leah takes off, I could collapse. Instead, I make my way to the cardio machines. I gaze longingly at the row of StairMasters before claiming my favorite elliptical. Corbin grabs the one next to me, then glances down at his knees.

"Man, sometimes I wish I could still do the Stair-Master too."

Nostalgia tugs at my chest as well. "Yeah, and stair drills, the kind that make you feel like you're going to die," I say with fondness for those exercises we used to do—were *allowed* to do.

He tosses his towel on the dashboard, nodding in solidarity. "The kind that makes your legs feel like a five-alarm fire."

"Fucking miss those," I say.

"So damn much."

Corbin's logged nearly a decade in the pros—not quite as many as I have, but close. After a while, your knees just aren't the same. Even if you can skate like a Ferrari on espresso, you've got to be careful with the other exercises.

Corbin sighs, long and contemplative. "Aging is hard," he says.

Three words. No bullshit. No ribbing.

Just a truth that gnaws at me.

"You're telling me," I say, but that doesn't mean I'm going to slow down. I'm going to stay a step ahead. I pump my feet on the elliptical as I build up speed. "You push hard, you do the right things, eat healthy, stretch, practice yoga, get your sleep...but Father Time comes for us all."

"And it comes for athletes fast and hard," he says as he hits the start button. "But I take solace in one thing."

"What's that?"

He flashes me a dickhead smile, his dark eyes twinkling. "You'll always be older than I am."

I shoot him a deadpan stare. "And wiser. I'll always be wiser."

He laughs. "That's probably true."

But not always. I find myself texting Skylar later that day while I head to the team plane for the flight to Los Angeles. I want to let her know Mom said yes to the before-and-after for Skylar's podcast.

Skylar replies in more exclamation points than I can count.

As I settle into my seat, I give her the code to the door and let her know she can shoot the before video anytime. I take the opportunity to touch base with her on other items, too, like the upcoming furniture delivery. As we taxi, I ask if we should fix the countertops. As we take off, I inquire about her opinion on lighting.

It's important to stay on top of the details. To make sure my parents' house is done right. That's all this is.

Well, mostly.

Before we reach the clouds, I send one more text about plants. Just because it'd be nice to have some. Then I turn off the phone and ignore the sliver of hope that when I land, I'll find a reply about plants.

11

THE GUY NEXT DOOR

SKYLAR

"This is awful. Just awful," I pant out as I round the edge of Alamo Square Park, talking to my brother on the phone while Simon lags behind me on his leash. Even the Painted Ladies can't make up for the pain of running. "I think I might be dying."

"That makes two of us," my brother deadpans as I slow my pace. Or slow my pace even more, since I wasn't going that fast in the first place.

"Please. You're not suffering," I say as my lungs seize and my legs bark at me.

Simon barks too—nothing but canine expletives as he waddle-trots alongside me, expressing his displeasure with exercise.

"Oh, I would say it's suffering, listening to you breathe as you run," my brother says.

"Hey, not everyone is naturally aerobic like you. You were born part cheetah," I say.

"And you were born half hyena. Why are you even calling me while running?" he asks.

"To be nice?" I retort as my heart threatens a mutiny. It's beating so fast from ALL THIS CARDIO.

But that's not true—I'm calling to be nice. And I'm calling to gloat about my handywoman accomplishments at his home.

"Also, why are you running with Simon? I thought he hated running," Adam says.

I slow even more. Fine, I'm walking now. "He does," I say, and my dog side-eyes me. "But humped the neighbor's dog, so it seemed like I should try to get his excess energy out, and I read that exercise could help. He can't do the elliptical with me. Ergo...running."

"Wait. Did you just say your dog humped the neighbor's dog?"

I didn't see what was confusing about that. Even so, I give a simple: "Yes."

"Skylar," my brother chides because he has never not played the role of the older brother who knows best.

"It's fine. It was over a week ago. He's not even upset anymore," I say.

"But he was then? Is it the hockey player?"

"Yes, but everything is good," I reassure him. "Plus, it turned out he's my brand-new client," I say, then quickly explain the coincidence.

I leave out that I might also find Ford Devon ludicrously handsome, surprisingly entertaining, delightfully sarcastic, and full of layers that are fun to peel back. I was legitimately touched to learn about his care for his parents and impressed, too, that he's as fond of his mom and her overbearing ways as he is. He's a kind man underneath a rough exterior, and somehow, that's hot to me.

"But everything is fine, right?" Adam presses.

"Of course it's fine. Why are you so worried? Is it

because of Jessica?" I ask, wondering if there's more to his crush on the artist neighbor.

"No, it's just...well, I was cautious to pursue something with her because," he says, then sighs, and I can tell this is hard for him. "You never know when you're going to need a neighbor's help, you know? I have friends who've gotten into arguments with their neighbors. They argue over yard signs and such, and then before you know it, it turns into a fight over property lines and other things, and then someone's stealing your mail and your packages. And they know too much about you and could hurt you."

He's always been the bossy big brother, but I hear real worry in his voice. Good thing he doesn't know I like to check out the neighbor when Ford's shirtless on the back porch. That I touched his arm the other day in the store. That I maybe have thought about him late at night when I was alone.

"Look, it's all good. We were literally texting last night about plants. Ferns, Adam. *Ferns.* We're not arguing about property lines or putting dog poop bags in a neighbor's bins."

"See? That's another thing to worry about. People don't like it when you use their bins."

"But again, I'm not using his bins."

"Things can go south quickly," he says.

I hate to admit it, but Adam's not wrong. "Yes, Dad," I say.

"Skylar," he chides.

"I hear you," I concede. "But don't worry. It's all good." I shift gears, finally getting around to gloating about my accomplishments. "Adam, have I mentioned the rod in your closet fell yesterday, and I hung it back up?"

"Um, thanks."

"Exactly. You're welcome," I say as Simon drags me to a grassy knoll in the park.

"Well, did you break it, though? I mean, you're the one using it."

"I don't use your closet. That's gross."

"I'm sorry, why is it gross to use my closet?"

"Because it still has some of your clothes in there. All those old radio station and coffee shop T-shirts you hang up—the rod must have finally given out. I wasn't going to mix my girl clothes with your yucky boy clothes, okay?"

"You are so ridiculous," he says, laughing.

"Don't worry. I'm taking care of everything. The house is fine. And Cleo also had a message for you."

"That so?" he says, sounding a little wary.

"She said she originally wasn't going to forgive you for moving, but now she has because she discovered she prefers me."

"You're the worst," he says, but there's laughter in his tone. "Why did I rent to you?"

"Imagine if you had rented to somebody you didn't even know, and then boom—they're stealing your mail and trolling you with yard signs."

"Yeah, yeah, yeah," he says.

I say goodbye and flop down next to Simon, who rolls onto his back in the grass. He has the right idea.

I don't sprawl on my back, but I do enjoy the rays for several minutes. I sit up, snapping a shot of my snoozing dog, then write a post for later with the caption: **Mom made me run today. I feel like she's trying to send me a message, but little does she know I'm not listening.**

When I turn onto my block, I run into my brother's crush checking her mail outside her townhome. I've talked to her a few times, since, well, nosy girl here. "Hey,

Jessica," I say to the pretty woman with the sleek black hair. She's wearing a T-shirt that catches my eye—there's a drawing of bees and the words Protect Pollinators on it. "Nice shirt."

With a small smile, she plucks at the blue V-neck. "Thanks. I designed this one."

I knew she was an illustrator, but had no idea she made cute T-shirts with sayings I love. "I hope it's getting" —I pause theatrically—"all the buzz."

She laughs kindly at my pun. "It is. I can't keep them in stock, but I found a local distributor of fair-trade T-shirts—" She breaks off and waves a dismissive hand. "You don't want to hear all the details."

O ye of little faith. "Actually, I do."

"Yeah?" She sounds enthused.

"One hundred percent."

We chat for another fifteen minutes about her business and how she sources her hand-printed tees. I can't get enough of the details. We're kindred spirits, it seems. Then, with a reluctant sigh, she gestures to her home. "I should get back inside and do some more work. But," she says, with a hopeful smile. "I'm traveling to Korea next week to see my mom. Is there any chance you could check the mail while I'm gone?"

"Absolutely," I say, then exchange info with her.

After I say goodbye, I head up the steps to Adam's home, my gaze swinging to another neighbor's home. Ford's place looks quiet. I don't notice any movement inside. I pause by the door, Adam's words echoing. He's wise about the importance of getting along with neighbors. The world has both become more global and much smaller. From Jessica's request to check her mail, to stories from friends of mine in Seattle who lost power after a bomb cyclone several months ago and took turns with neighbors charging each other's phones based on whose portable battery had the most power, it's common sense to get along with your neighbor.

Not to date them.

When my phone dings with a text later that night from Ford as I'm making cauliflower mac and cheese, I figure it's neighborly to answer. I'm just practicing good *getting-along* skills. I swipe it open as I sprinkle the cheese into the casserole dish.

> Ford: Remind me never to get on your dog's bad side.

> Skylar: Hate to break it to you, but you're definitely at the top of his burn book.

> Ford: I took him for a forgiving guy. My bad.

> Skylar: Just kidding. He loves everything, even ornery people. Well, everything except exercise. He rebelled today when I took him jogging.

> Ford: He can jog?

> Skylar: Is this a reference to his short legs? Your dog has short legs too.

> Ford: Fair point. But she also doesn't jog.

I'm tapping out a reply when I stop, wondering why he wrote. There's nothing practical in his note. It's...a remark.

A throwaway comment. Something fun. My lips curve into a grin as I dictate a response.

Skylar: Why don't you want to get on his bad side?

Ford: I looked him up. His commentary is withering.

That's too delightful. Opening the oven, I picture Ford checking out Simon's social. I imagine the smirk on his face. The roll of his eyes. The temptation to leave a like or a heart. It's a nice image.

Skylar: Scathing reality judges have nothing on Simon.

Ford: Truer words.

I close the oven and set the timer. The phone goes quiet, and something soft settles into my chest—the awareness that Ford had written simply to compliment...my dog. And to let on that he'd looked him up.

I peer out the back window, but there's only one light on in his home. Same as earlier. I check the hockey schedule. Ah, he's in Los Angeles. They played this afternoon—I hop over to the sports news—and won. I stay on the site to watch a few highlights. Then a few more.

Skylar: I'm making cauliflower mac and cheese. I bet it's not on your meal plan, but I can leave some on the front porch for you.

Ford: Sounds delicious. I'm landing soon. Will be home in a little while.

A little later, I put the food in a casserole dish and then write a note from Simon on his branded stationery. The one where he's lounging on his side, giving, naturally, the side-eye.

You're lucky. She serves me the same dry brown rocks every night.

As I head to the door, I feel a little fizzy knowing Ford wrote to me from the plane. Though I absolutely should not be feeling anything for my neighbor. Correction: My brother's neighbor.

But that's okay—nothing will come of this.

No matter how much I hope Ford enjoys the mac and cheese.

I trot up to the porch and set it down on the doormat... which has an illustrated dog and says *Wipe Your Paws*. There's just something about a man who loves dogs.

I turn around to head back to my house when I stop in my tracks. "Oh." My pulse speeds up. My chest...tingles.

Ford heads up the path, wearing a suit, walking his dog...

And looking straight at me, like I'm a good surprise.

12

STARRY NIGHT SNACK

FORD

In sports, timing is everything. The way you line up a shot, how fast you swing the stick, how long you're in the penalty box—in my case, hardly ever. I have the team's lowest PIM (penalty minutes) thanks to discipline.

I've played sports long enough to know that timing matters in life too.

Like the day a couple of years ago when I came home early from practice and found my ex's laptop open, a chat with the private chef still glowing on the screen. That was seriously good timing. Imagine how long the affair might have gone on otherwise.

As I walk across the stone path toward my house, Zamboni trotting faithfully beside me, I think about timing again. Because Skylar on my porch late at night feels like a shot lining up just right.

She could have dropped the mac and cheese off anytime. But she's here now. And right away, I know—I don't want her to go home yet.

"Lucky me—comes with personal delivery," I say.

Skylar smirks. "How else would it get here?"

"Your dog? Simon sounds like a man of many skills."

"True, but food delivery isn't one of them."

She bends to Zamboni's level. "Is it one of yours, girl? Can you do that?" She scratches behind Zamboni's big ears. The dog wags her tail, sniffing in Skylar's direction. Or maybe sniffing the food. I bet both smell good to her. They sure do to me.

"Missed opportunity," I say. "Simon could get even more work. Just another member of the gig economy."

Skylar pretends to consider that. "He'd look awfully cute with a little pack on his back, carrying mac and cheese on one side, a bottle of wine on the other, checking off deliveries on his app."

"I can see it now. At the very least, I can see him writing a snarky post about it."

Her eyes flicker with approval. "And thank you for a new idea for his social."

"You write Simon's posts? I never would have known," I say, dry as a desert.

"Don't tell anyone," she says in a conspiratorial whisper.

"Your secrets are safe with me."

She smiles, her eyes sweeping over me, lingering just a beat too long. There's something appreciative there, and I'm betting she likes the suit. I puff my chest a little in pride, as she says, "I didn't peg you for a Cabernet."

Or maybe I'm wrong. My brow furrows. "What do you mean?"

"Your suit. It's the color of a wine."

I glance down, running a finger along the lapel. "Huh. Thought this color was... Actually, I don't know what I thought it was—maroon?"

She shudders. "That is *not* maroon. It's a fine wine."

Colors aren't my strong suit. "Thanks. My sister picked it out. Hannah."

"Hannah has excellent taste. And I'm guessing she had a Cabernet from the Lucky Falls Winery in mind."

The wise move would be to say thanks, head inside, and tuck into the fantastic-smelling mac and cheese that's waiting for me. But that wouldn't be taking advantage of timing, or fine wine compliments.

"I happen to have a Cabernet. I don't think it's from that winery, but would you like to have a glass? Maybe some mac and cheese?" I ask, with some nerves—nerves I didn't expect—racing in my chest. I do my best to ignore them as I nod toward the wooden bench on my porch.

It feels like a porch kind of night.

"I already ate," she says, and I try to hide my disappointment as she pauses to pet Zamboni again, who shamelessly accepts the affection. But when Skylar looks up at me with those green eyes, I don't see the signs of a woman who wants to go home. Her gaze sparkles with… curiosity. Her lips part like she's forming an addendum to her answer, and I'm hoping she wants to stay.

I shouldn't want that. Truly, I'm fine with whatever she says next.

But when she says, "The wine definitely works for me though," I fight off a smile.

Five minutes later, I'm back with two glasses, a freshly opened bottle of wine, some napkins, and a couple of forks just in case. I've shed the jacket but not the tie. The cuffs on my crisp white dress shirt are rolled up.

We settle onto the bench, Zamboni flopping at my feet with a contented sigh. A few stars twinkle in the city sky. A car rumbles down the end of the street, then fades away.

Skylar tips her head toward Zamboni. "She came

home with you." It's a statement, but I understand the question.

"She stays at a dog hotel when I'm on the road."

"Stahp! Stahp! That's too cute. I need to know everything. Does it have heated floors, soft music, a swimming pool, and off-the-floor beds? Do they include bedtime stories, or is that extra? Can you order a biscuit to go under her pillow at turn-down service? Do they *have* turn-down service?"

"That's a barrage of questions."

She makes a rolling gesture with her hands, telling me to move it along, stat. "Answer them."

As I pour the wine, I take her questions one by one. "Yes, yes, yes, and yes. Also, yes, they have bedtime stories, but they are extra. Yes, you can order a biscuit, but there's no turn-down service. Next question."

Her smile spreads across the city block. "Can I stay there?"

I laugh harder. "Sure. I'll book a shared suite for you and Zamboni next time I travel. Sound good?"

"Simon too?"

Zamboni's ears prick, right on cue.

"See? She likes that idea," Skylar says.

I scoff as I hand Skylar a glass. "Pretty sure that look says *keep the mad humper away*."

"Excuse me. Simon prefers *happy humper*. Also, he likes peanut butter biscuits."

"Good choice." I lower my voice to a confessional whisper. "Sometimes when I get peanut butter biscuits, I eat them too. Well, I take a bite."

"Me too!"

"Speaking of, where is the happy humper?" I ask, looking around as if he might be hiding behind a bush.

Skylar lifts a finger. "He is not happily humping, you'll be relieved to know. He's sound asleep. Like I said, we went running earlier, and I'm pretty sure he's still recovering."

"Understandable," I say as I pour my glass, then set the bottle on the bench.

She lifts her glass, anticipation in her eyes. "Should we drink to..." She looks around at the small spread next to me.

"Late-night snacks," I say.

"They're always a good idea."

"They are."

"To late-night snacks...with your next-door neighbor then," she says, with the slightest bit of resignation over those last words. Is being neighbors an issue for her? I've got enough concerns of my own that it hadn't crossed my mind. But now that it has, it's probably a good idea to avoid entanglements with a neighbor. If things go south—and experience says they will—you'll risk seeing that person every time you turn around.

With that thought lingering, we clink glasses.

As she sips, I try not to stare too long at her glossy lips on the glass, at the column of her throat, at the way the porch lights cast a soft, silvery glow across her face. And at the freckles on her collarbone, exposed tonight in one of those T-shirts with the neckline cut out. A slouchy shirt that makes me want to dip my face and nibble on her flesh, then soothe the sting with my tongue.

A rumble threatens to work its way up my throat. I knock back some wine to hide the sound, then set the glass on the bench. Reaching for a fork, I dig into the mac and cheese and groan at the first taste.

After I swallow, I use the fork to point at the dish. "This is really good."

She blows on her fingernails. "I have some skills."

"Besides handling my overbearing, opinionated, tough-as-nails mom and making killer cauliflower mac and cheese, what else have you got?"

She waggles her mostly full glass. "I can make this glass disappear in about, oh, thirty minutes."

I laugh again. Come to think of it, I've laughed more with Skylar than I have in a long time.

Don't get used to it. She's your neighbor and she's a business associate. This is not the start of something else.

I eat some more and make small talk between bites as she nurses her wine. When I'm done, I say, "Thank you. This was way more fun than making or reheating something."

"Do they feed you on the plane?"

"Sometimes, but it was a short flight from LA, so nothing tonight."

"Good game this afternoon," she says, then sits up straighter, smoothing a hand down her jeans. "I mean, I didn't watch it. I didn't realize you were playing. I looked it up once we were talking."

Even on an inky blue night, I can see the flush crawling up her neck, as if she's embarrassed to have admitted all that. Or to have admitted something in particular.

"So you looked me up," I say, unable to resist teasing her.

"I just wanted to see how you did," she says, trying to make light of it.

"Of course. That's all."

"Shut up," she mutters.

"Admit it. You watched the highlights." I goad her, nudging her with my shoulder.

And that was a rookie mistake. Even her shoulder bumping mine feels good. I pull away. Don't want to tempt myself more.

She glances down the street as if the row of townhomes is the height of interest. "Just...I was curious," she says, then looks straight ahead.

Oh, hell. She's so damn cute now when she's...caught in the act of, well, looking me up. And since I looked *her* up too—well, her dog, but then her—I like that she did the same. But I like it more than I should.

Which means I should call it a night soon. I fold the napkin and set it on the bench with the fork on top of it. "I have to see my personal conditioning coach tomorrow."

"Cool. I should go." She moves to stand, but her wineglass isn't empty.

Without thinking, I set a hand on her thigh. "Stay. Till the picnic is over."

She swallows and nods in the dark. "Okay. I will."

With some reluctance, I remove my hand from her thigh, then sip more of the wine. For a beat, there's just the sound of cars cruising by a few blocks over and laughter carrying from down the street. I imagine the ocean crashing somewhere in the far distance.

"So, you have your own conditioning coach?" she asks.

"I want to play great this year—it's my last year—so I hired someone to make sure I'm operating at peak performance. Leah's one of the best. My agent, Shanita, found her for me."

Skylar tilts her head, her lips curving up. "Your agent is a woman, and so is your conditioning coach?" It's asked with a certain amount of delight.

"Yeah," I say, answering matter-of-factly. "So is my publicist. She gave me this tie—a lucky tie for the season."

"You have an all-female management team," she says, sitting up straighter, a pleased smile twisting her lips.

"I do," I say with an easy shrug, since hiring them was an easy choice.

"Was it intentional?"

"It happened organically. I wanted the best, and that's how I found them. Men dominate this business. It's eye-opening and, honestly, refreshing to have the support of people who see things differently."

Skylar brings her glass to her lips but doesn't take a drink. Instead, she just kind of smiles around it.

"What?" I ask, curious what's on her mind.

"I just...I kind of love that," she says, lowering the glass.

I'm glad, but I don't want the spotlight on me too long. "What about you? Do you work alone? Have partners? Have you always wanted to design?"

"I studied interactive design in college," she says. "I thought maybe I'd want to work with user interfaces and tech, but when I realized how much stuff they use—tech and the creation of it—I was overwhelmed with...guilt."

I stop mid-drink to process that. "I can see that. It does use a lot of resources."

"Exactly. And my whole family, one way or another, works in fields related to, well, the planet. My mom works in antiques, my dad runs a gardening store, and my brother's a scientist studying carbon emissions. I grew up loving, just loving," she says, for emphasis, "the grass and the earth and the trees and the sky. And, honestly, shifting my focus as a designer made sense. I'd felt so overwhelmed by this almost suffocating desire to save the planet, and one day a friend asked, 'Why don't you work in eco-friendly design?' and I thought, *that's it*. That's what I can do." She speaks with such passion, it's a little intoxicating.

"I love that. It's a gift to do what you love, isn't it?"

"It is," she says, then lets out a long, contemplative breath before turning back to me. "It's your last season. Is that going to be hard?"

After I set down the glass, I scrub a hand across the back of my neck and sigh. That's a good question. A great one, really. I take a beat to mull it over. It's not that I haven't thought about it being hard. It's that I've concentrated most of my energy on being the best.

I turn to meet her gaze, wanting to give her the most honest answer I can. It feels important.

"I want to go out on my terms. So yes, I think it will be hard to say goodbye. To walk away. But I think it would be harder if I stayed too long. You know? If I—" I pause. These words taste bitter, but they have to be said. Telling her is good practice. "If I wore out my welcome."

She gives me a sympathetic smile. "I understand that. And hey, I'm no hockey expert, but it sure looked like you played hard today."

I smile, appreciating that it was apparent. "That's the goal," I say, then reach for the glass again.

We finish off our wine.

But when she lowers hers, there's a tiny drop of Cabernet on the corner of her lips.

Ah, hell.

Before I think better of it, I reach for it, my thumb swiping it gently.

"Oh," she says, and a soft gust of breath seems to coast across her lips. The sound of it, faint, gentle against the night air, dances around me, drifting into my mind, burrowing into my soul.

Or maybe it's the feel of her skin, the dangerous proximity to her mouth, or the wish that I could taste the drop of wine right now. To kiss it off her lips. But that can't happen—romance is not in the cards.

I stand abruptly, gathering the dish, the napkin, the forks, and the nearly empty wineglass. "I should…"

"Get some sleep. Sounds like you have a busy day tomorrow. And every day. You have a big year ahead," she says, full of understanding.

Full of the reminder that I need to narrow my focus to hockey and *only* hockey. Romance is always fun at the beginning. But the deeper you get into it, the greater the chance you'll get screwed.

"I do," I say, then take the wineglass she's offering me. "I'll see you at the end of the week, though, when the furniture arrives. Well, if not before."

"Yes, if not before," she adds, brushing her hands down her shirt. "Good night, Ford. Good night, Zamboni."

The dog thumps her tail against the wooden porch. "Thanks for the mac and cheese, Skylar," I say.

Skylar turns to go but then spins around, her lips parted. "Your tie. You said your publicist gave it to you."

I run a finger down the pale-yellow silk. "Yeah. Camila did. She gives me one every year. She did when I finally played in my first game, so now I wear yellow to every game."

If I thought her smiles were big earlier, this one shoots to the moon.

"It's your lucky color? Yellow?" It sounds like she's uncovered a profound mystery.

"Yeah, it is."

She nods a few times, then says, "It's a good color on you."

She turns and walks away, and I watch her the entire time, savoring her compliment. And also this stolen moment with her. But late-night snacks with the neighbor aren't something I can let myself get used to.

I have a season to prove I can go out on top. And the sport that gave me everything demands the same discipline from me.

I pet my dog, and we go inside. Alone.

13

BIRD-WATCHING

SKYLAR

I shouldn't have a thing for apex predators, being a vegetarian and all. Still, there is just something about predatory birds that is so cool.

It's terrible of me to admire them.

Truly, it is.

But as I'm futzing around the kitchen a couple days later, fighting off a yawn while trying to crush my brother in Wordle—news flash: I'm not even close to beating his solve-it-in-three-tries average—a faint chirp floats through the open window.

Is that...my great blue heron love?

I race across the house in my fuzzy *Bees Are Cool* socks, complete with no-slip grips, to the front of the home, where I hunt for my opera glasses in the pile of paperbacks I keep meaning to give to my friends.

I hightail it back to the kitchen, past a curious Simon, who lifts his snout from his dog bed, then stretches and pads behind me.

While slinging the opera glasses around my neck, I

make it to the mudroom window as a chirp drifts past my ears again.

Hmm. That's not quite a squawk. But maybe herons chirp before they squawk? "Cleo, is there a great blue heron out there?"

But she says nothing. She simply sits imperiously in the corner, white paws crossed, gaze fixed on the live oak.

Well then.

If I'm going to become an amateur bird-watcher, no time like the present.

I swear I won't even look at the neighbor's home. I'll keep my focus firmly fixed on...the birds. That's what a new birder does.

I hoist myself over the windowsill, scanning the yard.

There's a mock orange tree in one corner, a red maple near the other, a California fuchsia in the middle...and is that a pack of hummingbirds in the fuchsia? Those birds are so tiny, it really is a good thing I have these opera glasses to check them out. But I should get closer, especially since someone is definitely chirping again.

With my blue jammies on today, I shimmy along the shelf, sliding closer and closer still to Cleo, while an annoying voice talks back in my head.

You're trying to spy on your hot neighbor.

Sheesh. My inner voice is super judgy. I try to reassure the voice that I won't look at Ford's porch. I really won't look to the east. I slink along on my belly, then bring the glasses to my eyes.

Whoa. Everything's blurry. It's all green fuzz. I adjust the opera glasses, focusing intensely on the California fuchsia. They're known for hummingbirds, I think. And look at all of them. Just look at them. Just look at...

That tanned skin. The smattering of golden chest hair. And that...is that...an eight-pack?

Five, six, seven...Oh god. Eight. And that treasure trail that leads right into...

Stop!

The man is simply saluting the sun, and I am salaciously, shamelessly...

Oh, is that a prayer twist now? Well, I am praying he holds this pose as I stare without intermission at those bare, toned, and muscular arms. Those sturdy shoulders, rippling and, I bet, firm to the touch.

Those strong thighs, looking far too good in those yellow shorts.

Ugh. My stomach twists. After he shared about his lucky color the other night, his all-female management team, and his focus and dedication, I should not be staring at his, well, focus and dedication. But my god, just look at his biceps.

The left one is Focus, the right one, Dedication.

And I think I'll name his abs Commitment and Discipline.

And...I'll stop after I name his pecs—

Oof.

There's a paw on my face. "Cleo," I mutter, waving my free hand to get the sleek creature off me, but when I yank the glasses away from my eyes, the feline's lunging across my face, her murderous paw aimed at a...bug in the screen. I roll away to get out of her line of fire—

And squawk out a wrenching, "Ahhh," as I topple to the ground and land on my...chin.

I'm moaning in pain, and groaning in misery as the ache lances through my freaking face.

How do you land on your chin, you might ask? By being the new breed of dodo bird who squawks as she tumbles.

"Everything okay?"

I cringe.

That's Ford. Can he see me all the way from his porch across my yard and down to the ground? *Dear goddess of the universe, please let the earth swallow me whole.*

The voice grows louder. "Skylar? Is that you?"

I glance around. Pretty sure I can't hide in the catio. I pull myself up, opera glasses in hand, and wave from inside the catio, figuring honesty is the best policy. "Sometimes I like to watch birds from the catio."

From across the fenced-in yard, he's standing on the edge of his porch, his handsome brow furrowing, clearly weighing my answer. Then, I swear I see his dimple flashing as he says, "That tracks."

I open the catio door—it has one, in case a human needs to, well, enter the catio like a civilized adult—and stroll casually across the yard in my fuzzy socks, like my chin isn't aching and there's nothing to see here.

Nothing at all.

I pad up onto my porch, offering a faint smile to Ford and Focus, Dedication, Commitment, and Discipline, then go inside.

Where the chirp is still chirping. "What the hell?"

I retrace my steps to the mudroom, look at the ceiling, and groan. The smoke detector's battery is low.

I've been bird-watching a battery.

* * *

Mabel studies my face as I sort through vintage doorknobs at one of my favorite shops later that day. "I hate to ask the obvious, but what happened to your chin?"

My chin still smarts, and I deserve it. I sigh as I look up from the options for replacements for the ones missing at Sofia's law firm in the Presidio. I set up all the retro lamps in her office a few days ago—she picked Tiffany-style ones, which delighted me.

"I had a battle with a smoke detector."

Mabel hums, then nods. "Sounds about right."

"Ford said the same thing."

"Sexy Reno Guy?" she asks.

I sigh, feeling foolish still. "Yep."

"What's going on?"

He's sarcastic and interesting, thoughtful and curious, and stern in a way I shouldn't like but do. Plus, he adores animals and seems to intrinsically get me. "I spied on him. Again," I admit, then tell her everything.

"I don't know whether to high-five you or warn you about getting caught."

"Maybe both," I say heavily.

We resume our hunt, and it's good to focus on another client.

Later that day, though, my mom calls to tell me the date of Landon's store opening so I know when to avoid that block.

I make a mental note of the day, then thank her.

Right. No looking back. No getting distracted. No bad decisions. Which means I should probably stop watching my hot neighbor—*my client, my very important client*—do yoga.

Fortunately, the bruise on my chin serves as a tender reminder.

I return to my couch, ready to focus, to draw up some plans. Then my phone pings with a message.

> Ford: This is last minute, but I have some tickets to tonight's hockey game. Want to go?

My chin says no, but my fingers say *Hell, yes.*

14

MY ASSASSIN PHASE

FORD

I ferry the puck down the ice, skates scraping, focused as a sniper. I dodge a giant New York defenseman, and in another second or two, I'll slap this bad boy past the goalie.

If I can just find an opening, I can break this infernal tie. And I can do it with the gorgeous, clever, amusing redhead watching from the stands.

But Karlsson, the New York defender, strips the puck from me, then flashes a smug grin as he spins around. "Slippery hands, old man," he taunts and races down the ice the other way.

"Fuck." I don't care about his insult—because fuck him, he's always been like that.

I care about me. And that? That's so not me.

I don't lose my concentration because of fans.

I block out the noise. I block out trash talk. I block out everything.

But now I'm on my heels, chasing Karlsson as possession changes. I've got to get it back from that asshole. I can't let a distraction interfere with my game.

No such luck though.

The shift changes ten seconds later, and I hop over the boards, irritated. Falcon claps me on the back. "We'll get 'em next time," the defenseman says.

I nod, grabbing my water bottle. "We fucking will." Shaking it off, I take a long, thirsty drink, trying not to look at center ice.

At the seats I got for Skylar.

I keep my gaze on the action, watching the opponents like I'm studying the penguins in that brain game I played earlier. The game that's supposed to help me keep my focus when it matters.

Like, say, now.

But another voice says, *Maybe just one look is fine.*

Then I think of Leah and what she said earlier today: *Your discipline is unmatched. But you don't have to do extra to play at peak performance. You're doing great as you are.*

While my teammates battle by the boards for the puck, I give myself permission to do ten reps...by stealing a glance at center ice at last.

Skylar's shouting, cheering us on, and—wait. Is she wearing a number fourteen jersey?

Holy shit. She is.

A dumb smile spreads across my face. I look down, so it's not obvious to everyone. Best if I look fierce, angry, glowering.

Then I read the words on my water bottle one more time before the shift change.

Surprise Them.

My mantra since I surprised the whole damn league by sticking around when no one thought I'd make it to the pros.

When it's time for the next line change, I hop over the

boards with Bryant and Falcon, locking in. New York barely sees it coming when Falcon strips the puck from their forward and flicks it to Bryant.

I am nothing but concentration as Bryant flings it my way.

I assess their goalie, watching as he sets up for me to bite on the slap shot. Then, at the last second, I switch to a wrist shot.

It slips right through his legs. He's...surprised.

The crowd roars, and Bryant bumps my chest. "You old dog. You *can* learn new tricks," he says.

"Right. I learned that from you," I say, but I can't even be sarcastic. We're ahead now, and all I want is to keep it that way.

This time, I don't fight the impulse.

Because focus isn't about fighting distractions. It's about not letting them get the better of you.

And Skylar, cheering me on in a jersey with my number? That's not something I want to miss.

I tip my forehead in her direction as she cheers louder. The woman next to her leans in and whispers something in her ear.

Skylar just smiles and keeps cheering.

And we keep winning.

When the game ends and my teammates cheer and high-five, I glide past center ice, mouthing to her, "*Nice jersey.*"

She gives a sassy pop of her hips. "This thing? Found it in a discount bin," she shouts.

I laugh. She loves to knock me down a peg.

And you love it when she does that.

The thing is, I really do.

Shame I didn't make plans with her for after the game.

But I dismiss that thought. We're...neighbors. Sort of friends. Definitely working together.

There's no need to make plans.

But I'm not annoyed one bit when I let Zamboni into the yard later that night to do her business and see Skylar across the fence with Simon running in circles.

The trouble is, Skylar's staring at her phone, her brow furrowed in tight concentration. Her lips are a ruler.

I strain to listen to whatever she's watching and catch a man's voice through the speaker: *"We're just so grateful that she was so supportive, and how the universe has brought us together to open our dream board game store."*

Skylar looks up, livid. I don't know what's on that video, but whatever it is, it just ruined her night.

I want to jump over the fence and comfort her. Instead, I step closer to the four-foot-high wooden fence that separates our yards, resting a hand on top of the painted wood, Zamboni parking herself dutifully at my feet.

"What's going on?"

Skylar flinches, then looks up from her phone. With a frown, she stabs the screen, ending the video. "Just my ex," she says with a shrug like it's no big deal. She shoves the phone into her pocket. "It's fine."

"You sure?" I ask, worried.

But embarrassment flickers in her pretty green eyes, visible even in the dark.

Simon yips, and she bends to pick him up. "It's fine, buddy."

The little brown and tan guy snuggles against her chest. Lucky dog. But I force myself to look up at her, not at the burrowing critter.

"Skylar." My tone is stern. I want her to tell me what's going on.

She draws a steadying breath, meeting my gaze with a cheery, "How are you? Great game. Thanks again for the tickets. It was so fun."

Ah, hell. She's trying to cover up her feelings. I appreciate the put-on-a-game-face routine, but the fact that she's not sassing me about anything says what her mouth isn't saying. She's hurt.

I nod to her pocket where the phone is out of sight but not out of mind. "What's going on with your ex and his *dream board game* store? And do you want me to have him poisoned? I can arrange for arsenic just like that." I snap my fingers.

A small smile teases at her pretty lips, and then she lets out a long sigh. "He talked to some local neighborhood site about his new store, that's all. I came across it on my social feed. It's opening soon, and it's honestly not a bad idea for a business."

She's right, especially with game nights becoming more popular. But I hate her ex on principle, so I am not going to concede this point.

"Would you like me to poison a game of Chutes and Ladders for him?"

"I have no idea how you would do that, but I love that you're thinking this way because—" She hesitates, weighing whether to say the next thing, then she gives in, "fine. He brought me up in the video. He said he appreciated how supportive I was of him and his dreams, especially because he's opening the shop now with his new girlfriend. That's what I was watching."

Anger lashes through me. My jaw tightens. I want to find this guy and throttle him. I don't even know what happened in their breakup, but I'm certain of two things —it was his fault, and he's an asshole. "Why did he bring you up in the video?"

"I was very supportive of him when we were together. His plans, his ideas," she explains, but it's clear from her tone that the memory hurts. "When we lived together, he kept saying he wanted to open this store, and I encouraged him to. But he never did. We were in a relationship for a long time, and then he broke up with me when he met someone else."

My own chest aches. I understand her situation too well. But I shove my feelings aside. "His loss," I say sharply, biting out the words as I clench my fists.

Zamboni looks up at me, thumping her thick tail in worry. She's always been an empathetic dog. I stroke her head so she knows I'm not mad at her. Never mad at her.

I lighten up on my frustration as I motion for Skylar to go on. "So they opened the store *together*?"

"It seems so," she says, lifting her chin, trying so hard to be tough. "And he said in the video that they appreciated my early support so much, they wrote my name on the floorboard in the vintage corner under the carpet in his shop. Said he hopes I find my own happiness like they have." She rolls her eyes. "I wish a cat would pee all over their store."

That's the Skylar I know. Completely exasperated and frustrated.

"I am *one hundred percent* going to poison him," I announce, meaning it. I'm ready to brew something deadly in a basement I don't have.

"Poison's too good for him," she says.

"You're right. He should suffer. But I'm positive some poison could do the trick. Something that guarantees a nice, long, painful death." I pause for a second to think. "We were talking about plants the other day. We could give him a potted poisonous plant as a store-opening gift and tell him it's edible."

And just like fucking magic, her frown disappears, replaced by a devilish grin I want to kiss right off her lovely lips. "I had no idea you were secretly—well, I knew you were secretly mean—but *secretly evil*? This is *really* something."

"Wait, it was a secret that I'm mean?" I ask, mock offended that she thinks I try to hide it.

"You're right. It's not a secret. It's obvious."

"I was hoping it would be."

"Terribly obvious. But this is actually kind of exciting." She steps closer to the fence, curling her hand around a wooden post. "What are some other ways you might poison him?"

"Well, considering I have *just* begun the assassin phase of my life, I need to do some research. But I'm good at research and incredibly committed to follow-through. When I say I'm going to do something, I do it."

"Like with your conditioning," she says, then dips her face and kisses the dog's head.

Simon peers up at her like she hung the moon. It's so endearing, their relationship. So familiar, too, though mine with Zamboni is different. But Skylar and I, we both seem to rely on our dogs. "How long have you had him?" I ask.

"Three perfect years. I adopted him from Little Friends. I always wanted a Dachshund mix. They're so cute and...spicy," she says.

Like you.

But I keep that thought to myself.

"That seems to sum him up perfectly," I say.

Skylar tips her head toward Zamboni. "And your perfect princess?"

I glance down at my loyal companion, sighing heavily as she settles deeper onto the soft grass by my feet. "She's a rescue too. Which might be obvious based on the fact that she's a weird mix. But I like it. Especially since she's all mine."

Skylar gives me a curious look. "What do you mean? All yours? Who else's...oh, did you share her with an ex?"

"Thank fuck I didn't." Just the thought sends a surge of anger through me. I do my best to douse it. "I adopted her a couple of years ago, as I was getting divorced." That word used to rankle. A reminder of my failure at marriage. Fine, Brittany was the one who left, but I still failed. But now, with some distance, I can see we were never going to last. Still sucks, though, that I once thought she was my forever. "Zamboni's been my main girl since then."

"My ex didn't appreciate Simon," Skylar says.

"I doubt mine would have appreciated Zamboni." I pause, unsure if I want to go there. But she's shared, so I say, "It ended for reasons...similar to yours."

She gives a small, sympathetic smile. "I'm sorry."

"It's for the best," I say.

"It is," she adds. It's a strange new bond between Skylar and me, but it's there. Real and true.

And there is her dog, licking her cheek. Once again, I find myself jealous...of a dog.

He licks her chin again. And again. And with each successive lick, I stare more closely.

Is her chin getting a little...bluer?

"Skylar. Are you okay?"

"Why?" she asks, a frown digging into her forehead.

I study her face, trying to catch enough slivers of moonlight to see. "What happened to your chin?"

Her free hand flies to cover it up. "Nothing!"

Oh, it's something all right, especially since she quickly adds, "I put on concealer. Foundation."

I lift a brow. "I think Simon just licked it off."

She winces, looking down before meeting my gaze with a touch of guilt. "He loves my makeup. And he loves lotion. And he loves licking me."

There's so much in that sentence I could respond to, but I start with, "How did you bruise your chin?"

For a long beat, a silent debate rages behind those eyes. "This morning," she admits. "I might have fallen in the catio. Go ahead and laugh."

But I don't laugh. I beckon her closer, saying softly, "C'mere."

I wait. I'm patient, and I hope she hears the sincerity in my tone.

She steps closer—tentatively, maybe, but still she does it. I reach out and run the pad of my thumb across her bruise.

Her breath seems to catch. The sound of it is a jolt of electricity down my spine.

"Does it hurt?" I ask.

She shakes her head. "No. Does it look terrible?"

I shake my head, but I don't stop touching her. I can't seem to. Stroking her chin will do nothing to get rid of the bruise. But she feels so damn good, and her eyes are soft, and her lips are parted, and she smells like summertime.

"No, it doesn't look terrible at all. I just wanted to make sure you were okay," I say as a breeze rustles the branches of the tree next to her.

She swallows roughly, and my chest aches with the

potent desire to run my hand down her throat, over her chest. I'd thread my other hand into her hair and pull her close. Then I'd kiss her chin, her cheek, her pink lips I can't stop looking at.

But I can't.

I let go of her.

"I'm okay. I actually feel a lot better now," she says, her gaze drifting down to my hand before she regards me like she wants to say something.

Nighttime surrounds us, the city lights glowing in the distance, the rattle of cars and buses drifting by.

She meets my gaze, and with a fresh new vulnerability, she says quietly, "I saw you doing yoga this morning."

It sounds like a confession, and I'm not sure why she would make it, so I lift a brow curiously and, like I'm piecing together details. "You mean when you were in the catio and I asked if you were okay?"

She gulps. "Well, yeah. And before."

"Oh."

For once, I'm at a loss for words. I don't know how to make sense of her admission or this charged air between us. This buzzy feeling in my body.

This crackling in my cells.

Instead, I give in once more. I slide my thumb along her jaw, then hold her face in my hand for a long beat. "Just make sure you don't fall again," I say, my voice low and smoky, "especially because we have a poisoning to plot."

She smiles, but it's subtle. A little sexy. And when she nibbles on the corner of her lips, my chest tightens.

My heart speeds up.

That hazy feeling spreads through me once again.

I'm not prepared to analyze it. To face it.

So I do something impulsive.

I lean across the fence, and I press a kiss to her forehead.

I tell myself it's friendly.

But the summertime scent of her hair—her perfume, her lotion, whatever it is—seeps into my senses, intoxicating me. She's champagne, and I want to drink the whole bottle.

I pull away, rasping out a "Good night, Skylar."

I head back into my house with my dog before I do something truly dangerous—like hauling my neighbor over the fence and asking her to come inside with me.

In the morning, I stand on my second-floor balcony, moving past the edge of the hot tub and drinking my morning smoothie—but really, I'm looking for her.

Fuck it, I'm spying. Shamelessly spying. Trying to get a sense of when she might walk her dog so I can casually join her like it's just a coincidence.

I down some more of the kale concoction, hoping the nutrients knock some sense into me, then...*finally*. I spot her moving around the kitchen with purpose—possibly getting ready to walk the dog. In no time, I dart downstairs, leash up mine, and head out the front door.

Yes!

Skylar trots down her steps, a hoodie sloping off her shoulder, jean shorts on, earbuds in. She holds Simon's leash in one hand, and the other gestures wildly with her phone. She's entirely focused on venting her thoughts to someone on a call. "Landon sent me an email this morning! They invited me to their opening!"

I growl. Poisoning is too good for her ex.

I walk the other way. I need time to think, but it doesn't take long, so I double back a few blocks later.

When Skylar returns home, I'm waiting on her front porch. "The store opening is next weekend?"

Startled, she stops on the stone path. "How do you know?"

"I googled new board game stores and found his," I say.

"Oh. Impressive."

"Not really. I'm determined." I hold her gaze. "If you don't want to go to it, no problem. But if you decide to go..." I pause for effect. "I'll be your date."

15

___

SEXY FROG
SKYLAR

Did my hot-as-hell, lucky-yellow-shorts-wearing, sun-saluting, stern-but-secretly-sweet, gruff-but-incredibly-giving, dog-loving, aspiring-assassin neighbor just ask me out?

"For the poisoning?" I ask, blinking...in shock, I think?

Yes, my heart is slamming against my rib cage. My skin is as hot as a forest fire. And my chest is tingling.

Wait, nope, you dumbass, that's not shock. That's—gasp—arousal.

Because...Ford Devon asked me on a date. Whether it's a poisoning date or not, who cares?

"We can bring a plant. Just for fun though," Ford adds, like he needs to keep the hitwoman in me in check. He rises from the stairs and strides closer while keeping Zamboni far, far away from Simon, who's wiggling on his leash like his tail is a high-speed metronome.

"Right. For fun." My head spins as I try to process this twist in my morning.

I drag a hand through my...ugh. The nest on my head. My hair is twisted into a messy bun, and I really need to remember to dress better for dog walks. Pretty sure that's one of the rules of having a sexy neighbor. You can no longer leave your house looking like you just rolled out of bed. Mascara is a must. Brushes are your friend.

"Yes, for fun, because that would be the point. To walk into his store opening that the prick invited you to and show him how much fun you're having without him."

Ford has a look in his eyes like he's ready to plow down any defenseman in his way on the ice. The idea is enticing, but my brain snags on one detail. How does he know I was invited?

Then, it hits me. "Oh! You must've heard me talking to Mabel when I was leaving the house."

"You were speaking kind of loudly, so I don't think it counts as eavesdropping."

"You're right. It's not eavesdropping when somebody is ranting at their bestie. That's fair game," I say.

But...does spying from a catio as someone works out come under the fair game umbrella? Do I need to tell him about that? I came close to confessing last night. I nearly blurted out all my voyeuristic transgressions. Then he was touching my chin and kissing my forehead, and I'm pretty sure my brain turned to pudding.

"And it's also fair game to take you on a date in front of your dickhead ex. *Landon*," Ford says, his lips twisting when he says Landon's name, then twitching up into a grin, as if he really likes the idea of...taking me on a date. My stomach flips in the best of ways. I think I truly like the idea too.

But I want to be sure I'm understanding him correctly. "Supposedly, there will be some press there. Well, from that neighborhood site that covered him already. You want to take me on a date to his store? Like a fake date?" I ask to clarify, while Simon tugs on his leash, desperately trying to say hi to the Shepherd Corgi.

The look on Ford's face could be entered in a contest to define the word *flummoxed,* as if he didn't entirely think this date through. But then he asks, with some concern, "Did I just break a neighbor rule? Or a client-designer relationship rule? No fake dates?"

"No, that's not a rule. Neither of those are rules," I say in a rush, because he'd better not take back a date, fake or real. I'd be crossing Adam's don't-date-a-neighbor line, but Adam doesn't have to know about this fake real date. Or this real fake date.

Whatever it is, it's mine, all mine.

"It's been a crazy morning. I've gone from an invitation to gaze at my name underneath the carpet at the board game store to the suggestion I attend the opening with my neighbor, and his biceps, Dedication and Focus."

I've probably said too much. I've definitely said too much.

Ford scrubs a hand across the trim stubble on his jaw, his blue eyes twinkling in...delight. "You named...my biceps?"

"And your abs," I admit.

"There's so much to unpack in that statement. But I have to get to practice. And no, I don't give a fuck who's there. So...is it a yes? To our revenge fake date?"

I smile, and when he smiles too, it does something entirely new to my heart—it feels light and glowy.

"It's a yes," I say.

His dimple shows up again. "Good." He heads next door, gives me a wave, then—a flex of his right biceps.

"Dedication," I say.

Another flex, the left this time. "Focus," I add.

He wiggles his eyebrows as he goes inside with his dog.

I have no idea how my morning went from a pity invite to a revenge fake date, but I'll take it.

* * *

"Bamboo is the new black. Fight me on this."

It's my opening salvo in today's podcast. I'm feeling all sorts of feisty after this morning's encounter with Ford turned my day around.

Trevyn arches a brow. "*Reclaimed* is the new black," he counters.

Mabel smiles, makes a rolling gesture, and says, "I'd better get some popcorn for this."

"Pay attention," I tell her. "Because you'll need to know this for your future bakery."

"She's not going to have a bamboo bakery," Trevyn chides from across the table, full of stern authority.

"Not least because *The Bamboo Bakery* is a terrible name," Mabel adds.

"One hundred percent," I agree.

"But she *is* going to have chairs made with reclaimed wood for her fabulous place someday, and here's why..." Trevyn launches us into a fifteen-minute debate about which design hack is better for both pocketbooks and the planet.

I feel energized. And, honestly, a little too excited about next weekend's...fake date with Ford. My mood must be patently obvious—especially to Mabel, who was on the receiving end of my rant this morning.

"You're in a *much* better mood than earlier," she notes. "The viewers can see that smile, but the listeners can't.

So...what's it for? You've been grinning this whole time, and let's be real—pretty much the only things that put you in a mood like that are great thrift finds, snarky comments from Simon, and ogling hot guys."

"Guess which one it is," I challenge.

Trevyn strokes his goateed chin. "Oh, this is gonna be good."

"I bet it's all three," Mabel declares, flicking a strand of light brown hair off her shoulder like she's just cracked the case.

My jaw drops, and I can't say a word as Mabel leans closer to the mic and whispers, "Is it *Sexy Reno Guy*?"

A tingle shoots down my chest, chased by a secret hope I haven't felt in a long time. I'm about to answer *yes* —but then I wonder if that would be saying too much. Is it admitting too much, even if it's just to our nine hundred thirty-one subscribers? Well, one thousand one hundred *fifty* now, since we had a bunch of new subs last week. *Yay us.*

But since I *did* tell Ford I'd named his muscles, it's not exactly a secret that I think a client is sexy. At least I haven't said his *name* on the show. And if he listened to it, or his mom did, they'd only hear that I think he's handsome. "Possibly," I say, twirling a lock of my hair.

"Oh, I do love possibilities," Trevyn says.

And the thing is—I like possibilities too. I'm eager for the possibilities for the first time in ages. But that eagerness also scares me. Dates lead to romance, which leads to opening up and getting close and realizing you've wasted *five years* of your life on the wrong person.

When the podcast ends, Trevyn takes off for an afternoon date while Mabel and I head to High Kick Coffee to meet some of our friends for girl time.

The bell chimes as we enter the coffee shop, passing the showgirl mannequin posed at the door in her boa and sequined dress.

I scan the café, spotting our skating instructor friend Sabrina first, her blonde ponytail cinched high on her head. She's already claimed a table by the window, right under a playful painting of two foxes, signed by local artist Maeve Hartley—another friend of ours. Leighton's here too. She's a photographer and an essential part of our extended girl gang.

After grabbing drinks, the five of us settle in at the table, and—just like Mabel did on the podcast—Sabrina dives right into the topic du jour.

"Is *Sexy Reno Guy* making you rethink your stance on dating?"

"You already listened?" I ask. "I *literally* just posted it."

"I listened too. On the way over," Leighton chimes in. "And that's saying something, because I hardly listen to *anything* when I walk around the city."

"We're just that charming," Mabel says, smirking.

"So, is he?" Sabrina presses, her eyes full of mischief. "Because you've been a little reluctant to get involved with anyone."

"Or a lot," Leighton corrects, because my friends know the truth.

I took a year off from dating after Landon took off. It was just *too hard* to put myself out there again. I tried online dating a few months ago, but it was a bust. All those questions I like to ask to root out red flags left me with...nothing.

And now I have this nebulous sort of fake date coming up with a new guy.

I blow out a breath, trying to make sense of what Ford is.

A *client.*

A *neighbor.*

And yet...he's also a type of *date.*

"He's making me think about a lot of things," I say diplomatically.

Sabrina wiggles her well-groomed brows. "I *hope* some of those thoughts involve getting naked with him. Because it's been a while for you, Sky."

"Shut up," I say, but I'd be lying if I claimed she was wrong.

I'd be lying, too, if I said I was thinking about slap shots and breakaways when I watch his hockey game the next night with Simon snoozing on my lap. How could I? The Sports Network shows the warmups, and I can't look away as Ford stretches on the ice.

He's kneeling, hands braced on the surface, shifting his pelvis up and down.

Up and down.

Up and freaking down.

I nudge Simon. "Look," I whisper. "He's..." My mouth goes dry. "It's like he's humping the ice."

Simon lifts his snout, side-eyes the TV, then gives a subtle nod—confirming what I'm seeing—before flopping his head back onto my lap.

"He looks like a frog," I say, then amend that to, "a *very* sexy frog."

And because that's a thought I *definitely* shouldn't keep to myself, I text Ford as soon as the game ends.

Skylar: Saw the warmups. You give new
meaning to the term 'sexy frog.'

A few minutes later, a reply lands. He must be in the
locker room now.

Ford: What did it mean before?

Skylar: It wasn't a thing before. You're
breaking new ground. And tomorrow, let's
hope we don't break furniture.

Ford: That sounds vaguely dirty.

Oh. He's right. It does. Maybe that's not the worst thing in
the world.

16

DID YOU KNOW?

FORD

It was a rough game last night, but I drag myself out of bed, let Zamboni into the yard, wait for her to finish, then step into the shower. It's early, especially for me, but the water wakes me. Once dressed in jeans and a polo, I grab my phone off the nightstand.

One missed call and a voicemail from Mom. Then a text.

> Mom: Did you know the Golden Gate Bridge was completed ahead of schedule? Construction began during the Great Depression and finished in 1937. It was also under budget.

I suspect this tidbit relates to the renovation—a not-so-subtle reminder of her expectations. When she couldn't reach me by phone, she resorted to a text message. The Sausalito house is on track for both deadline and budget, but right now I need to get over there and FaceTime with Mom to show her *everything.*

She'll be apoplectic if I miss our planned video call.

Skylar also texted this morning to say the delivery would arrive thirty minutes early. I barely have time to whip up a kale smoothie and pour it into my new to-go cup. A glance at the picture and caption makes my lips twitch up.

With a final goodbye to Zamboni, I head outside, half-wishing there wasn't this fizzy feeling in my chest when I glance at the townhouse next to mine.

A couple weeks ago, I thought my neighbor was a royal pain in the ass. Now I've come to enjoy the random morning sightings.

This morning is planned, however, and I've been counting the days, then the hours.

It's getting to be a problem.

A dangerously sexy problem.

Skylar's waiting by my car, a large canvas bag at her feet filled with what appears to be blankets. She looks effortless and edible in a pair of high-waisted jeans and a white top that reveals a sliver of flesh where it ends. My brain short-circuits for a second. How would her skin taste if I kissed just above her belly button? Or higher still, between her breasts?

Get it together, man. She's your designer, and you're about to spend the day setting up your parents' house with her.

I take a fortifying gulp of my kale smoothie to kill the thought and manage a rough-voiced, "Morning."

Skylar tilts her head, all faux skepticism. "Well, you sound like you just woke up. Which makes you an impostor because the Ford I know has been up since six."

I snort, hitting the unlock button on my car. "I am *not* an early riser."

"I don't believe it."

"I work at night a lot of the time. I think I'm allowed to sleep in."

"Of course you're allowed." She flashes me a grin. "It just seems completely antithetical to your personality."

I roll my eyes, open the door, and gesture for her to hop inside. "Get in, Skylar."

She grabs the canvas bag and reaches around the front seat to toss it into the back. I have to physically restrain myself from swatting her ass.

I really need to clear my head.

Once she's settled, I shut the passenger door and drag a hand through my messy hair. I take a breath, trying to reset my mind as I walk around the back of the car, get behind the wheel, and set the smoothie in the drink holder.

"Shut the front door!"

Skylar's shriek nearly startles me out of my seat. She's loud this early. "Are you trying to wake up the next county?"

"You got the OnlyPaws cup!"

I glance at the gleaming yellow thermos decorated with the image of Simon Side-Eye's back paws crossed— just the paws, that's all—and the words, "Starting an OnlyPaws page to help Mom pay the bills."

"Huh. Yeah. I guess I did." I rap my knuckles against the side of it. "Seems pretty solid so far. But you can't be sure until you stress test it by running into a mischievous pixie of a neighbor."

Skylar's smile seems to stretch forever. "Want me to

surprise you on the street someday and see how it holds up?"

"That won't be necessary," I say, then meet her gaze. "We both know I have good hands."

Her eyes twinkle and her breath catches. She swallows, then says, "I bet you do."

I'm about to start the car when she stretches across the console and drops a kiss onto my cheek. "Thank you," she says.

My head swims from the heat racing through me. From *that*. From her lips barely touching me.

She settles into her seat, and it takes me several seconds to get my bearings. Pulling away from the curb, I mutter a hot and strangled, "You're welcome."

But her summertime scent is setting up camp as I drive. Her kiss is lodged in my brain. I hunt for something else to focus on as we cruise along Scott Street, the bridge coming into view. "Did you know the Golden Gate Bridge was completed ahead of schedule? My mom texted me this morning to tell me."

Skylar gasps, laughing too. "Oh my god. She texted me too! To ask if I knew that the Eames lounger is engineered with a fifteen-degree tilt to relieve pressure from the base of the spine."

I shoot her an amused glance as we zip over the bridge. "That also sounds like her. She always wants to make sure furniture is good ergonomically." Then I narrow my eyes. "But the big question is: was that new information to you? Did you know that already?"

Skylar grins, confident and self-assured. "I did, Ford. I did."

There's something about how she says it—like a

woman who *knows* she's good at her job, who collects details like currency and keeps them handy.

It's scarily hot.

And I really, really need to stop liking her. There is zero space in my life for a crush. Especially considering where the last one led—to marrying the wrong person. An image of signing the divorce papers flashes through my head, and I wince, kicking the terrible memory into a dark corner.

Everything seemed great with Brittany at the start too, and I'd do well to remember that.

I focus on the road as we cross the bridge, the emerald-green hills of the Marin Headlands stretching out before us. We dip down into Sausalito, winding our way toward my parents' house as Skylar mentions she needs to be back in the city by four.

"I have to pop by a client's office at five," she explains.

"We'll be out of the home quickly," I say, though I wouldn't mind if she wanted to spend time there after we video call my mom. I wouldn't mind that at all.

"True. It won't take too long," she says, and do I detect a note of wistfulness in her voice? Like maybe she wouldn't mind hanging out there today too?

Doing what, you idiot? Staring at your parents' furniture together?

I shove away the thoughts of hanging out casually as I park the car.

A few minutes later, a truck from Twice Loved pulls up, and Skylar immediately starts directing the delivery guys. She doesn't second-guess; she just takes charge, telling them where to set each piece, from the dove gray couch to the pale yellow kitchen table, how to move things, and what needs extra care.

It's sexy.

Which is a problem.

Watching her handle this whole thing makes me like her even more. Apparently, I have a serious kink for competent women.

As the guys head to the truck to grab a bureau, Skylar wrestles a blanket from the canvas bag and artfully arranges it along the back of the couch.

"So that's why you had blankets," I say.

"Did you think it was for a picnic?"

"A man can hope," I say from the kitchen, watching her smooth out a corner. "Also, nice maroon."

She stops, stares sharply at me. "It's a Pinot Noir. See the light ruby color?" She strokes the blanket, slow and deliberate, and I'm mesmerized by the way she moves her hand.

Her hand.

I'm borderline turned on by the way she's stroking a fucking blanket.

"Nope," I rasp, shaking off the inappropriate thoughts as best I can. Then my phone vibrates with a new text from Mom, which is a buzzkill if I ever needed one. And I do.

I pace through the kitchen and open it.

> Mom: Did you have any idea how much cheaper Ubers are than cabs???

I start to reply, *Yes, Mom,* when I spy a ton of messages above the latest one. I must have missed them this morning when I only glanced at the Golden Gate Bridge fact. As I scroll up, my stomach sinks.

"No, no, no," I mutter, reading them all in horror. "She can't be serious."

Skylar shoots me a curious look. "Serious about what?" she asks with some concern.

A knock on the door interrupts my reply.

My mom's in town.

17

MOM BOMB

FORD

"How did you get here?"

My mother tilts her head, her platinum blonde, news-anchor hair barely moving as she gives me a look that says *Did you really ask that?* "I took an Uber. You'd know that if you responded to my texts. Now, is that any way to greet your mother?"

She holds her arms out wide, waiting for an embrace. My shoes stay glued to the hardwood floor, while Skylar stands behind me. I should hug my mom. I don't. "B-but you live in Seattle," I sputter.

"Only for a little while longer," she says breezily.

My shoulders bunch up. "We were supposed to do this on video, and you just *arrived*," I point out, like the absurdity of it will somehow undo reality.

"I called you as soon as I booked my flight."

"You flew down this morning?" I ask. That's exactly what the messages I just scanned said, but I'm struggling to believe it, even though the evidence stands in front of me in an Oxford cloth shirt, sensible flats, and her everyday pearls.

"Well, I don't think she took an Uber from Seattle, Ford," Skylar points out. "That's about eight hundred miles."

That's a reasonable point. Helpful, even. But is she taking my mom's side?

Mom, who's not even supposed to be here right now. The delivery guys are already gone, and it was only supposed to be Skylar and me. But now I know why she was texting Golden Gate Bridge facts this morning—probably because she was flying past it.

Mom turns to the designer, beaming. "Hello! So good to officially meet you."

She holds out her arms, and Skylar steps in, accepting a warm embrace like they've known each other forever. But that's Skylar. She has this thing about her that draws you to her...whether you want to be drawn or not.

"It's good that you're here. I can show you everything now," Skylar says, rolling with the changes the way I should be. But for some reason, I just can't.

I clench my jaw. "Mom," I bite out. "I can't believe you just showed up."

"I can't believe it didn't occur to me sooner," she says, like we're absolutely on the same page. "I woke up at four in the morning thinking—*What was I doing?* Letting you, young people with young bodies, test the furniture? I have a sixty-three-year-old ass."

Skylar snorts.

I snap my gaze to the redhead who's been living rent-free in my head.

She shrugs as if to say, *What's the big deal?* "What? I didn't think your mom would say *ass.*"

Mom winks at Skylar, then nods conspiratorially my way. "He still can't handle it." She turns back to me. "So I was in bed, in the dark, your father snoring, and I grabbed my phone and booked the next flight out of Seattle. And mind you, it was a *six-thirty* departure, so I had to hustle. I know you like your sleep, so I didn't call you until six, when I was boarding."

"I was asleep!"

"I *know.* Your phone went straight to voicemail. You really should get a landline," she says, *tsking* me.

Maybe this is why I'm annoyed. Somehow, she's twisting this around to make it my fault that she's appeared out of the blue. "I will never get a landline. Also, I had a game last night."

"And that was an excellent assist in the third period." She gives a fist pump.

My mother is fist-pumping me on her pop-in visit. Her *fly-by pop-in.* The world is upside down.

"As I was saying," she continues, admonishing me, "I called you and left messages. You really should listen to your voicemails."

"Oh, you should, Ford," Skylar says soberly.

"No one checks voicemail," I say, maybe a little louder than necessary and more annoyed than I should let on. "No one should leave voicemails."

"I thought you might think that too," Mom says evenly. "That's why I sent you *several* texts."

"Yes, I know. I just noticed them." I grab my phone and read from it like I'm giving court evidence. "*Ford, I'm on the plane. Ford, I got a window seat. Ford, did you know they have to-go boxes on flights? Oops, I'm wrong. The woman next to me simply asked for one. They don't actually have them. Can you imagine?*" I pause and look up. "I can't, Mom. I *can't* imagine."

"But it could prevent food waste," Skylar points out.

I cut her a look.

"To-go boxes on planes are an excellent idea," Mom says.

"No, they're not. They're a terrible idea." I blow out a breath, desperately trying to figure out why this treacherous ball of frustration is still running through me. "Mom," I try again.

"Hold that thought, darling. I just need to pop into the little girls' room."

Skylar brightens, pointing down the hall. "I put toilet paper in there this morning. It was in my bag with the blankets."

My mom beams. "I knew I liked you. I always carry tissues, because you never know."

She saunters to the bathroom while I stand there like a bomb's just gone off in the kitchen.

The most devastating kind of bomb. A mom bomb.

I drag a frustrated hand through my hair. I *really* need to let go of this annoyance. This is not who I am.

"This is...she just...crash-landed into my day," I grumble.

This is par for the course with Mom. Yeah, it throws me off, but I'm used to being thrown off. Opponents try to do it on the ice all the time. Defensemen do it every game.

So why does it bother me so much right now?

Skylar sets a hand on my arm, her tone gentle. "I've got this," she says. "It'll be easier with her here. And we can test all the furniture and know for sure it'll work for her."

I stare at her hand on my arm a little too long.

My heart rate settles a little at her touch, but then I look up, meet her green eyes, and it races again.

Thudding loudly.

I have my answer. I'm irrationally annoyed because I'd been looking forward to spending this time alone with the designer.

My mom just cock-blocked me.

18

AN UNBEATABLE PLAN

SKYLAR

I hold my breath as Ford's mother settles her sixty-three-year-old ass—her words—into the secondhand-but-looks-like-new chair.

She shifts around a little. Pats the arms. Leans her head back against the pillow. Takes an assessing breath.

Meanwhile, I am holding mine, praying Maggie Devon likes the chair. Sure, I'll roll with it if she doesn't, but I really want her to like it. If she doesn't like this chair, I'm not sure her rear, back, elbow, or any other part of her will like the other pieces I've sourced.

After a long, silent moment—or fifty million of them, who knows—she pushes up and issues a command: "Show me around. I've got a five p.m. flight to catch."

I blink. Okay, she keeps surprising me. "You're not staying overnight?"

She chuckles and shakes her head. "I have a gala here in San Francisco to prepare for in a few more weeks." That must be the one Ford mentioned—the last one she's throwing before retiring. "And I have a brunch meeting with the board tomorrow morning back in Seattle."

She doesn't say *chop-chop*, but I hear it in her tone. She hasn't issued a verdict on the chair. But now's not the time to ask. Now's the time to show her I read her right last week when I gave her the video tour at Twice Loved.

So, with Ford following quietly along, I usher his mom through the home. I show her the couch, the kitchen table, some nightstands for the bedroom, a fantastic vintage roll-top desk for the study, and a peach-orange sofa for that room too. We get to the chairs for the deck, which are made out of—yep—bamboo.

"Bamboo is the new black," I say, bright and upbeat. Then a fresh worry hits. What if she listens to my podcast? I did ask to feature her home on it. Worse, what if she knows her son is *Sexy Reno Guy*? Ugh. I should keep my ogling to myself, even though it's not the worst thing to say about someone's adult son.

For now, I keep my chin up and show her what I want to do with the lighting, flicking through the options on my tablet.

She whips a pair of reading glasses from her purse and sets them on the bridge of her nose to peer at my tablet. Meanwhile, I sweat.

Sometimes she feels like my best friend. Sometimes she's like the next Judge Judy, ready to sustain all the objections to my design choices.

When she takes off her glasses, she sweeps out an arm toward the kitchen. "The kitchen is a make-or-break," she says, mincing zero words.

"It is," I say. It's the one room I've had little to do with. "But I've been eager to hear what you'd like to do there, if anything."

I've kept the kitchen a blank slate. It's clean and mini-malist already, which can offer a lovely simplicity. But the second she steps into it, she shudders at the sight of the white cabinets. "I despise them," she says, shielding her eyes as if they're giving off rays.

I start to worry that she despises everything and is just waiting to tell me so, one item at a time. "In that case," I say, keeping my tone light, "I have paint options in muted earth tones."

"No. I hate *everything* about them."

Okay, that's fair. But she also wanted eco-friendly design, so ripping them out isn't ideal. Somehow, I need to deal with her hatred of these cabinets without throwing them into a landfill.

And I need to do it in about two seconds or I will lose this gig.

The day Ford showed me around the house, he said his mother hated the painter. That she wants everything done yesterday. That she's a woman who's not afraid to pull the plug on a project. I need to impress her.

Think fast.

Ford, who's been silent, clears his throat and says, "Tell us what your dream cabinets look like."

She turns to her son, beaming. "Excellent question."

And I could kiss him for the save. Just kiss him.

Instead, I focus on his mother. She rattles off details, and in a bolt of brilliance, I know what to do.

"I've got an idea," I say, then usher her down to the garage where I show her a bare wall, perfect for a work-bench and cabinets for storage. "We could take those kitchen cabinets and move them down here so we're not just ripping them out and sending them to the landfill. I know a carpenter, and she's fantastic. Then we can get some reclaimed wood cabinets for the kitchen."

For the first time since she arrived, Maggie beams. "Yes. Do that."

Then she breezes out. But first, she stops in the doorway, looks back at me, and says, "By the way—the chair is fantastic. I needed to see how my ass felt twenty minutes later, and I approve."

I want to punch the sky. As his mother heads upstairs, I turn to Ford, grinning in relief.

He squeezes my shoulder. Warm. Affectionate. And... lingering. "You're doing great."

"Thank you," I say, relieved. "I appreciate the save."

"You saved me, too, in your own way."

Did I, though? Guilt wedges into my heart. "I was kind of sassing you when she arrived," I admit.

"You were. But it saved me. My mom likes it when you knock me down a peg."

"You do too," I say, feeling a little like hummingbirds are flapping their wings in my chest as he strokes my shoulder.

His thumb slides slowly off the fabric of my shirt. Then, as if he's realized what he's doing, he pulls away quickly.

I glance at my shoulder. It feels radioactive, in the best of ways.

I want to stay here. Ask him to do it again.

But his mother's unexpected entrance rattled him earlier. The least I can do is handle the rest of her visit with aplomb, like we're a team.

His blue eyes look darker. Hungrier. My breath catches and the world blurs for a moment.

"I should..." I point upstairs.

"Yes. You should," he says, clearing his throat.

I tear myself away, my skin hot, my pulse rocketing,

and meet his mom in the kitchen, where she gives me a list of things she wants—the must-haves, from doorknobs to drawer pulls.

I can manage this. I *so* can.

When her list is finished, Maggie looks at her watch and says, "Well, that's done. Why don't we have lunch?"

At Gigi's Café, Maggie holds court, entertaining us with tales of drinks spilled on dresses at galas, of wrong names blurted out at fundraisers, and of veggie hot dogs that spurted mustard on shirts at picnics.

I laugh as I take the last bite of my arugula, mushroom, and sun-dried tomato salad.

She smiles, sipping her iced tea as a late October breeze drifts through the open windows and seagulls circle nearby.

"But one thing drives me batty," she says, setting down her glass. Her smile disappears. She huffs out a breath and shakes her head. "It's so annoying that my son is single again."

I perk up. I mean, I've been paying attention, of course, but now I *really* perk up.

"What do you mean?" Ford asks warily, arching a brow.

"Well, you're going to the gala," she says to him. "It's my last one, and you're not playing that weekend. It'll be here in town at The Resort." That's a hotel owned by the city's well-known billionaire Wilder Blaine, who built an empire with sports teams, hotels, and clean energy. Now his hotels are known for their sustainable efforts—a perfect synergy. "San Francisco has truly embraced our recycling initiatives throughout the city in office buildings and public spaces."

"Right," he says, crossing his arms.

Maggie heaves an aggrieved sigh and turns to me. "The thing is, everyone wants to set their daughters up with him."

Oh. Well, this got good. I lean in. "Tell me more."

Ford rolls his eyes. "Skylar, what did I tell you at Twice Loved?"

"That your mom loves you deeply and had the highway patrol check on you when you were eighteen and driving to college?" I ask innocently.

He drags a hand down his face. "What did I *really* tell you?"

"It was a reasonable thing to do," Maggie says with zero sarcasm.

"Of course it was," I assure her.

"So what did he tell you about me?" Maggie asks. No —she insists.

"Not to give you my number. Oops. Did it anyway," I say to his mom with a defiant bob of my shoulder.

Well, he *did* say his mom likes it when I tease him in front of her. Works for me. Teasing is my love language, and I can't help it.

He groans. "I said, don't feed steak to the tiger."

"I'm the tiger?" Mom asks sharply. "Ford, that's not nice."

"So tell me all about these dates," I cut in. I'm secretly hoping he turns them all down.

Unfair? Yes.

Irrational? Also yes.

But it's how I feel.

I'm dying for the details and praying he is not interested in these other women. As my neighbor and my client, he's a double-whammy of off-limits. I can't have him, but that means no one else can. Obviously.

"Cordelia Harrington wants him to take her daughter," Maggie begins with an even heartier sigh. "Kahlia Mayami wants to set him up with *her* daughter. Sunil Bakshi says his daughter is a huge hockey fan and would love to go with him. Honestly, it's endless. And, frankly, exhausting."

"Well, he gets proposals at games too," I point out, since I read that online.

"I'm *right here*," Ford mutters, pointing at himself.

Maggie waves a dismissive hand his way.

"But the thing is, I want to get them off my back. I can't have everyone hounding me about my single son. I have fundraising to handle. A gala to plan. A house to prep. I need a shield from all these date requests," Maggie says. Then she pauses, narrowing her eyes, studying me. Then Ford. Then me again.

Her smile turns Mona Lisa serene. "But I devised a plan this morning. An unbeatable plan."

"Do tell," Ford says dryly.

I'm on the edge of my seat.

Maggie's grin is her entire personality as she takes an even longer pause to drink more iced tea. She sets down the glass with a *plink*.

"Skylar will attend as your fake girlfriend," she announces. "I've watched you two this morning, and you look good together. It will be perfect. Say yes."

I freeze.

But Ford doesn't.

He turns to me, a slow, sexy smile forming on those lips. "Works for me."

I thought I was against dating. After I tried online dating and it failed, I figured I was content devoting all my attention to building my business. Happy to be hustling like no eco-designer has hustled before.

But from the way my stomach flips at his words, it's clear I'm not against fake dating Ford Devon.

"Yes," I say.

I was never saying no.

19

KISS ENGINEER

FORD

This fake date makes perfect sense. I'm already taking Skylar to the opening of the board game store. The gala next month is simply an extension of our plus-one-ing.

But I'm aware that my mother is a bulldozer. Sure, Skylar has handled her with nothing but the *aplombiest* aplomb. Still, I need to make sure Skylar's okay with this new twist. It's one thing for her to agree to a fake date with Mom managing my life over arugula salad. It's another for Skylar to honestly want to go.

Trouble is, after I pay the bill and we walk out of the café, Mom—surprise, surprise—commandeers the convo. With a furrow in her brow, she sets a hand on my arm, looking up at me under the awning of an illustration of the owner's tan Chihuahua she named the café after. "How long do you think it'll take to catch an Uber and get to the airport at this time of day?"

Right. She has a return flight at five. It's two-thirty now. And I wouldn't be a good son if I just let her catch an Uber. "I can take you," I tell her, "but I also have to drop Skylar off because she has an appointment." I do traffic math, but I'm not sure my chauffeur services will work for both women. The time it takes to dart over to Hayes Valley to drop off Skylar, then get Mom to the airport, will mean cutting it close for Mom's flight.

I grit my teeth, annoyed that I have to choose between being a good son and a good neighbor.

Skylar steps in and says, "I'll just catch a bus back to my place. It's not a problem."

My mother lifts a hand, her diamond ring glinting in the autumn sun as she waves us off. "Don't let me get in the way. You two need to figure out how this whole dating thing is going to work," she says, like she's been plotting this for a long time. And honestly, she probably has. She brandishes her phone like it's a prize. "I'm a pro with Uber after this morning."

"Mom, I'm driving you," I cut in. It's about the principle now. She rappels into my life like a CIA agent, then exits at her whim. I'm driving her because, one, I need to wrest control from her, and two, well, she's my mom, and as much of a bull in a china shop as she is, I love her. But I also don't want to leave Skylar in the lurch.

I raise a wait-a-minute finger and step away from them to open my Uber app and order a Green ride for Skylar. When I'm done, I say, "There'll be an Uber for you in a few minutes."

Skylar's smile is warm and genuine. "Thank you. That means a lot to me."

Mom fights off a cat-like grin.

A few minutes later, a car in the same model as mine pulls up, and Skylar arches a brow at the electric vehicle. "Nice choice," she says.

I give her a nod, one that says, *I get it. I feel the same.*

She slides into the plush back seat and waves as the

driver pulls out of the lot. I watch her until the red car slips onto the road and out of sight.

I turn back to Mom. "Ready for the airport?"

She's staring at me, arms crossed, lips twitching like she just swept the high-roller table in Monte Carlo.

"What?" I ask.

"Fake date," she says with an arch of her brow. "Hardly."

She's seen right through me, but I push back. I have to. "It *is* a fake date. You literally just set it up. I'm doing it for you," I insist. But am I too insistent?

She squeezes my arm, nodding in solidarity. "Keep telling yourself that, darling."

The woman knows me too well. "Mom, did you want a ride?"

"I did offer to take an Uber," she points out.

"And if I'd let you take one, I never would've heard the end of it."

"Ford, you should've driven Skylar. I can tell you want to spend time with her."

I let out a long, frustrated sigh. "Mom. Car. Now."

With a too-pleased grin, she slides into the passenger side. Once I'm behind the wheel, she says, "She's nice."

Something she never said about Brittany. Something I'm grateful to hear, even though there's nowhere to go with it. There's no room in my life or my hardened heart for romance, even with someone...*nice.*

"She likes you too," I say as I pull out of the lot and head along the main drag toward the highway.

"Well, she has very good taste," my mom says, then smiles my way, giving me a knowing look before saying, with genuine affection, "I mean it."

She's not only saying Skylar has good taste in liking

her. But I can't touch the other meaning—that Skylar might be into me.

Focus. Just focus.

I grip the wheel tighter and put all my concentration onto the road. But out of the corner of my eye, I see Mom peering sharply at my to-go cup. She picks it up and inspects it as I drive. "This is...interesting."

I say nothing. Just clench my jaw. The cup could open up a can of worms.

She clucks her tongue, grabs her reading glasses from her purse, and taps something into her phone. Probably looking up the dog on the cup. Probably learning Simon Side-Eye's "mom," the woman benefiting from his potential OnlyPaws page, is indeed Skylar. I brace myself for an inquisition.

Instead, Mom chuckles, then fights off a grin as I near the Golden Gate Bridge once more. She clears her throat and says, "Like I said—hardly a fake date."

But a fake date is precisely what it has to be. Because if it's fake, it can't fall apart. If it's fake, then there's no risk. No messy emotions. No future to ruin.

"Mom, do you honestly think I want to get involved again? My life is busy. I'm focused on hockey. I have an opportunity to go out on top. You know how much that means to me," I say seriously. I need the reminder as much as she does.

She gives me a sympathetic look, letting down her mother-knows-best routine. "I do, sweetie. I really do. And I want it for you—I want all the best, all the time for you." She was there through my early career, cheering me on at Minor League games, lifting me out of funks, always believing in me. Hell, she let me come live at home in the off-season when I was twenty-two, twenty-three. When friends of mine had pro contracts and I was just...hoping.

Mom returns her focus to her phone. "I should check out that podcast of hers. I've been so busy. Do you listen to it?"

"No," I say, as I merge onto the bridge. I have to set some limits. I already check out her dog's social, for fuck's sake. If I start listening to her design podcast, I might as well hold up a poster that says *I'm into you.* And since I don't want to keep discussing the woman I shouldn't be so into, I nod to San Francisco's iconic wonder of the modern world. "Did you know the Golden Gate Bridge was originally supposed to be black and gold?"

"Tell me more," she says, like this is the height of intrigue.

I appreciate her willingness to be distracted by the thought of a bumblebee-like bridge. It's like she knows I need a break from the romance talk. She knows how hard the divorce was on me, the way it shattered my trust. How I closed off parts of myself and vowed to trust only family, friends, and my dog.

And when my mom slides into a series of *did you knows*, it's exactly what I need. Because the more I talk about Skylar, the more likely I am to admit I want to date her.

When I shouldn't.

Really, I shouldn't.

Soon enough, I'm jostling through afternoon traffic at departures, trying to wedge closer to the curb of Mom's airline. I snag a free spot, flip on the hazards, then hop out for a quick goodbye. I give her a hug. "Glad you like everything. Can't wait for you and Dad to settle in," I say, meaning it deeply. She drives me batty, but she's always been there for me, especially when hockey wasn't. That matters.

"I do," she says, then breaks the hug, cups my shoulders, and steamrolls on. "You know, it's always a good idea to make sure everything's completely believable when you show up with a fake date. Like maybe a fake kiss? Think about it, practice it, and be ready for it. It was good seeing you. I love you, darling. Have a great day. Thank you for everything. The chair is great. The furniture is great. Keep up the good work."

She departs on a cloud of perfume, not letting me get a word in.

The thought digs in as I navigate traffic on my return to Hayes Valley.

The idea of a fake kiss taps on my brain like a woodpecker. It doesn't let go. I can't think of a thing that isn't connected to fake kissing my next-door neighbor.

Or really, real kissing.

Nope. Not even my audiobook does the trick. Not even the goddamn news. I try toggling over to another audiobook I downloaded—the inside story of how a once-promising tech giant sold its soul to the devil. But even the jaw-dropping, backstabbing tale of corporate greed and political ring-kissing barely registers as I weave through cars and the press of traffic.

All I can think is *fake kiss, fake kiss, fake kiss.*

When I finally arrive home around four, I march up my steps, yank open the door, and hold out my arms. "Did you miss me, girl? I missed you."

Zamboni bounds over, bouncing on her back legs, happily whimpering.

"Let's do it," I say, then rush through the house to let Zamboni out in the backyard.

As she does her business, I stare across the fence the entire time, shamelessly trying to catch a glimpse of Skylar. But the view from the yard isn't as good as from the hot tub.

Dammit.

Maybe I'll need a soak tonight. To enjoy...the stars.

Except...*wait*.

My pulse launches into the stratosphere. There she is, walking across the kitchen, phone in hand, dictating something into it while buttoning a blouse haphazardly. Pretty sure the sides aren't even lined up.

She's always getting things done—even in her reign of chaos. Maybe because of it. Skylar's a riddle. Wild and chaotic, but also focused and driven. Fiery and sassy, but also kind and thoughtful.

And I can't stop thinking about her.

She's got an appointment in fifty minutes.

I should leave her alone. But I'm a jack-in-the-box. I scratch Zamboni behind the ears, then wash my hands and say to my girl with finality, "Sometimes you just have to say *fuck it.*"

She barks her approval.

I leave, bounding down the steps, circling to my neighbor's yard, then heading up hers. I do it like I'm chasing the puck, hell-bent on scoring, refusing to let anyone get in the way.

And I knock on her door. Loudly.

20

ONLY ALMOST

SKYLAR

The man at my door doesn't look like the one who stood across from me in the yard the other night. He doesn't look like the guy who walked down the steps this morning with that easy swagger either. No, this version of Ford is the man from the day I met him—intense, tightly wound, ready to spring.

I can practically smell the frustration rolling off him like cologne. But it's a good cologne—virile, powerful, full of the quiet intensity you want on the ice when the game's down to the final minute.

He lifts a hand and rests it on the doorframe like he's trying to seem casual, but it doesn't work. He's gripping it. Hard.

I part my lips, unsure what to say or why he's here. I'm not used to someone showing up like *this*. In this state of... *need*. Simon's not either. Maybe that's why my dog hasn't even gotten up from his late-afternoon nap. He's upstairs in a dog-sized sleigh bed that's far too comfortable.

Ford's mere feet away, and he beats me to it, speaking first. "Your shirt's off."

I blink. "What?"

He jerks his chin at me, scowling. "The buttons. They're off. I saw you buttoning it."

I gaze down at my navy-blue blouse with tiny flowers on it. "It's not—"

Oh. It is.

"It's askew," he cuts in.

"So you came over here to help me button my shirt?"

"If you want help," he mutters.

I don't need it, but the thought burns me up from the inside. I'm so thrown off, I don't know what to say.

His frame blocks me from a view of the street. His eyes burn into mine. I reach down and start unbuttoning the shirt, one by one, my fingers skating across my heated skin, redoing each button as I go, methodically, like it's the most normal thing in the world to fix my shirt in front of my neighbor.

Ford doesn't stop watching. And I don't want him to.

When I finish, I glance back up at him, my heart racing wildly. "You saw me from the yard?"

"I did," he says—fearless, unashamed.

The thought of him watching me is...outrageously thrilling. A pulse beats between my thighs.

"You're helpful," I say in a heated whisper.

"Trying to be," he says, then licks his lips. "The fake date," he adds, like the words are heavy in his mouth.

"Which one?" I ask, carefully. I'm desperately hoping he's not about to back out.

Either one, both of them, they feel like...parties I get to go to. Like it's Halloween, and I get to dress up in the best way. I like these costume parties. I don't want them to end.

He nods tightly. "Both. But mostly the gala. Are you good with it?"

"I said I was," I answer, confused.

"I wanted to make sure."

"I'm sure," I add.

He stares at me, his blue eyes flickering with flames. He lowers his arm from the door, but his muscles are still tense, his forearms flexing. He's no more relaxed than when he banged on the door. He glances past me, toward the inside of my house. It hits me then—he's never actually been in here.

"Can I come in?" he asks, a new urgency in his voice. "Or are you going to be late?"

"I have ten minutes before I have to go."

"To catch the bus?"

"Yes."

"I'll drive you." It comes out like a command.

"I still only have fifteen minutes."

"That's fine." The click of the door shutting activates guard-dog mode. Simon barks, then hustles his little wiggling body down the stairs. He rushes over immediately, whimpering and circling Ford like they've known each other for years.

I think of Landon. Of the times he ignored Simon. Of the other guys I dated who didn't care, didn't even ask to see a photo on our first dates. But Ford? He crouches down and strokes Simon's long, soft ears with this gentle reverence that melts my heart.

"Hey there," he murmurs. "You're a good boy, aren't you? A *very* good boy, helping your mom with the bills."

My brain short-circuits.

He called me *Mom*. A dog mom, sure, but still—I love it too much. The stupid, silly designation that we dog lovers use is doing unfair things to my insides.

Once Simon trots off to his living room bed—shaped

like a cupcake—Ford rises slowly, his gaze locking with mine. "If we're going to fake date," he says, "we should probably..." His eyes drift to my mouth.

I feel it. The shift in the air. The way every nerve in my body goes on high alert. The pull.

He doesn't have to finish the sentence.

But he does.

"Fake kiss."

And all I can think is *yes, please, and now.*

"Don't make it fake," I say.

Ford lifts a hand, reaches for my face, and cups my cheek. He strokes his thumb along my jawline, and I gasp —a staggered breath that gives away every ounce of my unchecked lust.

His dimple flashes, but it disappears quickly as he studies my face like he's memorizing me.

He's focused, deliberate, every slow, tantalizing sweep of his thumb drawing me closer to the edge. Then he coasts it down to my chin. Holds me in place.

"Your lips...drive me fucking wild," he rasps.

I part them. For him.

And he shows me exactly how wild when he covers my mouth with his and kisses me fiercely.

His lips claim mine in some kind of proof of his statement. It's hard, hot, and full of tension. There's no prelude. No testing brush of lips. We've gone from zero to sixty in less than three seconds. I'd better buckle up since we're hurtling along this racetrack of a kiss.

And it's a thrilling ride.

He grips my jaw tighter, threads his other hand into my hair, and jerks me closer, tugging my chest against his, yanking my body flush to his.

So it's that type of kiss. Ford Devon kisses with his

entire body. He dives straight in with a hot, deep kiss and a full-on grind, and I am here for it.

For the hard ridge of him, insistent against my waist.

For the spark in my chest.

For the sizzle across my skin.

His tongue tangles with mine, and his sounds do too —his hungry, greedy groans. They match my whimpers and sighs.

And right when everything feels like we're on a collision course for the bedroom, he taps the brakes.

Slows down.

Runs his thumb along my cheekbone as he coasts his lips across mine. A sensual slide of his mouth now, a downshift into a different rhythm.

The change makes me hotter.

My mind blurs.

My body turns molten.

And Ford feels like...an inevitability as he spins me around, pressing my back against the door, then kissing the corner of my lips.

A prolonged sigh falls from his mouth. "Better," he rasps out.

"Better?"

"You taste better than I'd imagined," he murmurs, then groans, pressing another soft kiss to my lips. "But I'd better test that theory."

Excitement flares through my body. How he wants to test it, I don't know. But I'm up for it.

"You really should," I say, as he tugs at the collar of my shirt, exposing more of my flesh.

He inches back, looks me in the eyes, and traces his fingers along the freckles on my collarbone. "I'm a little obsessed with these," he admits.

"My freckles?" I ask, because holy shit, this man is observant.

"I noticed your freckles the day I met you," he murmurs, then flicks his tongue across them.

I gasp, my hips swaying of their own accord, asking for more...contact.

He thrusts back, licking across my shoulder. My knees nearly buckle. Steadying my waist, Ford laughs softly, clearly pleased by the effect he's having. And then he gives me more, coasting his talented mouth toward my jaw in a slow, deliberate slide. I move with him, stretching, offering him my neck to kiss as my bones melt under his touch.

My fingers curl into his shirt, holding on as this man turns me into a new state of matter—from solid to liquid in mere seconds.

I shudder out a breath as my fingers tighten. He hums —half cocky laugh, half needy murmur, and all desire— as he reaches my ear. Then he nips at the lobe.

I gasp.

He pulls back. Tilts his head. Brushes strands of hair from my face. "You taste like summertime," he says.

I pause, caught in the moment, in the fading sunlight as the autumn day winds down. As Ford nails it.

"It's my lotion," I say, my voice more feathery than ever. "It's called Summertime Crush."

He arches a brow, then dips his face, pressing his forehead to mine. "Good name," he whispers.

And the closeness. Dear god, the closeness. The way he goes from full-on crashing into a kiss to slow dancing into it? It's mind-bendingly good, and I want so much more.

I answer by grabbing his face and tugging him against me. It's my turn to kiss—hard and desperate. I twist the fabric of his shirt in my hand, sealing my lips to his, taking another hit of my neighbor.

Your client, you idiot. You're making out with a client.

This is wrong. This is so wrong.

But I keep kissing him anyway.

All the tension from the last couple of weeks crashes like ocean waves against the shore. And like them, this kiss is unstoppable.

So are his hands.

As I explore his mouth, his strong hands travel down my arms to my wrists, then to my waist. He drags his fingers along the hem of my blouse, untucked. Then he dusts them across my stomach.

"Fuck," I mutter.

Another laugh comes from him as he breaks the kiss. "Ten minutes," he says, his eyes dark and dirty. His lips, curved and curious.

His words—an invitation.

I close my eyes, breathe out, and try to think straight. But his fingertips are getting to know my waist, skating across the top of my pants, teasing at the button.

I'm already going to need to change my panties before this meeting. I breathe out and give in.

"You say you're good with your hands?" I ask, a taunt.

That devilish dimple comes out to play. "I do."

"Let's see what you've got then."

He presses a hot, quick kiss to my lips. "Be careful what you wish for, Skylar," he says, a filthy warning.

As he fiddles with the button on my pants, I consider stopping this. Saying we shouldn't cross this line. We'll be working on this house for a little while longer, and I want to make clients happy instead of my libido.

Things could go wrong. We could piss each other off.

He could leave a bad review. Plus, I have to see him so damn often.

But, on the other hand, we're not really involved. We can't truly hurt each other. This is…safe enough. We'll be faking it anyway, so what's the big deal if we have some fun?

And, wow. The second the zipper's down and his hand slides over my panties, I'm feeling exactly how fun this is. I shudder out a hot breath as his big hand covers me, sliding between my thighs, cupping the damp panel of my panties.

He groans. Taps a finger across the soaked cotton. Murmurs against my neck, "You're infuriatingly sexy."

Best. Compliment. Ever. "Same to you," I say, even though I'm aching for his touch.

With my panties still on, like he has all the time in the world, like he's confident that no matter how fast the clock ticks, he'll beat the buzzer, he strokes me. Slow, teasing circles through my panties. Winding me up. Making me shake. Making me tremble.

I grip his shirt harder. Clutching it. "Ford," I demand.

"Yes, Skylar?" He sounds far too happy to taunt me.

I glance toward the kitchen. A kitschy clock with rubber ducks on the ends of the hands ticks maddeningly closer to my departure.

"If you don't make me come in the next three minutes, I swear I will go upstairs, grab a toy, and take care of myself. I am not going to meet Sofia Ximena with a lady boner." I stare him down. Two can play his game. "Get moving."

His smile is bright, as if he's slightly thrown off in the best of ways. "You're fucking perfect," he says, then he finally—fucking finally—dips his hand inside my panties.

I shout in delight.

His fingers are magic. He slides them through my slickness, groaning so damn approvingly as he strokes, like he's never felt anything better than me.

That's a wild thought—that I could have this effect on him. But it's there, taking up space in my head as he touches me. Teasing my mouth with a barely-there kiss as he coasts his fingers across my hot center, then circles my clit.

I moan as I lean my head back. "Yessss," I say.

"No need to use a toy, Skylar," he murmurs as he draws dizzying circles right where I want him most. Making me rock into his hands. Making me chase my pleasure.

Making me hot and hazy and close to the edge already. My pulse beats mercilessly between my thighs.

I'm breathing out hard when he changes his pace, cupping me once again, rubbing my needy clit with the heel of his hand.

Holy fuck. That's good. That's so good.

What's even better is his mouth on my jaw. He's traveling across my face, leaving kisses all over me while he strokes.

And then—

I gasp out a long *yessss.*

His nimble fingers return to my clit once more with faster strokes, touching me just right, circling me just so. The whole time he's kissing my neck, my cheek, the corner of my lips.

And I understand the phrase, finally—he can't get enough of me.

Ford kisses me like his need can't be quenched, he fucks me with his fingers like once will never be enough, and I rock into his hand like nothing exists beyond this door.

Nothing but the way his body molds to my side. Nothing but the feel of him making me ache. Nothing but the pleasure roaring through my body as I seek the other side.

Or really, as he takes me there.

I'm hot everywhere, my neck burning up, my legs shaking as pleasure coils inside me, then all at once... explodes.

I cry out, dropping my head back, barely able to hold on, my vision blurring as I break apart and shatter into brilliant, beautiful pieces. Pleasure pulses in me for a long, delirious minute.

I'm panting, sighing, laughing, then opening my eyes —and, like a stupid, lust-drunk idiot, I blurt out, "I watched you do yoga."

His brow knits, and it takes him a beat to connect the dots. He tilts his head, curiosity seemingly piqued. "Right. The day that I saw you?"

I shake my head, too woozy, too drunk on pleasure to even be embarrassed. "Then, but also before. From the catio. There's a great view of your back porch, and you look really fucking good when you do planks."

"You watch me do planks from the catio?" It's asked with wonder, but also...cat-ate-the-canary delight.

And I laugh because I wonder if those words have ever been spoken in that order before. "In my defense, it's a really good show," I say, then smile. "And I needed to get that off my chest."

"Yeah?"

"I did. I felt...almost guilty, having watched you."

"Only *almost*?" he asks, catching me on that technicality.

"Well, not guilty enough to stop."

He doesn't seem mad, but I can't entirely read his expression. His jaw is set. His gaze is...calculating. I hope I haven't pissed him off. I brace myself for the fallout, holding my breath.

But then, in seconds, his blue eyes sparkle with mirth. More than I've ever seen before.

"Only *almost* are my two favorite words now."

I breathe out. "Good. That's good," I say, more relieved than I'd expected. "You were teasing me. Making me think you might be mad."

"Maybe I was," he says with an easy shrug. He licks his lips, seems to weigh something. "Or maybe I was figuring this would be a good time to let you know I watched you dance in the kitchen from my hot tub on the second floor."

I blink off the remains of my orgasm fog. Smacking his chest, I say, "You have a hot tub and never invited me over?"

He tips his head back and laughs. "I just confessed to watching you dance in your kitchen, and your concern is why I didn't invite you to have a soak?"

"Obviously."

He shakes his head. "You're too much." Then he smacks my ass, sharp and hard. "Go freshen up, you chaos demon. You've got an appointment to get to."

I've never been called anything remotely close to that before. And a smile steals its way across my face. I look down at my open pants and my useless underwear, then at his face—no man has ever looked more satisfied. And I can't stop having fun with him.

"Time me," I say.

"Really?"

"Yes."

Then I clutch the waistband of my open pants and bolt upstairs.

And two minutes and thirty-eight seconds later, I'm stuffing my feet into flats, smoothing out a new blouse, and grabbing my tote bag.

"Impressive." He whistles.

"So are your hands," I say.

He swats my ass again on the way out the door.

21

SEMANTICALLY AND OTHERWISE

SKYLAR

Like I'm riding off into the sunset, I slide into Ford's car, sling the buckle across my chest, and slam the door. "Giddy up," I say.

Before I can count to three, Ford hops into the front seat and hits the gas. "Yes, ma'am," he says in a howdy-partner voice, and I'm a little buzzed that this stern man occasionally lets a playful side show through.

I tap the address into the screen, and we're off as the car cruises silently, making my green heart pitter-patter.

I feel relieved. Not simply because of the orgasm—though that helps, undoubtedly. I mean, it's been a while. But mostly because there's a weird sort of relief in my honesty. Something raw and oddly intimate about those confessions. I've come close to getting it off my chest, but now it's out there officially, and he doesn't seem to mind.

But as he expertly darts through traffic, I wonder... what happens next? Were those fifteen minutes about convenience, lust, or something neither of us is ready to name? Namely, this crackling, sparking connection between us that I didn't see coming the day we met. The more time I spend with Ford, the more we, well, crackle.

And combust.

Was that combustion a one-time thing?

Well, of course it was. We're barely even fake dating. It's like fake dating lite. Fake dating with fewer calories.

"That was…" I say, pointing back at my house.

"An orgasm, Skylar. An earth-shattering orgasm that rocked your world."

I roll my eyes as I crack up. "Cocky much?"

"Am I wrong?"

"Nope." Then I glance at my nails, weighing whether I want to continue my confessions. But why not? After the truths I served up, I can handle this one. "It's been a while for me."

"That so?"

"Well, not solo," I explain. "I'm a big fan of those."

He growls, a low, hungry sound that makes me feel in control again, and I love it. "Hot," he says. "Just hot."

"Thank you for your appreciation of my solo flights." I pause. "But with someone else? It's been…quite a while."

At the light, he slows, then tosses me a dark look, his lips a straight line, his eyes glimmering. "Good."

As he turns onto the next street, he adds, "Same for me. I haven't been with anyone…in a long time. Since… my ex."

It's one of the few times he's mentioned her. Every time he does, I realize we have more in common than I'd first thought—back when I assumed we had nothing.

Maybe that's why the honesty bug takes over my vocal cords again. "Good. I'm glad too," I say.

He just smiles.

"And I didn't get to return the favor," I add—and then,

bam. It's like my mouth handled the setup for the awkward question: Will this happen again? I draw in a fortifying breath. "That was...a one-time thing, right?"

He's quiet for a block, his fingers curled tight around the wheel. The silence is thick and heavy with the weight of...decisions. Of consequences.

I want a good referral from his mother.

I want to honor my brother's wishes.

And Ford wants to focus on his career. Understandably. He said as much when he ate mac and cheese on his front porch.

Sex is distracting. It fries brain cells.

"It probably should be, don't you think?" he asks evenly, in a measured voice.

I blow out a breath. "Of course. Sex makes you stupid," I say.

He laughs again. "Yes, I suppose it does. Fake dating is one thing. Sex is another." He sighs, then furrows his brow. "But then again, is it sex when I fuck you with my fingers?"

A flush races up my chest to my neck—hell, to my ears. "That feels very semantic, Ford."

"Did it feel semantic when you came all over my fingers?"

"You know, maybe it did."

"We should try again," he says, deadpan.

And while I love that he wants to, I also know it's for the best that we don't. "But we shouldn't, right? Even though I didn't return the favor."

He cruises into the Presidio. "Sex isn't about favors. Or scorecards."

"What's it about?"

"How good I can make you feel," he says.

All the breath escapes my lungs. "You succeeded."

"Semantically?"

"And otherwise," I say as we reach the office building. He pulls up in front of the four-story brick building with two minutes to spare. "Thanks for the ride. I guess it'll be more believable now that we've kissed."

"And now that you've fucked my fingers." There he goes, stoking the fire.

"You really like saying that."

"Seems I do," he says, sounding wistful. He leans across the car, slides a thumb along my chin, and says, "You're fucking perfect."

The same thing he said earlier. It makes me feel... floaty in a whole new way.

I get out and go, still glowing from the unexpected afternoon orgasm, but also a little melancholic from the realization it can't happen again.

Even though that's for the best.

It really is.

* * *

"It's almost perfect," I declare, adjusting the vintage banker light in Sofia's new office. "Let me just move it a smidge over here."

The polished lawyer watches me with intense scrutiny, like everything is fascinating to her, including the way I position her new—well, old and now new again—lamps that were delivered today. I set them down next to a paper-back with a title in Spanish—looks like a romance novel.

"That is better, Skylar," she says.

I smile. "Glad you agree." Then I position some plants on her side table and add a pillow to the chair across from her. "I know a pillow doesn't scream attorney, but you want your clients to be comfortable."

"Of course I do," she says crisply. "And a pillow does the trick."

"I love pillows so much," I say, since, of course, I love pillows.

"What's not to love?" she replies, then gives me a look that says she's poised to say something. "Will you feature this before-and-after on your podcast?"

I freeze for a few seconds, then furrow my brow. "You follow my podcast?"

"Of course I do. I was hoping Ximena, Kuo, and Richardson would be featured."

Hell yes.

"Absolutely," I say, pulling out my phone to shoot some after videos. At least I can bring attention to my podcast by working with a client. That's something real.

Unlike the fake thing currently occupying my brain— fake dating the guy next door.

When I'm done, Sofia tells me she's meeting with a client from a labor union, and my mind spins with exciting stories of who she might be standing up for. Heck, I bet she'd defend the planet if Earth asked her to.

"Lucky client," I say.

"I'm pretty lucky to do what I love," she says. "You're the same."

And really, I am. I love my job, which is why I keep my focus on Haven Designs.

Not horny Haven.

Which means I probably shouldn't mention Sexy Reno Guy again on air.

Shame. Seems I've grown quite fond of the man I once hated.

22

NO SUCH THING AS TOO SHORT

SKYLAR

Mission accomplished.

Mission accomplished so hard that my friends are shocked I didn't once mention Ford on the show, even when they goaded me.

And they goaded me.

"Who even are you?" Mabel asks as we leave the studio on a Thursday afternoon.

Trevyn seconds that with a: "What she said."

I spin around on the sidewalk, walking backward, holding my arms out wide. "When you're good, you're good."

"But you've never been good at keeping your mouth shut," Mabel points out.

"Are you sure you're Skylar? And not her, I dunno, alien replacement?" Trevyn asks.

"I understand it's hard to accept defeat. But don't even try to get out of it," I say, turning around now and walking with them. "You both need to pay up. You said I'd fold."

Trevyn whistles in appreciation. "We sure did."

"I was positive you'd cave," Mabel says with a shrug.

I drape one arm around her, the other around Trevyn. "And I was a badass babe. Time for you two to buy me an outfit for a board game store opening."

* * *

But the thing about thrifting is it's hit or miss. A few laps through Champagne Taste, we come up empty. With a beleaguered sigh, I pick up a pink tweed blazer with gold buttons and frown. "It's all Emily Gilmore here today, friends," I say.

"And old rich white dudes who golf," Trevyn says, brandishing a pair of green plaid pants and a matching cap.

"Thrifting is shopping roulette. But you can't win if you don't play," I say as I return the jacket to the rack, while Trevyn does the same.

"Another time," Mabel says on the way out, pushing open the door, the chime of the bell signaling our exit and our failed mission.

"I'll just have to thrift my own closet," I say, shielding my eyes from the afternoon sun. "So what exactly does one wear to your ex's board game store opening?"

Mabel taps her chin, her eyes intense. "Something ridiculously hot."

"Outrageously sexy," Trevyn says.

But that doesn't add up. "For my ex?" I ask, doubtful.

They both laugh, and they both shake their heads. "Oh, sweet summer child," Trevyn begins. "When a hot-ass man who scores goals for a living insists on taking you on a fake date to show your douche-canoe ex what he missed out on, you'd better look—" He turns to Mabel, like they've planned this one-two delivery.

"Edible," she says, "you need to look edible."

With that brief in mind, I collect Jessica's mail the following evening, setting it on the entryway table as I picture my closet and its possibilities. I hustle upstairs and hunt through my clothes, assembling option after option for my friends on FaceTime.

As I'm tugging on a pair of vegan leather shorts, Cleo sashays into the bedroom and hops on the pile of clothes. Of course. Her cat radar for things to leave fur on is strong. But first, she must bathe. Right as she's licking a toe bean and I'm buttoning the shorts, my mom's name flashes across the phone screen. "Let me call you back," I tell my friends, then switch over to Mom.

"Oh," she says, jerking away from the screen.

"Mom! You've seen me half-dressed before."

"I've seen you in your birthday suit too. I just wasn't expecting it."

Of course, because I was the one who answered on video. I lie on the bed next to Simon, who's lounging like he's prepping for an upcoming *Playgirl* photo spread, then button the shorts. "I'll make myself decent for you."

When the shorts are on, along with a tight top, I pick the phone up again. "Want to switch to a regular call?"

"Well, the damage has already been done. But no, this is fine," she says. Her screen bounces as she sets towels on a shelf in her closet. "I just wanted to see if you'd like to do a bookstore and dinner night tomorrow. Wander around An Open Book, then get some naan and chana masala at our favorite place. Since it's the Games People Play opening," she says sympathetically, then rolls her eyes. "And I just saw another piece from a reporter at *San Francisco Life* about it."

Oh. That's thoughtful of her. But I am a bad daughter. At our lunch this week, I didn't tell her I'm attending the opening after all. "Actually, Mom, I'm going," I say with a smidge of guilt.

The stack of washcloths in her free hand wobbles. "What? Why?"

"It's kind of a long story." I sink onto the edge of my bed and tell her, finishing with, "And then he insisted on taking me."

Her smile is too many shades of delighted. "That's so sweet."

Sweet? Is it sweet? It felt more sultry when Ford offered. More feral. More demanding. A hot spark curls down my chest as I remember the dark look in his eyes, the intensity in his voice when he asked. Still, she's not wrong. It was hot, and heady, and also...sweet. "I suppose it was."

"Well, have fun on your date then," Mom says. I can hear the hope in her voice.

Better nip that in the bud. "It's not a real date, Mom," I say.

"Right," she says, but her smile calls bullshit.

"It's not," I say again.

"Of course not, dear."

But I can't have her thinking it's real, especially since I know she still feels bad about Landon, even though I've told her a million times not to. I can't let her think it's authentic since she'll get her hopes up.

Or will you get your hopes up?

I shush that voice in my head that came out of

nowhere. This date is for fun, for show, for getting even. That is all. "It's just a revenge fake date."

Mom waves an airy hand, then reaches to a shelf out of the camera's range. "Hanging out. Revenge fake date. Your generation has such funny terms for dating."

When she lowers her hand, there's a stuffed toy in it. Her dog barks in the background. "I should go," Mom says.

"Tell Taco I hope he enjoys Friday Night Monkey."

"He always does."

When I hang up, a new text from my sexy next-door neighbor lands on my phone. Isn't he at a hockey game? He's been on the road this week, having played in St. Louis on Tuesday night. Tonight, he's playing in Vegas.

The game starts in about an hour. My alarm is set to go off so I can settle in on the couch with my pillows, popcorn, pup, and the remote to watch it.

> Ford: Can you do me a favor?

Skylar: Sure. But you're not home, so another hot tub peep show is probably out of the question.

> Ford: I'm taking a rain check on that. Mark my words. But the favor is this—I ordered a special plant for tomorrow night's opening. It arrived earlier today. I'd rather not leave it unattended on my porch all night.

Skylar: There has been a rash of plant thieves in the neighborhood. You really can't be safe enough.

Ford: It needs water, Skylar. I won't be home till after midnight.

Skylar: So it needs water to activate the poison? How much? Be precise. Be very precise.

Ford: Unfortunately, going to prison for poisoning would make it hard to win the Cup in my final season. However, I am not above being an asshole, so I found a plant that smells like cat pee.

Skylar: I could kiss you for that. Nope. Let me revise that—I could get on my knees for that.

Ford: That image will be indelibly etched in my head even when I hit the ice in an hour. But for now, can you water it?

Skylar: Of course. The pee plant must be cared for like it's a precious thing till tomorrow night. I will water it with a dropper all night long if I have to.

Ford: Just a quarter cup should do. Also, you can leave it in the metal bin on the front porch. The one for Styrofoam recycling. That way, critters won't be able to nibble on it. Just don't bring it inside.

Skylar: Yes, Ford. That was clear.

I've already poured the water from the sink, and I'm racing up the steps to his home when an idea lands. One nearly as nefarious as Ford's. Or maybe more nefarious. But it's good to be sure things work. I water the plant, double back to my house, and take care of one last pre-revenge detail.

* * *

On Saturday night, I'm feeling almost *too hot*. This outfit is a little...how shall we say, in your face? The shorts are short, the corset is tight, and there's so much skin on display. I really should see if this is what my friends meant.

But right when I'm about to convene an impromptu meeting on my phone, I stop. I can hear Mabel's voice, loud and bright in my head. *"You'd better look edible."*

Then Trevyn calling Ford a *hot-ass man*.

Maybe theirs aren't the opinion I want. Maybe they're not the ones I'm dressing for. The hot-ass man *is*.

I text Ford.

> Skylar: Can you tell me if these shorts are too short for tonight? I can take a pic.

> > Ford: The answer is there's no such thing as too short. But how about that hot tub peep-show rain check? Go to your kitchen window right now, and I'll check from the hot tub level.

A stupid smile spreads across my face. This is the kind of game I want to play. With a breathlessness I didn't expect, I head downstairs and rush over to the window. I pace back and forth, like I'm playing Pin the Tail on the

Donkey, trying to find the spot where he can see me best when a text lands.

Ford: I was right. Also, wear heels.

I was right too. He's not too sweet at all.

* * *

The pee plant doesn't smell terrible as we walk to Games People Play, but we are outside.

"Are you sure this works?" I ask, peering at the small plant in the terra-cotta pot. It's a shockingly pretty plant. But that's typical, I suppose. Pretty things can be deadly.

"I'm not a botanist, but if you'd like, I can stop by Landon's store in a week and check."

"You really would do that?"

He stops at the corner, studies my face, and nods. "I would, Skylar. I would."

Goosebumps erupt across my skin. "You're hot when you're evil."

His lips curve, and he never takes his eyes off me as he says, "Same for you, Skylar. Same for you."

As we walk, I can feel his eyes on me the whole time. Yes, I'm glad I dressed for him, because I like how I feel right now. Pretty and deadly.

23

ALL THE BYGONES

FORD

The shelves of board games are artfully arranged. The location, just past a record shop in Hayes Valley, is top-notch. The music is, begrudgingly, a good playlist of alt rock and pop.

Ergo, I hate this place and Skylar's ex even more.

I'm guessing he's the guy striding over to us with a proud papa look on his bearded face. It's the stupidest beard I've ever seen. There is literally nothing I don't despise about this man.

"Skylar! You made it," the guy says, beaming as he eyeballs the redhead at my side. Really eyeballs her.

Sure, she's hot as fuck in those black shorts. That sexy top. Those heels that make her legs look endless. And all that flesh I want to kiss, suck, bite.

But the dude is a cheater, and his eager eyes say he'd cheat again.

I loathe him to the end of time.

"Wouldn't miss it for the world," Skylar says, all sugary as she inches closer to me, her bare shoulder bumping my arm. I don't hate that though—the contact.

Landon holds out his arms, asking her for a hug.

Oh hell no.

As guests mill about, sipping on champagne, checking out Trivial Pursuits and Twisters, I step forward, cutting off the potential hug like it's a pass to the other team I'm stopping. I thrust the plant at Landon. "Here's a store-opening gift for you."

"Wow. A plant. This is amazing," Landon says, taking it from me while still staring at Skylar.

She points to me. "This is my...date. Landon, this is Ford; Ford, Landon."

Landon looks my way this time, then does a double take. "Aren't you—?"

Skylar never mentioned her ex was a sports fan, but the way he's gaping at me with fanboy recognition tells me he probably is.

But I'll wait for him to make the connection.

"Ford Devon," he says a second later, his eyes sparkling.

Landon sticks out his hand, and I take it, as a man with a well-groomed mustache and an affection for dapper clothes moves behind us, snapping a picture of the handshake. Probably the guy from the local neighborhood site. Skylar said he'd be here.

"That's me," I say, crunching Landon's fingers. I'm a couple inches taller. My handshake is much stronger. I consider squeezing harder. Then I go for it. "Yes. I'm Ford."

He winces, and a few satisfying seconds later I ease up, then let go.

After he blows out a relieved breath, he blurts out, "Holy shit! I love the Sea Dogs," he says to Skylar. "You never told me you were dating a hockey star now."

Not a player, but a star. Don't hate that either.

"Well, we don't talk now, Landon," she says, with a saccharine smile.

"And that should change. I'm all about letting bygones be bygones," he says like they're both responsible for the fallout.

And sure, rationally, two people are in a relationship.

But fuck him. Just fuck him.

Before I can say *you're the bygone, asshole,* a high-pitched gasp lands on my ears. Landon whirls around to meet the gaze of a blonde woman wearing gold-rimmed glasses. With wide, accusatory eyes, she's pointing to a nearly empty tray of crudités on a table. "Landon, I told you to get more."

"I told you to get more," he tosses back.

Her eyes flare. "I told you. Don't you remember?"

He sighs heavily. "Shoot. You're right. Excuse me," he says. Chastened, he cups her elbow and guides her to the back of the store.

Skylar turns to me, her eyes twinkling. "Trouble in paradise?"

"But not in fake paradise," I whisper, and we didn't plan this. Hell, we barely plotted anything besides the care and feeding of the pee plant, but I slide an arm around her waist.

Her breath hitches.

She moves against my hand like a cat, seeking touch, her back arching against my palm.

Here in the corner of her ex's quirky shop, next to a stack of vintage Monopoly games, I angle my body close to my revenge fake date.

Tuck a strand of her red hair behind her ear.

Watch her lips part.

Drag my finger along her jawline.

Observe her fighting off a shudder.

Then, fuck it.

"We said it shouldn't happen again, but that doesn't include a kiss, does it?"

"It doesn't," she says, turning her face so her lips graze mine. It's a teaser kiss but it's hardly enough for me.

I press my fingers firmly on her back, kissing a little deeper till she opens for me. *Yes.* She tastes so good. I forget we're in public, at a party, surrounded by guests.

Until someone bumps an elbow into my back, and we wrench apart.

"Sorry, man," says a guy in skinny jeans and a plaid shirt.

"It's all good," I say, and the dude weaves past us to join a group in the corner of the store.

I try to clear the fog of that kiss from my head, but it's hard with the way Skylar's looking at me with glossy eyes that say she wants more. With a hungry tilt in her pretty lips. I'm about to toss her over my shoulder and say *fuck that one-time thing* when a throat clears from behind me.

I turn around.

My fists clench, reflexively. It's Landon again, with the woman in glasses by his side. "This is Gretchen," he says. "Just wanted to introduce everyone."

"Oh, great! I was so hoping you would," Skylar says, laying it on thick.

But Gretchen just offers a simpering smile, missing the sarcasm.

After the intros, Landon rocks back and forth, saying, "How did you meet?"

Shit. We didn't practice our story. It never occurred to me anyone would ask. Which is a huge fuck-up on my part. It *should* have occurred to me. Of course people ask.

But my job is to react and to react really well. "She's my designer," I say.

Too bad Skylar answers at the same time with: "My dog humped his dog."

I snap my gaze to her, and we stare wide-eyed, nonplussed.

Landon arches a brow. "So, you're not quite clear on how you met?"

"That's funny," Gretchen says with a simpering laugh. I'm not sure if she's saying the way we met is funny or Landon's question is hilarious, but I am sure of one thing —they're not winning.

"We met when her dog humped mine," I say confidently to the asshole and his girlfriend. "And it also turned out she was interviewing later that day for a project as my designer." I turn to Skylar again, playing up the hearts and flowers. "I guess you could say...it's fate."

And when playing it up, you go for the gold. I loop an arm around her waist and bring her close. She fits so well against me, especially when she gazes up at me with her green eyes flickering with over-the-top adoration.

"Yes, it was fate," she says, roaming a hand up my chest. "I was sure he was going to turn me down. It's not every day when your dog goes full doggy-style on a hot hockey player's pup," she adds, then turns back to them with a carefree shrug. "What can you do?"

I laugh, brushing my lips against her hair because why the hell not? "I did the only thing I could. I hired her, then asked her out on a date."

"Really?" Landon still sounds doubtful, and I hate him more.

"Yes. Right away. I was taken," I say, dusting a kiss to her cheek just to prove how taken. Also, because I can.

"That's sweet," Gretchen says in her milquetoast tone, but clearly buying it.

"And then we started dating," Skylar says.

"Where did you go? On your first date?" Landon doesn't want to let up on the grilling. Does this ass think he's besting me? He doesn't know who he's dealing with. I don't relent. I push till the bitter end.

"We went to yoga," I say, then shoot my fake girlfriend a lovey-dovey grin. "Remember that class?"

"Sure do. It gave a whole new meaning to hot yoga," she says, with a purr in her voice and a dirty gaze just for me.

"So did the hot tub," I add, then cuddle her even closer.

"But it was definitely when we went to my favorite consignment shop and touched the same couch at the same time, like—"

"*Lady and the Tramp*," I cut in, because cute new couples finish each other's sentences adorably.

"Exactly. That's when I knew."

I turn to Landon, puffing out my chest. "So, thank you," I say. "If you hadn't walked away from the best woman ever, I might have been—"

Gretchen emits a tiny shriek. "We're out of champagne, Lan! I told you to get more. You never listen to me."

"I do too," he insists.

"You don't."

"You don't listen to me."

"Landon," she seethes. "Now is not the time. You need to fix this!"

"You're right. You're right. Sorry." With a frown, he surveys the table with empty bottles, eyes flickering with worry, whether for disappointing Gretchen or the guests it's hard to say.

Aww. The poor, unhappy couple. I feel so bad for them. So bad I want to rub it in their faces.

"We'll get you some," I say, fixing it for them. And fine, we both have public images, so it doesn't hurt to be a nice guy. But it really doesn't hurt to show them how happy and helpful we are while they're...bickering like rats fighting over sewer crumbs.

"Dude! You'd do that?" Landon asks.

"Of course. Sky and I—" I stop as if I just realized that rhymes, shooting her another lovestruck grin, before cooing, "We rhyme, baby."

"We do," she says.

I blink away the haze of happiness I'm floating on. "Where was I?" I clap Landon's shoulder. "Right, bro. We love to help others who need it." I drop my voice to a man-to-man whisper. "I can tell things are rough. We've got you."

The second we're outside, I say to Skylar, "I hope you don't mind—"

"Us rubbing in how much happier we are?" she asks, like the prospect is sweet sugar on her tongue. "I don't. Not one bit. Their sour relationship has turned out to be the best revenge."

As I turn those last words over in my head, it occurs to me I've no idea if Brittany's still with the chef. No clue if she's happy in her new life. But I know this much—*I'm happier than I was with her*. And right now, that's because of this woman by my side. Tonight, Skylar feels like my partner in mischief. And I couldn't ask for anything more. "Let's celebrate being happier without our exes," I say, holding her gaze for a long beat. Her eyes flash with that familiar playfulness that's so very her. But also...something more. Something that feels starkly real. Like we're in this whole thing together. Well, I suppose we are. "Since, if you think about it, living well is the best revenge."

"It is," she says.

We pop into a gourmet market down the street, grab two bottles of champagne, and return to the board game shop.

As we're heading in, the guy with the mustache, checked shirt, and snappy vest strides in our direction.

Purposefully.

He stops a foot away. His smile is warm but professional. "Hi there. I'm Ryan Goldberg with *San Francisco Neighborhoods*," he says. "I took a picture of you two earlier and I'd love to run it, with your permission."

Wow. I'm not used to lifestyle reporters asking. When I was with Brittany, a few pics of us out and about had appeared here and there—I knew this only because my mother would call and say *did you know you and Brittany are on the socials*? But no one asked our permission most of the time.

"Is it okay with you?" I ask, turning to Skylar.

"Absolutely," she says. After a pause, she fiddles with her bracelet before she finally asks him, a little sheepish, "Do you need my name too? Or just Ford's?"

With a smile, Ryan shakes his head. "I know you. You're Skylar Haven. I listen to your podcast," he says, then turns to me. "And, Ford, you must be Sexy Reno Guy?"

I'm not easily surprised. Comes with the territory of being a pro athlete. But...this? This was not on my bingo card. "Excuse me?"

Skylar sets a hand on my arm, squeezing my biceps. Is that Focus she's squeezing? I'm not sure but she's sending a message, and it says, *shut the fuck up.* "Yes," she says. "He's Sexy Reno Guy."

There's a story there, and I'm going to get it out of her *tonight.*

Ryan looks to me. "Great. And will Skylar be at your next home game?"

Oh.

Oh.

Oh hell yes. Like a good teammate, Mister Friendly Neighborhood Reporter just set up the perfect pass. I snag the puck and shoot.

Because...I don't want to stop faking it with Skylar. I just don't.

I wrap my arm around Skylar, possessively. "Of course my girlfriend is coming to our game against Phoenix. Want another picture of us?"

"I'd love one," he says.

I smile for the camera one more time.

Ryan thanks us and we move on, heading toward Landon and Gretchen, who are chatting with another couple by a display of Clue board games. Fitting. The dude needs a clue. The other couple peels away as we arrive, and I hand him the cheap bottle of champagne. "For you."

"Thank you. You saved my ass," he says, then his voice pitches up. "Maybe we can hang sometime?"

I smile, but it's my media grin—the kind I reserve for asshole reporters. "I'm busy."

As if to emphasize my point, I drop a quick kiss to Skylar's cheek.

She shudders, then says to Landon, "Yes, he's very busy with me. Good luck with your store." She nods to the champagne. "And cheers! Be sure to have a toast on us."

I reach for her hand, and we leave, but not before Gretchen whisper-seethes to Landon, "Great. Your perfect ex-girlfriend had to save us. *Of course.*"

Skylar squares her shoulders and struts out, looking like sin and mine for tonight. Or, really, for a little while longer since, thanks to the game she'll be going to and the gala. It sure looks like she's my fake girlfriend.

Outside on the sidewalk, I waggle the bottle of the good stuff. "The expensive one's for us. I want to hear all about this Sexy Reno Guy."

"I bet you do."

"In fact, I'll make you a deal."

With an arch of her brow, she says, "I'm listening."

"We drink it in the hot tub."

"The same one where you spied on me?"

"You love that I spied on you."

Her jaw comes unhinged, all over the top. "I could say the same to you," she says. It's cute how she pretends she's outraged.

"And you'd be right," I say, admitting that much.

Her lips curve up. "Then I accept your offer."

Warmth spreads through my chest, chased by something that feels dangerously like happiness every passing moment with her. I drape an arm around Skylar as we walk away from the shop, heading into the next part of the night.

"By the way, I didn't want to take any chances. So I

made sure the plant would smell," she says, with an impish grin.

Color me intrigued. "How'd you do that?"

She wiggles her eyebrows. "I sliced up an onion and put it in the plant."

I stop in my tracks, shaking my head in amazement. She's deliciously nefarious and it's going to my head. I drop a kiss to her pretty mouth, murmuring, "You're so evil, and it's outrageously sexy."

24

AL FRESCO DINING

SKYLAR

I dip a toe in the bubbling warm water while Simon watches me with avid eyes from the floor of the deck— upper deck, really.

"I'm surprised you let him into your home," I say.

"Yeah, me too," Ford says, then shoots me a stern look. "He'd better not try a thing."

"I know, I know," I say, but so far, so good.

Simon's been a gentleman, maybe because we walked both our dogs when we returned home. Mine trotted the entire way, burning off his humping energy. Nearly killed me with his enthusiasm, but I'd switched from heels to flip-flops, so I was at least able to try to keep up.

Zamboni's watching us too, albeit from the other side of the hot tub, keeping her eye on the humper. Smart girl.

The water's nice and toasty as I step into the jacuzzi in my orange polka-dot bikini that Ford can't stop looking at me in. I sink down into the welcoming tub, letting the water kiss my skin. I can't complain about Ford's hot tub attire—black swim shorts that give me a view of the ladder of his abs, the breadth of his chest, the strength of his arms.

It's a good sight.

After he sets down an ice bucket with the bottle of champagne and two glasses on the edge of the tub, he sinks into the water too. As his abs disappear, I pout.

"What's that for?" he asks.

"I was enjoying the view of Commitment and Discipline."

His brow knits. "I thought it was Focus and Dedication?"

I shake my head. "Those are your biceps. I named your abs too."

A smile tips his lips. "Right. I nearly forgot," he says, then holds my gaze for a confident beat as the water gurgles around us. "Which means it's about time we talk about Sexy Reno Guy."

I knew this was coming. I'm glad he's not mad though. "Champagne first," I say.

He grabs the champagne from the ice bucket, then, as he holds the bottle above the water, he shoots me a panty-melting look—one that says he knows where my eyes will be. *On him.* After he removes the foil, he drapes a linen napkin over the neck. Holding the cork and cage, Ford slowly twists the bottle. "Gotta release the pressure gradually," he says, in a smooth voice that's making me think about other kinds of pressure.

Naturally.

That's what he wants me to think about as he unscrews the cage but doesn't remove it. With the napkin-covered cork and cage in one hand, he slides his other hand around the base, taking his sweet time and reigniting memories of how good he is with those fingers.

Beads of condensation line his ropy forearms. Drops of water slide down his chest. I stare at his hands, a little shamelessly.

Oh, who am I kidding? I stare *a lot* shamelessly as he points the bottle toward the yard, and away from us and the dogs, twisting the bottle until the cork falls with a soft pop.

It lands in the napkin.

It's not theatrical, but it ensures no dog freaks out from the noise. And my heart thumps harder because of that.

I fight off all the smiles as he sets down the napkin and the cork, then pours and offers me a glass. I take it, stealing a glance at Simon as I do. He's now settled on the wooden deck, resting in the night air. Zamboni's watching us, but her eyes start to float closed.

I'm wide awake. I feel as bubbly as the hot tub. As full of anticipation as the corked bottle moments ago.

Ford lifts the flute, his brows arching up. "A toast."

"To living well?"

He smirks. "Yes. And to your podcast."

And here we go. "To my podcast."

He clinks his glass to mine, and I feel glowy and warm from both the temperature and his heated gaze. I watch him as he takes a drink. I do the same, then he sets down his glass. Slides closer on the bench, but not close enough.

My skin prickles and I want more. So much more than I should want, but I can't think about *shoulds and risks* anymore. I left those behind at the board game store when Ford bestowed a fake kiss on me that wasn't fake at all. When he spun tall tales about us that felt entirely true. When he had a blast rubbing in our happiness.

Most of all, I suppose I left the risks behind when he asked me on yet another date. Another fake one, yes. But a date, nonetheless.

He's all darkened gaze and raspy voice as he says, "So, I'm Sexy Reno Guy?"

Damn, this man really likes foreplay. I'm all wet and I *am* wet. "Well, I named your muscles. Is this really a surprise you have a nickname too?"

A small laugh falls from his lips, then it fades. He's a man on a mission. "What did you say about me on your podcast, Skylar? Tell the truth."

It's hardly a question. It's more of an invitation to... confess.

My breath comes faster. My chest rises and falls. And I'm heating up so fast from his hungry stare. "That I'd been checking you out," I admit.

"For how long?"

"A long time," I say, my insides flipping from his stare.

"When, Skylar?" he presses.

His intensity is such a turn-on. My thighs clench as I part my lips and whisper, "Since the first day."

His smirk is so pleased. He slides an arm across the back of the hot tub, closer to me. An excited breath coasts past my lips. My arm aches for him to touch me. Just to run a finger down my wet skin. Even though I want so much more than that.

"The day we met?" he asks, his voice low and smoky as he toys with me, like he wants to hear me admit every detail.

"Yes."

His dimple flashes. The bubbles brush against my thigh as he leans closer to me, dipping his face so I almost, *almost* think he's going to kiss me senseless in the hot tub.

But instead, he reaches for his drink. Takes his time lifting the glass. Swallows some champagne. Leaves me wanting even more. I'm aching everywhere for my next-door neighbor.

When he sets down his glass, he nods to mine. "You've barely touched yours, Skylar."

Because I'm too distracted by the way this man moves. "Your fault."

A tilt of his head. "Why's that?"

"Because you've been staring at me the whole time."

His lips twitch, but he still doesn't move any closer. "How was I staring at you?"

This man. He's making me work for it, the sexy jerk. But two can play this game. I sit up straighter, so my breasts rise above the water.

His breath hitches. A rumble that drifts across the steamy air.

Well, I guess I'm doing this foreplay thing too.

I rest my elbows on the edge of the hot tub, knowing the move draws even more attention to my tits. With a sensual sigh, I raise a hand from the bubbles and slide it through some strands of hair, making them wet.

I stretch my neck to the side, exposing more of my collarbone—the place he's obsessed with. Finally, I meet his eyes again and answer his question. "You were staring like you wanted to eat me up."

His blue eyes turn to flames, a flare against the night. His shoulders bunch. He's holding back, and I'm not sure why. Maybe because he likes to play games with me. Reaching for my glass, he commands, "Take a sip, Skylar."

I'm curious where he's going, so I take the flute, but he wraps his hand around mine. "And you should know I plan to kiss it off you." I shudder as he pauses, then adds even more seductively, "Everywhere."

Sign me up.

I lift the flute with excited fingers, holding it tightly so it doesn't slip out of my eager hands. I take a drink, my mind racing with wonderfully lurid images of this man devouring me.

He moves so quickly, I can barely catalogue how it happens. The images are no longer pictures. They're reality.

I place the glass on the edge of the hot tub. His lips keep crashing down on mine, and I'm moaning into his mouth. Water sloshes around us, bubbles licking my shoulders as Ford claims my mouth in a searing kiss.

Curling around my head, his fingers scrape through my hair as he tugs me close, his lips exploring mine. My lips part for his, inviting more of these deep, hungry kisses. He sucks on the tip of my tongue, nips on the corner of my lips, tilts my head back. Like he needs more of everything—more of *me*. I'm dissolving into this kiss. The steam from the hot tub mingles with the heat between us and I'm not sure what's warmer—the water or the need coursing through my body. My pulse is shooting to the sky, beating between my legs.

He slows the kiss, skates his mouth along my neck till I'm boneless and mindless with want. Then his lips travel to my ear, where he whispers, "You taste better than I imagined. But I really need to be sure."

My mind pops with questions like *What do you mean?*

But the answer comes in his hands roaming down my body, along my arms to my waist. Lighting me up with every touch till they settle on my hips.

With a cocky grin, he lifts me up and sets me on the

edge of the hot tub, my calves and feet still in the water, the rest of me exposed.

Awareness hits me right as he settles between my legs on the bench, spreading them apart. Sliding his hands up my slick thighs, he parts my legs wider. The look in his eyes is mischievous and molten. And I think...I've met my match.

But thoughts break apart as Ford brushes his mouth along my inner thigh, roaming those lush, hungry lips higher and higher still. It's in the sixties, so it's not cold, but it's not summery at night either. Goosebumps rise on my arms, and I'm not sure if it's from the evening air or the sensations whipping through my body. But when he reaches the apex of my thighs, heat blazes through me. He kisses the wet panel of my bikini and I gasp.

Simon lifts his snout.

"I'm fine, honey," I reassure him.

Ford laughs against my center. "You call your dog honey."

"Of course I do," I say, then curl a hand around Ford's head, shooting him a fierce stare. "Stop talking and get back to work."

"If you insist," he murmurs, giving me another kiss right where I want him.

My bathing suit is slick from the hot tub. But that hardly matters. He yanks the material to the side, and presses a slow, sensual kiss to my clit.

I'm panting, grabbing his head, rocking against him in no time.

He groans low in his throat, a sound that vibrates against me. I can *feel* the sound as he flicks his tongue through my wetness. My toes curl in the water. Wrapping my feet around his back, I tug him closer, grip his hair harder, roping my fingers through all those thick, damp strands. Needing more.

He stops for a second. "It'll be easier like this," he says, then maneuvers my wet bikini bottoms off me.

I've never been happier to be half-naked than I am right now.

His breathing is ragged and carnal as he eats me on the edge of his hot tub. My nipples are pebbling in my damp bikini top. I let my head fall back, giving into the pleasure as Ford licks and sucks me voraciously. Jets of water froth around us, fizzing against my legs.

Sparks fly under my skin, all through my cells, then they speed up when he flicks his tongue in a long tantalizing line down, then back up. When he sucks my clit into his mouth again, I am lost.

Loud too.

I don't know when I started, but I'm moaning his name over and over. Both dogs notice, watching like little horndogs. But I don't bother correcting mine. I'm too far gone from my neighbor's mouth owning my pleasure to even think about saying *down, boy*.

Ford's groans are addictive as he eats me. They mingle with mine, a new chorus of need and want. Soon, I'm gripping his head harder; he's swirling his tongue faster. I'm raking my nails through his hair. He's digging his fingers into my flesh. And we are communicating without words.

With just all this pent-up desire.

That spirals higher.

That spins faster.

That takes over my body and mind. Bliss coils in my belly, then spreads like a pinwheel. And in seconds, I'm falling over the edge.

"Yes, yes, yes," I'm chanting as his hungry lips and talented tongue work me over to the other side.

Pleasure bursts inside me, bright and strong.

And so damn loud that I briefly wonder if other neighbors hear the two of us. But I can't hold on to thoughts long enough to care. A minute later, maybe more, I blink open my eyes.

One very smug man is gently kissing my legs, running his hands soothingly along my calves. Two dogs are standing on their back feet, wagging tails, asking with big eyes if I'm okay.

"I'm very okay," I tell Simon, and Zamboni too.

Ford laughs, then dips his face and bites my thigh.

"Ouch," I yelp.

He lets go, looking unrepentant. "Yeah, you taste better than I'd dreamed." He rises up in the hot tub, shorts tented gloriously. And, well, pointedly.

"I want that," I say, gesturing to his enormous erection.

"Good. Because. I really need to fuck you, Skylar. So get naked and get inside."

I shiver in excitement. "But not in that order?"

That earns me a swat on my thigh. "Inside. Now. I have plans for you."

I swing my legs out of the tub, grab a towel, and knock back some champagne. "What are they?" I ask, with more excitement than I feel when I spot the perfect vintage dress in my size.

"You're about to find out."

He drops his shorts, and now I want him more than anyone has ever wanted a thrift store treasure.

25

BETTER USES FOR CHAMPAGNE

FORD

This has never been my fantasy.

But it's top of the list now. Skylar, laid out naked on my bed on a big, fluffy bath towel, me holding a bottle above her. I drizzle some of the frothy liquid between those pretty, perky tits.

Yup. Brand-new fantasy unlocked.

"Fuck. What a perfect fucking view," I say, in utter, filthy appreciation of the sight in front of me. A stream slowly trickles down the valley of her breasts. I lick it off. A long, slow slide of my tongue from her belly up to her tits. She tastes like chlorine and celebration, like summer and sex. She shudders as I lap the drink off her sweet skin, the taste going to my head, an unexpected cocktail that's driving me wild. "So fucking good," I praise as I flick my tongue above her belly button, licking off the last of the drink.

She stretches, arching under me. "Do it again," she urges.

I sit on my knees, bring the bottle to my lips, and then

drink some. After I swallow it, I nod to the redheaded beauty. "Turn over."

Her eyes flicker, and with a sexy smile, she complies, craning her neck and watching me.

And that's all I want to do—gaze at this sensual, gorgeous woman in my bed. I run a hand down her back, admiring the lines of it, then over her sweet ass, palming the curves.

She drops her face to the pillow, trembling as I squeeze the soft flesh. My bones rattle with the desire to take her. To have her. To fuck her hard and good into next year—the way I know, I just know, she'll want.

But I give her more of what she wants. This foreplay. "Living well, Skylar. We are living so fucking well," I say as I position the bottle above her back, then slowly pour some onto the pale skin, freckled here too.

When did I become obsessed with her freckles?

When you met her, you dumbass.

A stupid smile teases my lips—but I'm smiling at my goddamn inner voice when I really should be licking champagne off my neighbor.

"What's so funny?" she asks, sounding a little nervous, maybe because I stopped touching her.

I set the bottle on the nightstand, dip my face to her back and lick the champagne from the top of her ass to her shoulder blades. As she shivers under me, I answer her at last with the reassurance she deserves. "Just thinking about your freckles."

"I have a lot of them," she murmurs.

"And I'm obsessed with them all," I say, then run a finger down her spine slowly, savoring each shudder as I travel. I can't look away. I'm too mesmerized by her. I kiss a constellation of freckles near her upper back, then another, then one more.

With each press of my lips, she murmurs, wriggling under me. With every move she makes, an urgent need hums through my cells. Like my bones are vibrating with want. "Can't wait anymore, chaos demon," I say roughly into her hair.

"Thank god," she says, full of filthy relief.

She's so free with her desire. So outgoing. So confident. It's intoxicating and so very her—a woman who's unafraid to be exactly who she is.

Is this what I've needed? This fearless energy?

Maybe, but now's not the time to dwell in my head.

I flip her over and run a hand down her neck, amazed in some ways that she's here with me, arching into me.

"Ford," she whines. "You're such a tease."

I smile. "Can't help it. You're fucking perfect to tease," I say, then stop the teasing. After reaching into the nightstand drawer, I grab a condom, but then stop. "Um," I say, unsure how to break this to her.

"What is it?" she asks, with heightened concern.

"Your dog is staring at me."

Skylar rolls her eyes, but pushes up in bed, peering at the little Doxie mix. The long, little guy is sitting on the floor next to the bed, his ears hanging adorably, while Zamboni snoozes in a corner. But Simon's big eyes are locked on us. It's a little...unnerving. I'm not used to a canine audience.

"He knows all my secrets," she says as Simon thumps his tail. "He hears the videos I watch when I play with my toys. It's what he does—watches. It's okay. A dog keeps his woman's secrets. Just get inside me and stop thinking about Simon's voyeurism."

My head pops with so much delicious intel. "We're going to circle back to those videos real soon."

"Later, Ford. Later. I've been admiring your dick since you took off your swim shorts. Now I need to feel that nice big cock fucking me into the mattress."

Masculine pride floods me. I don't care what her dog does. I only care about giving her exactly what she wants.

I settle between her thighs, tear open the wrapper, and roll it on. My dick jumps as I cover it. Skylar's watching me the whole time, licking her lips, eyes flickering with a lust that matches mine.

This is almost too much.

I roam my hands up her legs, my chest heating to supernova levels as I admire the woman under me—the woman who speaks her mind. I'd tease her all night, but my storied patience makes a fast exit when I rub the head of my cock against her wetness.

It's like a match to kindling. I'm on fire in seconds, a roaring blaze in my cells. I sink into her, groaning savagely at the tight, welcoming feel of her.

The way she lets out a breathy gasp.

How her thighs fall open, inviting me to fill her.

As I do, everything turns electric. She reaches for me, holding my face, all her vulnerability suddenly shining through as she strokes my jaw.

It's a tender moment amid the lust, and it floors me. Hits me right in the heart.

"I want you," she whispers. It's soft and sweet, and the sound of those three words sends a hot tremor shooting down my spine.

"Have me," I rasp, as I ease out, pausing to let her feel the emptiness without my cock in her. When she's whimpering for more, I thrust into her again.

I slide a hand to her hip, hitching her thigh against my ass. Finding the perfect spot to fuck her good.

My mouth catches hers, and I give her quick, rough kisses as I fuck her into the mattress like she wants.

Till she's crying out.

Till she's wrapping her legs tighter around me.

Till she's grasping at my hair.

Arching her back and letting go. It's outrageously breathtaking in a way I never expected.

But then I never expected her.

Lust barrels down my body as I swivel my hips, then thrust back into her. Her breath comes faster, her moans needier, and I'm sure she's almost there. But a man should never assume.

"What do you need, baby? Tell me what you need to get there."

Her eyes fly open. Her cheeks are flushed, her breathing staggered. "Put me on my hands and knees."

Say no more.

I ease out, flip her over, and move behind her. And… yes. Fucking yes. She's beautiful like this as I sink back into her sweetness. My brain melts, and I'm pretty sure I won't last much longer.

I rope an arm around her waist, then coast my fingers down to the paradise between her thighs.

"Oh god, yes, do that," she instructs.

"I've got you, baby," I murmur as I play with her clit while I fuck her.

She moves with me, rocking back, dropping her head, muttering desperately, "I'm close. Don't stop—please don't stop."

My legs shake. My mind blurs—the tell-tale signs an orgasm is imminent. But I grit my teeth and fight it the hell off. She must come first. And the woman has made it clear what she wants and needs—for me to go the distance.

I follow her orders to the letter. Fucking and rubbing, thrusting and stroking. Staving off my own pleasure until she shouts a long, glorious *yes* that shatters into incoherent sounds of pleasure in seconds. Finally, I stop fighting it. I follow her there, giving in to the white-hot pleasure coursing through my body.

And...to something else.

I'm not sure what to do about these...feelings. Right now, though, I don't honestly care. I kiss her shoulder, then several of those freckles that have somehow knocked me to my knees.

She murmurs happily, like she's sex drunk, and it's the best sound ever.

Too bad it comes with a growl.

What the...?

I peer over the side of the bed. One little dog has a very big opinion. Simon's staring at me from the floor. "Your dog. He's definitely giving me the side-eye," I say.

With a soft laugh she says, "Well, that's because he wants to be on the bed, silly."

I look down at the crown jewels. "Pretty sure I don't want him on the bed right now."

"Like I've said before...you're mean."

I tie off the condom, grab the fluffy bath towel from the bed, and pad to the bathroom. When I return a minute later, Simon's resting dog face is even stronger, directed squarely at me. "My god. How do you deal with that?" I ask Skylar, feeling a little admonished by her pet.

With an easy shrug, she says, "I make money off it."

"Reasonable," I concede.

She takes her turn in the bathroom, and as I straighten up a little, the Doxie mix stares at me with canine contempt.

I feel...shamed by him. "I didn't disrespect her," I say, pleading my case to the dog.

He's unrelenting though. Just stares harder. It's weird, since I'm naked. I grab some boxers and stuff my legs into them. There. I feel a little better. Still, I'm compelled to defend myself to the judge and jury of one. "I swear. It was all consensual."

Skylar cracks up from the doorway. "Are you trying to reason with Simon?"

"Yes!" I say, thrown off by the pup staring at me from the floor. "He's freaking me out."

"You have a dog too," Skylar observes.

"I know, but she doesn't stare at me like that," I say, flapping my arm toward Zamboni, who's curled up peacefully in a fluffy gray dog bed in the corner of the room.

"That's also why she doesn't have a line of merch. Simon has a lot of opinions, okay?"

"What is he judging me for? I didn't defile you," I say, worked up more than I expected over a dog's consternation. But then again, I've never experienced anything like this before.

"You kind of did, and I liked it," she says in a sexy purr that nearly makes me forget the dog's watchful stare.

"Yeah, I suppose you're right. I did," I say, then move closer, looping an arm around her naked waist and pulling her close.

She sets a hand on my chest. "But he's probably critiquing you."

"For what?"

"Ford, you critiqued him, now he's critiquing you! You

even did doggy-style, and you expect him not to have notes?"

That's it. She can't go home tonight. I scoop her up, toss her over my shoulder, and carry her back to bed. When I set her down, I brace myself on my palms on either side of her shoulders. "Stay the night."

"Give me a T-shirt and I will," she says.

"You drive a hard bargain." I hustle to the bureau and grab a Sea Dogs T-shirt with my name and number. I toss it to her. With a pleased-as-punch smile, she tugs it on.

It's my turn to growl. She looks good in my number. She looks good in my gear. A streak of possessiveness I didn't expect hits me square in the sternum as I return to the bed. I roam my hand down her bare leg. "So, you get off to me while watching videos of who knows what, you mention me on your podcast, you spy on me from your catio..." I blow out a satisfied breath. "Did I get that right?"

She shifts onto her side. "You checked me out from your hot tub, demanded I join you in it, then gave me the first of many orgasms on it. Did I get that right?"

"Many? I gave you two. But sure. We'll call it many."

With a wicked grin, she tap dances her fingers up my bare chest. "I say many because I'm pretty sure you'll give me another later tonight."

Heat floods my chest. My dick perks its head up. "Yes, you can call it many."

"And your point is?" she asks.

That's a good question. What is my point? To prove she likes me?

Ah, hell, that's exactly what I'm trying to do. I want to goad her into admitting she's into me too.

But this isn't a real thing. We're doing a fake dating thing. I should recommit to the fakeness. Here in my bed, as moonlight streams through the open door to the deck, I ought to clear my throat and say, "That was a one-time thing, right? We shouldn't do that again. We're working on the house together. Not to mention, I'm trying to have the best season of my life."

But the words that come from my mouth are: "Was it hard seeing your ex tonight?"

Fuck. What was that all about? Why the hell am I bringing up exes...*in bed*???

Skylar takes a beat, her forehead creasing, as she considers. "I thought it would be hard. I spent five years with him," she says, regret flashing in those pretty green eyes. "That's a long time."

The touch of self-loathing in her voice strikes a chord with me. "I was with my ex for four. I get it," I say.

"And sure, I wanted him to see that I'm on the other side," she says. "But as I was getting ready for tonight, I wondered *why* I wanted that."

I turn closer to her in bed, wanting to both protect her from whatever she might be feeling and to understand her more deeply. "Yeah?"

She meets my gaze with a soft expression. "I was asking myself why it mattered. Don't get me wrong," she says hastily, explaining herself. "It was fun. But in the back of my mind, I kept thinking about *why*."

Tension grips me as I wait for her answer. "And did you figure it out?"

"I think I needed to go, not for him. But for me. I needed to know I was happier. I was better off," she says, looking in the distance before turning and meeting my face again. "Because for a while there, after he left, all I could think about was how I was second best."

It's like she's holding up a mirror to all my walls, to the

ways I've had to protect myself after Brittany took off. "Know that feeling well," I admit, and it's easier to speak the truth with her than I'd expected. Opening up feels like second nature when we're together.

She gives a sympathetic smile. "I learned a lot from everything that went wrong. I never want to be second best. And honestly, I deserve the best."

My heart warms from her certainty, from the way she knows herself. "You do, Skylar. You really do."

"Thanks. I spent a while with him. I felt like I had all the time in the world to fall in love, like my parents had. I thought a love like theirs was inevitable. But it takes work and risks. And I need to be with someone who thinks I'm worth the risk," she says. Then blinks. Shakes her head. "I mean, down the road. Someday. I'm totally focused on my business now. Romance is just scary…"

She's talking too fast. Racing through the end of the convo like she's said too much.

Doesn't feel like too much to me. "I'm the same. Romance is scarier than a puck flying at your face."

A laugh bursts from her. "I'll have to trust you on that."

"I promise. I'm not wrong." Then I reach for her hand. Yeah, I need to erect walls, but I also really, *really* like touching her.

I thread my fingers through hers, looking at our joined hands for several seconds. We fit in such an unusual way. A way I didn't anticipate. On paper, we should despise each other, like we did the first time we met.

She's chaotic. I'm controlled. She's carefree. I'm anything but. She's a go-with-the-flow person. I'm a structured type of guy.

So why, universe, why the hell do I feel this almost soul-deep connection with my neighbor?

My chest twists. My heart races almost too fast, too out of control. I stare at our hands, like the answers lie there. Only, I can't find them, so I do the dumbest thing for a guy trying to avoid romance. I open up.

"I'm glad you felt that tonight—that you're better off." I swallow uncomfortably. "Because I did too. I felt that. Not just the whole 'living well' thing." I tap my sternum. "But I feel it here, deep inside me. Even though he's your ex, I still felt this sense of...moving on from my past. From Brittany."

With a bright and buoyant smile, she asks, "Yeah?" Like she's enchanted by the idea of us both letting go of the people who've hurt us.

I tug on the hem of the shirt of mine she's wearing. "I did. It's been a while. But yes, I felt it. And sure, I don't want to go down that path again. Not one damn bit," I say. "The thought of opening myself up again is—"

"Like a puck to the face?" she says lightly, masking the real worry underneath.

I lean over and drop a quick, firm kiss to her lips. "Exactly."

But the truth is, I don't want to be replaced, like I was in my marriage. I fought like hell to be a good husband, just like I work my ass off to be indispensable on the ice.

As I stroke this lovely woman's hair and talk with her late into the night, I'm starting to think I could feel that way again—vulnerable, hopeful, and most of all, *ready*.

My chest tightens uncomfortably at the thought.

I need to enjoy this thing with Skylar for what it is—a fake romance. "That's why it's a good thing this is fake, right?" I ask, forcing myself to sound easygoing when my heart feels the opposite.

She tenses under my touch. But it seems to pass with a quick, decisive nod. "Absolutely," she says. "With everything going on, it just makes sense."

"And *this*," I say, doubling down with a gesture from her to me, "will make our fake romance more believable."

She's quiet for a beat. "Because your dick's been inside me?"

Ah, hell. I'm an idiot. Time to walk this back. "I didn't mean it like that. I meant the sex helps the fakeness," I sputter.

With a *did you really say that* smile, she waits for me to dig my hole deeper.

"I meant...I just meant...we seem believable."

I'm not sure that's any better. But as I search for forgiveness in her eyes, I find humor dancing there, delight at my faux pas. She's not offended by my remarks. She's having fun with me, the way she does. Because she wants a fake romance too.

I sigh with relief. "I thought you were pissed."

"Because you just implied fucking me makes a fake romance more plausible?"

When you put it like that..."Yeah," I say, utterly chastened.

She gestures to her dog on the floor, staring at me again with disdain. "Don't worry. He's got enough side-eye for both of us."

I laugh. I've been exonerated, but I know I was kind of a dick. "You can mention this on your podcast."

"Your dick? My dog's judgment? Or how you just put your foot in your mouth?"

There she goes, calling me out fearlessly. It makes my

stupid heart beat faster, and I'm back to where I was an hour ago.

Falling for her.

Correction: falling even further.

I shut myself up by kissing her, then sliding between those warm thighs and giving her one more of the many orgasms she deserves. Then, another.

Sometime after midnight, she curls up in the dark under the covers, and I do something that surprises me even.

I scoop up the little dog and let him sleep on the bed.

Well, it's only fair. Zamboni's already at the foot of the mattress, that perfect little pooch.

* * *

The next day I'm walking Skylar to the front door. It's surreal and weird at the same time, saying goodbye to someone who lives fifty feet away. "Do you want breakfast?" I ask, trying to prolong the inevitable.

She shakes her head, her red hair even wilder in the morning. Well, lots of sex and little sleep will do that to you. "I'll grab some nuts and a piece of fruit. I have to head to the Dogpatch District anyway to pick up some items for other clients."

My shoulders slump. I even took both dogs out first thing, hoping she might want to linger here with me. But I've got to stop hoping for things that won't happen. I slough off the disappointment as we reach the door. Along the way, she tosses a knowing glance at the sleek living room couch, covered in charcoal cushions and sporting brushed metal legs. Then the electric fireplace with its marble mantel, home to a few sleek candles, then back at the kitchen, its white counters pristine.

"I was right, by the way," she says.

"About how many times I could make you come? Yes, you said many, and I delivered. Four, Skylar. Four," I say, then blow on my nails.

Yeah, we were busy last night.

She laughs, and it sounds like *Oh, you silly boy*. "No, about your house. I predicted it'd be neat and clean, with metal accents, and a minimalist look."

I pfft. "That's not hard to guess. Also, what's wrong with being neat?"

"Nothing. But I also suspected," she says, scanning my living room once more, her gaze landing on the tiny plants that don't need much watering, "that you'd have plants. And I spy all sorts of succulents."

I bristle a bit. I don't know if I love or hate that she nailed the brief of me. Maybe both. "You were right," I concede, then curl a hand around her waist, pressing my palm firmly to her back. "But I'm right too—I only saw your living room, but I bet the rest of your home is bursting with every color of the rainbow, books everywhere, and more mugs than any person should rightfully own."

Her eyes widen to moons.

Yup. I'm right.

And I don't hate that. I love it.

26

ME? OBSESSED WITH YOU?

FORD

"Dude."

That word can mean a million things, but Wesley's tone later that morning, after I gave up a yawn the size of Wisconsin, I can translate.

What did you do last night?

"Yeah?" I ask while I lace up in the locker room. I barely glance at him, not sure I want to talk about Skylar as the whole team gets ready for practice. Wait—I *am* sure I don't want to. I'm not a kiss-and-tell type of guy. Besides, last night felt private. Just for Skylar and me.

"How does it feel?" Wesley asks, tugging on his jersey while Miles sets his watch in the stall next to him.

"How does what feel?" Something doesn't compute. "Yawning? Having better stats than you?"

Across from us, Asher whistles as he tapes up his stick. "Man, that's gotta hurt, Bryant."

Wesley scoffs, grabbing his phone from the stall, then turning his attention back to me. "One, you don't. Two, you're on the socials."

I blink, tension slamming into me. No one likes to

hear that. With my skates laced, I sit up straighter. "What do you mean?"

Max lumbers over from his locker, wiggling his fingers. "I hate social media, but this I have to see." He already looks pleased at whatever's happening to me online.

Wesley hoards his phone. "Now I'm not sure I want to show you," he says.

"Yeah, that's a brilliant idea, Bryant," Miles says, rolling his eyes. "Hide your phone like he can't find it any other way."

Now they're worrying me. Is there a trade rumor on social media? Did someone see Skylar and me in the hot tub? I grab my phone and get ready to start scrolling through...I don't even know where to look. "What's going on? Just serve it up," I say evenly. I'd rather know bad news than be blindsided later.

"When you admit my stats school yours," Wesley tosses back.

"Don't do it, Devon," Tyler calls out from the bench as he pulls on a jersey.

"Boys, enough games," Miles declares in his captain's voice, then motions to Wesley. "Just show us."

With a huff, Bryant finally swivels the screen around. I peer at the headline: **Hockey Player & Designer Save The Day.**

That must be the *San Francisco Neighborhoods* site.

I read on.

At last night's opening of Games People Play, hockey star Ford Devon and his new girlfriend, savvy podcaster and designer Skylar Haven, saved the day when the party ran out of champagne...

My first thought is that *girlfriend* is a really nice word.

My second thought is *Get it together, since she's not your real girlfriend.*

My third is I'm so glad the reporter identified her by name and occupation. Not simply as *my* girlfriend. Because any woman is so much more than her relation to a man. Fucking love that she earned as much attention as I did in the piece. Love it so much an irritating smile tugs at my lips. Irritating because my teammates are going to notice it in three, two, one—

"Aww. Devon's happy, boys," Wesley says to the whole damn team, pointing at me before leveling me with a sharp stare. "When were you going to tell us about how happy you are, dude?"

That *dude* says they're never going to let me live this down. *This* being finding out on a neighborhood site that I'm...dating.

Fake dating, you ass.

Shit. The voice in my head is right. I'm fake dating. And I'd do well to remember that.

I square my shoulders. "What can I say? You've seen the marriage proposals I get from the fans. I'm just...irresistible."

I leave, texting the article to Skylar before I hit the ice, knowing she's the one who's irresistible.

* * *

When practice ends, I practically jump on my phone, hunting for a response from Skylar. And there it is.

> Skylar: We're famous!

Ford: I saw.

Skylar: Also, we look hot.

Ford: You do.

Skylar: Shut up. You do too. Say it. Say 'I look hot.'

Ford: You look hot.

Skylar: That's not what I want you to say.

Ford: Fine. We look hot.

There's a pause—just bubbles dancing—then a reply.

Skylar: I'm practicing our cute couple pose for the Phoenix game.

It takes me a beat, but then I connect the dots. Right. Our next fake-dating appearance. Because that's what this is. We look hot as a fake couple. We're believable as a pretend romance. But isn't that what I said last night? We're good at faking it.

That's fine by me. Faking it is totally fine with me.

Only, I don't quite buy that the way I used to.

* * *

That afternoon, I leash up Zamboni and take her for a walk, then hop into the car. I need to drop her at the dog hotel so I can catch a flight out of here for a short road trip. As I head to the car, though, my gaze strays to Skylar's home.

Is she inside right now? Working on a plan for the cabinets for my parents' place? Dreaming up new merch for her judgy dog and his doggie-style critiques?

Stop. Just stop.

I tear my gaze away from her home without any answers and drive off. On the team jet, I listen to the audiobook my sister recommended—the one on the soulless tech giant. It's a riveting story, but I can't stop thinking of my neighbor.

I check my texts more than I should. But it's just a fake romance. There's no reason she'd be writing to me.

And when a text finally lands that night, I open it so fast in my hotel room.

Skylar: Your mom likes these cabinets.

A picture is attached. Another note lands seconds later.

Skylar: I figure it'd be easier to write to her directly than bug you about every detail. Hope that's okay!

Oh. Right. Because we're working together. Because I'm her client. That's why Skylar's writing to me with details of the interior design project.

I tell myself it's fine. She's efficient. Professional. Focused on the job. It's what we talked about last night. We're both devoted to our businesses, not to romance.

But my heart's a little heavy. Her note still feels like a door quietly clicking shut.

Ford: Of course.

I turn off the lights, wishing she'd bug me about every little detail.

In the morning, though, there's still no text from her about anything, and I shouldn't do this. I know I shouldn't. But as I stretch my neck in bed, I go to my podcast app and check for new episodes of *Hot Trends, Classic Spends*.

I sit up straighter. It shows one recently posted episode. Like a gleaming prize. A treasure I've been seeking.

I bolt out of bed, brush my teeth, and yank on workout clothes. I shouldn't want this so much, but the second I step onto the elliptical at the hotel gym, I hit play—and five minutes later, the grin on my face is ridiculous in size.

Skylar's voice is playful, full of laughter as she counters one of her friends with, "I admitted it! I told you I'm dating Sexy Reno Guy."

"Oh please. You didn't tell us. You were outed," her friend says. That must be Trevyn.

"Also, ahem, use his name. You were in the news with him," Mabel says. "We know who Sexy Reno Guy is."

Is Skylar smiling? Are her eyes twinkling? Is she

tucking a strand of hair behind her ear like she does when she's feeling sort of feisty? I have to know.

I switch to video and watch it there as I work out harder and faster.

There she is in the studio, a secretive smile tilting her lips as she says, "And what can I say? He bought me champagne and then"—there's a spark in her eyes—"we drank it."

Mabel raises a brow. "You drank it?"

"Yes, that's what you do with champagne," she says primly, and a smug smile owns my face as red-hot memories of the way the drink tasted on her come crashing back.

"Then why are you blushing?" Trevyn asks.

"It tasted good," she says, all demure and so thoroughly fuckable I can barely stand being away from her.

But she never reveals anything tawdry, and soon enough, she moves into design hacks, discussing how to use plants like succulents for eco-friendly decor.

She keeps talking, and I keep watching.

Before I know it, I've binged most of the episodes from when we first met. The more I watch or listen, since I switch back and forth, the harder it is to remember that this is just a bit, something to entertain fans. It's a storyline. Not my real life.

Even so, I think it's safe to say I'm a little obsessed.

27

NEIGHBORLY ACCESS

SKYLAR

Is this what it's like to be lucky?

To strut through life, to point perfectly painted nails at anything you want, and say, *I'll take that.*

Then to have it?

If so, sign me up. Because that's how the last several days have gone.

My podcast numbers are climbing higher and higher—we passed seven thousand subscribers yesterday. Who knew a fake romance would align so perfectly with podcasting? The show's basically dating and design now. And that's fitting, since my dating is by design.

Other good things include the hot sex I had last night when Ford came home from his road trip. I may have just happened to be out in the backyard, letting Simon out shortly after he returned. Deliberate, of course. But what's the point of having a fake fling with a neighbor if you don't let yourself enjoy neighborly access? It didn't take any convincing—or engineering—for him to come over.

The second he spotted me, he walked right up to the

fence, rested his strong arms on it, and roamed his eyes up and down me, undressing me immediately. "What are you doing right now?" he asked.

I glanced at my dog, then jutted out a hip, asking, "What does it look like I'm doing?"

"Getting ready to head inside so I can fuck you up against the kitchen table."

I ran through the door so fast.

But Ford didn't only bang me against the kitchen table —he bent me over the bed too. After, he curled up with me and confessed he'd listened to every episode of my show since I'd met him. I told him I'd watched all his games in the last few weeks. Then, he asked me more about the show, and how I started it, and I asked him about the stretches he does. I hardly wanted to go to sleep. This morning, he whipped up a pineapple smoothie at his place and brought it back over to me, chiding me for not having a doormat. That was so him—both the smoothie and the chide.

Honestly, it's really good to be me right now.

Especially on the work front. My carpenter friend Priya managed to get the kitchen cabinets removed from the Sausalito home and moved them down to the garage. Everything is coming up roses. Or autumn leaves, really. Golden and ruby ones crunch under my feet as I play Wordle with my brother—he solves it in fewer tries, the smarty pants, then he texts me to *make up the guest room* since he'll be coming home for a few days later in the month for a symposium on carbon emissions. *I'll give you the big dog bed and some kibble*, I tell him. We rib each other for a few more texts. When I turn the corner onto Fillmore Street, heading to meet my friends for coffee, my phone rings.

Mama Devon.

My spine goes ramrod straight. I still want to impress her. Even though we've been getting along just fine, she's still—for all intents and purposes—the client. And if she refers me to her friends? It'll be huge.

I answer right away as I pass An Open Book, the holiday display in the window catching my eye. I should probably grab a Christmas romance later today. I eat them up and then watch them on Webflix too. Does Ford watch Christmas movies? Has he seen my favorite one—*Merry Little Kissmas*? Would he want to?

I shake off those thoughts with a cheery, "Hi, Maggie."

"Hello, Skylar. I just wanted to tell you that those photos of the reclaimed wood cabinets are very nearly perfect."

The operative words being *very nearly*. We talk through the tweaks she wants—just a few changes here and there, maybe a different door handle style. I duck under the awning of a perfume shop and take notes on my tablet.

"That's not too much, is it? Just a few little changes?" she asks, her tone making it clear it's not a question.

"That won't be a problem."

"Lovely. So many other designers said my vision was a problem. But it's so much easier with you."

"That's the goal—to make things easier *for you*," I say with a smile. It's a genuine one. Sure, Maggie is an opinionated client. Sure, she likes to make changes too. But it's her house. It should feel like a little slice of heaven to her. My job is to make her dreams come true.

"Speaking of easy things...do you know what you're going to wear to the gala?"

That's a good point. It's coming up soon. "I guess I need to figure that out in the next week."

She launches into suggestions, then adds, "Will you mention it on your podcast too? The gala?"

I blink. "You're...listening to the show?"

She chuckles. "Of course I am. I've been listening *and* watching from the beginning. How do you think I knew that you and my son would be perfect for fake dating? It was clear you had a crush on him."

Oh. That makes shockingly perfect sense. She would do that—she's nothing if not the ultimate mastermind. There's something deliciously ironic about the fact that we're not entirely faking it for her.

Except, of course...we are. She doesn't know about the things that happen between us—late nights, pillow talk, endless texts, and all those tasty smoothies.

But those late nights and early mornings aren't turning into anything permanent. They simply can't.

"Well, that was brilliant of you," I say, forcing myself to focus on the fakeness, not the feelings.

"Thank you. I thought it was too. And send me some pictures of the cabinets when they go in," she says.

"I will," I say, wrapping up our conversation right before I reach High Kick Coffee. Stopping outside a cute tchotchke shop, I pause before I go into the café. Something about that interaction has thrown me off a little, like I've had too much caffeine and it's making me jittery.

Am I afraid of disappointing her? That can't be it. This thing with Ford is like reverse fake dating. We're not faking it for his family—his family knows we're faking it.

I'm not sure why my stomach feels a little twisty. Maybe because she said she knew I had a crush? Does that mean she thinks this will turn into something more? That she...wants it to?

My heart sits up, dares to hope. My mind races ahead to...days and nights spilling into weeks and months.

But that's foolish. All the roadblocks to our romance still exist. Even if we weren't neighbors, even when we stop working together, we'll still be a man and a woman who have dreams other than love.

I push open the door of the coffee shop and leave thoughts of fake and real dating behind when I head inside. I'm the first one here, but that's no surprise to me. Everyone expects me to be late. People don't expect a creative type to be on time. But I didn't launch my own business—or my dog's—because I'm a mess. I launched them *in spite* of my messiness.

I sail over to the counter and order a vanilla latte.

"You're going to want a toffee brownie too," says Birdie, the owner of the shop.

"Twist my arm, why don't you?" I say.

She winks, a smile coasting across her red-lipsticked mouth. "What's the story with Sexy Reno Guy?"

My jaw drops. "You listen to—?"

She scoffs. "My grandson told me about it," she says, and I'm guessing she means Miles, who plays on the Sea Dogs with Ford. He's also Leighton's boyfriend. "Couldn't resist. It's too cute when you narrate your dates."

Fake dates, my head autocorrects her. "I'm glad you're enjoying it," I say—and maybe I need to check my numbers again.

Is it really seven thousand forty-five?

After she makes the drink, I grab a table to wait for my friends. Mabel's coming, along with Sabrina and Leighton

too. As I take a sip, I toggle over to the podcast dashboard
—then nearly spit out my drink.

We're at eight thousand six hundred forty-four now.
"Holy smokes," I say.

"It's good, isn't it?" Leighton asks.

I look up to see my friend with the pretty brunette hair
and tattoos of flowers snaking down the fair skin of her
arm. "I didn't hear you come in."

"That's usually my line," she says wryly.

"True," I say with a smile. She wears hearing aids, and
I love that she's able to make light of it while living her
best life too.

"What's so funny?" she asks, meeting my gaze as she
settles across from me.

"My podcast. It's over eight thousand," I say in a
whisper—like if I say it too loud, it'll break this...luck.

"That's amazing," Leighton says brightly.

"I know, but..." I say, but I also feel...like I'm walking a
tightrope. The show is clicking, business is steady, and the
Sausalito home is coming together. But I'm also balancing
that all while faking a romance with a client. A romance
the client's mother engineered. My head's spinning as I try
to keep track of what's fake and what's real. I scrunch my
brow, trying to put words to this antsy feeling.

"But what?" Leighton asks with some concern written
in her tone.

I flash back over the last few nights with Ford, my
chest warming as I think about the texts we send, the
chats we've had, the way he invited himself to spend the
night after we collapsed onto my bed in a hot, sweaty
mess. He's such an interesting mix of intense and tender.
He's strong, almost stoic, but then he has this soft side that
he shows me—the Ford who kisses his dog's snout, who

cuddles under the covers, who makes me pineapple smoothies in the morning. I'm about to tell Leighton the truth—that something's shifting, tilting—when the bell chimes and in bursts a flurry of noise, fabulous hair, and bright voices.

Mabel and Sabrina whoosh past the sequined mannequin greeter at the door, beelining for us. I kick my wobbly feelings to the corner. Now's not the time to dissect them anyway since Mabel's chatting loudly about a douchey broker who said he'd heard about her *spotty* history.

I stand at attention. "Who is he? Because we ride at dawn."

"Damn right we do," Sabrina seconds with a crisp nod.

Mabel smiles softly, but it shifts into a frown. "Love the sentiment. But I'm not sure I'll ever be able to get a place besides the ghost kitchen, which isn't really a place, of course," she says, and now's not the time to talk about my good fortune.

We chat about her bakery situation while Leighton and Sabrina grab drinks. When everyone returns, I figure we can focus more on Mabel and strategizing some plans to help her.

But as she snags the cup of coffee that Sabrina slides her way, the steam wafting around her face, she shoots me a playful look. "So, tomorrow night you're going to the hockey game as Ford's...*girlfriend*."

Just like that, I'm the center of attention again. Maybe that's why I feel like I'm walking a tightrope. Because the spotlight is on me now in a big way.

Well, girl, you said you were dating a local sports star to a reporter.

The remark felt offhand at Landon's party, but it's not

so offhand now. But if I let myself believe this romance is real, I'm setting myself up to get hurt all over again. And after investing five years of my life in one person and then watching that relationship vanish, I don't want to get hurt again. Since I don't even know how Ford feels—surely, he's not tying himself in knots like I am over these fake-slash-real questions—it's best if I don't get caught up in the meta-ness of it all either.

"Mabel, are you keeping track of my romance?" I ask, trying to keep things light.

Sabrina lifts her fingers and sketches air quotes. "Your 'fake real romance.'"

They're my friends, so they know the whole reverse fake-dating thing. But with those words, my stomach cart-wheels again with nerves. Everything feels topsy-turvy—maybe because things don't feel entirely light. Or fake.

But a part of me wishes it were—because the more real it gets, the more it might hurt when it ends.

And it will.

Fake romances always do.

* * *

Later that day, I walk up the steps to my brother's home, then stop in my tracks at the door. There's a new doormat on the porch, and a white piece of stationery beneath it.

The doormat is beige with a black silhouette of a Doxie mix and the words—*Knock to See My Wiener.*

A laugh bursts from my chest. No, from deep within me. I don't even have to pick up the card to know who it's from. But I grab it fast, anyway, unfolding it just as quickly.

It's Simon's stationery. He bought my dog's stationery.

My heart climbs into my throat. I feel like I'm going to cry. A good cry, like when I watch a figure-skating competition, or a, well, a Christmas romance. The note reads: *I saw this at a garden store and thought of you.*

That's it. That's all. But it also says so much more.

I clutch it to my chest as I head inside.

28

SAPS LIKE US

FORD

Whenever I hit the ice for pre-game warmups, I usually keep my head down. I shoot the breeze with my team-mates, but then I focus on the stretches. Hell, that's why I play brain games.

After I run through a round of River Ranger in the locker room—spotting animals I pass in the on-screen water, then recalling them in order—I'm ready to tackle Phoenix. Tucking my phone into the stall, I grab my stick and head down the tunnel alongside Miles and Tyler, who's currently describing his new foster kitten's latest antics.

It's hilarious how obsessed the guy's gotten with kittens since he started fostering them with Sabrina. But I guess a woman will do that to you—make you feel all sorts of new things.

Like the woman who's already here at the arena, *for me*.

I flash back to Skylar's last text.

> Skylar: Should I blow a kiss during warmups? You know, for all our new fake-dating fans? Wait—I've got it. I'll come to the glass, press my fingers against it, and you can skate over and kiss the glass. Make it look desperate.

> Ford: A wave will do.

> Skylar: You're so not fun.

> Ford: I'm so fun. Like I was last night when you begged me to spank you.

> Skylar: Great reminder! I'll hold up a Spank Me sign.

I laugh, shaking my head at the memory as I push open the gate and skate onto the ice. Honestly, I wouldn't put it past her to actually hold up a *Spank Me* sign. As I glide across the cool surface, I can't resist. My gaze drifts to center ice—right where she's standing, waving, and holding up a sign.

And I nearly trip on my skates when I read the big, bubbly letters—yellow, outlined with black. **I'd Knock So Hard To See That.**

I fight off a smile the entire time I'm warming up from the insider joke. But also from the color. And when it's game time, I do everything I can to channel my River Ranger mentality and push her out of my mind.

* * *

We're down by one with nine minutes left in the game. I'm battling it out in the corners with a Phoenix defenseman, who's shoving me into the boards. He jams an elbow into my ribs. A sharp, bone-rattling ache lances through me. But I put it out of my mind and jab my stick toward the puck.

Ha. *Take that, asshole.*

I'm off and racing away from the big guy. I'm faster—that's the job as a forward. I leave him in a spray of ice, passing the puck to Bryant in the neutral zone.

My teammate flies down the ice, full speed ahead. Bryant closes in on the net with our defenseman Rowan Bishop flanking him. With one swift move, Bryant lifts his stick, and smacks that little black disc. In no time, it zips past the goalie and lodges into the twine.

"Yes!" I shout, racing down to high-five Bryant as the lamp lights. "Let's do it again," I shout, since we're not there yet.

"We're gonna get another," he says.

"We fucking will."

We skate over to the boards for the line change. Once I hop over, I hazard a glance across the ice.

Skylar's on her feet, cheering the goal, jumping up and down.

My chest floods with endorphins. From the goal, I think. Or maybe not.

Because these heady feelings don't dissipate. They seem to spread as Skylar's red hair tumbles around her heart-shaped face, her cheeks bright, her eyes probably full of mischief and excitement. She looks so damn good in my jersey.

I just can't stop looking at her.

Briefly, I remember Brittany coming to games. She

always wore my gear too, but looking back, there was something performative about it. Something she seemed to enjoy about being a hockey wife.

With Skylar, it feels real. Like that joy over the goal came from deep within her.

I have to keep reminding myself it's not real. But it's getting harder especially when we win, and I impulsively skate over to her and do the very thing she asked me to do. I blow her a kiss.

Well, it's for *San Francisco Neighborhoods.*

That's what I tell myself.

But I know the truth. It's for me.

* * *

"Yup. Called it. Our boy is *hap-hap-happy,*" Bryant sings in the locker room, flinging his jersey into the laundry bin.

I scowl. "Never pretended I wasn't."

Miles scoffs as he unties his skates.

Tyler laughs, while icing his shoulder.

"What? I'm not the team grump," I argue, nodding toward our defenseman Rowan Bishop—the one who took that title from Max Lambert.

"That's right. I *own* that," Rowan deadpans as he stretches his neck from side to side.

Wesley rolls his eyes. "Not the point, boys. Not the point." He turns to me. "You were always sarcastic as fuck. Always steady. Always a grinder." He smirks. "Now you're a fucking *sap.*" He claps his hands together and cackles like a madman. "And I *love* it."

"Because he's a sap like you." Lambert grunts as he tugs on a T-shirt.

Wesley points to Max. "And you." Then to Asher. "And

you." Then Miles. "And you." Then Tyler. "And you, and you, and *you.*"

I roll my eyes and wave a dismissive hand, turning my back so they can't read my face while I change. Because they're not wrong. I am raring to get out of here and see Skylar.

But before I can do that, the team publicist, Everly, knocks on the door, and calls out, "Are you decent?"

Max—her fiancé—shouts, "Never."

She pokes her head in. "Ford, can you join Wesley for the press tonight? With your assist and all, it'd be good to have you there."

"Of course," I say.

After I pull on a T-shirt, shorts, and slides, I head into the media room and run through the usual game-day questions. Easy stuff. How did you feel out there, what were you thinking late in the game, and so on.

Until Gus—grizzled, sharp-eyed, and probably born in a press box—leans forward. "You're having a great season—and it's your last one. How does it feel to be a month in and playing like this?"

It's a simple question, but it's loaded with meaning.

If I say I feel good, I invite hypercritical attention. If I hesitate, they'll read that as doubt. Either way, it's a trap. I sidestep. "Any player wants to have a strong year."

Then another reporter pipes up—a younger guy from *The Sports Network*. "Is your new girlfriend the reason?"

It catches me off guard. My brow furrows. "I don't think she has anything to do with the assist," I say, but that sounds callous. "But I'm glad she was here."

It's true. Every word. Yet it feels like I've changed the narrative—moved our fake relationship one step closer to real by acknowledging it out loud. Here, in front of the sports press. Not just the lifestyle media.

And that raises a question I hadn't fully faced until now: What happens when it ends?

It's a sour thought, one I don't want to sit with.

* * *

I skip the polar plunge this time. I shorten my post-game bike ride to ten minutes. A truncated routine now and then won't hurt me. Besides, I am more than ready for the rest of the night to begin. By the time I'm showered and suited up, all I can think about is taking Skylar home and doing very bad things to her. Just like that, the game, the press, and the quiet dread I've been wrestling with fade into the background. With a one-track mind, I find Skylar chatting in the corridor with Sabrina and Leighton, as well as Everly.

I hope she doesn't plan to hang out with them for long.

I head over to them, with Everly catching my eye when I'm a few feet away. She tips her head toward the other side of the corridor, the sign she wants to talk.

"Hey, Ford," she says quietly, and I'm running through potential issues she might be drawing my attention to. Something I said wrong to the press? But that's doubtful. I'm pretty bland—deliberately so—when I talk to them. "I didn't want to say this in front of everyone," Everly adds. "But we have family night next week when we play Vancouver here, and if things are going well, it'd be nice to have you two there."

Oh. *Oh.*

That's the game where players bring their partners

and kids, if they have them. Where the team takes all sorts of pics for social media. Everywhere we turn, it's like the universe wants us to keep pretending.

Or maybe you do.

I school my expression, reining in the cat-who's-got-the-cream smile. "I'll check with Skylar, but it sounds good to me," I say.

"Great."

We return to the other two women, and this time Skylar peels away from her friends as I approach, flashing a flirty grin my way—a grin that says we're on the same wavelength.

"Want to go home with the star of the game?" I ask, sliding my arm around her shoulders—a very *possessive* arm.

She grins. "I do."

But as we leave, footsteps grow louder behind me. The loud *clop-clop* of someone jogging in work shoes. I look back. Damn. It's Ryan from the neighborhood site heading our way. We can't leave just yet.

"Hey, Skylar. Hey, Ford," he begins, as I hit pause on my *do bad things* plans. "I couldn't make it to the game—my partner was sick. But I sneaked off when he fell asleep. Can I get another picture and maybe ask a few more questions for our site?"

It's just a neighborhood site. It's small on the scale of things. But then again, I was just a Minor League player for a long time. An undrafted guy. Here's Ryan, clearly hustling for a living.

"If it's okay with Skylar," I say.

"I'm up for it," she says, and if that doesn't sum her up, I don't know what does. We talk with Ryan for a bit, answering easy questions and smiling for the camera.

When we're done, he offers a grateful smile. "Appreciate you sticking around, man."

He didn't mean it this way, but his words remind me of my goal for this year—*to stick around*. As I leave, I start to wonder if romance and sticking around are as mutually exclusive as I'd once thought.

29

SPANK ME AND LOVE ME

SKYLAR

I can't wait.

I can't wait so much I nearly blurt out my plans on the drive home. But I'm a good girl, keeping my mouth zipped as Ford drives and pulls up in front of our houses. We hop out together, and for a brief moment, my mind spins forward.

This action—pulling up together at our homes—is so...couple-y.

It's almost like we live together.

What will it be like when this ends? We won't be driving home together. But how will we behave when I run into him in the front yard? On the sidewalk? In the backyard?

My brother's concerns weigh on me.

But then I think of my plans for tonight, and what's waiting in the bedroom, and I kick those concerns to the curb.

Best to stay in the moment. *To enjoy.*

After we take our dogs out for a walk, we head up the steps to my home. Before I unlock the door though, I set a hand on his chest. "I have something for you. Leave the suit on."

His lips quirk up. "Whatever you want, baby."

"But take the jacket off," I say, then I don't bother waiting. I push it off his shoulders myself.

"Someone's eager," he says, grabbing the material before it falls to the ground.

"So are you, so be good and wait here for me for a few minutes," I toss back as I unlock the door, then take off for the staircase.

I can picture the scene. I nearly giggle at the thought of what's to come. I fly upstairs, little paws slapping on the floor behind me, since Simon must be a part of everything. I wash my hands, change quickly into a sexy black bra and panties, grab my supplies, and position myself at the edge of the bed—Simon staring avidly from the floor, because of course he does. I do a double take though. Cleo's lounging on the pillow, all stretched out and lithe. She probably knows Ford is here. She's always had a thing for him.

"I get it, girl," I whisper, then I call out to Ford. "It's safe to come upstairs."

A trail of laughter follows his voice. "Is it ever safe with you?"

"Reasonable question," I call back.

His bare feet pad along the hardwood floor, growing louder with every step. Anticipation climbs the stairs inside me. I feel bubbly and frothy. My chest flips as I wait.

The second Ford turns into the room, he stops cold. "Fuck yes," he murmurs.

The praise zips through me, and I wiggle my hips—

though there's not a doubt in the world it's the only place he's looking.

I'm in position, bent over the bed, holding the sign over my ass. I crane my neck to watch his reaction, savoring every second.

He shakes his head. He looks to the ceiling, like he's asking the universe *are you even real?* Then he reads the sign out loud:

Spank Me.

"Are you glad I didn't bring it to the game tonight?"

"I'm very glad you saved it just for us," he says, and those last three words echo in my head and heart—*just for us.*

That shouldn't hit me as hard as it does. Raw, full of meaning, full of a future. But this thing between us isn't about the future. It's about the present and there's no place I'd rather be than here in this moment.

Ford closes the distance between us, then bends so his face is close to me. He cups my chin, and claims my lips in a hot, searing kiss. My head goes hazy as his fingertips slide along my jaw, his other hand roaming down my lacy bra and over my stomach. His kisses are deep and hot and full of something pent up. Like he's been holding back all night and doesn't have to anymore.

When he pulls back with a long, appreciative sigh, he takes the sign and sets it on the bed. He moves behind me and slides a hand up my back, along my neck, into my hair. He curls his fist gently around the strands. I tremble, my breath catching.

A charged moment. The air vibrating. Cleo watching.

Then Ford's hand comes down on my ass in a sharp smack. I yelp as the sting spreads through me in a painfully delicious way. Simon barks.

"It's okay, buddy," I reassure him as I drop my head, catch my breath, then lift the sign again.

Once more Ford laughs, raises a hand, and swats the other cheek. The bark is quieter this time, but the pleasure is even greater. I raise the sign a third time.

Ford gives me the same treatment a few more times until I feel a little sore and a *lot* turned on.

Setting the sign down, I turn around, grab his tie, and loop it around my palm. "Did you wear your lucky yellow shorts tonight during the game?"

"Always."

"What color are you wearing now?"

"Find out," he orders.

"Yes, sir."

My eager hands travel down his white shirt to his beige slacks. I undo the button, then the zipper, and tug them down.

I lick my lips. My body hums. A pulse beats between my thighs as I take in his sartorial choice. "When did yellow become so sexy?"

But I already know the answer—when I met him.

"You tell me, baby," he says, curling a hand lightly around the back of my head.

Nothing has ever been sexier than his yellow boxer briefs—especially with his hard cock straining against them, a drop of liquid arousal giving away exactly how he feels.

I drop to my knees.

Roaming my hands up his rock-hard thighs, I lift my chin, locking eyes with this man as I tease him with my eager fingers. His blue eyes darken, and in them I see heat, desire and something else. Something I've been seeing in them lately—a passion that goes beyond the bedroom.

A passion that matches mine.

He lets go of my head and runs a finger along my jaw. A new vulnerability spreads inside me. I think I sense it in him too.

Or maybe I just want to? Hard to say, especially in *this* moment when lust has the wheel.

I tear my gaze away from his handsome face. I like looking at his dick too. And touching it, so I peel down his boxer briefs, inch by inch, enjoying the moment when his hard cock springs free, pointing right at me.

I bite the corner of my lips, and stare at his long, pretty pink dick. Yes, I *could* draw him into my mouth right now. But I think I'll toy with him first. I fist his cock. His breath hitches. I rest my cheek against his shaft, rubbing him against my face.

"Fuck, baby. You have no idea how hot that is," he mutters.

I smile wickedly. "Actually, I do. That's why I did it."

His fingers rope through my hair. "Do it again then." Like a cat marking a person, I rub my face along his cock, like I'm saying *he's mine.*

Mine. It's a strange thought, but it feels strangely true.

I tease him some more, then brush my lips slightly against the head. I flick out my tongue. He groans. I squeeze the base with my palm. He shudders.

I press the gentlest kiss to the tip.

He snaps, saying on a rough groan, "Suck it, baby. Suck it now."

"What a good idea," I say, then draw him past my lips.

His breath is ragged. The staggered sound of his moans sends sparks of pleasure through my body, settling between my thighs as I fill my mouth, enjoying the view of him in his post-game suit—the slacks undone, the shirt untucked, the briefs half down, the jacket gone. Somehow, the messiness of his attire makes me hotter. I suck deeper. Harder. Take him all the way in while curling my fist around the base.

He sucks a breath of air through his teeth. Cups my head harder this time. Rocks into my mouth.

Want pools in my belly. I wriggle around, like I can find some sort of relief from this ache between my thighs.

But then I concentrate fully on him, murmuring against his cock, scraping my nails along the coarse hair of his thighs. His muscles are like steel, and this isn't the first time I've felt his legs, of course. But to feel them now while his dick's pulsing in my mouth, thrusting into my throat, gives me a particular thrill.

All day, this man is so strong, so stoic, so steady.

Yet when we're alone, he seems as lost to the pleasure as I am.

That thought spurs me on. I grab his firm ass, then take him deeper.

"Fuck yes," he grunts.

He fists my hair with one hand, his other hand moving down my face, his fingertips dragging along my cheek. I swirl my tongue around the head then relax my throat, letting him drive deeper.

With a throaty moan, he fucks my mouth, his gaze locked on my face as he pumps. My lips stretch around his length, and I will myself to open wider. It's not easy. He's a little rough, a lot big. My tonsils are getting knocked around, and I'm not sure how long my throat can handle this.

But I'm also growing wetter from every thrust, every grunt, every tight grip of his fingers in my hair. Most of all, from his eyes lasered on me. His attention is a match, and it lights a fire of lust inside me. I'm rocking my hips now too, moaning as I lick and suck.

"Look at you," he grits out. "With your pretty lips wrapped around my dick. Just look at you. So fucking turned on from sucking me off."

My brain pops. No one has ever spoken to me like this. I'm used to being the chatty one, to talking too much, to speaking my mind. But here he is, reading me right. Seeing through me. *Knowing* I love touching him and turning him on too.

And saying it.

That's freeing as well—the fearless way he names what's happening between us in the bedroom.

I feel fearless with him, so I let my right hand fall from his ass, and I shove my fingers inside my panties.

Yes...

I've been aching for contact, and in seconds I'm riding my hand while I suck him.

"Ah, hell, Skylar. You can't keep that sweetness to yourself. Gimme," he demands. "Gimme some of that right now."

Arousal gathers hotter and faster as I fuck my fingers, then remove them, lifting that hand. Offering it to him.

He pulls his dick from my mouth. I whimper from the loss of contact, but not for long. He kneels so we're eye to eye as he sucks my slick fingers, licking my desire off each one, his eyes rolling back in his head. When he lets go, our gazes hold each other, flickering with so much need, so much urgency.

There's passion in his irises but also pure vulnerability. "You're doing something to me," he murmurs. "You're just doing something to me."

My heart thumps harder. We're talking about sex, but we're also talking about us.

"Let me keep doing it," I plead. "Want to taste you coming down my throat."

It's not the first time I've blown him. But it's the first time I've felt this...desperate to touch him like this. To give just to him. I lean into the mood, the athlete on a victory lap after a win. The athlete enjoying his spoils. "You know you were thinking about it at the game," I tease. "And you deserve it for that assist."

But Ford's expression is stony. He holds my face, cups my cheeks, and shakes his head. "You're wrong."

I freeze, my mind racing with worry.

He reassures me quickly with a deep, rumbly answer. "I was thinking about how fucking badly I want you to sit on my face."

My neck flushes. "I really better finish you fast then," I say, then point to the bed, since, well, a very curious dog is staring too closely at us from the floor, with all these naked parts on display.

In no time we're on the bed, and I'm between his legs, sucking him deep again, with loud slurps.

Ford's noisy too. Grunting, groaning, biting out a long string of *fuck yes*es and *just like that*s.

He's reckless and uninhibited, and the sound of his pleasure sends sharp, hot waves of pleasure cascading through me. I love how he lets go in the bedroom.

He's gripping my head, thrusting into me, and I'm this close to gagging. *This close.* But when Ford unleashes a low, feral moan like a warning, I hold the hell on even though I'm on the verge of coughing. He shakes. Grips me tighter. Roars my name in a deep rumble. He comes, the warm salty taste like TNT to my own desire.

I'm dying for his touch. Aching everywhere.

When he eases out, he makes good on his promise. He yanks off my panties and gives me an order. "Fuck my face now, Skylar. That's what I really want."

"I better not deny you," I say, breathless and wild as I comply.

Briefly, as I straddle his face, I'm struck by the easiness of our intimacy. Sex can be awkward and weird, complicated and lopsided. But when it comes to Ford and me—we just fit.

It doesn't take me long at all. Soon, I'm gripping the headboard, shouting his name, and falling apart.

When I open my eyes in a haze of pleasure, Cleo's slinking off the bed like she's had enough.

Ford hasn't though. Gently, he moves me off his face, tucking me close to him. He wraps an arm around me. Kisses my shoulder. Runs a hand over my hair. "Yeah, I was definitely thinking about eating you out at the game," he says, then takes a weighty beat. "Among other things."

He sounds serious as he says those three words—*among other things.*

"What sort of things?" I ask.

He inhales. Stares at the ceiling thoughtfully. Then at me as he shrugs and speaks with such vulnerability that it feels like something's cracking—in him. "How much I like spending time with you, Skylar."

My heart glows, warm and bright in my chest. "It's the same for me. With you," I say, an admission for an admission.

He dusts another kiss to my forehead, then hums—a happy but wistful sound. "Good. That's really good."

"It is," I say softly, snuggling against him, feeling safe, and feeling like there's no place he'd rather be.

That's how Ford makes me feel. Like I'm his priority. It's a new feeling. A welcome one.

But then he glances down at his clothes. "I should..."

The way he trails off makes me think he's going to say leave. Instead, he says, "Change. Make some food. Then tell you about the next date we're going on. Everly asked us to come to family night."

I smother a full-blown smile. He didn't use the word *fake*. He just called it a date.

I'm not surprised Ford can cook. He's a competent man. A man who gets shit done.

What surprises me is that he's stashing fake bacon.

"You have Facon?" I ask, even though the evidence is right in front of me as he unpacks a grocery bag onto my counter.

"Of course I do," he says, all nonchalant as he pulls a tomato from the canvas bag, then some lettuce.

My mouth waters as I stare, slack-jawed, at the magic bag.

"But—" I sputter, unable to put into words how I'm feeling. What I'm thinking. The thought behind the gesture. "You have..."

I just point, flailing, flapping my hand like a fish out of water.

He slides behind me in the kitchen, wraps his arms around my waist, and kisses the back of my neck. "You don't eat meat, so I picked up a few things I thought you might like."

Which is thoughtful in and of itself. But it's also *calculatingly* thoughtful, because he just popped over to his house, changed into shorts and a T-shirt, and returned with this bag. Which means...he planned this meal.

"When did you get all this?" I ask.

"Earlier today," he says, then lets me go and offers a confident smile. "What can I say? I figured we'd both be hungry and would want a late-night snack. So I picked up some things."

The detail. The thought. The planning.

Does it matter so much that he's my neighbor? What would happen if I just took a risk...with a client? Maybe. Maybe I can. Because Ford isn't just some guy. He feels like he could be *my guy*.

I rise up on tiptoe and cup his cheeks, sighing affectionately. "A neat freak who drives a Swedish car and plans midnight dates."

"I know. I'm awesome," he says, then swats my ass. "Now get out of the way so I can cook for you."

I set out a cutting board, knife, and pan, then trot over to a stool, park myself on it, and enjoy the front-row seat to a hot hockey player making me a veggie BLT—complete with fake bacon.

As he slices the tomato, I sigh happily. "What'll you do when you finish playing hockey? Open a late-night grilled cheese and BLT pop-up shop? A girl can dream."

"Not a bad idea."

Which brings up a valid question. "Seriously though. What will you do? You're a planner. You probably have three priorities for retirement."

He nods. "I do."

But that's all he says. Hmm. Is it a secret?

I debate leaving it alone, but I've never been good at that. "What are they?"

As he washes the lettuce, he says, "My health—always

a top priority. Second would be keeping busy doing something I love. Third would be…" His gaze goes slightly wistful, almost dreamy, as he opens the package of Facon and drops a few slices into the pan. "Third would be spending time with my dog. So to answer your question—for two, I'm debating between going into broadcasting and opening a smoothie shop."

I sit up straighter. "Really?"

"Really. I think I'd like both. I'll decide after we win the Cup this year." He pauses, his gaze contemplative, spatula midair. "That's the first time I've shared that with anyone."

My heart does a little flippy-flop. I'm all sorts of giddy. "Thanks for telling me."

"You're easy to talk to, Skylar," he says—offhand, but full of meaning.

My chest is warm as I respond in kind with a, "You too."

After he slices some sourdough bread, he asks, "What about you?"

"I'm not retiring anytime soon, buddy," I tease.

"Is this your dream? The eco-friendly design?"

"Yes. I'm doing exactly what I want." I pause, giving my own question some thought. But I already know the answer. "I suppose my dream is to keep doing more jobs like this —the full house, where I have the chance to really make a difference with my brand of design."

"You'll succeed," he says, then finishes making some delicious-looking BLTs.

He plates one for himself and one for me, then slides onto a stool beside me.

In my pajamas and tank top, I indulge in the most delicious late-night snack—made just for me.

Later, we go back upstairs, with my dog under the covers, his in one of Simon's many beds, and Ford in mine.

"Ford," I whisper quietly as moonlight streaks through the window, illuminating his handsome face. "Is the third priority really just your dog?"

"Ah, you noticed that," he says, with a soft laugh—one that says he knows he was caught.

"Yeah. I did."

He sighs. Hesitates. Then finally, he says, "I was going to say...spend time with people I care about. And my dog."

My heart thumps harder. "Why didn't you?"

He's quiet again, his brow furrowed. "It seemed..."

But I think I know the end of that sentence. Or at least I *hope* I do. *You're one of those people.* I don't want him to feel pressured to say that though. So I jump in with a save. "It seemed like too much?"

He takes a beat, and when he answers, his tone is just shy of somber. "Maybe, Skylar. Maybe it seemed like too much."

But too much *what*? Too much to want? Too much too soon?

I don't press.

Not tonight.

It's safer that way.

30

VERY SERIOUS LOOK

FORD

"Ten. I did exactly ten," Corbin gloats to Leah, then tips his chin to me as I do another lateral hop. "He just did thirteen."

Shit. He's right. I did more reps with the medicine ball than Leah wanted.

"I noticed," the conditioning coach says.

Why didn't you stop me? I want to say to Leah. But that's a weak excuse. I can fucking count.

Fact is, I stopped counting.

"Just seeing if you were paying attention," I say to my buddy, deflecting with an even weaker excuse.

Corbin scoffs, eye roll included. "You were off in la-la land."

Leah gives me a stern look—but it's chased with concern as she adds, "I think you were too."

I swallow, then square my shoulders, trying to shrug it off. "Just thinking about the next game," I say, owning it as best I can. "Won't happen again."

But the game was the furthest thing from my mind.

The truth is...I was daydreaming. Goddammit. I was

thinking of the gala. Of Skylar. Picturing undressing her after the event. Letting slim straps fall down her shoulders. Kissing those freckles that drive me mad. Hiking the soft fabric of her gown up to her hips. Fucking her against the wall as neither of us could be bothered to take off all our clothes.

Then making her a late-night snack. *Again.* Taking our dogs for a walk together. Watching her clever brain spin up a social media post for her dog, like she did the other morning when she posted two pics. One was a shot of herself, looking tired and sad, with the caption: *I've been working all day. He hasn't worked since I met him three years ago and doesn't want a job. He expects me to make dinner and clean up every day, doesn't help, and gets upset when I leave the house.*

Followed by a photo of Simon, lounging on a pillow, looking smug, saying *Talk about wrapped around my paw.*

It's seriously cute watching her brain work.

"And now?"

Huh? Oh, shit. Leah's talking to me again.

I snap my focus to her, "And now what?"

If a laugh could say *busted,* hers does. "And now are you thinking about it too? Or did you want to do one hundred Russian twists?"

I have to stop thinking about how every little thing Skylar does is magic. "Yes, ma'am," I say, then drop down to the mat and start twisting my arms side to side while keeping my feet off the floor.

Corbin stretches his arms, preening like a peacock. "I did better than him, right?" he says to Leah.

"Would you like a gold star?"

"As a matter of fact, yes. My daughter loves those," he says, a note of pride in his voice.

I jump on that—partly so the conversation doesn't snap back to my distracted-as-fuck brain. "Better get some for her. Let her know how good you are at working out."

"Yes, I'm sure a—what, fourth grader?—will be so impressed," Leah deadpans.

"As a matter of fact, I was planning on giving her one," Corbin says.

"Then I'd better go get some. Now join Captain Distraction," she tells Corbin, then shifts her gaze to me, "who's busy thinking about the next game."

Her lips twitch in a grin, and she might as well point at her eyes and say *I see you*, because that's exactly what she's doing. But at least she's not saying it out loud.

I'll take that victory as my core burns on the way to one hundred.

When we're done, Corbin heads off to fill his water bottle, and Leah gives me a chin nod. "Everything okay?"

I bristle. "Course. Why wouldn't it be?"

"Just making sure," she says gently, but with a shrewd look in her eyes. "Life has a way of being busy."

It's said like some aphorism Yoda would drop while training Luke. I should probably take it as such. Still, I say evenly, "It can, Leah."

"Finding balance is equally important," she adds, not letting this go. "Are you doing your yoga?"

I snap my fingers. Fuck. She's right. I skipped yoga this morning to make Skylar breakfast, then I had to rush off to practice. "Good point. I'll get back on it."

She gives a crisp nod. "Good. I'll see you next week."

After she leaves, I head to the cardio machines with a renewed focus, Corbin joining me. He's chuckling at something on his phone.

"Anything good?"

"Just a note from Charlotte reminding me what time my game is," he says.

"Your kid's the keeper of your schedule?"

"She's the keeper of everything. She's set up a color-coded calendar for all our activities. I swear I don't know what I did to have a child so organized. But I'm not complaining."

As we claim our ellipticals, he tells me about the way she's even set up digital stickers for completing tasks each day. For both of them. It's sweet the way he talks about his young daughter, and the sticker for *workout completed* she sent him recently. I'm about to pop in earbuds and listen to an audiobook—a new one on improving your focus, which I definitely need—when Corbin gives me a *very serious* look.

He rarely breaks it out, but when he does, it lands. "What's going on? You stressed about the season? You're having a great one."

It's reassuring. Friendly. And totally off-base. But I'm not about to admit I'm too caught up in the woman I'm fake dating, even though it hardly feels fake.

"Nah, I'm all good," I say. "Just an off day."

But as I work out, the lie lingers—like the scent of smelly socks.

And it reminds me of the end of my marriage. The lies my ex told me.

Just took a nap.

Just out with friends.

Just an extra Pilates class today.

All to cover up the fact that she'd been spending time not-cooking with the private chef.

When I hop off the machine, the lies—by omission—I'm telling now gnaw at me.

As I push open the door of the gym, heading out on Fillmore Street, I turn to my friend, my gut still churning. "And the other thing is—this woman? The one I've been..."

I don't even want to say *fake dating*.

But he gives me a reprieve by asking, "Yeah?"

I heave a sigh. "I fucking like her."

Corbin claps me on the shoulder, his smile sympathetic. "Had a feeling." Then he adds, "What are you going to do about it?"

I shrug. "That's a very good question."

* * *

I haven't devised the answer yet, but that night I text her in bed, hunting for another answer.

Ford: Show me.

Skylar: You think I'll bend that easily?

Ford: You love when I give you orders.

Skylar: In bed, Ford. In bed.

Ford: C'mon. Just a peek.

Skylar: Aren't you supposed to be in bed? You have a game tomorrow. Get some sleep.

I've got five more minutes till it's lights out. Told myself I'd focus—and with a game tomorrow, I *need* to focus. That means no sleepover tonight. Too bad being without her is making it harder to fall into the land of nod.

> Ford: But I'll sleep better if you show me a picture of what you'll be wearing to the gala.

>> Skylar: I would never have pegged you as the kid who peeked at his Christmas gifts before Christmas morning. I'm going to be discussing this with Mama Devon at the gala this weekend.

> Ford: I did not peek.

>> Skylar: I don't believe you.

> Ford: I still don't see that picture, Skylar.

I sit in bed and wait. And wait. And wait. My chest is tight. My fingers are busy, scrolling articles I'm not really reading on a news site. A few minutes later, a text arrives —with an image. I open it so fast.

It's not the dress I expected. But it's her, right now, on the other side of the bridge working late at night. Skylar's standing triumphantly in front of the new cabinets at my parents' home, with the words: *Just finished!*

She's wearing a black T-shirt, the neckline sloping just right. On the front, there's a picture of Princess Leia and the words: *A Woman's Place is in the Resistance.*

Her next text reads.

Skylar: I'll wear this.

I don't tease or goad. I simply speak from the heart.

Ford: You look stunning.

At last, I turn off the light and set down my phone. But I miss her. More than I should. And this is getting to be a *problem*.

* * *

I adjust the lapels of my charcoal suit. Run a hand over the purple tie. Adjust the cuffs and give my girl a kiss on the snout.

"Be good, Zamboni," I tell her as I settle her into her dog bed with a new stuffy Skylar gave her—an armadillo with a plastic-free squeaker.

Zamboni bites into it. The noise must be satisfying, because she does it again.

"You love that toy, don't you, girl?"

She answers with another love bite. I ruffle her fur one more time.

After grabbing a gift I picked up for Skylar earlier today, I leave, shutting the door behind me. Outside, I draw a deep, soldiering breath in the crisp autumn evening, then walk down the steps.

It's surreal strolling across the path to the sidewalk

and then doing a one-eighty to head up my neighbor's steps.

My heart is beating so fast, I feel like a teenager on his way to the prom. My palms are sweating. I tug at the tie. Skylar told me not to wear yellow, so I listened.

Before I knock, though, I briefly consider playing one of my focus games.

Hell, I need it with my skyrocketing pulse. But I'm not about to break out my phone on the porch and start playing a game just so I can handle a damn date to a gala.

I play professional sports at the highest level—I can get my nerves in check.

Briefly, I picture navigating the penguin through the maze. Even though I'm not actually doing it, the muscle memory and the mind memory somehow settle my nerves.

I square my shoulders and knock.

The first time I met Skylar, she was wearing a floral bathrobe, her jammies underneath covered in martini glasses, and gardening boots.

When she opens the door now, she's dressed to the nines. I grab onto the doorframe—because if I don't, I'll fall flat on my ass.

I let out a low whistle of appreciation. "Holy shit."

I didn't know what to expect. I don't really think about dresses. But instantly I know: this is *so her.*

She's wearing some kind of 1920s flapper dress in a shade of yellow so soft, so subtle, it's like the color of a lemon cookie.

And I want to take a bite.

Her shoes are pale gold, I think, with a thin strap down the top of her foot. I can't wait to undo them later, then press a kiss to her ankle. My gaze roams up her legs, taking in strong calves peeking out, then the dress.

I'm not even sure what's happening with it, but it's got floral embroidery and tiny see-through sleeves, and it falls beautifully on her body.

She juts out a hip and says, "What do you think? Can I be your lucky color?"

Goosebumps erupt across my skin. *Goosebumps.* When was the last time I felt goosebumps?

Did I ever feel this way with Brittany?

But she's the last person I ever want to think of, so I dropkick thoughts of her to the curb as I take in Skylar, with glossy lips, long eyelashes, and auburn hair falling in soft waves, styled like she's stepped out of *The Great Gatsby.*

I can't even stand how beautiful she is. "You are definitely my lucky color."

She plucks at the fabric. "Can you believe I found this at Champagne Taste?"

I have no idea what that is, but I'm guessing it's a thrift shop. So I just say, "Yes, I can. Because you find everything."

Including...me.

Before I say that, I thrust out the box, blinking and still trying to take in this vision in front of me.

She flicks it open and gasps. "Ford," she says softly, reverently.

She told me she was wearing a vintage dress, so I went to a jewelry shop and asked for a matching necklace. A vintage choker with a blue topaz pendant.

"It's beautiful," she says, then lifts her hair, her bright, big eyes full of vulnerability as she says, "Put it on me."

My fingers are normally steady. They're supposed to be. But I slip undoing it.

My mouth is dry, and my voice is hoarse as I say, "Turn around."

She complies, hair piled into her hands, her summertime scent drifting under my nose and intoxicating me. I loop the necklace around her neck, willing my heart to settle, and I manage to clasp it without making a fool of myself.

But I can only be so strong. I lean in, press a decadent kiss to the back of her neck, and say, "You're incredible."

It's easier than saying *I'm falling for you.*

Maybe soon, I'll have the guts to say that. For now, I take her hand, and we go.

* * *

When we arrive at the nearby hotel, we walk through the sleek lobby, with a modern waterfall structure set against a black stone wall. Mirrored panels reflect opulent chandeliers above. I'm holding Skylar's hand the whole time, running my thumb between her fingers, unable to stop touching her.

This is a fake date. For my mother. To ward off hungry matchmakers—from the Cordelia Harringtons, Kahlia Mayamis, and Sunil Bakshis who were exhausting Mom with date offers.

But fending off romantic setups feels like a distant reason for this date, one born of another era. As I walk toward the ballroom with Skylar, nothing about us feels fake. There's no ruse. There's no facade. There's only this...new reality.

"Thanks for coming to this. Mom appreciates it," I say. But that's not the reason I'm saying it.

Skylar must know it, too, because she says, "I like her, but I don't think that's why you want me here."

Ah, fuck. She can see right through me. Her honesty excites me. And steadies me. It does something warm to my heart. "You are right," I say. "And I know they're your favorite words."

"They are," she says with a happy shrug.

I give her a quick kiss, then walk in, buoyed by the same kind of can't-lose attitude I carry with me every damn time I hit the ice for a game.

As servers weave through a glittery crowd, offering trays of caprese-stuffed mushrooms and cranberry baked brie bites along with flutes of champagne, I nudge Skylar. "I know you like champagne," I whisper.

"I know *you* like champagne," she counters.

"On you," I say, stopping to grab two flutes and thank a server.

In the middle of the ballroom, with a string quartet in the corner playing pop tunes, I hold up my flute in a toast.

"To..." I stop before I say *fake dates*. Because fuck it. Just fuck it. "To real dates."

A smile ignites on her beautiful face. "Real dates, Ford Devon? You sure about that?" she asks with a sassy challenge.

"Positive," I say, then I kiss off her lip gloss. When I let go, I tip back the flute and drink some, like the very satisfied man I am. Champagne has never tasted better.

She does the same, then adds, "Good. Me too."

That's it. That's all. And maybe it's just that easy—moving on from the past, and the hurts, and the things you're afraid of.

Sometimes you just...let them go, one fall evening when your next-door neighbor wears your lucky color.

But as much as I want to spend the night in this bubble with her, I know we're here to put on a show—a show that hardly feels like one anymore.

Still, I scan the crowd for my mother. I spot her easily in the middle of the room, holding court with some donors, and we make our way to her.

She's elegant and in charge, but thoughtful too, clearly listening as others chat. When I reach her, she gives me a mama bear hug, then says, "This is my son and his new girlfriend, who I might even like better than I do him."

I roll my eyes at the mom dig, then introduce my girlfriend to all the people who allegedly wanted to set me up.

I'm not sure if Skylar *is* my girlfriend. But I am sure this isn't fake for either one of us anymore.

We stay and make small talk, and as some of the donors chat with Skylar and ask questions about her business—which, of course, dovetails perfectly with my mom's charity to bring recycling initiatives everywhere—she's asked for her info for possible work.

Skylar might gain referrals. That's an outcome I didn't see coming, but it's one I love.

As Skylar chats with Kahlia about the work she does, my mother tugs me aside, whispering, "You should marry her."

I nearly spit out my champagne. "Mom."

"What? She's so much better for you than your ex. I knew it from the start. A mother just knows these things," she says, then sails off to mingle with another donor.

Right as Skylar returns to me.

We've done our job for the night, but the night is young—and it's time to simply enjoy the gala.

We walk away from the crowds, heading for the bar, when I see a mirage. *That can't be. Why is she here?* Like a ghost I didn't summon, my ex-wife strides over in a jet-black dress that brushes the floor, earrings glittering, head tilted with a very curious look on her face.

She locks eyes on me. Then on Skylar.

I grip Skylar's hand tighter, one thought taking up all the space in my brain—*she's not going to ruin our night.*

31

STURDIER THAN A SUITCASE

SKYLAR

Before she even introduces herself, I know who she is. I see it in her gaze. In the possessive way her pretty brown eyes—of course she's pretty, but I don't care—roam up and down him.

"Ford, so good to see you," she says, with a smile so falsely sweet it makes my teeth hurt.

"Brittany," he says tightly, giving a crisp nod.

But how is he really feeling? What is he thinking? I wish I knew. Does she want to win him back? Fuck her. Not going to happen, lady. Not today. Not on my watch.

Before he can ask why she's here, Brittany answers the unspoken question. "I've become a big supporter of your mother's charity. I wondered if she'd told you." She bats her lashes.

Sucking up to his mother? I'm ready to take off my earrings. Instead, I turn to Ford and mouth privately, "*Hold my smoothie.*"

Then I turn to Brittany. "That's funny. I've had a lot of conversations with Maggie Devon, and she didn't say a thing about that."

Ford squeezes my hand, and I feel the touch as a *thank you.*

Brittany whips her head toward me so fast it gives me whiplash. "You must be Skylar," she says, eyes wide and smile bright.

Wait. She knows who I am?

"Yes, I am," I say, trying to keep it cool, but I'm definitely thrown off. The mother-charity opening line wasn't her real intention?

"I'm actually starting a new line of upcycled furniture, and I thought it would be such a fun thing for us to talk about!"

Ford scoffs. "You're here to suck up to my girlfriend?"

I love his protective side—truly, I do. But I'm also so damn curious about her furniture I can't help myself. Nosy by nature wins. "I'd love to hear about it," I say.

Ford shoots me a *what the hell* look. But I give him one right back that says *Trust me.*

"I was really hoping we could chat," Brittany says, offering her hand.

I take it. Her handshake is limp. I bet her ideas will be too.

"I'm already envisioning ways we can potentially partner, since we're both in the sustainability space. I just absolutely love what you're doing," she says, sounding exactly like the kind of fake-bubbly person who would do...exactly what she's doing.

"Oh, right. Of course. Because we have so much in common," I say, egging her on.

"Exactly! When I heard you two were a couple, I immediately thought we could work together. Women supporting women, eco-friendly entrepreneurship—it's so important. That's why I thought it'd be great if I could develop a partnership with you."

"Tell me more," I say, dripping with faux enthusiasm. "Tell me all about what you're designing."

She rolls her lips like she's holding in all her excitement. "I'm designing a line of furniture made from old suitcases!"

Did she really just say that? "Suitcases?" I blink. "Like...actual luggage?"

"Isn't it brilliant? Just think about it—so many suitcases wind up in landfills. But instead of throwing them away, we can turn them into furniture. Can't you just imagine an entire house full of couches that used to be suitcases? And we'd be saving the planet together."

"That's...incredible to envision," I say, smiling like I mean it.

"I'm so glad you're excited! Maybe we could set a time to meet and talk more?"

"Why don't you have your people call my people?"

She claps like an overeager cheerleader. "I'm totally going to do that! Would you give me your number?"

"Of course, of course," I say, then shrug apologetically. "I don't have my phone with me right now, but go ahead and take my number and text me. I'll answer it later."

Ford knits his brow. Then I rattle off a number that Ford will instantly know is fake. He snickers as Brittany taps it into her phone.

"I can't wait to talk more, Skylar," she says.

"I can't wait for you to roll out your line of suitcase furniture," I add with a sugary smile.

"Yay! Me too." She turns to Ford. "You look different," she says, tilting her head. "But I can't quite figure out what it is."

Ford doesn't even pause. "I'm happier, Brittany." Then once more, for good measure, he says, "I'm happier."

My heart soars. Last week, I'm pretty sure I started letting go of my worries about getting involved with a client and a neighbor. Now, with that lovely word— *happier*—I can feel myself letting go of the bigger one.

The one that has lived inside me.

Without a second look at his ex, Ford drops a kiss on my cheek and says, "Let's go, sweetheart."

I wave goodbye. "Can't wait to see the chairs made out of carry-ons."

And soon, we sail off into the night.

* * *

The second our dogs are let back into my place, Ford is on me. He's cupping my cheeks and devouring my mouth. No —he's claiming me, kissing me so thoroughly, my head spins. Everything's a beautiful blur. My body's awash in lust. In happiness. In him.

His tongue tangles with mine, then he nips the corner of my mouth and moves down my throat, murmuring praise. *So pretty. So beautiful. Want you so much.*

His words hit differently this time.

The need in them.

When he looks up, he grabs my chin. "I had this fantasy of fucking you up against the wall. Of you in some...dress. Of us...just—" His words rasp, like he can barely get them out in the right order. Then he picks me up, tosses me over his shoulder, and carries me to the couch.

It's not made out of suitcases. But it's sturdy enough to survive this man manhandling me. When he sets me down, he makes sure I'm straddling his lap and the very hard, very insistent ridge of his erection.

I shudder at the feel of him. Then he's kissing me again, blazing a trail of open-mouthed caresses down my neck till he reaches the top of the bodice. The whole time he's inching up my skirt, sliding the material along my legs, then bunching it at my waist.

When my panties are revealed, he lets out a feral groan. "Fuck, baby. You're too much."

They're pale yellow. "Want to get lucky?" I ask playfully.

He doesn't smile—he just shakes his head, maybe in amazement, and says, "I *am* lucky. I'm so lucky I met you."

My heart feels like the sun is shining from inside me. "I feel the same," I say, my voice wobbly with emotion.

"Yeah?"

"I really do," I say, my throat tightening as nerves wing through me along with all my deep-seated fears. Fears of being second best. Fears of being left behind. But he's only given me reason to believe I'm one of his priorities.

And it's a feeling I relish now.

So much that I say, "I'm on protection, and I've been tested. Negative."

He goes quiet for a moment, his blue eyes flickering with passion and promise. "Me too," he says, blowing out a weighty breath. "I want to feel you with nothing between us."

Hastily, I tug at his pants, undo his tie, and unbutton his shirt as he maneuvers off my panties, and in no time his hard, throbbing cock is free and beautifully ready for me.

Just like I'm ready for him.

I sink down on him, my eyes falling closed, my breath stuttering, and my world narrowing to just him and me.

"Skylar," he groans, my name said like he cherishes me.

And that's how he fucks me.

With a white-hot need and a deep, tender passion. He holds me tight, guides me up and down, and kisses me fiercely as I ride his cock until we're both falling apart.

Later, we're in bed, and he says, "It was good to see Brittany tonight."

I tense. "Um, why?"

"Because it's good to know when your past is truly behind you."

My heart's beating outside my body. "It is. It really is."

Then he kisses me like I'm his future.

32

OUCH

FORD

Before I head to the game, I slip over to Skylar's house. "I'm leaving in fifteen minutes. But I got you this." I hand her a new jersey—one of mine. "I wanted you to have a second one. You need two."

The implication had better be clear—*you are coming to as many of my games as you can.*

"I sure do." She holds it up against her chest, modeling it with a sexy sway of her hips. The jersey falls to mid-thigh. She'll swim in my number fourteen.

"I want you to wear *mine*," I add.

She shoots me a sly look. "But should I still wear undies? It's kind of like a dress. You want access?"

I growl. "You'd better wear undies. So I can rip them off you later."

"Well, if you insist."

"I do."

I plant a searing kiss on those sweet, glossy lips. She tastes so damn good. "It's a good luck kiss," I say.

She tugs at the tie I'm wearing, wrapping a fist around

it and holding me in place. "Then I'd better give you another. You should have double the luck."

I happily take another kiss from her, my head swimming with endorphins, my body supercharged with lust.

I feel like a goddamn superhero thanks to this woman, to her faith, her spirit, her bold confidence, and her delightful chaos. I could lift the fucking car. I am so crazy for her. But I've got to get to the game. I tear myself away. Before I head down the steps, I wheel around. "Oh, Mom said next week works for her for the after-episode of your podcast. Where you're going to live stream and show everybody how the house looks."

"Perfect. Those do so well," she says.

"Good. You deserve it," I say. She's already gained a new client from the gala. I'm so damn proud of her and the way business is growing for her. But now, it's time for me to get in the zone. I hop in my car and head over to the arena for family night.

* * *

Two hours later, Skylar's there on the ice right next to me as the Sea Dogs pose for photos for our social media—the players and their partners. Wesley's here with Josie. Max with Everly. Asher with Maeve. Miles with Leighton. Tyler with Sabrina. And now, this time around, Skylar's here with me and everything feels right in the world.

Once the photos are taken, I return to the locker room with the guys and go through the motions of getting ready for the game. This time, though, is different. This time she's here as mine for real. Knowing I'm playing for her is a whole new feeling. One I want to hold on to for the rest of the season.

As I stretch on the ice, I visualize the game. The way I'll have to be on my toes, looking behind me, playing ruthlessly.

Vancouver has been one of our toughest opponents. Canadians don't fuck around when it comes to hockey. Their defense is stacked with big guys, like Long Neck John, a six-foot-seven-inch D-man with a neck like a giraffe's and shoulders like a tank's. He sees every play and plows down anyone who gets in his way.

In short, I plan to evade him.

That's easy enough in the first period. I'm faster and smoother. I'm flying down the ice. Hell, I feel like I've got wings. I lose him every time he comes near me. Nine minutes into the first period, I'm guiding that puck down the ice, lifting my stick, then sending it right into Vancouver's net.

Yes, fucking yes.

It's early and I've already put a point on the board. I can't resist. I spin around, turn toward center ice, and tip my forehead toward the gorgeous redhead in my number who's cheering for me. I'm subtle enough, but I give her a look and a smile that says, *"That one's for you."*

I head over to the boards and hop over it for the line change.

On the bench, Tyler gives me a fist bump and I knock right back. I grab my water bottle, down some, and blow out a breath, feeling pretty, *pretty* good. All the conditioning, all the time with Leah, all the yoga, all the medicine balls, all the box squats, all the kale smoothies, all the Penguin Mazes and River Rangers, and more than a decade in the pros is paying off.

I feel loose and easy still in the second period, even

though Long Neck John keeps breathing down *my* neck. But I strip the puck from him on a rebound, briefly glancing toward center ice again. The thought that she's watching me, cheering for me, is electrifying. I'm playing for my woman for real. Maybe soon, I'll blow her a kiss and the whole world will know that this guy, this undrafted guy, has made it to the top—not just in hockey but in life.

When I skate behind the net, Long Neck John swipes the puck from me.

Shit.

I didn't even see him coming.

All of a sudden, we're jostling for the puck, with Falcon and Bryant flanking me. I've got to get it back. It was my fault I lost track of it. I was thinking of...her.

Must focus like it's my fucking life.

I jab at the puck in the fray, snagging it once more when Long Neck John slams into my shoulder. The hit sends me barreling right into the boards, my torso smashing against them. It's like a car rear-ended me. My teeth clench, my bones rattle, and my ribs scream as I wipe out, stumbling backward onto the ice.

I can barely catch my breath. Pain lances through me. My abdomen is on fire. I try to breathe, but I can't. She's out there though. Mere feet away in the stands. I can't get distracted by her again. Or by thoughts of her. And I don't want her to see me like this. *Hurt.*

I glance at the action—Bryant's wrestled the puck from Long Neck John, so I scramble, getting back on my skates and racing after them...even though everything screams inside me. My ribs feel like they're poking through my goddamn abdomen. They're shouting at me, but I ignore the noise, chasing Vancouver, chasing the puck, chasing anything until Vancouver scores. I curse as I try to hop over the boards.

"You okay, man?" Tyler asks.

I nod. "Yeah," I grit out as I make it over, more gingerly than usual.

"You sure?" he asks again.

I grit my teeth as another sharp, stinging wave radiates through my abs. Is that Commitment? Or Discipline? I don't even know. Everything is a painful blur. I lower my face. I don't want Skylar to worry. I can't have her thinking I'm failing—then she'll replace me.

You're failing because of her.

I really need my thoughts to shut the hell up. I try to clear my head. To extradite all these irritating ideas racing through my mind.

A hand lands on my shoulder. "Hey, buddy, we need to check you out."

It's the team medic.

"I'm fine," I say, waving her off.

"No, you're not."

"I am," I say, then raise my face. "Score's tied. I'm fine."

"We need to check you out," she says, more forceful this time.

Leaving now feels like giving up. I don't give up. I'm a grinder. I fight it out till the bitter end.

But one more shooting pain—one I can't fight—and I give in, leaving the game. I don't look Skylar's way as I go.

* * *

"I'm fine," I insist, agitated. The clock is ticking. I need to get back out there with my team. "I'm really okay."

In the athletic trainer's room, Doctor Booker gives me

a funny look. I'm on the exam table in my shorts, my jersey and my lucky—no, unlucky—T-shirt off.

She's a no-nonsense woman with short, coiled hair and light brown skin. "You're not fine, Devon."

"I am," I say, but I hiss in a breath. Damn, breathing hurts.

"I'm giving you ibuprofen. You're going to go home. You're going to rest and not do anything to aggravate the pain. You'll ice it tonight," she says.

"Fine," I grumble. "But tomorrow I can work out."

She laughs, and it's a very doubtful sound. I don't like it one bit. "No, you're going to rest. Tomorrow too."

Fine. We don't have a game tomorrow, so that's not a problem. But we do have a game in two days. She hasn't said anything about that, so I might as well let her know I plan to be in the lineup. "I'll be ready to play against Montreal."

She sighs heavily and crosses her arms. "You need at least a week's worth of rest. Your ribs are bruised. They need time to heal. You're going to apply ice packs to the injured area for ten to twenty minutes at a time, several times a day. It'll help reduce the swelling. You're going to take some over-the-counter pain medication. And if you feel like you're going to cough, hold a pillow against your ribs. It will lessen the pain."

But all I can hear is *at least a week*. And *at least a week* can turn into two. I haven't been injured in years. I played every single game last year, and the year before. I'm the healthiest guy on the team. That's—no. *No*. "That just doesn't work," I say, digging my heels in.

"You'll be back on the ice soon," she says. "It'll go by before you know it. Do you have anyone who can drive you home tonight?"

I drag a hand down my face. Close my eyes. I hate asking for help. I don't want to. My team is going to go on without me, and I'm going to go home because...I didn't pay attention on the ice. My mind was hanging out in my heart, and I was thinking of a woman.

Now I have to ask her for help. When I'm...broken.

* * *

Skylar breathes out a relieved but upbeat breath after she parks the car outside our homes. "Whew. I did it. See? I'm not a bad driver," she says, and she's been chatting nonstop on the drive home, clearly trying to make me feel better. To distract me from the pain.

I don't deserve that either.

I wince and push open the passenger door just as she scurries around the back of the car and offers an arm. I wave her off, frowning. "I'm fine."

"You're injured."

That word rankles me. Not quite like *divorced* did, but it's close. She tries again to help me, but I shrug off her hand on my arm. "I can walk. I just wasn't supposed to drive."

"You're a grouchy man, but I'm still going to help you get inside," she says, flashing a smile and clearly trying to make light of my mood.

"I don't need help." I grunt.

"You do, Ford," she says, insistent and strong.

But I don't want it. Even though everything hurts as I walk up the steps, punch in the code, and head into my house where Zamboni bounds over to me. Her tail wags as she presses close, whimpering her hellos.

"Shit," I mutter.

I need to walk her with my bruised ribs, and my chest is aching.

"I'll take her out," Skylar says before I can even ask.

"Thanks," I say, guilt shooting through me along with the pain. As she leaves with the dog, I grin and bear it over to the fridge, grab an ice pack, and gently lower myself to the couch. Those polar plunges have come in handy—this ice is nothing.

Except five minutes later, my ribs feel frozen. Skylar returns with Zamboni, then hustles over to me. My dog comes, too, whimpering and nosing me. I pet her. "I'm okay, girl," I say.

Skylar side-eyes me. "You're not."

I don't look at her. I can't. It hurts too much.

She sits on the end of the couch and gently sets a hand on my shin, rubbing slow circles. "What can I do for you?"

She's so caring. So giving. But all I can think is how I want to be able to finish the season on my terms. That was my goal—to finish what I started when I was twenty-four and nobody wanted to take a chance on me. To play out the rest of the year. What if this injury leads to another? What if I don't heal right?

How can I recover when I'm so distracted that I lose sight of the puck?

This isn't anybody else's fault but mine. My head started wandering to her just like it did at training with Leah and Corbin. These last few weeks, it's always wandering to her.

The more that happens, the less I can focus on the job. I'm going to bring down the team. They're going to bench me before I even finish out the year.

What will my legacy be then?

I'll just be some guy who stayed beyond his prime. A

player who hobbled out onto the ice when he should've retired.

I scrub a hand across my jaw. The last thing I want is to hurt the woman I'm absolutely falling madly for. But now I'm injured, and it's my own fault.

Love makes you annoyingly vulnerable. I'm better off white-knuckling it myself.

This woman? This caring, giving, kind, considerate woman who's looking after me, who's taking care of my dog? This woman who bought a toy for my dog? Who puts up with all of my mom's quirks? Who stood up for me in front of my ex?

She deserves better than a guy who'll get distracted on the job. A guy who gets distracted isn't dependable.

"Skylar," I say heavily.

In a heartbeat, tension radiates from her, and everything must be obvious from my voice.

"Yes?"

I breathe out. Breathe in. Let the pain from my ribs shoot through me. "I made a promise to go out on my own terms. To not let my team down. Tonight, I let them down because I was distracted."

Her brow furrows. Her voice is filled with concern as she asks, "How were you distracted?"

I swallow past the guilt. "Because I was looking at you. I was thinking of you. I can't stop thinking about you." The words should be positive, but it feels like I'm wrenching up my guts, and *that's the problem.* I can't manage all of these feelings and deliver on my top priority. *My team.* "But the thing is, I think about you so much... I can't concentrate on hockey."

She nods a few times, absorbing my meaning. "You

really can't?" she asks carefully, perhaps making sure I mean what I'm saying.

"Yeah. I think we should take a—" I wince. My ribs ache. I brace my arm around them, coughing, because I hate what I'm about to say. She grabs a pillow and hands it to me. I hold it tight as she says what I can't.

"A break?" Her voice sounds like it's breaking too, and I grab hold of the lifeline she's giving me.

"Yeah." But I don't want to be a complete dick. "But you can still—you can still shoot the podcast at my mom's."

She gives me a look of disbelief. I can't believe I said it either. But the damage is done, so when she says a harsh, "Thanks," I just mutter, "You're welcome."

And I don't stop her when she leaves.

Instead, I pet my dog.

Because Zamboni stays. No matter what.

33

THE FULL TONGUE TREATMENT
SKYLAR

I'm starfished on the living room carpet, bathrobe flared open, trying futilely to reach for my coffee cup when I hear it.

A squawking comes from the mudroom window. Sounds a little like a *roh-roh-roh*.

Rolling listlessly to my side, I face Simon. "Can you go check?"

He wags his tail.

"It might be the great blue heron."

His tail thumps faster. He tilts his head, his floppy ears sweeping the hardwood.

"Do it," I urge, nodding toward him. "I have faith in you."

He slides over to me on his belly and drags his tongue down my face. I squeeze my eyes closed, like that's enough to fend off the full tongue treatment. "Seriously. You're my only hope. Do it and let me know."

He swipes my other cheek.

I open my eyes, then lift my right arm, grunting. Or is that a whimper? Maybe it's both. "Ungh. Ungh." I slump back down, my shoulder smacking the wood. "I can't. Go on without me."

Simon bolts to attention, clambering onto my chest. "Seriously. Save yourself," I tell him, then flail my arms around. "Your food is in the pantry. I'll let Mabel and Trevyn know."

The squawking grows louder. Simon barks, then licks more furiously. I fling a hand over my eyes. "I can't. I'm too sad."

It's been thirty-six hours since I was dumped. And dumped rudely, with a casual *you can still do your podcast* send-off.

"I knew I hated him for a reason," I mutter, but inside I'm aching. I didn't even get a chance to argue with Ford about the split. To fight for him, and for us. He was so... certain in his stupid nobility.

I death-moan again. That earns me more licks.

"I don't want to get up," I whimper. The thought of answering Mabel's messages is too much. The prospect of seeing Ford's mom in a couple days for a wrap-up video call—*her* words—is horrifying. Meeting with a new client the day after that is unthinkable.

The slamming of a car door from the sidewalk catches Simon's attention, and he shoots off me, scurrying on determined little Doxie legs to the front door, barking his head off.

"Shit," I mutter, then push up. What if it's Ford, and he's coming up the steps because he forgot...I don't know...a lucky tie? Did he leave something here? I already gave away the mug I let him use for coffee—the one his strong hands wrapped around the other morning. Does he want the necklace back? The rat bastard! I'm going to sell that necklace so hard. Even if I only get five bucks for it, I'll use that five bucks, buy a kale smoothie, and pour it on his porch.

Ugh.

That sounds like too much effort. I try again to reach for the coffee, this time forcing myself to sit up.

But Simon's still barking.

I swear, if Ford comes to the door while I'm in a state of feeling sorry for myself, I will pee on a plant and leave it on his porch.

I down the rest of the lukewarm swill and crawl to the front of the house. When I reach the Captain of Barking, I peer out the front window like a Peeping Tom and then duck down, all the hair on my arms standing on end.

It's Ford, tapping on his phone, standing next to a white Prius, looking all put together in khakis and a polo that hugs his strong arms. I hate them too.

But whose car is that? Brittany's? Someone else's?

The car pulls away, and he walks to his house, his lips in a straight line and his jaw set hard.

Oh. Did he just take a Lyft somewhere? To the doctor? That should have been *me* taking him—the stubborn, stoic jerk. I swipe at my eyes, my heart hurting as I look at the man I was falling in love with as he walks up the steps, wincing once, but not even looking my way. Of course. I'm second best. To hockey.

But when he reaches the top step, his gaze drifts left... and is he checking out my porch? Probably trying to avoid me. His peripheral vision surely isn't good enough to see inside the window while I stare furtively at him.

I duck down when I hear the squawk again.

Well, I'm already halfway up. I drag myself to my feet, grab my opera glasses from the hallway table, and trudge to the mudroom, then poke my head out of the catio. Cleo's lounging on her corner shelf, but she deigns to glance my way, shooting me a look that says I'm fashion roadkill. Like I didn't already know that.

I scan for the heron, and my shoulders sag. "Are you kidding me?"

He was here, and now he's flying away.

Fitting.

* * *

"No. Just no. You do not look good in a bathrobe."

That's Trevyn's declaration as he shuts the door behind him and Mabel the next day.

"Well, you're not supposed to be here," I say defiantly, as I tie the sash of my robe tighter. At least I changed out of yesterday's robe.

He struts in with his Labrador mix, Barbara-dor, who's looking pretty sassy with a new pink rhinestone collar. Simon wraps himself around her legs since they've been friends for a while.

"Can I let them out in the backyard?" Trevyn asks.

"Now you're asking my permission for something? You showed up unannounced."

"Sweetheart," he says. "You've barely responded to any texts. This is a welfare check."

"Feels like an intervention."

Mabel gives a guilty-as-charged smile. "If you call friendship an intervention, then yes. Yes, it is."

I wave to the back porch. "I'm not going to sit out there though. Ford might see me, and that is not happening. I *almost* ran into him yesterday. Also, Simon's too little to be in the backyard by himself."

"Let me just take them outside real quick, and then we'll let them sit on the back porch and sunbathe."

I sigh but relent, because that is a really good idea. There's little a dog likes more than a sunbath. As Trevyn heads outside—protecting me from the possibility of running into Ford—I turn to Mabel. "I guess my brother was right. It really is messy to get involved with your neighbor. You can't even leave your home. I mean, imagine what it's going to be like when I'm literally living inside here for the rest of my life."

Mabel gives me a sympathetic look. "You have really entered the dramatic phase, haven't you?"

"Yes, and I'm still in the bathrobe phase, so you can see why this is a problem."

"I'm pretty sure you're always in your bathrobe phase," she says, then heads to the kitchen table and pulls out a chair, patting it for me. "I think I know what you need."

I slump down in the offered seat. "What do I need? And don't say the podcast—I don't know if I have the energy to do that."

Even though it usually energizes me—talking about design hacks.

As Trevyn comes back inside, Mabel announces, "We need to redecorate."

I go still, then slowly—like I'm transfixed—I bring a hand to my heart. "Don't tempt me with something so beautiful," I whisper.

"Something simple. A little forgotten corner of your brother's place—maybe the mudroom. We can spruce it up with a mirror. Like a vintage mirror."

I gasp. "You're a witch, teasing me with a vintage mirror."

"We know you love them," says Trevyn, getting into the goading.

"I do. Like Emma Thompson loves Joni Mitchell in *Love Actually*."

"Ain't no love like that," Mabel says.

Trevyn moves behind me and squeezes my shoulders, whispering seductively, "We could even hang a reclaimed chandelier somewhere in the house."

I clasp my hand over my mouth, then whisper reverently through my fingers. "Healing begins with lighting. And a good mirror."

Mabel reaches for my hand, her big eyes full of kindness as she says, "And a shower."

Five hours later, Simon and Barbara-dor are playing tug-of-war with a stuffed alligator, and I'm wiping clean with a rag a gorgeous secondhand Turkish handcrafted tiled decorative mirror from Reflective Showroom that Amika set aside for me when I called her earlier. Post-shower, of course.

I stand back to admire it, Mabel by my side. "It makes the mudroom look bigger," I say, smiling with pride. "Why didn't I think of this sooner? Mirrors always make rooms look bigger."

"It looks seriously good," Mabel says approvingly.

"So good I'm taking a picture, and you're adding it to your socials," Leighton instructs, since Mabel enlisted her to join us. "We can't let your marketing suffer just because you're deep in your feels."

My heart squeezes for them. I love the way they're thinking of me even when I can't think of anything but how much I'm still hurting over missing that jackass. But with them, I don't feel second best.

"I love you all. So much," I say, as Trevyn adjusts the newly acquired French chandelier behind us, then climbs down the steps of the ladder.

"Ta-da," he says, gesturing to the antique that looks like it belongs in a French farmhouse. It was missing a few teardrops, but I fixed it quickly. This girl is handy.

"I love it too," I say, and I'm way up in my feels now, because I stare at my friends, gathering them all close, "but not as much as I love all of you."

They come in for a hug, and it feels like maybe I'm starting to outrun the hurt. Since they're reminding me that I can be first...for me.

34

THE DOUBLE AMBUSH

FORD

I love doing yoga in the living room instead of the porch.

Said no one ever.

But like I could go out there now. I don't need the temptation of seeing Skylar. Or the fucking embarrassment of her seeing me like this.

In a goddamn child's pose.

Since it's practically the only yoga pose I can do right now with my broken, pathetic, flimsy-ass ribs.

Fine, they're not broken. But...feels like they are.

I stretch out my arms in front of me on the yellow mat in the living room while Zamboni circles me, nudges my hair, then slides next to me, slinking into a proper downward dog with utter ease. "Are you trying to make me jealous? Because it's working."

She wags her tail, still happy to see me, even though I'm not sure I deserve nice things.

I am sure of this—my vaunted discipline is long gone. I don't even fight the impulse to look for Skylar. I turn to peer out the sliding glass doors. Not that I can see her from inside. I just wish I could, even though I don't want her to see me as I move into cat-cow.

Four days after injuring my ribs, and I'm feeling better. The pain's no longer persistent. The ice is doing its job. Time is working its magic.

But kale smoothies don't taste as good as they used to.

After I finish the weakest of weak yoga sessions, I plod past the kitchen, glancing at the remains of my smoothie, only half-drunk, in a to-go cup that had nowhere to go.

Even with fresh-picked kale from the farmers' market that I had delivered, my morning pick-me-up still tasted like disappointment—my disappointment in myself.

The pile of dishes in the sink is teeteringly high. Huh. I wonder how many more plates till it crumbles? Maybe it'll topple onto the unwashed blender.

Later. I'll deal with it later.

I pop in my earbuds and hunt for my newest audio-book—the one on focus that Hannah sent me. I've been trying to get through it for more than a week now. I should be able to get through it. I have nothing but time as I recuperate from a stupid, self-inflicted injury.

This is all my dumbass fault, but as I find myself wandering aimlessly up the stairs and through my bedroom, I have no clue what the narrator just said about ways to improve your attention in the present moment.

"Fuck me," I mutter as I stare at the second-floor deck.

And the hot tub.

And the temptation.

I've never been good at resisting my neighbor. Not sure I can stop now with my self-control having vacated the premises. Like some master puppeteer is controlling me, I turn on the tub, and minutes later I don't even bother stripping off my yoga shorts. I step into the hot tub with them on.

I won't watch her. Seeing her will only make me want what I can't have.

The woman I fell in love with.

The woman I need to stop thinking about.

I try again to focus on the moment—the warm water, the bubbles surrounding me, the soothing sound of the jets. But the hot tub doesn't ease the lingering sting in my ribs, or the ache in my heart.

And, evidently, I possess zero focus. Because before I know it, thirty minutes have passed and I've spent the whole time staring forlornly at my neighbor's kitchen windows, desperate for a glimpse of her.

But there hasn't been one. I don't deserve it anyway. I close my eyes, and somehow, I fall asleep in the hot tub.

I wake up groggy, in tepid water, to the sound of laughter.

I peek over the edge and freeze up. Skylar's on the porch, her red hair pulled into a messy bun, dancing with the dog and her podcast friends. Pretty sure I saw them arrive yesterday, too, in Trevyn's car. Not that I've been staring out the windows like a pathetic creeper. Watching everything going on. Hoping for a glimpse.

I grit my teeth, jealousy thrashing inside me that I'm not the reason she's having a dance party. Then guilt strides in next. I shouldn't be butt-hurt that she's having fun. *Two days in a row*. I should be happy for her.

But as the song ends and she heads inside, my heart plummets like the stock market on a bad news day.

Here I am, sitting in a lukewarm vat in my shorts, stealing a glimpse of my neighbor—who I broke up with.

I might have pulled the trigger, but she's the one

moving on. I need to move on too. I made my choice—to focus on my career. Now I need to do just that.

My phone buzzes with a message, and I grab the device. What if it's her? My pulse sprints for the first time in days, then slows when I read it.

> Mom: Did you know that the flowers on your front porch need water? The plants too.

What? How would she know? I start to reply when another message lands. This one is from my sister.

> Hannah: Did you know that brothers who get book recommendations from sisters and then do dumb things don't deserve recommendations from sisters?

Hold on. What the hell is happening with this ambush from the women? My fingers fly as I try to reply to...well, both of them.

> Mom: Did you know that Zamboni is happy to see me?

I pop out of the tub so fast. Of course Mom would fly down to give me a piece of her mind. I change into sweats and a T-shirt, then rush down the stairs, checking to see if I've missed any other messages from her.

As I scroll through our thread, I arrive at the bottom of the steps, where my traitorous dog is waiting hopefully by the door, tail wagging.

As I open the door, I metaphorically duck, sure she'll be lobbing mom-bombs with her bare hands the second she sees me.

"Ford, I can't believe you made me come down here. I'm nearly done packing up my good china," she says with an annoyed huff.

"Why don't you have someone pack it for you?" I ask, then instantly regret it. Of course she's not going to let anyone touch her good china.

She gives me a dismissive wave of her hand. "Let's pretend you didn't ask me that."

"Fair enough," I say as she sweeps in and shuts the door. I scratch my head. "Also, how did I *make* you come down here? I didn't see any messages from you saying you wanted to talk. Or warning me that you were coming."

Not that she'd ask for permission, but still, this is out of the blue, even for her.

With a pfft, she whisks past me. "I didn't bother to send one. Sometimes an ambush is what you need."

I arch a brow. "What's going on?"

She strides over to the couch, sits down, and arranges herself neatly with crossed legs, setting her red purse on the coffee table. "How are your ribs? Do you need anything?"

I blink, taken aback. I figured she'd come to reprimand me. "They're okay." I flash back to three minutes ago when I ran down the stairs—they actually didn't hurt at all. "But you've been texting and calling about my injury. We've talked a few times. You didn't need to come down here to check on my ribs."

"That's true. I didn't. But I did come down anyway. Do you need anything? Ice? Ibuprofen?"

I shake my head. "I saw the doctor two days ago. She said they're actually healing."

"Did you drive?"

"I took a Lyft." I'm still thrown off by her questions and the fact that they're so...normal. She's not tearing me apart. But there's time for her to launch a mom attack.

"That's good. But it's also sad. You could've asked Skylar to drive you."

"Mom—" I start, but I haven't even told her. I join her and slump down on the couch, the weight of all my mistakes dragging me down. The next words scrape my throat. "We split up."

She simply nods and says, "I know, dear."

I sit up straighter. "How do you know?"

"I had a meeting with her earlier today."

"She mentioned it?" That doesn't sound like Skylar. She's good at keeping our secrets.

You don't have any secrets with her anymore, you dumbass.

"Of course not. I was able to figure it out."

"How?" I ask tentatively. But then again—this is my mother. She figures everything out. Her mind-reading powers are next level. I shudder at the thought.

"It was obvious," she says. "She was trying hard to be upbeat. And she's not someone who has to try hard. She's naturally cheerful. I asked if everything was okay and she said it was great—*just great, absolutely great, totally great.*

She said the same when I asked how you were doing. The three 'greats' made it clear. Then she had to end the meeting."

Mom gives a sad smile, and it's like a vise to my heart knowing I did that to Skylar. I made her...fake it. Was she faking the dancing a little while ago? Or is she just trying to fake it till she makes it through the breakup? I feel worse, knowing this. I say nothing, because I'm not really sure what to say except—I'm a selfish dick.

"So why did you break up with her?" she asks calmly. I was not expecting calm. Not after the *"Did you know?"* barrage of texts.

I draw a deep breath, hunting for the guts to tell her the truth, when she says, "Because you're afraid."

Thank fuck. She gets it. Relief floods me. I scrub a hand down the back of my neck, admitting it as I say, "Yeah. Can't let the team down, you know? I really don't want to do that."

"Ford," she says, gentle and caring, so I keep going, unspooling everything inside me.

"That's the thing—I worked so hard to get where I am. To stay where I am. To fight for everything. I made a mistake the other night in the game, when Long Neck John was trying to strip the puck from me. I didn't focus, and that's how this whole stupid hit happened." I gesture to my midsection. I debate telling her the full truth, but then—I've come this far. I let the rest out. "And honestly, I was kind of distracted with Skylar. She was there and she was all I could think about..."

Mom squeezes my shoulder sympathetically, then ruffles my hair. "You've always expected the best from yourself."

"Exactly. You understand, right? I couldn't let the team

down. I couldn't take a chance on continuing to be distracted this season. There were reporters who speculated I should've retired last season, when I was thirty-five. Thirty-six years old in the NHL...just like when I was twenty-four and people said I wouldn't last. But I did last. I'm still here, and this is going to be my best year. I have to do it with no distractions."

I'm winding myself up. My ribs ache a little with each word, but I need to say this through the pain. "I'm so glad somebody gets it."

She ruffles my hair again, nodding like she truly sees me this time. It's a relief—finally talking to someone besides my dog. It feels like something in me is loosening. The tension, maybe.

She sighs. "But sweetheart. That's not what I meant."

My brow knits. "What did you mean, then?"

"What I meant is—you're afraid of getting your heart broken. You're afraid of being replaced. And you're terrified of truly opening up to another person, like you did with Brittany," she says, leveling me with a sharp but thoughtful stare. "Because what if they leave you? That's what distracted you. That's what scared the living hell out of you."

My mouth opens, but then I snap it shut. I should tell her she's wrong. But the thing is—she's not.

She's completely right, and I didn't even see the truth that was right in front of my eyes.

No, man. You did. You were just afraid.

After I draw a soldiering breath, I turn to her and shrug, helpless.

"Did you know I have no idea how to fix things?" I look down. Then I force myself to say the hardest part, "Or if I even can."

35

I'D EAT THEM TOO

SKYLAR

I'm finally ready to drag myself out of the house. I can't hide any longer. And really, I don't want to.

Maybe Ford didn't put me first, but I fully intend to put *me* first. That includes my business. I put on the blazer I bought for my first meeting with him, grab the tote I nabbed that day too, and head to the door so I can meet with a new client—one I gained from the gala. A woman named Carmen Santorini wants me to redo her home office with an upcycled *Gilded Age* vibe.

I'm just a little excited.

I'll be early, but that's okay. I'll grab a coffee and be ready when she is. Then, I'll catch a ride with my friends to Ford's parents' house for the podcast where we do the "after." That won't be easy, but my friends will be there, so I know I can handle it.

As I'm heading to the door, though, my phone buzzes with a text. A flurry of hope ignites in me. Maybe it's Ford. But that's too much to ask for. He hasn't reached out since the night he dumped me. I haven't seen him either, besides that day when he emerged from a Lyft. I've only texted to confirm I'd be doing the live stream at his mom's house to show how it looks *after* its makeover—and that was a group text with him and his mother. He didn't reply.

I toggle over to my messages as mid-morning sun streaks through the living room window.

> Adam: My flight landed early! Literally just slid into a car now. Is the dog bed ready?
>
> Skylar: Yup! I left out a bowl of water next to it and some kibble too.

I check the time again. Well, I guess I'll wait here.

Thirty minutes later, Adam arrives, and I fly out the door, then race down the porch steps to tackle-hug him the second he emerges from the car. I didn't realize how much I needed to see him until right now, and I don't let go. Even if things didn't work out with Ford, I'm so glad I met him and had a brief and beautiful love affair—thanks to my brother, who made it possible by letting me live here.

"Whoa. Everything okay?" Adam asks when I break the hug.

I frown, my eyes welling with tears. "I fell for your neighbor. I'm sorry...but I'm also not sorry."

With a protective gaze, he glances next door, then cups my elbow and ushers me inside, passing a brown paper bag on the front porch. I didn't notice that earlier, but I'll grab it when I leave in a bit.

Inside, his green eyes—a similar shade to mine, and

bright behind his glasses—hold mine with concern. "Is it the hockey player?"

"Yes," I say through tears. But once we sit on the couch, Adam reaches for a tissue from the table and offers it to me. I take it as Simon hurls himself into Adam's lap. Adam pets the shameless boy, who offers his belly to my brother.

I dab at my eyes. "I started seeing him, even though you said it was a bad idea. But I promise I won't make things awkward as neighbors. I'll be civilized. You have my word."

Adam's expression is soft, his voice gentle as he says, "Don't worry about it. All I care about is if you're okay. Are you? And do I need to beat up this jerk?"

The prospect of Adam taking on the burly, sturdy Ford is amusing but unnecessary. "No. He was worried he was distracted by...me," I say, then I blurt out the whole sad story. But when I'm done, I add, "But it's fine. I'm moving on. I have my friends, and my dog, and you and Mom and Dad. Everything is fine."

"Good," he says, then cocks his head. "But did you ever tell him how you felt?"

I shoot him a *what do you mean* look. "Well, no. He ended it."

"Right, but when you explained how you broke up, it sounds like he started to say *'take a break'* and you finished the sentence. So you didn't even tell him how you felt."

I open my mouth to protest, but...he's not wrong. "I don't know that it would have made a difference though," I say.

But then again, would it have mattered?

"You also don't *not* know," he says. "Sometimes in science, you have to test things."

I purse my lips and narrow my brow. "Look at you, turning science around and using it against me."

"Science just works. What can I say?" he says with a smile.

I say goodbye to him and Simon, then leave, shutting the door behind me, wondering if I should have told Ford how I felt. I bound down the steps, then stop.

Right. The paper bag.

I trot back up and grab it.

Oh.

There's a drawing on one side. A simple line sketch of a dog. And the words:

For Simon—his favorite.

And yours too.

I miss you so much.

My heart nearly bursts in my chest as I flash back on the moment on his porch when we confessed our love for this type of dog biscuit.

Sometimes when I get peanut butter biscuits, I eat them too. Well, I take a bite, he'd said.

I'd replied with an excited *me too.*

My throat tightens as my fingers curl tighter around the bag. I turn toward Ford's house, hoping—stubbornly, deeply—that this means something.

When I head down the steps, I look to another house on the street. Jessica's. And I start wondering about her as well.

But first, I go to the meeting.

* * *

I steel myself as I arrive at Ford's parents' house in Trevyn's car. He pulls into the driveway, turns off the engine, and gives me a supportive smile. "You've got this, girl," he says.

"Of course I do," I reply to my good friend.

I push open the door and step outside, the sea salt air from Richardson Bay drifting under my nose. I told them about the dog biscuits Ford left on my porch this morning —eager to dissect the meaning, but also wary of reading too much into the words *I miss you.* They're not the same as *I want you back.*

"What do you think?" I ask again.

"I think you need to get your butt into the house. We have a show to do," Mabel says, then shoos me toward the front door. She hauls the podcast equipment, but it's not much. Just our lavalier mics and phones. We're pretty DIY. The Internet is like science—magical.

"Fine, fine, make me suffer," I say.

"We can spend the rest of the day *after* we shoot dissecting what it means. Does that work for you?" Mabel asks as we head to the home's entrance.

"Yes, thank you very much. You get me."

"We so do," Trevyn says.

I punch in the code and open the door.

The place is warm and welcoming, but I knew it would be, since I designed it. I've seen it, too, since it all came together, but it's still gratifying to take everything in —from the couch to the lamps to the kitchen cabinets. To —wait. What is this? There's another bag by the front door. A big brown one. And am I losing my mind or is that a fluffy, fleecy dog bed that's longer than it is wide?

It's wiener-shaped, and I can't stand how cute it is. I pull it out, stroking the obscenely soft material, then gasp when I read what's been embroidered on it.

Property of Simon Side-Eye.

"Shut up. He made Simon a personalized dog bed," I say, my heart swelling in my chest. This man is up to something, and I'm eager to know what, or what's coming next in this trail of gifts.

Mabel bends to inspect it. "Okay, that's adorable. But get moving."

I arch a brow. "You're awfully eager to get this going."

"You got us past twenty-eight thousand subscribers. They expect us to show all the design stuff," she says.

"They were tuning in for the dating drama," I say with a sigh.

"Yes, but they stayed because we're good," she adds.

"Also, I bet you can still be dramatic," Trevyn throws in.

And fine, fine—I haven't lost my touch in that area.

A few minutes later, we're ready to go, streaming live on our YouTube channel as I say to the camera, "Who doesn't love a before and after?"

Then we show our podcast viewers the house—from the dove gray couch to the pale-yellow kitchen table, the blanket on the back of the couch, the counter in the bathroom, the Eames chair, the rest of the office, and the plants in the living room.

"What do you think?" I ask, turning to my friends and co-hosts. "Do we like the after?"

But before either of them can answer, there's a loud knock on the front door. I shoot Mabel a quizzical look. "Are you DoorDashing while we're going live?"

She rolls her eyes. "Yes, Skylar. I'm getting cookies." She pauses. "It's probably, oh, I don't know, your client. I'll go let Maggie Devon in."

But seconds later, it's not Maggie walking in. It's Ford. And my heart beats faster than it does in a thrift shop.

A million times faster.

36

THE BEST THING

FORD

When I'm on the ice, I wear all sorts of protective gear—shoulder pads, a mouthguard, a cup. They help protect you from the hits.

In life, though? You can't really protect yourself. Not with a stoic attitude or an emotional shutdown.

So, with no armor—just my heart on my sleeve—I walk into the middle of their live stream.

I've been watching it online from the driveway for the last fifteen minutes. About five thousand people are tuned in. Fewer than the number of fans who come to a Sea Dogs game, but far more than I ever expected to witness the hardest thing I've ever done: ask for another chance.

With a curious glint in her gaze, Skylar stands in front of the dove gray couch she picked out one afternoon last month, when I started to realize I could fall for her. Probably already had.

I square my shoulders, ready to say the hard stuff. I should've scripted this. But some things are better unplanned.

"I miss you," I say, my voice steady even if everything

inside me is trembling. "And I was completely wrong when I thought you distracted me from playing."

Her bright eyes are fixed on me. I hope her heart's still open, too, but it's hard to tell. She's saying nothing—just waiting for me to keep talking.

"It was fear that distracted me. The fear that you might not feel the same as me. The fear that you might not want the same things I do. And I let it masquerade as something else."

Trevyn smothers a smile. Mabel rolls her lips together, trying to hide hers. They're in on this too. I called and asked when they were going live, and they told me.

"I'm sorry," I continue, my chest cracking open. The fear's still real, but I have to push past it. She's worth the risk. "I'm so sorry I didn't realize this the other night. I'm sorry it took me almost a week. But I know it now. And if you'll take me back..." I pause, my heart stuttering with hope. "I'll always put you first. Well, sometimes I might put your dog first, but I think that's one and the same in your eyes."

Her eyes shine—hopefully from happy tears—as Mabel keeps the phone steady, capturing every word.

"It is the same," Skylar says, her voice wobbly. Her lips quirk up and she can't seem to fight off a smile.

"Good. Because I love you," I say, and that was hard, but it's also freeing. Like getting back on the ice after an injury. Like stepping out of an ice bath. Like finally, *finally* letting go of the past for real. "I love you so much. When I met you and your dog humped my dog, I thought you were a complete pain in the ass. But I couldn't stop thinking about you—and I haven't stopped since. And now I know that's not a bad thing. It's the best thing. *You're* the best thing."

She shakes her head slightly, and for a second, I worry she's going to say no. But it's more like amazement. She steps forward, grabs the collar of my shirt, and says, "You beat me to it."

"To what?"

"To saying *it*," she says, and I hope so hard her *it* means what I want it to. "I realized I kind of ran away too," she says, apologetic, but she hardly needs to be. "I didn't tell you that you were an idiot the other night. I didn't tell you that you were wrong. And I definitely didn't tell you that I've fallen in love with you too."

My breath hitches. My chest warms, and I feel drunk in the best of ways. Those words are all I want.

"I want to be there for you," she adds. "I want to take care of you. And let you know I'm not going anywhere. You can't get rid of me."

"Well...you are my next-door neighbor," I say.

She smirks. "Exactly. Which is why you really better be nice to me. In *every* single way."

I grin. "So will you take me back?"

She lifts a brow. "Only if you'll eat a peanut butter dog biscuit live."

"That's all you're gonna make me do?"

"Okay, fine. Get down on your knees and tell me I'm amazing."

"That's easy." I drop to my knees, look up at her, and say, "You're amazing. And even when you drove me crazy, I was falling in love with you. I want to keep falling in love with you. Every single day. Will you let me?"

She offers me her hand and pulls me to my feet, grinning that sassy, signature Skylar grin. "I accept your groveling. You may kiss me now."

Nothing can distract me from the way this woman makes me feel. *Happy*. And happiness like this is worth it.

This won't be our first kiss in public, but this one feels like the start of our forever.

* * *

Back at my house, she tugs at my shirt, her nimble fingers yanking it off. But then her eyes widen with worry. "I didn't ask. Did that hurt?"

"Why would it hurt?"

"Your ribs, silly."

I scoff. "You think I'm going to let some bruised ribs stop me from fucking my woman?"

"Ford," she chides.

"Fine. You can be on top, okay?"

"Seriously. Did you ask your doctor?"

"No, and I'm not going to. But if it makes you feel better, I'll seriously just lie there and let you bounce on my dick. Now, get on me," I say, tipping my forehead to the king-size mattress in my bedroom, where she belongs right now, and really, all the time.

She gazes ceiling-ward. "Seriously. He's so stubborn," she says to the sky.

"I am," I say, then kick off my jeans, skim off my boxers, and lie the fuck down, my hard cock pointing right at her.

With a playful shrug, she strips, then comes over and straddles me, sinking down.

I shudder out a ragged breath as I wrap my hands around her hips, savoring this connection that I've missed fiercely. Savoring *her*.

"Everything okay?" she asks.

I shake my head. "No. Everything is perfect."

Because I'm sure she's perfect for me. And sometimes you don't get the girl right away. Just like you don't get into the NHL on your first shot. But when you get her, you hold on tight and keep her.

As she rides me, I make a promise to myself—to keep her close and treat her like the gift that she is.

Later, as she settles in next to me between the sheets, with Simon testing out his new bed, Skylar runs a gentle hand over my abs. "Are you sure it didn't hurt?"

"You can ride my dick again to make sure," I suggest helpfully.

"I will." She snuggles tighter, her auburn hair spilling across my chest. "Thanks for the gifts."

"Thank you for taking me back," I say. And as I stroke her hair, I add, "In case it wasn't clear, the dog bed is for here. So Simon has someplace to sleep when you're sleeping over."

Her grin is electric. "Really?"

"Yes," I say, dropping another kiss to her pretty lips.

She murmurs against my mouth, and when she breaks the kiss, she says, "Does this mean I can still spy on you from the catio?"

"I don't think you ever stopped."

"You're right. I didn't."

"I didn't stop checking you out from the hot tub either," I admit.

"Good. Spies unite," she says, then rests her head on my chest. But a second later, she lifts it again. "You didn't eat the peanut butter biscuit."

"Next time," I say. "That's a promise."

"You're just angling to come back on my podcast."

"You are right."

"My three favorite words," she says. "Wait—actually, I think I have three new favorite ones."

I'm pretty sure I know what they are, so I cup her cheek and say, "I love you."

"I love you too." Then she gives me a once-over. "By the way, you grovel well."

As Simon thumps his tail, and Zamboni curls up into a tight dog ball on her bed, I blow on my fingernails. "I play to win, Skylar."

And this win is better than any I've ever had on the ice.

EPILOGUE: ONE FINE DAY
SKYLAR

Do I have everything? I scan my suitcase, then my carry-on, then Simon's bag. I have his dog bed, his toys, and some peanut butter biscuits.

We're all set.

As I head to the door, I wave goodbye to my brother's house. I'll be back, for sure—but as a guest.

Adam moved home from Europe and is taking over the place again. Right now, he's at work, but later he'll return to take care of Cleo.

And, well, his *new girlfriend*.

Like I could resist playing matchmaker with Adam and Jessica. Besides, Adam finally got over his whole "don't date a neighbor" thing when I showed him how well it can turn out. They went on a date when he was home last fall, and then she visited him in Amsterdam in the winter. I checked her mail while she was gone. I'm just a good neighbor like that.

I leash up Simon and open the door...to find my boyfriend waiting on the front porch. Ford is standing there, grinning and looking so damn good in shorts and a polo.

He sticks out one hand and takes my suitcase, then Simon's with the other. "Like I'd let you carry your own bags."

"Not when you have Focus and Dedication, and they helped you win the Cup," I say, still proud of him for finishing his final season exactly the way he wanted to— on top of the world.

With no bruised ribs. No injuries. Just joy.

He's been noodling on what to do next. Maybe that smoothie shop. Maybe broadcasting. Or maybe he'll open a dog hotel, he mused the other night.

For me, I'm busy with the podcast, which has kept growing, but so has Haven Designs. I've been decorating so many homes with secondhand, refurbished, and vintage looks that my little green heart is growing bigger every day. For now, the next thing is a trip.

He carries the bags to his car, loads them in the trunk, then helps Simon into his dog seat in the back, right next to Zamboni.

Before I get in, I spot Jessica in her front yard and wave. "I'll be sure to check the mail," she calls.

"Have fun with my brother," I say.

"I will," she replies with a wink.

Then we head off—to the dog hotel first, where we check in two very spoiled dogs into one special suite.

They're practically living together now. They will be officially when we get back from our trip, and I move in full-time with the guy next door.

For now, though, we're headed to Italy.

On the plane, I say, "You never told me—are you the

kind of guy who sets out for a day in Tuscany ready to see what he stumbles across, or do you hire a tour guide?"

His dimple flashes. "I guess you'll find out."

A few days later, I do—when we're wandering through a vineyard, the sun shining bright across the grapes, my boyfriend relaxed and happy, and then...

He gets down on one knee.

"Marry me, Skylar," he says. "Marry me and be mine always."

My heart soars to the sunlit sky as I say *yes*.

From strangers to neighbors to forever—you just never know what might happen when you take your dog out for a walk in your bathrobe one fine day.

Ready for more hot hockey heroes and the women who bring them to their knees? Check out single dad Corbin's romance with his best friend's little sister Mabel in **JUST BREAKING THE RULES** coming to KU January 2026! It's available to preorder now, and if you want to read it in KU, sign up for my newsletter and follow me on Amazon to be notified whenever I have a new release! Turn the page for the first ever sneak peek!

If you haven't binged the Love and Hockey series, all six titles are available now to download in KU!

EXCERPT: JUST BREAKING THE RULES

Corbin

Sometimes you just need to pivot. Like when you're skating backwards, but you need to open up to receive a shot.

Or, say, when you're at a Webflix event with your buddies before a game, and one minute you're checking out cookies, and the next, you spot your best friend's little sister landing in the middle of the cake she'd been making.

Sure, Mabel was ad-libbing like a pro, but a good teammate has your back. That was all I'd wanted to do back there.

Now, I shut the door to the closet-sized trailer and place the towel Ronnie's assistant gave Mabel on the few square inches of counter. There's a tiny couch, a doll-house-sized table, and a bathroom smaller than one on an airplane. The sink there is too small to be useful, but there's a bigger one between a microwave and a coffee machine. That'll do to get her ready for the pic.

Tossing my suit jacket on the couch, I turn to Mabel and finally ask, "Smash cake, huh?"

"It's a thing," Mabel says with a little jut of her pretty chin.

"That save you attempted was worthy of a top goalie." Even if that faux-badass judge wasn't impressed with her song and dance, I sure as hell was.

"Thanks," she says dryly. "But I'm pretty sure I'll need a new career after that." Her shoulders drop, and she shudders out a heavy breath, slumping against the trailer door and groaning like a wounded creature. "What have I done?"

Ah, hell. Can't let her go all woe-is-me. "Hey now," I say, reaching for her shoulders, cupping them to reassure her. "You handled that with aplomb."

She peers at me, the corner of her lips screwing up. "Aplomb? Seriously? More like *I bombed*."

"Nope. You fell down and you picked yourself right back up." I rub her shoulders through her T-shirt. I'm not usually a shoulder man, but hers feel damn good under my palms, strong and toned, probably from lifting heavy bags of flour and mixing batter. But I probably shouldn't be rubbing Theo's sister's shoulders with so much—I look down at my hands—*gusto*.

I drop my arms to my sides.

"Didn't do much good. I'll never get my—" Mabel's voice catches, and she doesn't finish the thought.

"Never get what?" It sounds important to her, what she didn't say.

She blows out a breath, then shakes her head. "It's nothing. I'm fine. It's one contest. I'll move on after the photo opp."

I want to reassure her that no one will remember what just went down. But I don't like to make empty promises.

She waves toward her brown waves, the swoopy tendrils tumbling out of her hair clip. "I'll move on if I can ever get this frosting out of my hair, that is."

Now *that* I can promise. "Let's do it."

She lowers her hand and studies me with narrowed eyes. "Don't you have a game to get to?"

"Yes, but the arena is three blocks away, and for a six-fifteen puck drop, I don't need to be there till four-fifteen."

But that doesn't satisfy her. "What exactly *are* you doing here, Corbin? Did you come with Theo? Is he looking out for me? That would be just like him."

True. Checking up on her is her brother's style, but I'm not here with him. Officially, I'm here for my teammate Riggs, who has a dangerous crush on the hostess of *Romance Beach*. This morning in the weight room, while scrolling socials in between reps, the left winger blurted out *Holy shit, my future girlfriend is in town.* I'd bet a hundred bucks she'd never give him the time of day. Our goalie, Miller, got in on the action. So, we're here to check on our investment and, fine, wingman if Riggs needs it.

But I have ulterior motives too. Retirement from the ice is still a couple years away, but someday, when I hang up my skates, I'll open a bakery in Cozy Valley like my mom always wanted but wasn't able to. It never hurts to keep up with trends in the baking world.

I flash her an easygoing grin. "It was field-trip distance from the rink," I say, then move the hell on from my *why*. I hold out a hand so I can get her to the sink. "Let's de-cakify you."

Mabel gazes at her arm, coated in frosting, which is... hmm. Sort of gray, maybe white? "Goodbye, cake," she says to the remains of her creation. "You were a good cake. One of the best. You would have served me well."

Ah, hell. There's real sadness in her cake eulogy. She'd been working hard on that confection before it all went south with a rogue butterfly. I can't let her wallow.

I swipe a finger through the sugary mess coating her arm. "You're right. It did go out in a blaze of glory." I bring the frosting to my lips for a taste. "It's fantastic."

Not the first time I've said that about her baking. I've tried the caramel chocolate brownies and chocolate chip candy cane cookies Theo's brought to hockey games. Mabel and I even made raspberry lemon ricotta cupcakes together for the surprise party she threw for him last year. She's magic with dessert, and her frosting is almost, *almost,* as good as sex.

"Thanks," she says. "The universe giveth and taketh away. Good baker, but a terrible competitor." She shakes her head in obvious frustration.

"Good thing baking isn't a—" I'm about to say a competitive sport, but there's no such thing as a competition-free job. I backpedal. "You can be a great baker without winning fancy competitions. And I bet you'll start a smash-cake trend. Now let's get you cleaned up. I'm under strict orders to return you in"—I check my watch—"thirteen minutes now."

And I'm the kind of guy who follows orders. Well, most of the time.

But when Mabel shifts her gaze to me, her frustration shifts with it. "Look, I appreciate the whole knight-in-shining-armor thing you have going on. It's on brand and all. But you don't have to stay. I can clean myself up."

"I know you can," I say evenly. She radiates independence. I swear I see it shimmering, like waves of heat. I'm not going to treat her like she can't manage the situation on her own.

"Why are you helping then?" She's skeptical, but I realize I'm not the target of her suspicion. Just the bystander.

"There was a whole crowd out there *not* helping," I explain, because it's that simple. "Didn't want to be like them. That work for you?"

She squeezes her eyes shut for a few seconds, dragging her hand through her hair, and oh shit...Before I can stop her, the damage is done. She's combed frosting all over her pretty locks.

I wince but then school my expression when she opens her eyes.

"It's not you," she begins, her tone tinged with sadness. "It's, well, my ex just told everyone that watches *Romance Beach*, which, for the record, is pretty much the entire world, that I suck at life."

What the fuck? I'd tuned out the *Romance Beach* promo and lasered in on Mabel's mad cake skills, so I missed that. But I'll deal with it later.

"He's wrong." I hand her the towel from next to the sink. "Now, let's get you ready for the photo. Show the crowd out there that when you fall, you get back up."

She frowns apologetically. "Sorry. I shouldn't have argued with the one person being nice to me."

"I've been hit harder in hockey games. I can take it."

"Stop trying to make me smile," she mutters, but she's smirking, and that's good. I'd rather see that than her feeling sorry for herself.

She tosses the towel over her shoulder and scrubs her arms over the sink. Once they're clean, she dries them off, then wipes most of the frosting from her apron too. She peers around, like she's looking for a mirror before she asks, "I think there was some in my hair?"

I stifle a laugh. "*Some* being the operative word."

"Seriously?"

I point at her hair. "Remember when you got so annoyed with yourself you shoved your hands in your hair, oh, about three minutes ago?"

She lets out a low moan, like a tire leaking air. "Noooo."

"Yesssss."

Since there's no mirror, she has to rely on me. "How bad is it?"

I should resist touching her again, but my hands seem to have a mind of their own around her today. Maybe I have a thing for cute women in aprons with llamas kissing on them.

Maybe you have a thing for the woman you wanted to ask out the day you met her.

Setting a palm on her shoulder, I spin her around and...wow...it's a fucking nest of frosting and cake. "On a scale of one to desperately-in-need-of-a-wash, I'd say it's one hundred."

The sound that emanates from her is now death-moan level. But Mabel's undeterred, and that's nearly as sexy as her attempt at a smash-cake save. The woman doesn't let the small stuff get her down. She beelines for the locker-sized bathroom and squeezes in to deal with the problem. She attempts to wipe off bits of frosting from her hair with her towel, but her elbows bump against the wall. The bathroom's so small she can't quite get the right angle.

She turns back to me with a look of surrender. "Fine. Go ahead. Be nice if you insist. *Help.*"

I give her an *I told you so* look as she emerges. "I insist," I say.

When she's standing in front of me a second later, I pace around her, reviewing the damage. Once I've done a full loop, she meets my eyes and says: "Level with me. Is it time for a buzz cut?"

"Hmm," I say as I take the towel from her. "Have you got clippers in that apron pocket?"

Her brown eyes pop. "It's that bad?"

I don't mince words. "Mabel, you *are* the smash cake. It's everywhere." But I'm fast on my feet and quick with a solution. Years of taking care of my mom, of raising my little girl, and of executing plays on the ice mean I don't fuck around when it comes to taking care of people or problems. "I have an idea."

She holds up her hands, but she's not defeated. Her words crackle with a spark that hasn't been snuffed out from a rough day. "Let's see what you've got."

"Game on," I say and reach for the clip in her hair.

"That's my lucky clip," she says.

"Why's it lucky?" I undo it, letting her waves fall in a dark mess, a contrast to her fair complexion. She looks... good. Even with frosting and cake guts all over those strands.

"I wore it to my first big wedding catering gig," she says as I set the clip down on the counter. "It's been good to me. I have another wedding coming up soon."

"Then I'll make sure to take good care of it," I say, glancing at the hair clip. I wet the end of the towel under the faucet and dab the frosting off the strands near her face.

As I touch her hair, she shudders in a breath, then goes quiet, and I work steadily.

I wet the towel once more, then clean the sugar and cake bits from the back of her hair. I check the time. She's due out in eight minutes for the picture. "Done."

"Is it all gone?"

"Yes. But your hair's damp now."

"Does it really matter? No one's going to be looking at the llama-kiss ex," she says with a snort.

I spin her around, shaking my head. "You're wrong. They will."

Her look says she doesn't buy what I'm selling. "To stare at the five-car pileup on the side of the road?"

I scoff. "Not in the least."

She parks her hands on her hips. "Why, then? Why will they look at me?"

The question hangs in the air, taking up the very small space between us.

The mere inches between us.

It's the first time I've been *this* close to Mabel. I've seen her a few times over the years. At hockey games. At barbecues. In the diner, when she stops by Cozy Valley to see her family.

With her shiny hair, her expressive eyes, and her bow-shaped lips, Mabel Llewelyn's always been pretty. I've thought so ever since the day I met her at a fundraising event for the local fire department in Cozy Valley—her hometown, and now mine too.

But I knew it in an empirical sense.

Now I take a beat to drink her in, and the answers to her question are clear and bright.

Why? Because freckles dance across the bridge of your cute nose. Because your lips are so lush. Because your eyes shine with fire and humor. And because you're so fucking brave.

"Because...you're you," I say at last.

There. That's safe enough. Just because I'm thinking things about her for the first time—or, really, the first time since I learned who she was—doesn't mean I'm going to say them out loud. Let alone act on them. Our lives are too...connected. It'd be messy, and I hate messes.

But helping her right now? That's easy, so I keep going. "Which means you're going to have the best French braid ever."

She blinks. "You can *French* braid?"

"Of course."

"Really?" She sounds like she'd be more surprised if I said I spoke French.

"I have a twelve-year-old daughter. Now, turn around."

"Yes, sir." Mabel spins around once more. I take the clip and run the teeth of it through her hair, combing out the wet strands, then separating them into three chunks.

Checking the time on my watch, I put the clip on the counter, then grasp the right chunk in my hand. Her breath hitches.

That's an interesting reaction, but I need focus to do this quickly *and* well. I weave that handful over the middle section, then loop in the left chunk. I gather more locks on the right, add it to that strand, and weave it into the braid. I do the same on the left side, then slowly, steadily work my way down her hair, crafting a tight French braid.

As I go, I sneak a whiff of her sugary scent. No surprise—Mabel smells like the treats she makes. It's the best kind of smell, like candy and butter, with a hint of vanilla.

When I reach the nape of her neck, my thumb slides across her pale, creamy skin. I don't want to stop touching her, and this is a problem.

A problem I like far too much. My chest heats as I steal another touch, grazing her neck once more.

She stifles a gasp, and I pause, absorbing the realization that she likes the way I'm touching her hair, maybe even the way I have to pull on it to braid it. When I near the end, she goes still, as if she's holding her breath. I fight the urge to tug on the end of her braid. But I focus on finishing, neatly looping one strand over the other until I'm down to the middle of her back with little hair left.

"I don't have a hair tie," she says quietly.

"But we have a lucky clip." I grab the clip once more and use it to secure the end of the braid. "Done. And with four minutes to spare."

She turns around, and there's something in her brown eyes that wasn't there before. It's not gratitude, though there is some of that. It's more like curiosity with a touch of heat.

A part of me thinks that's good. Another part thinks it's a problem that this temptation seems mutual.

"Thank you, Corbin." She lets out a laugh, then adds, "I should bake you a cake to show my appreciation."

"That's not necessary. I'm just glad I was here."

"You don't like cake?" From her tone, indifference to cake would be blasphemy.

"I ate some off your arm a few minutes ago."

"But did you like it?"

I'd have thought that was proof. "Of course I like cake."

"Why of course?"

"Because I like things that taste..." I pause, trying not to look at her mouth, but failing, "really fucking good."

Maybe that came out a bit naughtier than it sounded in my head. Maybe I'm flirting with my best friend's little sister. Didn't have that on my bingo card for today.

"Like what?" she counters.

This woman doesn't back down. And there are so many reasons I shouldn't answer that question. Her brother's the acting general manager for my hockey team, filling the role after the longtime GM retired last season. As if that's not enough, with the season barely underway, a rough end to last year's playoff hopes, and my daughter extremely busy with middle school in the city, my life is complicated enough.

But there's something about the space in this trailer, or the lack thereof. There's something about the flirty way Mabel asked, *Like what?* And there's definitely something about the way she's waiting for my answer like she *needs* it.

My gaze drops to a tiny bit of frosting still left on her forearm, then returns to her eyes. "Things like frosting."

Read on...

THE RIVAL UPGRADE

Dear Reader,

I'm so excited to share this short story with you! I just wasn't ready to leave the Love and Hockey world, so I wrote another romance! If you've read my Virgin Society series, you'll recognize the heroine — Camden. She's a rising star singer in that series and she never got her own romance. I brought her into my hockey world and gave her a hot, sexy love story with a British athlete, and you also get to see Karlsson finally get his comeuppance! I love a revenge romance and hope you do too!

Xoxo
   Lauren

LOVE AND HOCKEY

THE
Rival
UPGRADE

26

#1 New York Times Bestselling Author
LAUREN
BLAKELY

ABOUT THE BOOK

They say the best way to get over someone is to get under someone else.

I say the best way is to get under his rival.

Enter Shaw: smooth, sexy, British—and my ex's biggest enemy on the ice. What was supposed to be a one-time revenge fling turns complicated when he invites me to his game… and catches me in my lie.

Turns out, nothing turns him on more than payback.

And now I've got a hockey player who won't stop chasing me.

A LOVE AND HOCKEY SHORT STORY

By Lauren Blakely

1

NO BIG DEAL

CAMDEN

Everybody has an annoying trait.

Or three.

And you just have to remind yourself...*it's no big deal.*

For my boyfriend, the question he's asking just happens to be one of those three.

"Hey, babe, where's my protein powder?"

I look up from the sage-green couch in the living room of my West Village rooftop apartment, where I'm reviewing the final details for the kickoff of my music club next month, and meet Erik's concerned gaze. He's a few feet away in the kitchen, his brow a furrowed line digging into his thick forehead as his gaze darts from the blender on my sleek white countertop, then to the cupboard, then to the blender again.

It's just one of those things—him never remembering where he left his protein powder.

"The cupboard. Above the stove. Where you left it yesterday," I say helpfully, since there's no point getting pissy about it.

He shakes his head. "That's not my whey protein

though. I need the whey for muscle recovery. I just worked out," he says, flipping open another cupboard as he hunts.

"You left more than one type of protein here?" I don't ask how many types of protein one needs because I can't bear another conversation about the differences between egg protein and whey protein and who-even-cares protein.

Erik Karlsson is good at a lot of things—being a sweetie-pie and having great stamina—but wowing me with the fine details of his post-workout regimen is not one of them.

"Yes. I leave all my protein here because one, you're my girl, and two, I come here after the gym. The season starts in a month. We have a shot at the Cup finally, but you can't be a top defenseman in the NHL without working out hard," he says, like it's a gift he marks my place with his tools for getting ripped.

I suppose it's sweet, in a very Erik Karlsson way.

He yanks open another cupboard when I spot a huge white container on the other side of the stove.

"There it is," I say, my bracelets sliding down my ink-covered arm as I point to the in-your-face treasure he seeks.

"Damn, babe. Look at you," he says with a big smile, then stalks over to me, cups my face and declares, "You're the best."

"Thanks," I say to my teddy bear of a boyfriend, then adjust my black strappy tank top.

Erik returns to his protein mission, measuring and dumping powder and spirulina and spinach and other get-bigger-faster this and that into my blender, which I'll need to fumigate later because...gross. But I can manage that annoying thing too.

It's not a big deal, like the other things aren't a big deal.

When he's finally done, he points finger guns at the appliance. "Kapow," he says. To no one. Or maybe himself.

Okay, fine, that's another annoying thing. Actually— make that two, if we're counting both the finger guns and the talking to himself.

Like he's doing right now as he mutters, "Gotta have better stats than Coleman this season."

Right, right. That's his rival. The guy on the other New York team that he's obsessed with. He can't stand the fact that some other player makes more money, was picked ahead of him in the draft, and has more points.

But I'm doing my best to ignore both the finger guns and the muttering as I email the general manager for Goddess, the new club that I funded with the proceeds from my platinum album, letting her know the plans for the launch are not only approved but that they're goddess-level beautiful.

When I close my laptop, Erik's lounging against the counter, downing some of his shake—a white, milkshakey line above his lip. His phone buzzes on the coffee table, and he lowers the tumbler. "Oh! Can you grab that? My agent's booking an interview for me on a lifestyle show," he says, lips curving in a satisfied grin. "You don't see Coleman getting those opps, do you?"

I smile placatingly. "No idea."

"You don't, babe. Because your boyfriend is the hottest fucking commodity. Especially since sports talk gurus are saying the New York Red Hawks are going to go all the way this season."

Okay, that's a little annoying too. The way he's his own hype man. But I ignore that as well, grabbing his phone as I pop up from the couch, then I startle. Blink. Stare.

The hair on my neck stands on end. What the hell is this on his screen?

A photo from the neck down of a woman in a red-lace baby-doll nightie with a demi-cup bra? Next to a bunny avatar and captioned with the words: *Are we on for tonight*?

My smile disappears. I grip his phone so tightly I could break it. "Does your agent want you to wear some sexy lingerie for the interview, Erik?"

His tongue pauses mid protein-mustache lick. *Oh shit* flashes in his blue eyes. He gulps, but his guilt lasts only a few more seconds. He straightens his spine. "Babe. I can explain."

"Is it part of your muscle recovery to wear a baby-doll nightie?" I march into the kitchen, brandishing the evidence, waving the phone at his face.

"No, obviously," he says, quickly recovering, and I guess that powder does work since the next words from his mouth are: "It's from my...publicist."

Wow. That was scarily smooth. But also, I'm not fooled. "You don't have a publicist," I point out, my tone icy.

"Camden, babe. I just hired one."

"Did you now?" I seethe as I spin around and stalk the other way. "Let's see what sort of *image* advice she's giving you."

"Cam," he sputters, and maybe, just maybe, he's not so smooth.

I scroll down the thread as I race into the living room.

He follows, darting out a thick, muscled arm, reaching for the phone. He's bigger and stronger than me. But I'm madder, so I win the first round of keep-away as I weave around the coffee table with the same take-charge attitude I possess when I strut across the stage during a concert. I scroll through the text chain. "*Counting down till I see you tonight. Can't stop thinking about the way you taste. Your mouth is fucking heaven.*" I pause, then bite out: "You use the same lines on her as you do me!"

"That's just...*no*. That's just me telling her how much I love you."

"Of course. Your publicist ought to know how much you love me." I read more of his greatest hits as red billows from my eyes. "*Your body is insane. The way you feel under me drives me fucking wild.* You said all this to me. You're not even original!"

Erik works his jaw back and forth, his eyes flickering like he's trying to figure out how to play this unexpected bust. He drags a hand through his frosted blond tips, then blows out a breath. "Look, I can't fucking help it— being this in demand. And I definitely can't help if you were so into my dick you let me keep two containers of protein powder here just because you like climbing me. Consider yourself lucky, Cam. Most women would be seriously grateful to get even one night with me in their lifetime."

Forget seeing red. I am the fire of the sun as I hurl his phone against the door. It lands with a loud smack, then clatters to the floor. "Get out, and take your stupid protein powder too."

Erik tuts. "That's not very nice," he says, scrambling for his phone. "That was a new screen protector."

I rush into the kitchen and grab his dumb protein containers myself, then chuck each one at the door."

Grabbing them with an aggrieved sigh, he says, "You're

giving crazy-ex-girlfriend vibes right now. But it doesn't have to be this way. We can still fuck."

I breathe fire. "Go fuck the baby-doll-nightie woman!"

"Her name is Tiffany. And you know what? She wasn't mad at me for blessing you with my dick too. She knew it was her only chance to get with a hockey star. I figured you knew the same."

That's enough. "I was faking it! Every single time. Now go."

That's not true. I have way too much self-respect to fake an orgasm. Besides, I like to help myself along with my fingers. Life is too short to have *O*-less sex even if you need a little assistance. But his ego wouldn't believe they were all real thanks to *me*.

The way his eyes turn to ice tells me I've hit below the belt though. "Not cool, Cam. Super not cool."

"I bet Coleman doesn't cheat on his girlfriend," I throw out, since why not hit even lower.

Erik groans like he's been wounded, but then comes back with, "Coleman wishes he could pull like I do."

"Doubtful. I bet his girlfriends don't have to fake it," I say, though of course I know nothing about this other player. He might be married. He might be gay. No clue.

With his free hand, Erik grabs the door handle and sears me with a stare. "I will always do better than him. And I'll do better than you. I was faking it too."

I roll my eyes. "Yes, you fake came on my tits. Go fuck a protein shake, Karlsson."

"You'll regret saying that."

"I won't," I say, crossing my arms.

He leaves in a huff.

So much for his protein powder obsession being his most annoying trait.

He is his most annoying trait.

Later that night, I'm equal parts enraged and hurt when out with my friend Jules at Gin Joint, drowning my break-up sorrows while also toasting good riddance to my ex.

"Let's drink to the next guy being hotter, richer, smarter, *nicer,* and better in bed," Jules says, lifting her champagne.

I clink my flute to hers. "To upgrades."

"To upgrades."

I swallow some of the bubbly, and when Jules sets her glass down, her phone buzzes. She grabs it, then clicks on what looks like a text. She takes a few seconds to read it, her face turning white. "Camden," she says in a heavy tone that tells me I'm not going to like what she's looking at.

"Yes?" I ask, warily.

When she raises her face, she says, "Ethan just sent this to me."

He's a good friend of ours who always knows things first.

Worry crawls up my spine as Jules spins her phone around and taps a video of...my stomach plummets. It's Erik's lifestyle interview. He must have done it a little after he left my place. I can't hear it above the music in the lounge, but I don't need to. I can read the captions.

"And how are things going with Camden?" the perky interviewer asks, using only my first name, since that's what I go by professionally. She flashes her bright smile, her blonde bob shining under the stage lights. "You and the rising pop star have been a thing for a couple months now. Will we see you at the opening of Goddess next month?"

"Nah. That little music club that caters to women musicians? Please. Like anyone wants that. She'll *regret* having opened it."

At first, I'm angry. Then later, as I'm walking home, I pass Doctor Insomnia's Tea and Coffee Emporium. A memory flashes before me. I go there most mornings. I went there most mornings in the spring, too, and there was a guy there who looked familiar at the time. He had magazine model good looks—the kind of cheekbones that were carved, the kind of jawline that was chiseled, the kind of scruff that made you think dirty thoughts.

The type of body that made it clear he probably played pro sports.

And the most interesting brown eyes I'd ever seen. Warm, kind, and soulful.

Some days, he'd look my way as he waited for his order—always an English Breakfast.

But nothing happened, and when spring rolled into summer, he was gone. Didn't matter much anyway since I'd just met Erik and we'd started dating then.

As I flash back on the coffee shop guy, though, the memory fills all the way in. I'm pretty sure I know why he felt familiar—I'm pretty sure the coffee shop guy is a hockey player too.

But on the city's *other* team. The team that won the Cup last season. The New York Ice Kings.

The guy Erik's obsessed with.

A wicked smile forms on my lips.

I know how to exact my revenge. When the season starts, I'll get Erik Karlsson's biggest rival to ask me out on a date.

2

YOUR ENGLISH FRIEND

SHAW

One month later

If I'm lucky, the redhead will be a creature of habit. And I've been very, very lucky in my life.

Well, not just lucky. I'm pretty fucking good too. And disciplined. You don't win a Cup without either luck or discipline.

Maybe today, as I stride down Christopher Street, beelining for the coffee shop I've been going to every day before morning skate so far this pre-season, both luck and discipline will pay off.

And yes. Fucking yes. There she is, bang on time. A thrill races through me since the redhead is here. I thought about chatting her up in the spring last season, but I was so damn focused on the game, the strategy, the chance to win it all that I didn't want to risk being distracted.

Problem is I regretted that.

That regret ends today.

I've been running into her every morning for the last week, just like I did last season. I haven't found the right time to speak to her yet, but now's my chance—I just know it.

I finger the soft envelope in my back pocket, reviewing my strategy as she orders her coffee at the counter. Her fiery red hair falls down her back in a wild tumble. She wears black pants, painted on. Her top is silver, sleeveless, and shows off the creamy skin of her arms, the right one covered in ink of flowers, vines, and words. A leather jacket dangles from her fingers.

I push up the sleeves of my Henley, since it's warm for early October, then check my fitness watch. Plenty of time to make it to the arena of the best team in the city. Our cross-town rivals—the New York Red Hawks—would say otherwise. They've been talking shit about us during the pre-season. Ironic, since they didn't even make it out of round one of the playoffs last season. But that hasn't stopped the team's reigning arsehole, Erik Karlsson, from his nonstop trash talk. He's despised me since I went ahead of him in the first round of the draft years ago—the Brit who has better stats than him.

Well, he's right.

I am better.

And more disciplined. And that discipline has brought me here every day. And luck has put the redhead in my path this morning.

The sound of my boots clicking must catch her attention since she turns around.

The sight of her is like a shot of red-hot desire straight into my veins.

That face. Strong cheekbones and a spray of freckles

across her nose. Those lips. Red, lush, and full. Those eyes. Dark green and merciless.

My pulse spikes. She's been the best part of my last few days. "We meet again," I say.

She gives a small smile. "Lucky us."

"Indeed."

The barista sets a coffee tumbler on the counter in front of her. "Here's your pour-over with oat milk. For Jane."

Jane. I've got to wonder if that's her real name, or her coffee name.

She turns back to him. "Thank you," she says, then makes a move to lift her phone to pay for it.

Nope.

I step forward, waving her off, fast reflexes and all. "I've got it." I turn to look at the beauty, then enjoy myself as I say her name—fake or real, I don't care. "Jane."

Her red lips curve up. Then, playfully, she says, "In that case, I'll have a few bags of beans. A couple sesame bagels. The roasted almonds and the morning oats with chia seeds."

Little does she know I'd get it all for her. The whole shop if she asked. "Whatever you want. It's yours."

She takes a beat, her eyes sparkling. "Coffee will do," she says, then gives a slight tip of her head my way. "And thank you, *sir*."

It comes out sensual, a little husky. It goes straight to my brain, which quickly flashes images of her saying that in other ways, other places.

"You're welcome," I say, then step back in case she wants to leave. And if she does, fine. I'm not in the business of pursuing women who don't want to be pursued.

But if she opens the door, I'll kick it the rest of the way.

She spins back to the barista but tosses me a coy look, her red waves catching the morning light through the window, looking coppery and shimmery. "And my English friend will have his usual. An English Breakfast."

I fight off a smirk. She's noticed me too. I set down my to-go cup, and the barista takes it to fill with hot water.

"We really do need to stop meeting like this," I say, and fortunately, I have a solution since I pride myself on solving problems. Teammates not getting on? I sit their arses down and make them talk till they work it out. Brownstone runs out of hot water one morning? I fix the water heater myself. Missed my chance last season with the woman at the coffee shop who likes to flirt too? I've got a plan for that *today*. I reach into the back pocket of my jeans, sliding a finger along the soft envelope once more.

"Do we though?" she counters.

"That's a fair point," I say, then thank the barista as he hands me the mug. I turn to go, and in perfect sync, Jane walks with me. "We don't have to stop."

She roams her clever eyes over me. Judging by her smile and the way her gaze lingers, she seems to like what she sees. "Go on," she says as we leave the shop and stand outside in the Manhattan morning.

I take out the envelope with the tickets in it. "We could meet again later this week. I'd love it if you'd come to the home opener. I have a VIP ticket for you, Jane…?"

I wait for her to supply a surname. There's something teasingly familiar about her, but I've never been able to place it.

She's quiet for a beat, her green eyes sparkling, her lips curving into a grin she seems to try to fight off. Maybe she's trying to place me too? Hard to say, and hockey players aren't always recognized, which works fine for me. I'd rather let my stats speak for themselves.

She licks her lips, takes her time, then says, "Jane Smith."

Right. Sure. But I'm not about to call her on that. "Jane Smith," I say, accepting her coffee name.

She takes the envelope with her polished nails, gunmetal gray. "It was nice meeting you..." She lifts her chin, her eyes widening, waiting for me.

"Shaw Coleman. Defenseman on the New York Ice Kings," I say. "But you can just call me *your English friend*."

That smile? It widens, and it looks almost...conspiratorial.

No idea why it would. But maybe she's been wanting the same thing I have—the chance to meet again.

"Thanks for the coffee. And the invitation, *Shaw Coleman*." It's said like it tastes good on her lips.

I bet her lips would taste good on mine.

"There are actually two tickets in there. Bring a friend. Don't bring a date, Jane," I say, locking eyes with her, making my intentions clear. "Since you'll have one *after* the game."

Her smile spreads, pleased and sexy.

Then, out of the blue, she steps closer, her honeysuckle scent wafting around me, and she presses her lips to my cheek unexpectedly, leaving a faint trace of a kiss as she whispers, "I'll be there for the game and *after*...my English friend."

With her lipstick on my cheek and her honeysuckle-infused confidence trailing behind her, she takes off, walking the other way with a defiant click-clack of her boots, leaving me on the street with the thrill of watching her go.

But this time I have no regrets, since thanks to luck and discipline, I'll see her again in a couple more days.

3

A KIND OF PLOT

CAMDEN

Would you look at that? I've got a date to the first game of the season for the New York Ice Kings. Shame it's not against the Red Hawks, but you can't have everything.

"It's almost like the universe wants me to get a little revenge," I say to Jules as I flick through a rack of clothes two days later at my favorite thrift shop—Champagne Taste in the West Village.

"I'll say, but let's be honest. You did kind of plot it." She grabs a lavender vest, then holds it up. "This is hot. But maybe not best for a hockey game?"

"Might be too cold," I say, then make grabby hands. "But I can wear it at the club one night." Before I get too caught up in how Goddess is coming together—swimmingly, thanks to the lineup of amazing female artists and musicians slated to play there next week—I rewind to what Jules just said.

A kernel of guilt wedges into my chest. I didn't just *kind of* plot the date with Shaw. I premeditated it. I flirted with him. I showed up at the shop every morning till he started coming back—I'm pretty sure he spends his summers in his hometown of London, which is why I didn't see him all summer. Yes, I googled him.

And I did nearly everything I could think of to get the man to finally ask me out. "Is it my fault that my plot worked?"

Jules shakes her head, laughing. "No, I'm just impressed. You really had it all mapped out, right down to the pseudonym."

"I don't usually give my real name at the coffee shop," I say, defending myself. I'm not a household name yet, but with two successful albums out, I'm often spotted. Though, to be honest, I'm usually spotted by my core demo—young women in their teens and twenties. Guys, less so.

"I know, sweets," she says, then shoots me a serious stare. "But that's not why you didn't give him your real name."

Ugh. Best friends. Why do they have to see inside your soul? "Fine," I grumble as I move to another rack, this time spotting a sweater. "I just...well, I don't want him to think of me as Karlsson's sloppy seconds."

"Camden," Jules says, sympathetic now.

"But it's true," I admit, my gut twisting, right along with the second thoughts that swirl up in me. "Besides, maybe this whole thing is a bad idea. He doesn't know I used to date his rival, and he doesn't know who I really am. Is it a good revenge ploy if I'm using someone?"

"First, you're not using him. You're genuinely attracted to the guy! And secondly, it's a damn good revenge ploy, especially if you can get him to kiss you over the boards," she says.

"Now you're an enabler."

"I've always been an enabler," she says. "I'm also brutally honest. I say go to the game and kiss him, and if the kiss is good, then fuck him, but not before you tell him who you are."

"You're already having me bone him?"

She stares deadpan at me. "He took his time asking you out. I bet he takes his time in bed." She wiggles her brows suggestively.

Hmm. I wouldn't mind a man who likes to savor his food. But I'm getting ahead of myself. "When you say tell him who I am, do you mean—"

"That you, Camden Tinsley, used to date his shit-for-brains rival."

"So it's truth before sex. I hate you." I pout.

She wraps an arm around my shoulders. "You love me."

I sigh. "I do."

"And you're really going to love me now," she says, breaking the embrace to dip a hand into her canvas bag. "I bought this for you!"

She takes out...a New York Ice Kings jersey with the name Coleman on the back underneath the number twenty-six.

"Noooo," I say.

"Yessss."

And really, I suppose she's right. This jersey is a definite *yes*. Especially when I spot a short, vegan leather skirt to pair it with.

Well, revenge is best served half-dressed at your ex's rival's hockey game. As I buy the skirt, I feel both devious and brilliant.

When I get dressed for the game, though, I'm not thinking of Erik at all. I'm thinking of the deliciously confident and heart-stoppingly gorgeous Brit who invited me to watch him play a game.

As I head to the arena with Jules, my chest flutters. It has nothing to do with my ex. And everything to do with the guy whose name I'm wearing.

4

FIRST DATE

CAMDEN

I'm not a rock star by any stretch, but a few years ago I worked in a lounge as a bartender, moonlighting there as a torch singer. When my good friend Ethan invited me to perform one of my songs with his popular band one night, I jumped at the chance, singing "Whiskey Memories" with Ethan harmonizing along. A few days later, a video of our performance went viral. A few months later, I released an album called *First Times*. It struck a chord with my demo—sexy, playful tunes about women owning their lives, their bodies, their romances. It was the right music at the right time with the right marketing. My label sent me on tour, where I performed for big crowds under my first name only.

Camden.

I didn't use my last name—Tinsley. It's never really felt like mine anyway.

My second album, *Rebellious*, did even better, and the tour was longer. But being on the road hurt my heart. All those nights in different places reminded me too much of my childhood, being bounced from home to home without a place of my own, ever. I decided that before I tour again I want to build something stable. Something that'll give me security. I've poured some of my money from the tour and the second album into a business idea over the last year—the club.

That's why Erik's insult hurt so much. When he was with me, he'd acted like he supported my dream, and then he undermined it. Maybe that's another reason I didn't tell Shaw who I am. I don't want another dismissive comment about my business. He doesn't seem like the kind of guy who'd do that, but who knows who you can trust?

Who even knows if Shaw will truly want to hang out after his game? He might be tired. Erik often was. The date may end when the game does, and I'll be fine with that. Hopefully, though, Erik knows I'm Shaw's special guest.

I walk into the arena with Jules, heading to the center-ice seats.

The players are doing warmups, taking easy shots on goal or stretching their legs. I'm not sure if Shaw sees me or not, but after Jules pops out to go to the restroom, he skates my way.

I'm behind the glass, so he beckons for me to come close to the players' bench. I move over a few chairs, and he hops the boards where there's no glass. In full uniform, he walks over to me, skates on, leaning across the edge of the bench.

"You made it," he says, sounding charmed.

I bob a shoulder. "I said I would."

Tugging off his gloves, he nods at my jersey with something like...heat in his eyes. "I would have sent you one."

The implication is clear. I didn't give him my name, so

he couldn't send it to me. Still, I can't resist teasing him. "You could have sent it to the coffee shop yesterday," I say, then slide my teeth along my lower lip.

"Or brought it myself and waited for you to show."

I blink. "You...did?"

He shrugs, like it was nothing to wait for me. Like it was just part of the chase. "I rolled the dice."

My breath catches. He showed up. He made an effort. I wish I'd been there. "I didn't make it there yesterday. I had a morning meeting."

"Shame," he says.

"Or maybe not," I say, fingering the hem of the jersey. "If I'd been there, then it wouldn't have been a surprise for you to see me in it now."

"True," he says, roaming his gaze shamelessly up and down me. "And it's a very good surprise...Jane."

One word, and the guilt swirls in me. I should say, *I'm not Jane Smith. I'm Camden Tinsley, and your rival thinks my club is a bad idea.*

But Shaw leans in closer, and I catch a hint of his soap —clean and woodsy—and it knocks my senses loose. So does his warm voice and his unbearably sexy accent as he murmurs, "Confession: I saw you at the coffee shop last season. Wanted to ask you out then but I was too focused on the game and the playoffs. Wasn't going to let my chance pass me by once I saw you again this last week. There. Now you know."

My heart both soars and caves in. He's being so honest and really, he deserves the same from me. But is now the time? Before his first game of the season?

But my thoughts scatter when he leans in and presses a kiss to my cheek—the mirror of what I did the other day. It catches me off guard in the best of ways. I feel floaty.

Tingles race down my back. My stomach flips. "Oh," I murmur.

I feel him smile against my face, then hear him mutter, "Fuck it."

And before I know it, my ex's rival is kissing me.

Soft, confident lips brush mine. A strong hand grabs the neck of my shirt. Scruff scrapes against my soft skin. So many delicious sensations and they all go to my head, zapping my thoughts as Shaw Coleman takes his sweet time with a soft, thorough, sensual kiss that makes my head swim, my pulse race. I reach for his jersey, fisting the material just to hold on. If I don't, I'll wobble. The kiss is that good.

But soon he breaks it, curling a hand around my shoulder. A shudder hits me as his fingers dust over the exposed skin of my neck. He bends, his mouth danger-ously close to my face as he whispers, "Been wondering something since last season."

"What?" I ask, my voice sounding as blurry as my mind.

"If you tasted as good as you looked."

It's like a jolt of molten pleasure shoots down my body. "And the verdict?"

He pulls back and locks eyes with me, his beautiful brown-eyed gaze strong, steady. "Better."

I thought I held the cards, but my body says this man might hold the cards to me.

Get it together, girl.

"Then, enjoy your good luck kiss," I tease, then make a mental note that "Good Luck Kiss" would make for a good song name. I can hear bits and pieces of the melody—a dreamy, lush sound.

"Yes, I'm feeling very lucky, Jane."

There's my chance, but then he adds, "Meet me in Corridor D after the game. Tell security you're here to see me. I'll put you on the list, Jane Smith."

The way he says my name with a lopsided grin tells me he knows it's fake, and maybe likes it. Or perhaps that's wishful thinking, so I clear my throat so I can clear the air. "I'm—"

But his teammates catcall him, and the sound of my voice is drowned out as he's off, jumping over the boards and returning to his stretches.

The kind where he's working out kinks in his groin, stretching like he's almost humping the ice, and my mind is thinking about *after*.

After the game.

And how Jules is probably right—he'd take his time. And honestly, I see no reason why I shouldn't fuck my ex's rival.

Tonight.

5

CHALLENGE ACCEPTED

SHAW

She's nervous. Distracted, maybe, as we head out into the Manhattan night. I reach for her hand. But she's been fidgety since she met me near the players' exit after the game. Hmm. Fidgety won't do. I want her to have a fantastic time with me tonight. This is the chance I've been waiting for since last season, and I don't want it to slip through my fingers again. Trouble is, outside the arena is not the place for a blunt conversation. Half of New York is here it seems, and the sidewalks are packed with fans in purple and gold Ice Kings jerseys. As it should be.

I usually take a subway home to the West Village after games, and that's fine when it's just me. This woman is far too lovely to sully with a subway ride at night. She deserves a limo, so I ordered one.

"I got a limo."

"For our—"

"Date," I supply.

She swallows, like something is throwing her off. "Okay."

Did I misread that kiss? The coffee shop flirtation? The wearing of my jersey? "Was that too presumptuous? This is a date, isn't it?"

She licks her lips. "Yes."

"Yes, it was presumptuous?"

"Yes, it's a date. No, it's not presumptuous," she says as we weave past a pack of drunken guys. "It's just—"

But right as she's about to say something, one of them stumbles toward her. I haul her close, keeping her out of the line of fire.

I hold her hand tighter. "The car's not far from here, but the traffic's too bonkers to have the driver pick us up at the arena, so I asked him to meet us a couple blocks away."

I'm vaguely regretting that. Idling in traffic would be better so we could talk easily, but a block later, I spot the limo. The driver hops out to open the door, but I wave him off. "I've got this."

I open it for Jane, then slide in, following her. When I shut the door, I tell the driver to head downtown. But I don't offer my address. I don't want to presume. I hit the partition for privacy then turn to her. "You seem out of sorts. Want me to take you home?"

She blows out a breath. "I'm not Jane Smith."

I laugh. Is that what's got her so flustered? "I figured as much." Then I lower my voice. "Also, I never thought you were."

But she doesn't breathe a sigh of relief. Instead, she seems to take a soldiering breath. "I'm Camden Tinsley," she continues. "I'm a singer. I go by Camden on stage."

Oh.

Ohhh.

I've heard of her, seen her name pop up, but I pass

most music by. "I knew you felt sort of familiar. I have to confess I don't know your music though. I'm more of an audiobook bloke."

She smiles, but it vanishes quickly. "It's okay. Most of my fans are young women. But what I really wanted to tell you is..." Her tone sounds serious. "You might also know me as Erik Karlsson's ex."

I sit up straight against the seat, my smile erased. "You were involved with that prick?" My lower lip curls, and I can't mask the distaste in my mouth.

"Yeah," she says, wincing, like she's embarrassed.

And...I'd better rewind. I set a hand on her bare thigh. "I didn't mean it like that. I'm not saying you chose badly. I'm not blaming you because he's a prick. We all tend to get involved with the wrong people at some point. So let me amend that. I'm so bloody glad you're not with that arsehole anymore." I squeeze her thigh. She shudders. "Since it means you can go out with me."

Now I'm really being presumptuous, but I'm okay with that.

A smile shifts her lips. "Really? I was so worried you'd think I'd tricked you."

I roam my hand down to her knee, savoring the way she trembles under my touch as I counter with, "Well, did you? Trick me?"

I expect an immediate no.

What I get is a shrug. A guilty one. An admission. But it's kind of a sexy shrug. It's chased with a sparkle in her pretty eyes. "How did you trick me, Camden?" I'm intrigued, and maybe a little wary. But mostly curious.

She tilts her head, holding my gaze straight on. Her lips are parted, but she takes a beat before she finally answers. "I didn't tell you who I was because I didn't want it to ruin my grand plan."

"Okay, now I'm really intrigued. What's your grand plan?"

She doesn't look away as she says, "I have to admit, I thought it'd be really hot to fuck Erik's rival."

My jaw drops.

I'm not normally surprised. Being quick on your feet comes with the territory of being an athlete. But I'm not sure how to take that invitation at first.

Until she slides a hand up the buttons on my dress shirt, coasting toward the collar. "Especially since your kisses make me so much hotter than his did."

And now I know how to take her invitation since I can't resist a competitive challenge.

I cover her hand with mine, haul her close. "Then by all means, let's make this grand plan of yours happen right fucking now. And I can show you exactly how much better I am than him. At everything."

6

INSPIRATIONAL FUCK
CAMDEN

I'm down to my bra and panties and I'm soaked. This scrap of lace between my thighs is utterly useless since Shaw Coleman is a king on and off the ice.

I'm spread out on his big bed in his highline penthouse, with a view of the Hudson River lit up at night, and I'm a hot, wet mess as this man tugs down the cups of my bra. Caresses my tits with his mouth. Kisses my stomach. Roams his hands along my sides. Then brushes his mouth across the top of my panties.

I'm aching. "Please," I moan.

He flicks his tongue across the lace. "Please what?"

"Please take them off and—"

"Fuck you with my tongue?"

Sparks shoot across my skin. "Or your fingers. Or your cock. I don't even care. I just need something."

Shaw pushes up and moves over me, bracing himself on his palms and looking down into my eyes. "Camden, don't just pick *something*. With me, you can have everything. I can make you come all night long. And if you can't choose, I'll just start with a nice, slow, wet kiss," he says, then slides the tip of his tongue along his lips, "along your very pretty cunt."

I gasp. This man. His mouth is sinful. "Yessss."

He drops a tease of a kiss to my throat. "Lie back, princess. Let me show you what getting fucked by the rival feels like..." He slides a hand down my stomach right between my thighs. "Especially since you're so ludicrously wet."

That's the word for the way I feel right now—ludicrous.

But when he skims my panties off, the new word is a long, needy *ohhhh.*

He presses a soft kiss to my pussy, then flicks his tongue down, like he's lapping up all my wetness.

I arch my hips as he travels back up, the flat of his tongue worshipping me.

He roams his hands down the back of my thighs, then pushes my knees up to my waist, opening me, making me feel so damn vulnerable and wildly aroused at the same time as he eats me like I'm a decadent crème brûlée and he's licking every last drop off the spoon. He pushes my knees higher up, opening me even more while he draws a dizzying circle around my pussy with his wicked tongue.

I'm grasping at the covers, clawing at the sheets, bucking against him. For a second, he stops. "Grab my hair, princess. You can fuck my face while I fuck you with my tongue."

Sensations bathe every cell in my body. I feel loose and warm as I lace my fingers through his thick, dark strands, tugging him closer.

The sounds he makes—the hums, the murmurs—are obscene.

And so are mine as he goes down on me like my pleasure is his only goal. He flicks his tongue around my clit, then sucks it.

My hips jump up. "Oh god," I gasp.

Everything feels electric.

"Better?" he whispers before he dives back into his feast.

"Better?" I repeat, then it hits me what he's asking. Is this better than my ex? "It's in a different league."

I can feel him smile, pleased, satisfied as he French kisses my pussy till I'm writhing, crying out, then falling apart.

My world is white-hot and hazy for a long while, and when I finally come down from the high of my release, I expect Shaw to be hovering over me, ready to fuck me.

But the man doesn't abandon his position. He simply lowers my legs to the bed, slides his hands under my ass like he's scooping me closer, then looks up and meets my gaze. "Let's see about another one, shall we?"

I gulp. But I can't say no to this. "We shall. Oh, we definitely shall."

He shakes his head, clearly amused, but then he returns to my center seconds later. I'm so sensitive that he has to slow his pace. He's more tender this time, with teasing little licks at first. But once I settle back down, he turns on all his talents, this time slipping a finger inside me. My breath catches.

Then two.

Now three.

Oh god.

Oh fuck.

He crooks them, hitting a spot that makes me see supernovas. Light bursts behind my eyes, and before I know it, I'm coming again. It's a shorter, sharper *O* than the last one, but no less good.

When I come down, he crawls up me, wiping a hand across his mouth, then unhooking my bra.

"There," he says like a declaration. "Now, why don't you sit on my cock for a good long while, princess?"

I nibble on the corner of my lips, leaning into the moment. "Only if you think you can make me come harder than I ever have before."

He scoffs, but it ends on a smirk. "Princess, I *know* I can."

He hops out of bed, strips down to nothing, and grabs a condom from the nightstand drawer.

He sinks down to his back, rolls the protection on his hard cock, and offers it to me.

Yes, it's an offering indeed. Because it's a beautiful dick, long and thick.

"I could write a song about this dick," I say as I straddle him.

He arches one playful brow. "Then I guess I'd better make sure this is a really inspirational fuck."

I laugh. "Oh, I'm pretty sure it will be, Shaw."

I straddle him, sink down, and then yes, I sing his praises for the next half hour as he fucks me good, and hard, and better than anyone has before.

By the time we're done, I've lost count of my orgasms.

And the reason for my grand plan too.

As I lie there in his bed, spent, with this attentive, obsessed-with-me Englishman, I'm not thinking of revenge. I'm thinking of living well.

I turn to him. "Do you want to come to the opening of my club with me next week?"

The corners of his lips curve up. "Like a date, Camden?" It's a question full of delight. "A real one?"

"Was tonight *not* a real date?"

"It was a revenge fuck," he says. "But it sounds like I revenge fucked my way right into your calendar, didn't I?" The man is simply too pleased. But it's well deserved.

I laugh. "You definitely did, Shaw."

He leans over and kisses my cheek. "Good. Stay the night. I'll be taking you out tomorrow too. And fucking you to another hat trick again."

"Yes, sir."

Shaw is a man of his word. He takes me out the next night for a walk along the Brooklyn Bridge, then to dinner at an off-the-beaten-path bistro before he has me again for dessert.

The next week, he joins me at the opening of my club and wraps his arms around me as we watch some of the most talented female singers perform on my stage before a packed house, thank you very much.

When the last one is finishing, I tell Shaw I'll be right back.

"Don't take too long, princess."

"I won't," I say, then weave through Goddess, down the hall to the wings, and enter the stage to sing a new song.

"This is 'Good Luck Kiss,' and it's for Number Twenty-Six."

Shaw's eyes spark. His smile touches something deep inside me. And his gaze never leaves mine as I sing about his inspirational kisses.

The next morning when we wake up at my place, he

asks me to come to another game. "It's our first game against the Red Hawks this weekend," he says, "And I would love for my girlfriend to be there when we take on your ex."

My ears perk. My heart dances. "I'm your girlfriend? That didn't take long."

He smiles. "Princess, I'm not the kind of man who fucks around."

His meaning is crystal clear, and it does not go unappreciated. I show him how much I like it with my mouth on his long, pretty dick.

When he leaves, he kisses me at the door. "I have a new jersey for you. I'll send it over before the game."

"There's nothing wrong with the one I have," I point out.

"True, but this one is better."

Better. There's that word again. Everything is better with him.

Including the jersey, which arrives right on time, and I can't stop grinning as I put it on and wear it to the game as requested.

It has Shaw's number on it. But the name is different.

And when Shaw knocks Erik into the boards in the first period, my boyfriend flashes my ex a satisfied grin. I can't hear what he says, of course. But it looks like, "She never fakes it with me."

Erik parts his lips like he's about to say something, but he's become a fish evidently. He just opens and closes his mouth, like Shaw's taken away the power of speech from him. Well, Shaw is better at everything. Sex, love, and hockey.

Then Shaw turns to me and blows a kiss.

I blow one back, and turn around so everyone can see the name on my jersey above Shaw's number.

Upgrade.

THE END

Be sure to check out the entire Love and Hockey series starting with **The Boyfriend Goal**, a roommates-to-lovers, teammate's little sister hockey romance available now to download in KU! And mark your calendars for January 21, when my brand new hockey series Hockey Ever After begins with Just Breaking The Rules!

BE A LOVELY

Want to be the first to know of sales, new releases, special deals and giveaways? Sign up for my newsletter today!

Want to be part of a fun, feel-good place to talk about books and romance, and get sneak peeks of covers and advance copies of my books? Be a Lovely!

ACKNOWLEDGMENTS

Thank you to Rose for believing in The Flirting Game and loving it from the start. Working with you is a dream and I love your support, encouragement and wonderful ideas!

Big thanks to Michelle for making this possible, to KP for understanding everything, including me, and to Lo, Kim, Sharon, Sandra, Kara, Claudia, Kara for all your eagle eyes and big hearts!

Thank you for Lauren and Rosemary for making this story better.

Thank you Kayti for all the chaotic brainstorms! Big love to my author friends who I rely on daily — Corinne, Laura, AL, Natasha, Lili, Laurelin, CD, K, Helena, and Nadia, among others.

Thank you to my family for making it all worthwhile.

And thank you to you — the readers — for picking this up! I've loved writing every single book in the Love and Hockey series and I'm thrilled you're enjoying it!

I've written more than 100 books! **All of these titles below are FREE in Kindle Unlimited!**

The Love and Hockey Series

The Boyfriend Goal

A roommates-to-lovers, teammate's little sister hockey romance!

The Romance Line

An enemies-to-lovers, player and the publicist, forbidden romance!

The Proposal Play

A brother's best friend/marriage of convenience romance!

The Girlfriend Zone

A coach's daughter romance!

The Overtime Kiss!

A single dad/nanny romance!

The Flirting Game!

A neighbors to lovers, fake dating romance!

Holiday Romances

Merry Little Kissmas

Fake dating my brother's best friend at Christmas!

My Favorite Holidate

Fake dating the billionaire boss at Christmas!

The My Hockey Romance Series

Hockey, spice, shenanigans and cute dogs in this series of

standalones! Because when you get screwed over, make it a double or even a triple!

Karma is two hockey boyfriends and sometimes three!

Double Pucked

A sexy, outrageous MFM hockey romantic comedy!

Puck Yes

A fake marriage, spicy MFM hockey rom com!

Thoroughly Pucked!

A brother's best friends +runaway bride, spicy MFM hockey rom com!

Well and Truly Pucked

A friends-to-lovers forced proximity why-choose hockey rom com!

The Virgin Society Series

Meet the Virgin Society – great friends who'd do anything for each other. Indulge in these forbidden, emotionally-charged, and wildly sexy age-gap romances!

The RSVP

The Tryst

The Tease

The Dating Games Series

A fun, sexy romantic comedy series about friends in the city and their dating mishaps!

The Virgin Next Door

Two A Day

The Good Guy Challenge

How To Date Series (New and ongoing)

Friends who are like family. Chances to learn how to date again. Standalone romantic comedies full of love, sex and meet-cute shenanigans.

My So-Called Love Life

Plays Well With Others

The Almost Romantic

The Accidental Dating Experiment

A romantic comedy adventure standalone

A Real Good Bad Thing

Boyfriend Material

Four fabulous heroines. Four outrageous proposals. Four chances at love in this sexy rom-com series!

Asking For a Friend

Sex and Other Shiny Objects

One Night Stand-In

Overnight Service

Big Rock Series

My #1 New York Times Bestselling sexy as sin, irreverent, male-POV romantic comedy!

Big Rock

Mister O

Well Hung

Full Package

Joy Ride

Hard Wood

Happy Endings Series

Romance starts with a bang in this series of standalones following a group of friends seeking and avoiding love!

Come Again

Shut Up and Kiss Me

Kismet

My Single-Versary

Ballers And Babes

Sexy sports romance standalones guaranteed to make you hot!

Most Valuable Playboy

Most Likely to Score

A Wild Card Kiss

Rules of Love Series

Athlete, virgins and weddings!

The Virgin Rule Book

The Virgin Game Plan

The Virgin Replay

The Virgin Scorecard

The Extravagant Series

Bodyguards, billionaires and hoteliers in this sexy, high-stakes series of standalones!

One Night Only

One Exquisite Touch

My One-Week Husband

The Guys Who Got Away Series

Friends in New York City and California fall in love in this fun and hot rom-com series!

Birthday Suit

Dear Sexy Ex-Boyfriend

The What If Guy

Thanks for Last Night

The Dream Guy Next Door

Always Satisfied Series

A group of friends in New York City find love and laughter in this series of sexy standalones!

Satisfaction Guaranteed

Never Have I Ever

Instant Gratification

PS It's Always Been You

The Gift Series

An after dark series of standalones! Explore your fantasies!

The Engagement Gift

The Virgin Gift

The Decadent Gift

The Heartbreakers Series

Three brothers. Three rockers. Three standalone sexy romantic comedies.

Once Upon a Real Good Time

Once Upon a Sure Thing

Once Upon a Wild Fling

Sinful Men

A high-stakes, high-octane, sexy-as-sin romantic suspense series!

My Sinful Nights

My Sinful Desire

My Sinful Longing

My Sinful Love

My Sinful Temptation

From Paris With Love

Swoony, sweeping romances set in Paris!

Wanderlust

Part-Time Lover

One Love Series

A group of friends in New York falls in love one by one in this
sexy rom-com series!

The Sexy One

The Hot One

The Knocked Up Plan

Come As You Are

Lucky In Love Series

A small town romance full of heat and blue collar heroes and
sexy heroines!

Best Laid Plans

The Feel Good Factor

Nobody Does It Better

Unzipped

No Regrets

An angsty, sexy, emotional, new adult trilogy about one young
couple fighting to break free of their pasts!

The Start of Us

The Thrill of It

Every Second With You

The Caught Up in Love Series

A group of friends finds love!

The Pretending Plot

The Dating Proposal

The Second Chance Plan

The Private Rehearsal

Seductive Nights Series

A high heat series full of danger and spice!

Night After Night

After This Night

One More Night

A Wildly Seductive Night

Joy Delivered Duet

A high-heat, wickedly sexy series of standalones that will set
your sheets on fire!

Nights With Him

Forbidden Nights

Unbreak My Heart

A standalone second chance emotional roller coaster of a
romance

The Muse

A magical realism romance set in Paris

Good Love Series of sexy rom-coms co-written with Lili

Valente!

I also write MM romance under the name L. Blakely!

Hopelessly Bromantic Duet (MM)

Roomies to lovers to enemies to fake boyfriends

Hopelessly Bromantic

Here Comes My Man

Men of Summer Series (MM)

Two baseball players on the same team fall in love in a
forbidden romance spanning five epic years

Scoring With Him

Winning With Him

All In With Him

MM Standalone Novels

A Guy Walks Into My Bar

The Bromance Zone

One Time Only

The Best Men (Co-written with Sarina Bowen)

Winner Takes All Series (MM)

A series of emotionally-charged and irresistibly sexy standalone
MM sports romances!

The Boyfriend Comeback

Turn Me On

A Very Filthy Game

Limited Edition Husband

Manhandled

If you want a personalized recommendation, email me at laurenblakelybooks@gmail.com!

CONTACT

I love hearing from readers! You can sign up for my newsletter today! Find me on Instagram at LaurenBlakely-Books, Facebook at LaurenBlakelyBooks, or online at LaurenBlakely.com. You can also email me at lauren blakelybooks@gmail.com

Made in the USA
Las Vegas, NV
14 December 2025

36384887R00236